ASHWOOD

AND

BRIMSTONE

E. A. OLIVIERI

Content Warning

Death, murder, death of a child/infant, descriptions of violence, gore and torture, descriptions of battle and killing, discrimination, alcohol use and addic-
tion, on-page sex and sexual acts.

Paperback Second Edition ISBN: 978-0-6454677-4-1
Paperback ISBN: 978-0-6454677-0-3
Paperback Global ISBN: 978-0-6454677-3-4
eBook ISBN: 978-0-6454677-2-7

In the spirit of reconciliation I, E. A. Olivieri, acknowledge the Traditional
Custodians of Country throughout Australia and their connections to land, sea
and community. I pay my respects to their Elders past and present and extend
that respect to all Aboriginal and Torres Strait Islander peoples today.
This book was written on Whadjuk Nyoongar Country.

For Daniel and Aidan,
My biggest supporters.

CONTENTS

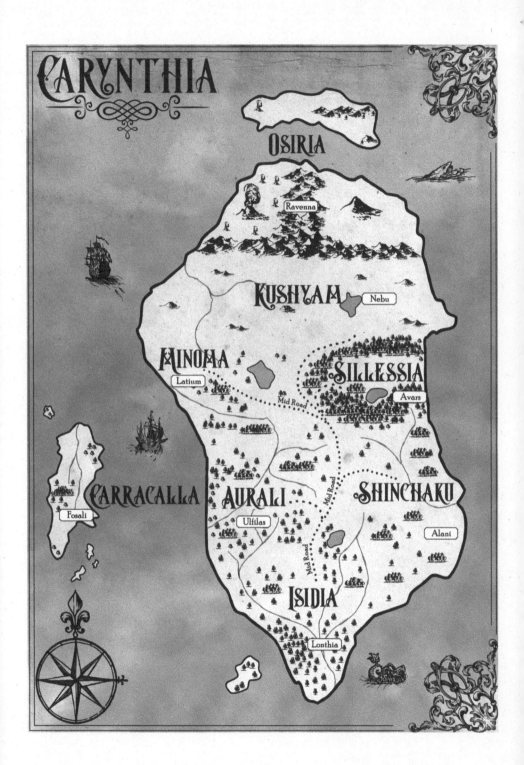

PROLOGUE

I kept my hood up as I entered the town. The white buildings of Lonthia would all look the same were it not for the differentiating wood timber work on the exteriors, some had panels of crossed wood and others framed rectangles. The richer houses had more detail, small square designs and protruding windows that cut into the street, flower boxes full of wilting blooms.

For a moment no one noticed me, I was just another rider on the road. Then came the gasps, the whispers, the too-familiar sound of slamming doors and shutters. Parents calling for their children, and the children, being the pure curious creatures that they are, ignoring them and stopping to watch the stranger ride through town, probably wondering what the adults were fussing about.

Then one of them straightened in alarm as they caught sight of my face beneath the hood. Fear smothered their expression and the others quickly followed suit and dispersed upon noticing their friends' distress. The frightening tales of my people that their parents no doubt filled them with rising to the surfaces of their minds.

I continued on, unperturbed. Though my fingers tightened their grip on the reins.

The reaction was the same the further I rode through town, the only businesses not closing their doors, the questionable ones. The ones that cared more about money than their own personal prosperity—or imminent death.

The buildings of this sort were not white like the others, they were discolored and stained, the wood detailing splintered and lifting, never to be nailed back down.

I got down from my horse, tied her off and entered the ramshackle tavern. I placed my flask on the bartop. "Fill this."

The keeper rushed to fill it, their hands shaking as they snatched it from the counter and stepped away as quickly as they could. Perhaps I could have been

1

more polite, but the filling of my flask was more important. I would need its contents today more than ever.

I peeked out one of the grease-coated windows up to the palace. It wasn't what I'd been expecting at all. The stones were dull, the garden unkempt, it didn't at all resemble the splendor I'd been told of. It was the first confirmation of the Isidian Queen's struggle.

"D–did you need a room, sir?" The barkeeper asked, sliding my flask across a scratched wood bartop.

The thought of staying in another cheap, dirty tavern did not appeal at all, especially not when the palace was up the hill and already expecting me. "No. How much for the drink?" I pulled my coin purse out and waited. The barkeep was staring past my shoulder when they spoke next, an outdated Isidian custom of not looking someone of higher status in the eye. I pulled my cloak closer around myself to hide my family emblem.

"One Silver."

I left it on the bar and turned to leave. Now that they knew who I was they would spread it like wildfire. I had been planning on milling about the town more before heading up to the castle but now, now I had to hurry up the hill—and face what I'd been dreading.

"H–hey," a slurred voice called from behind me. "I didn't hear you say thank you."

I ignored it and continued to the exit, I didn't want trouble.

"Hey, I'm talking to you *Deathbringer*!"

A hand slapped down onto my shoulder. I paused.

"Dorrick, just leave it." the barkeep said. "A–apologies s–sir, he's had too much to drink."

"No, if he's going to swagger in here like he owns the joint, disrupting our lives and disgracing your business, the least he could do is thank you for your service." Dorrick ended the speech with a belch.

I turned to face him, my hood slipping down and truly revealing my identity.

"Now, now sir, there's—there's no need for trouble, your payment is thanks enough." The barkeep pushed, rushing over to pull his patron away from me, minding the distance between us.

As I continued out I left a handful more silvers on a table by the entryway.

CHAPTER ONE
ALIVE BUT DEAD

Carrot. Chew. Wine. Swallow. Sprout. Chew. Watching my mother eat was like watching the hands of a clock go round its face. Predictable. Monotonous.

"How did the meetings go today, Evalina?" She asked.

"Everything is as it should be." I scanned her thin face. "There's nothing for you to worry about." If she felt anything from my words she didn't show it.

I sat back in my chair and sipped my wine, staring at the wall just past my mother's shoulder. It was littered with portraits large and small of past rulers of our Queendom. Family I'd never met.

We sat in silence as my mother slowly ate the remainder of her dinner.

Parsnip. Chew. Wine. Swallow.

This was how our lives had been for the last sixty years, since my father was killed; though I'd only been attending council meetings in her stead for the last twenty. Every day was the same, as if my mother couldn't bear to stray from her routine. Sometimes I wondered if it was the only thin thread holding her mind together.

"Lorkin is taking to his new position well."

"I suppose so," I replied, trying my best to sound indifferent.

Since accepting his position as Captain of the royal guard Lorkin hadn't said a word to me, outside of duty, and my mother and I hadn't spoken of it since she'd offered him the position.

Had it not been for Lorkin, I would have lived a very solitary life confined to the castle since my fathers' death. Thankfully, our parents had been close friends. So, when his parents had died in an accident, Mother and Father had taken him in, allowing us to grow up together.

So I'd had one friend, until we were more … and then we were nothing.

"You knew he wanted it, you can't be angry at me for giving him what he wanted," my mother added. She'd given him what he'd wanted but driven a wedge further between the captain and I, and she knew it.

3

"Can we change the subject please?" I asked, running my hands over my face.

"Fine, Evalina, now that you're heir, how about we discuss the subject of your marriage?"

"All right," I said, pushing away from the table. "I'm going for a walk."

"Evalina, you can't keep avoiding this." mother called after me. I waved her off and stormed from the room and out into the woods.

Slumping down onto a fallen tree I held my face in my hands, massaging my tired eyes. My head was pounding, I'd had to get away from my mother, the council, my life, but the woods were as far as I could go. Once I was Queen it would all be easier—I hoped. There'd be no need to hide my mothers' affliction anymore, and I wouldn't have to trick her into competently ruling her Queendom, signing trade treaties and laws that she seemed to read differently, that took her back to a time of war and loss. Trying to keep the council from noticing as best I could. Soon, it would be over soon. I had been named Heir now.

My head snapped up as I heard a rustle in the forest before me. At this time of night I would surely be alone. The servants would be preparing for bed and none needed to come this far into the woods. I prayed it wasn't an issue with the wards; our mages had made enough mistakes of late that soon I wouldn't be able to talk my mother down from executing them.

I hopped off the fallen tree and stepped toward the creek, the half moon reflected in its surface, looking for anything hiding in the bushes.

Our guards were trained not to make a noise while patrolling, if it was one of them I would have to report them to the Captain and punish them tomorrow in front of the rest. If it were one of our wall patrols, they'd be wearing plated armor and the moon would be shining off it; up ahead, I saw no such thing.

Without much thought, I leapt over the creek and crept forward, like a predator stalking prey. I heard another rustle to my right and quickly ducked behind a tree; as I peered around the trunk, I was hit with a Mother awful smell—like meat that had been in the cold room for too long.

Then I saw it, stumbling through the brush, half-rotted and covered in a mix of dirt, blood, and waste. A human, but it couldn't possibly be alive, not with the gaping wounds I saw.

I swung myself back behind the tree and looked for something, anything, to use as a weapon. About five paces to my right there was a large branch, but if I went for it the thing would see me. I'd have to be quick.

I peeked around the tree again, it was about six paces away from where I stood, stumbling blindly as if it should have found whatever it was that it was looking for by now. I took a deep breath and prepared to run. Bending my left leg in front of me, stretching my right leg behind, bracing it on the tree so I could push off it for an extra boost forward, I counted myself down from five.

Four ... three ... two ... one!

I pushed off the tree and bolted for the branch.

The second I leapt out from behind the tree I heard a wet snarl. Definitely not human.

4

I reached for the branch as the thing leapt for me. I twisted and swung the branch at the creature's head, causing it to fall back, giving me enough time to straighten. I gripped my branch like a sword and prepared to swing again. The creature straightened and I got a good look at its mangled, rotting face; its eyes were whited over and its skin was peeling away from its jaw. The little clothes it was wearing were tattered and barely covering its wound ridden body, and its feet were bloody and torn from walking barefoot from wherever the pit it came from.

The creature darted for me and I swung at its head, again and again, blood splattering all over me and the forest floor. I dipped and swung my leg out into the thing's legs, knocking it to the ground. I forced my foot onto the creature's neck, pinning it to the ground. It writhed under me and I dug my branch into its stomach making it squeal.

"Do you speak, creature?" It struggled against me so I dug my branch further into its stomach, making it scream again, black gunk oozing from the delicate, dead flesh pierced by the end of my makeshift weapon. "Do you speak?" I demanded, disgusted at the creature's appearance and gall to wander into my home.

"Yes! Yes, I speak!"

I cringed at its voice. "What *are* you?" I asked, unable to hide the disgust in my tone.

It coughed blood onto my boot and I dug my foot further into its throat, making it gasp for breath. "I am a servant of The Life Bringer," it spat with its gravelly voice. "Here to do his bidding, to start his great mission." It turned its head to the side and spat more blood on the ground.

I held my foot steady on the creature's neck, though dread filled me. "What mission? Who is he?" I asked. The creature struggled against me again, I removed the branch from its stomach and thumped it over the head. "What mission!?" I repeated, desperation creeping into my voice.

"You Elves," the monster drawled, "think you own everything, you couldn't be more wrong. The Life Bringer is going to sort you out, starting with you pale, uppity bastards."

"He's human then?" I snorted. "He will be easy enough to dispose of." One lone human could do nothing against an army of Elves.

The creature chuckled. "You can try, she-elf, but The Life Bringer has survived much."

"He has not had to deal with me yet," I said before removing the branch from its stomach and hitting the creature over the head again, this time hard enough to render it unconscious. My false confidence faltered as the creature's eyelids fluttered shut.

What could I really do?

I removed my foot from its throat and took a better look; it was human, or had been. I didn't know if it still counted as human if it had already quite possibly been dead. Its body was covered in wounds that were still leaking blood as if it had just walked through every obstacle it had encountered. The smell this close was torturously bad, the little food that was left in my stomach threatened to resurface,

I swallowed it down and bent to pick the thing up and flung it over my shoulder, I wanted it to be interrogated and I wanted the mages to study it so they could fix our damn wards.

I carried the body of the thing back through the forest, its blood covering me. As I walked through the tree line a few guards began to rush for me. I dropped the creature on the ground. "Get the Captain, now!"

One of the guards darted away toward the servants' quarters, the other guard stopped just in front of me and looked me up and down—checking for any injuries.

"I'm fine, it didn't touch me. Just bind it."

He got to work tying the arms and ankles as I saw Captain Lorkin and the other guard rushing over.

Lorkin bolted straight for me, grabbing my shoulders violently and looking me over. "Are you hurt?" He said looking me in the eyes frantically.

"Lorkin—"

"ARE YOU HURT?!"

I'd never seen Lorkin so wild.

I struggled out of his grip. "I'm *fine*, Lorkin!"

His shoulders relaxed. "What happened? Why were you alone?" He was still looking me in the eyes.

"I went for a walk," I avoided mentioning my need for a break, "and found him stumbling around the forest. I want him interrogated and studied by the mages right away."

Lorkin snapped back to normal and focused on a random point just past my shoulder, our ridiculous customs forbidding him to look me in the eye. "Of course, Your Highness, I'll get on it right away."

I placed my hand on his arm. "I'm fine Lorkin, you've trained me well."

He quickly glanced at my eyes and away again, running a hand through his hair.

"What do you think it is? And how did it get through the wards?" I asked, watching the guards bind the bloated corpse, gagging at the putrid smell as they did.

Captain Lorkin sighed, "I don't know what it is, but it was already dead when it crossed the wards. That's why it didn't set them off."

My back straightened. "What?"

"The human was alive but ... dead when he crossed the wards."

"What do you mean? Alive and dead? And how do you know?"

"This isn't the first one," he continued confidently, despite my obvious frustration. "There was another one, earlier this week. I didn't kill it, so when the watch told me what they'd caught I didn't believe them. I thought it was some stupid joke ... until now."

I straightened and turned to the guards behind me. "Leave us, and take that … thing to the mages." The guards turned at once, lifted the body and trekked back toward the castle. I faced Lorkin. "Why am I only hearing of this now?"

He closed his eyes and took a deep breath, staying silent for a moment before he continued, "Like I said, I didn't believe them. I didn't want to add more stress if it was nothing."

"Well, clearly it wasn't nothing." I chided. "Any reports, even ones you think may be pranks should be reported to me, Captain."

"Of course, Your Highness. I apologize for my misjudgement." he said, his eyes downcast, shoulders slumped.

"Work with the mages to discover what it is, and inform my mother of it, with care." I added, not that Lorkin needed the reminder. "I want to know what it is, where it's come from and what it wants."

"I can handle that, Your Highness," Lorkin said.

"Can you? You couldn't even pass on important information."

"I didn't pass it on because I didn't think it had any merit," he argued, something he shouldn't be doing.

I pinched the bridge of my nose in frustration, attempting to reign in my temper. He should be punished for speaking to me like that, but I couldn't do it. I turned away from him and stormed toward my chambers. "I'm going to bed."

"Princess Evalina," he called, rushing to catch up with me. "I don't want you wandering around the woods alone again, or the grounds. Clearly it's not safe."

"Yes, thank you for that observation, Captain," I snapped.

"Evalina."

I paused, noticing the dropping of my title. I faced him, his expression was bleak.

"I'm sorry. If anything had happened to you … I–I don't know—"

"Lorkin." I placed a hand on his shoulder, it was the most contact I would allow myself. "I'm fine. Just don't hide things from me. I'm going to be Queen, I need to be able to handle the pressure."

"You don't have to do it alone, I'm here to help."

"I know," I said, and left him standing on the steps of the east wing of the palace.

CHAPTER TWO
BAD BLOOD

I stalked through the gardens to the mage's tower, furious with myself that I would be so careless. Of course, I should have told Evalina. Of course, I should have taken the threat seriously. I felt like a damn fool. And if anything had happened to her … I didn't want to think of it.

"Captain Lorkin!"

"What is it now?" I snapped at the guard running toward me.

"Apologies, Captain, the Osirian Prince has arrived," the guard huffed. "He's waiting at the gates."

For a moment the world around me faded to nothing, then, a lone face filled the black, a wanted poster of the man who'd killed my King. The only other Dark-Elf I'd ever seen. "He's not meant to arrive for three more days," I said, more to myself than the guard. "All right, let's get this over with, then."

I diverted my path to follow the guard to the gates, mentally preparing to meet the Prince.

"Also, Captain, we were given this directive from the Queen weeks ago, she asked us to keep it from you until the Prince arrived." The guard added sheepishly.

I glared at her as I snatched the letter, it was written in the Queen's shaky handwriting.

My gut dropped, my grip on the letter tightening until it was at risk of ripping. "You've got to be kidding me." I looked toward the Queen's quarters. *What are you planning?*

"I want extra guards *everywhere*, he goes nowhere without my knowledge." I directed. The guard nodded and headed toward the barracks to pass on the order.

I spotted him as soon as I grew closer to the gates. His hair, unlike our black Isidian hair, shone white in the moonlight like a beacon, and his yellow eyes glowed as I'd imagine a Pit Creature's would. He stood holding the reins of his horse, tight enough that for a moment I thought perhaps he was as nervous as

I was—or he was struggling to rein in his power, to keep from killing us all as we'd been told Osirians did.

"Your Highness." I bowed, locking my hands behind my back to hide the shaking. He towered over me and the rest of the guards stationed at the gates. "Welcome to Lonthia."

"Thank you, Captain," he replied, bowing back to me. I worked to hide the confusion that threatened to creep onto my face. Royalty did not bow to soldiers. "I was going to stay the last few nights in the town, but the palace looked so inviting I just couldn't pass it up."

"And I'm sure you're exhausted from your travels. Grenfield will take your horse to the stables and I'll escort you to your room."

The Prince nodded and silently followed me through the gardens; if he had any weapons on him, I hadn't noticed them. Though it wasn't weapons I was worried about but the second his hands had left the reins he'd stuffed them deep into his pockets. Extra guards had already stationed themselves through the gardens and inside the palace and I was thankful that I hadn't had to spell out what I'd meant when I ordered it.

We reached the hallway to his room quickly, I was anxious to begin interrogating the creature.

"Are there always so many guards posted?"

I gazed back quizzically at the Prince, my hand resting on my sword.

"I only ask because it seems … excessive." He added, a knowing tone coating his words.

"The Queen is wary of guests and we are expecting many," I said simply. The Prince's eyes darkened, catching the true meaning of my words. "Your room, Prince Thanatos. Dinner has already been eaten but I'm sure the kitchens can put something together for you."

"No need," he said. "I should like to meet with the Princess tomorrow, can that be arranged?"

My eyes narrowed. "She is indisposed until the afternoon."

"Tea then, if you could let her know—"

"Of course, Your Highness." I bowed and backed away from the door, waiting until it was closed before I moved down the hall.

Ten paces and I was at her door. The Queen had ordered the Prince be placed ten paces from where her daughter slept. I rested a hand on Evie's door. I would not disturb her again tonight, it had already been difficult enough.

The tower was hidden at the back of the castle, behind the kitchens so they could store their ingredients in the cold stores if they needed it.

My legs were already burning from rushing to find Evalina and the stairs in the tower were not helping that at all. I could hear raised voices and quick movements echoing down from the rooms above and prepared myself to deal with the chaos.

"Hold it down!" Hemfain called over the struggle.

The creature was bound by its arms and ankles but it was still fighting with the guards, having woken since they'd left Evie and I. Fiona was attempting to hook its arms to the top of an examination table and failing. I darted over to help.

"Thank you, Captain," she breathed. "He was out cold when he first arrived, we didn't even think to properly restrain him." She brushed her hands down the front of her green mage robes leaving streaks of inky black blood.

"That should have been the first thing you did," I chided.

Fiona flinched at my words and moved away to fetch parchment and a quill. Hemfain began examining the creature, as did I.

It resembled the one my guards had previously killed. Decayed and wound ridden. Its rotten smell was quickly filling the tower. The smell was not new to me; I'd dealt with death before when disease had spread through the city and mass disposal was needed, after executions, and on expeditions through the forests beyond the palace walls. There were always dead things on the forest floor. But this was different.

"What is it, Hemfain?" I asked the Head Mage, he looked no older than our Queen but he was centuries beyond her.

"It looks to me to be a Corse."

Fiona gasped.

"Corse?" I frowned at the unfamiliar term.

"The creation of a Necromancer. Dark magic, Captain," he explained, prodding the writhing creature with a small cane, causing it to gasp in pain.

"Necromancy," Fiona whispered. "The returning of the dead through dark magic. It doesn't heal as our magic does, only returns the soul to the corpse."

"Depending on the skill of the Necromancer." Hemfain corrected.

"Wonderful," I said, pacing around the table. "Can it be questioned?"

Hemfain's eyes locked with mine as he nodded. I pushed my sleeves up and requested that Fiona leave. She may be a mage but she didn't have the constitution to witness what I was going to do.

"Right," I said after the last of the mages had also left the tower and it was only Hemfain and I, "Let's get started."

"You speak, creature?" Hemfain asked.

"I already told the wench that I do," it replied, its voice almost sending shivers down my spine.

"How do you want to do this, Lorkin?"

I took a deep breath, "I want answers no matter what it takes."

The Head Mage nodded and retreated to a back room, returning with a roll of healing tools. I rolled out the leather pouch onto a bench behind me and selected a thin metal poker, no longer than my middle finger, with a wooden handle and a pair of sharp cutters.

Turning back to the creature, I asked, "Where did you come from?"

"The Life Bringer sent me."

10

"From where? Last chance before I start removing toes," I said, walking to the end of the table.

"The Life Bringer summoned me back from ... brought me back." It seemed to struggle with its words. "He—" The creature screamed in pain as I closed the cutters around its smallest toe, blood oozed from the wound I was inflicting, slowly creeping its way down to mix with the blood already drying on the torn soles. The feet were already destroyed, I was surprised it could feel pain at all.

"Answer the question and I'll heal you," I said, removing the cutters from the fresh wounds. "I'll make the pain go away."

"If I may, Captain," Hemfain cut in. "Perhaps it's the wording of the question that needs adjusting." He turned to the creature and in a firm voice asked, "Where did you come from before The Life Bringer?"

The creature paused its whimpering and seemed to fall into its own mind for a moment. "I–I—" it struggled, trying to remember. It seemed to be warring with itself, fighting through a blockage.

Hemfain caught on as I did and placed his hands on either side of the creature's head, the loose skin on its jaw flapping as it tossed. Hemfain called his power, the familiar white mist manifesting in his palms. "Where were you born? Where did you live your *first* life?" He asked.

The creature stilled, its eyes glowed white as Hemfain's power flowed through its mind. "Minoma," it said, its tone dull and hollow. "I was born in Minoma."

"And where did your second life begin?" Hemfain asked. The creature seemed to balk at this as if he'd forgotten that he'd died and been resurrected. The white glow of his eyes flickered as Hemfain fought to keep control over his mind. "Someone, much more powerful than I, has compelled this creature beyond what I can do. I don't know if we'll get much more from him."

It was Minoman. I couldn't leave it at that, I needed to know more. "We keep trying," I ordered. "Compel him as I cause pain and maybe it'll snap him out of his master's control."

The Head Mage nodded and we continued.

We learnt that we could heal him, almost back to normal. Hemfain informed me that this meant we were dealing with a highly skilled Necromancer. To bring the corpses back is one thing but to bring them back enough that they can be healed is another.

So we healed him, and then we broke him and then we healed him again.

I lost count of how many times I removed toes and fingers, before stitching them haphazardly back on and healing them only to remove them again, the tower filling with the dead man's screams. It was possible to compel things to not feel pain but, clearly, the thought to do that did not occur to the creature's creator, or they were not strong enough. This was all evidence, evidence to support the idea that the Necromancer, though powerful, was indeed a human.

It wasn't until we moved away from removing toes and up to sawing limbs that the creature divulged more information.

The saw was slick with blood, practically slipping from my hand as I pulled it through the skin and bone of the creature, my muscles screaming with the effort.

11

Hemfain had asked for the fourth time what the Necromancer wanted and it had finally responded, "Isidia's downfall!" It gasped. "The Life Bringer wants you all dead, gone … all of you." He trailed off, his voice rougher than it had been when we'd started. "Elves," he spat. "The lot of you should die. You only cause trouble. Especially you pale fucks and the Deathbringers in the north!"

"Are the Osirians the next target?" I asked. The light of Hemfain's magic again flickered in the dead man's eyes. I began sawing again, the screams echoing off the walls, filling my head.

"I don't know!" The creature sobbed. "I don't know." It added once I stopped sawing.

"Captain, I don't think we'll get much more from him tonight, or any night," Hamfain said, resting a hand on the saw. I nodded, my breathing too heavy for me to speak. I removed the saw unceremoniously, the creature screamed once more before returning to sobbing.

"Minoman, the Necromancer is most likely human and it's targeting Isidia— possibly all Elfkind," Hemfain concluded, running a hand through his black hair. "This could be war, Captain."

I nodded.

"You must tell the Queen as soon as possible, and Princess Evalina."

"The Princess is aware," I said. Something in my tone must have given the situation away.

"I would advise against informing the Queen of *that* detail." The mage and I shared a look.

"I'll send someone up to remove the body," I said, reaching for a rag to clean the blood off my arms and face. "I'll inform the Queen at once."

I rushed back to my rooms to clean myself more, and change my blood-soaked tunic, before seeking out the Queen, the early dawn sun peeking through the trees. I hadn't slept and, with the Prince now here, I probably wouldn't get a chance to. My eyes stung with tiredness, my arms almost limp at my side from exhaustion.

I'd been told the Queen had eaten dinner alone and I wondered why Evalina hadn't eaten with her mother, why she'd been in the woods alone, but I didn't want to push my luck with her. She'd been distant, more so than I'd expected. Though it wouldn't surprise me in the slightest if she said the same for me.

It was complicated between us now, and it was both our faults. In trying to do what was best for ourselves, we'd done what was worst for *us*.

I knocked on Queen Islina's door before entering. "It's just me, your majesty," I called.

"Lorkin?" She had her back to me. "It's quite early for a visit." She didn't turn to face me, just continued writing at her desk before the window.

"I'm sorry, but something's happened and I had to inform you urgently." I crossed the room to stand beside her.

"Has something happened to Evalina?" She asked almost frantically.

"No, no, she's fine, but there was an attack on the palace." Her eyes widened for a moment and I paused, giving her time to process. Speaking to Islina required patience, it was why I did it and not Evalina.

When she'd calmed, I continued, "I've been informed by the Mages it was a Corse—"

"A Necromancer." She interrupted, her eyes glazed, her mind traveling to some other time.

I waited for her to return again. "We believe so. Hemfain and I have gotten what we could from the creature and, unfortunately, it wasn't much." I paused again, allowing the information to soak in. "The Corse was Minoman in life, and it seems this Necromancer is targeting Isidia, for what reason, we do not know."

"Humans are a jealous race, it could be anything." She waved off, uncaring. "We'll deal with it."

"Also, Your Majesty, the Osirian Prince has arrived." At this, she straightened and turned to face me, but her expression was not what I'd expected. I'd thought she would react with fear, or anger, or retreat into her memories so deeply I'd need to send for the mages to calm her, but she was excited, beaming.

"Early? How wonderful."

"Majesty, should we not send him away in light of last night's events?"

"No, we mustn't. And our other plans will proceed as arranged," she urged, her eyes bright and clear for the first time in a long time. "We need these events to take place now more than ever, but take any other precautions you feel are needed."

"I have him heavily guarded already."

"Good. I will break the news to Evalina today. I will need you there, you know how ... explosive she can be."

I nodded. I'd spent the last sixty years of my life prying the mother and daughter apart when things got explosive. "He's requested tea with the Princess this afternoon," I cautioned.

To my surprise, the Queen's smile only broadened. "Excellent," she purred.

We shared a look, her eyes softening as she rested a hand on my cheek. I felt my eyes grow wide for a moment before I could compose myself and excused myself from the room.

CHAPTER THREE
UNTIMELY ARRIVAL

I sat in an armchair, head in my hands and massaging my eyes with my fingertips. The bloated corpse from the night before flashing in and out of my mind's eye. I'd tried to think of what it could mean, what purpose it could have served, but came up with nothing.

Carynthia had been in a state of peace for almost two hundred years, the last war ending when I was just a child, and we certainly hadn't done anything to warrant an attack from anyone. I just had to hope that somewhere in my mother's troubled mind there would be some kind of answer.

I was perpetually tired from having to cover for my mother. Lorkin and I had been hiding her declining mental state for decades, keeping it from the council and others that would use it as an excuse to usurp her.

And now, on top of everything, my mother had somehow organized a ball without my knowledge. I'd been shocked when I'd found a note waiting for me when I'd returned to my rooms last night. I glanced at the note still sitting on my tea table,

Evalina,

You stormed out before I could tell you in person so this is how you will find out.

In three days time we will be hosting a ball in your honor, with foreign Kingdoms and Queendoms in attendance.

Lord Fallows will be coming to your rooms in the morning for a fitting, I expect you to be there to meet him.

My mind had gone blank for a moment. *A ball?*

14

We'd never held a ball in Lonthia in my lifetime, had rarely had visitors at all, not even my father's kin from Carracalla. I'd kept in contact with them mainly through letters, though even those were few and far between; my life was too busy to simply spend time writing about it.

A ball. I didn't know how to conduct myself at a ball. I'd barely learned to waltz, let alone anything more. The tutors had tried, but I'd been more interested in weapons training and my father had indulged me. He never would have let me be the prim Princess the Isidian people had been used to, and I hadn't wanted to be.

My hands tapped impatiently on the arm on my chair—Ashby was late.

What would my people think of me? They hadn't seen me since I was a child, since before my mother had hidden me away from the world.

The image of the corpse flashed into my mind again. Two days, we had two days before the palace would be full of Carynthia's most important people.

Two days to hope my mother would cancel the ball.

The doors to my room burst open with a crash. I jumped, my heart racing at the sudden noise.

"Your Highness! So sorry we're late, we had breakfast with the Queen and went over time." The Palace Dresser bellowed loudly while swooping into a low bow, his voluptuous, multi-coloured robes sweeping around him. I rolled my eyes. Of course, my mother would demand I wait for him and then hold him up. I'd tried to sleep in that morning, to relax so I could act like nothing was out of the ordinary, but all night I'd been tossing and turning, dreaming of dead things coming to life and ripping me apart.

"It's fine, Ashby," I said, accepting his warm embrace.

Ashby had worked as the Palace Dressmaker for as long as I could remember and longer still. He'd dressed my grandmother, my mother, and now me. According to Ashby, my mother and grandmother had been very particular about their clothing, using it to show our people how they should feel regarding certain events. I did not care. While my mother would request certain necklines and patterns depending on the occasion, I gave Ashby complete freedom. I didn't know what the fashions were outside of the palace, so my input would not be of much help.

"I've had a vision of your dress, a dress that will stun the masses!" He made a grand gesture with his arms, his vast sleeves sweeping through the air dramatically. "My people will come and get you ready for the night. Don't let any of your mother's stylists near you, they'll only do you a disservice."

I nodded. It was the same thing every time Ashby dressed me. He had a vision, and it had to be executed exactly as he had seen it or the world would end.

"You know I trust your judgment above all else," I said with a bow.

"Good, we've got something a little different for you this time, but it's a surprise! For your coming of age." He bowed low and ushered me to a platform his assistants had set up and began taking my measurements.

I closed my eyes and listened as he artfully described the location of his recent travels, painting a perfect picture in my mind of Latium, the metropolis of Minoma. He often did this for my sake, to give me a taste of the outside world, and today it was a welcome distraction from recent events. Some would think it cruel, but Ashby had a way of sharing what life was like outside of these walls that made it feel as if I wasn't really missing out on anything.

After an hour of measuring and double-checking measurements, Ashby was finally forced to let me go when I was summoned by my mother, though it wasn't to her chambers that she'd summoned me to but the throne room. Which could only mean she had finally spoken to Lorkin about the alive but dead human.

The throne room had always been my favorite place in the palace. It was vast, giant columns topped with archways ran from one end to the other, stopping at the dais where three thrones sat. The roof had been destroyed in a war that had taken the lives of my grandparents long ago, and had been replaced by a powerful ward that blocked even the elements from getting through. Stained glass windows covered the walls from floor to where the ceiling used to sit, depicting kings, queens, and battles from thousands of years ago. The floors, walls, and columns were all made of the same white stone as the rest of the castle and, to complement that, the three thrones were carved from white ashwood.

To add to the overall beauty of the room, the mages had spelled the 'ceiling' to reflect the seasons as they were happening. Autumn leaves were falling from the open ceiling but disappearing before they could hit the floor, adding an orange glow to the parts of the floor that weren't already glowing with colors from the windows.

My mother sat on her throne, her stark white skin almost blending into the wood. Were it not for her ebony hair, you wouldn't have even noticed her sitting there. She wore a shimmering white gown that glittered gold in the autumn light. I could already feel her frowning at my attire from the other side of the massive hall, I was dressed casually in a white blouse and my brown leather training pants. After this meeting, I had planned to go to the training pits.

"Mother." I kneeled before her throne, dipping my head as low as I could. In Isidia, the greatest insult you could give is to look into the eyes of someone in a higher social class than you without their permission. It was a custom I hated.

"Evalina, I have spoken with the Captain and the mages and we have all come to the same conclusion—we seem to be dealing with a Necromancer. The first one in three thousand years." Necromancer? I had never even heard the term before.

"Is it a human mage?"

Humans have had magic since elves granted them our knowledge, but they rarely used it for more than healing the wounded or promoting growth in crops. High-Elves are the only race capable of bringing the dead back to life, and even that comes at the risk of losing our sanity.

"Ah yes, I forget how young you are. We can only assume that it is a human. It was a human three thousand years ago when this last happened. The Necromancer had thought an army of the dead could overthrow the elves in Sillessia, so they could take the rich land for themselves."

That must have been a desperate time for the humans. Of all the elven races, they had the best relations with the Wood-Elves of Sillessia, you would not believe that they had once tried to destroy them with dark magic.

"Do you believe they wish to do the same here? Take our lands from us?" I asked.

"I am not sure. It seems the dead have not attacked our villages, only Lonthia."

"Then we are the target, the royal family. Why else attack the palace?"

"Precisely. Now I must ask that you keep this knowledge to yourself until after the ball. I do not want our guests to think they are in danger."

"Should we not cancel the ball?"

"No, after the ball, while our guests are still here, we shall have a meeting with the rulers of the other lands and discuss what to do about the threat."

I wished to argue with her, to demand she cancel the ball for our safety as well as everyone else's, but it was so rare for her to make a decision without me that I couldn't bring myself to start it.

"As you wish," I said, simply bowing my head again and moving to stand.

"One more thing, Evalina. Along with the human lords, *all* of the Elven kingdoms will be present at the ball."

I froze. My heart raced and my breathing had stopped. "You're letting Osirians in our home. After what they did to Father?" I could sense my mother's flinch as the words came out of my mouth.

"Pirates killed him," she whispered, as if she were still trying to convince herself, "not the royal family." She took a deep breath but her hands shook on the arms of her throne. "I expect you to treat them just as well as you treat the others, excuse me."

I held my head down as my mother stood and left the hall through a side door that linked to her chambers. I knew I should follow her, beg her to cancel the ball and make sure she was all right, but my legs had frozen.

"You know she hates the idea of them being here just as much as you do, Your Highness," Lorkin said. I hadn't even heard him come in.

"I know but it's still … unexpected, Captain." I stood and faced him. He looked as if he'd been up all night with the mages.

"We're taking precautions, extra guard patrols of the grounds and living quarters, especially near the Prince's room."

I pinched the bridge of my nose, my head was beginning to throb. "Have you begun interrogating the creature?" I asked.

"We have, but he just keeps blabbing about the life bringer and how Isidia will be the first to fall. We did, however, find out that he is, or was, Minoman," Lorkin replied, his hands clasped together behind his back, shoulders squared, his guard stance.

"It would make sense for the Necromancer to be in Minoma, he was probably studying to be a mage. But why? Why get rid of elves when we gave them magic?"

Minoma was the home of the human Mage college and, though they try, humans could never be as powerful as elves. It would be futile for the humans to start a war with us; the Necromancer had to be working alone.

Lorkin shrugged. "I don't know, Your Highness, but that's all we could get out of him. The Necromancer seems to have blocked our compulsion abilities somehow."

"Have you told my mother about all this?" I dreaded the thought of my mother knowing I had been in any kind of danger.

"I have, but I left out the part about you facing it alone. I thought it was best she didn't know that part."

I smiled, the old Lorkin was still in there somewhere.

"Thank you."

He gave a small smile, now looking back past my shoulder.

"Well, hopefully there's not an ambush halfway through the ball," I said with a sigh.

"We will have guards everywhere and the mages are working on new wards as we speak."

"Excellent." I sighed and rubbed my face. I couldn't believe mother hadn't given me more notice. "And when can we expect our guests to arrive?"

"That's why I'm here." Lorkin shuffled backwards slightly, putting some more distance between us. "Prince Thanatos of Osiria has arrived and has asked if you would join him for tea."

I didn't know what my face looked like but all the color drained from Lorkin's.

"What?! He's come three days early and he expects me to just drop what I'm doing and have tea with him?"

I had heard stories of Prince Thanatos of Osiria. He was apparently quite debauched; supposedly very good looking and very ill-mannered, and that I could already attest to.

"Apologies, my Lady, he arrived early and thought the palace better lodgings than the town and wishes to meet with you before the ball. If you'd like, I can tell him to wait for dinner."

"No, tea will be fine. Might as well get it over with." I motioned for Lorkin to follow me out of the throne room. "We'll take tea in my chambers, make it seem more intimate—like I don't see him as a threat."

"Forgive me, my Lady, but do you think that is wise, given his reputation?"

I glanced sideways at him. "Are you questioning his honor or mine, Lorkin? I am sure the rumors are true about him being good-looking, but I doubt he's good looking enough that I can't control myself."

"Pardon, Highness, I didn't mean it like that or to offend. I just don't trust him."

"Neither do I, but we need him to think we do so we can get through this mess. If this Necromancer ends up being more of a hassle, it would be handy to have the Osirian army on our side."

"Just be careful, and, Evalina … Evie, please, don't go walking alone again." Hearing him say my name made me freeze on the spot. It had been months since he'd last said it, the last time we had been alone together. Since then he had only addressed me as Your Highness, Lady or Princess.

He looked me straight in the eyes and, behind the soft look he was giving me, I sensed the same frantic worry of last night.

"Lorkin, I … I won't, I promise."

"I'll see you in the training pits for our afternoon session."

I watched as he turned and stalked away, still frozen in place. That was the first thing he'd said in months that hinted at him feeling the way we did before my mother named me heir.

I'd be lying if I said I didn't miss it, miss him, but it was impossible. I'm the heir. I'll have to marry a prince or lord to keep the royal line going. We both knew it would happen eventually, but we'd expected to have at least five hundred years before my mother would name me.

When I got to the hallway before my chambers, I was surprised to see servants frantically changing bed linens, scrubbing floors and beating rugs. I supposed there'd be guests staying up this end.

I'd been the only one living in this wing since Lorkin had denounced his family title and become Captain of the Guard. He used to have the room at the end of the hall from mine, though he had spent most of his time in my room.

I called for my handmaids to set the room for tea. I re-brushed my inky blue-black hair and made sure the doors on the left-hand side of the room that led to my bedroom were firmly closed before I then sent for the Prince.

I was about to settle into my armchair by the fire with a book to sneak in a few minutes of reading, when there was a knock at the door. Thinking it was Ashby for another measurement, I stood and walked over to answer it myself.

I opened the door and came face to face with the Prince of Osiria.

CHAPTER FOUR
HEIR AND GRACES

The Prince swept his arm out and bowed low. "Your Highness."

He looked exactly as I had expected a Dark-Elf prince to look. His skin a light purple, the color of the sky at twilight, with snow-white hair that fell past his shoulders and bright, glowing amber eyes. He was dressed in what I could only assume were his traveling clothes: a simple, white, flowing shirt tucked into tan riding pants with a pair of heavy, black, knee-high boots.

"Prince Thanatos." I bobbed and dipped my head. "I did not expect you so soon, were you waiting for me?" I had to admit, the rumors about him being attractive did not do him justice. He was extremely attractive. His eyes were almost cat-like in shape, his nose straight and slightly hooked, cheekbones sharp enough that they shadowed the lower half of his face. He was a head taller than me, his shoulders broad and hulking. He looked more like a warrior than a prince.

"No, Princess, I was just unpacking when your maids came to get me. As it turns out, I am in the chambers next to yours—and quite thankfully, at that, as I am quite starved from my journey."

My heart skipped a beat. My mother had let our enemy not only into our house, but practically into my own bedchambers. Perhaps she was playing the same game I was, friends close and enemies closer.

"What great fortune, shall we sit?" I gestured to the table that had been set in the living quarters of my chamber. "I, too, am quite famished." I bowed again and he stepped past me into the room.

He smelled of ash and freshly fallen snow, a strange mix that reflected the strange land he was from. Osiria was half volcanic waste and half icy tundra; as far as the outside world knew, they had no resources and relied heavily on Kushyam and Sillessia for food and other necessities.

"My apologies for arriving so early, no one in my lands was quite sure how long it would take to get here by horseback, it has been many years since any of my kin has traveled this far south."

The room filled with an air of awkwardness. Our kingdoms had been on opposing sides of wars for millennia.

"Horseback? Did you not ride with an escort?"

"No, my family could not make it, unfortunately, and it's easier to travel alone than with twenty soldiers."

It also makes it easier for us to kill him if he tries anything.

"I can only imagine."

He gave me a sad, knowing smile, as if he knew I was a prisoner in my own home, *bastard*.

I rang a little bell that was placed in the center of the table and within seconds servants were streaming in carrying trays of tea and sweets. The Prince had not lied when he said he was starved; I don't think I'd ever seen so much food on one plate. We ate in silence for a while, both of us only saying something when we wanted more tea from the servant standing five paces behind me, his broad physique betraying his true reason for being here. Lorkin had kept his word about guarding the Prince.

Then it clicked.

Lorkin had known the Prince was going to be in the chambers next to mine, that's why he said he was going to have them guarded and why he was worried about the Prince coming to my chambers for lunch. I must not have hidden my realization and anger very well at all because the Prince put his fork down and stared at me intently.

"Is everything all right, Your Highness?"

I took a deep breath. "Yes, everything is fine." I gave him my best attempt at a cheerful smile.

The Prince sighed. "Look," he said, sitting forward, "I know this is a mess and I know you'd much rather I not be here right now. In fact, I argued with my father to not make me come right up to the moment my horse stepped through the gates of Ravenna. He said if he didn't get a letter telling him that I'd arrived here within three weeks of me leaving, he'd send an assassin to cut my balls off and have them hung from the watchtower."

I sat back in my chair with my arms crossed and eyebrows raised waiting for him to finish. I was surprised by his crass words but found it … refreshing.

"I know you dislike my kin because of what happened to your father, but you must believe me when I say that the pirates worked alone, and the second we got news that they had landed back in Osiria they were executed, no questions asked. My father asked to visit but was ignored, we tried to send gifts but they were sent back. For as long as I can remember my family has only ever wanted peace between our lands."

I sat forward, now that it seemed propriety was out the window. "I'm sure you can understand that we took the death of my father quite hard. And, given the history of our peoples, a touch of bitterness is expected, no? We recognize that it was a lone act, but the fact remains that your King did nothing to stop Orrick and it was left to my father to rid the seas of scum like him. But, look, Your Highness, you've come, you've seen, we've had words. I think you've done everything your father wished, so why don't you just go? Pack up your shit and get out of my castle."

His eyes were wide for a moment at my outburst then he chuckled. "Unfortunately, there are other parts of my person on the line if I don't attend the ball." He leaned back in his chair with his arms wide, as if asking me if I had more to say.

"Then I guess I'm stuck with you."

"I guess so," he said with a forced smile, and stood to leave. "I'll try to behave and keep any *companions* quiet, though I don't make any promises," he said, with a touch of bite to his words as we walked to the door.

"Pig!" I called after him before slamming the door. I spun around to the guard still standing behind the chair I had been sitting in. "Tell Lorkin I'll be at the training pits in five minutes and he'd better be ready."

After changing into the rest of my leather training clothes, I ran to the western wing of the castle grounds where the training pits were. I'd needed to train today, anyway, but after that lunch I needed to work off my temper. My body hadn't stopped shaking since my moment of realization. I had controlled myself much better than I thought I would. Granted, the Prince had been more refined to start with than I'd expected, after hearing stories of him getting blind drunk in human taverns and taking lovers in alleyways like a common sailor. Though I could definitely see why people found him charming. He'd have them falling at his feet.

Lorkin was waiting at the base of the pits, in a large flat area that was reserved for sparring. I watched him as I walked down the spiral ramp, passing royal guards lifting various weights and stretching as I went. At the end of the ramp was an alcove the size of my bedroom filled to the brim with weapons racks and training armor that beginners used. I had never given myself the luxury of using the training armor, I wanted to feel every bit of pain I could until I was numb to it, that way if I ever was in a battle and was injured I could carry on.

Lorkin was still talking to the guard from lunch, probably obsessing over every tiny detail, trying to find a threat in anything the Prince said. When I reached them, both Lorkin and the guard bowed low,

"Your Highness."

I didn't wait for Lorkin to prepare, didn't wait for him to formally start training before I punched him square in the jaw. His head twisted to the side and he staggered a bit, but remained upright.

"Why the fuck didn't you warn me that he was going to be practically sharing my room?!"

He dodged the next punch with a duck to the left. "I didn't think I needed to. I told you he'd be guarded."

He bent back to dodge a kick aimed at the right side of his head; I twisted and hopped to land on my left leg then kicked my right leg backwards and hit

Lorkin in the gut. He stumbled back but caught my left hand before it made contact with his jaw again.

"I'm sorry, I should have told you ... Your Highness." He added the last part as if he had realized who he was talking to. He let go of my hand and took up a fighting stance.

I did the same. "Yes you damned well should have. And how long have you known about the ball? Thanatos said his father gave him three weeks to get here, why was I the last to know?"

We were circling each other now, each waiting for the other to make the first move.

"That you'd have to ask your mother. I've known for about two weeks. She surprised us all." And, with that, he swung with a right hook.

I ducked and went for an uppercut, which he dodged.

We spared like that for a while, punching and kicking, all the while dodging, until we moved to blocking. It was the same routine we'd been doing for months, dodging then blocking then breaking out of holds.

I caught Lorkin's right hand as he went in for a gut punch and twisted him into a chokehold, he hooked his leg around mine in the blink of an eye and pulled me off balance. I fell backwards with him landing on top of me, forcing the air from my lungs. Before I could gulp down any air Lorkin was straddling me, pinning my hands above my head. I took a deep breath and bucked my hip to the side using all my weight to knock him off balance, we rolled so that now I was on top of him. I twisted my hands so that I had hold of his wrists. Pinning his hands to his sides I moved my knee up so that it was hovering just above his groin.

"Very good, Your Highness," he said between pants. "You're learning very quickly."

Our faces were so close I could feel his breath on my lips.

Without even thinking I said, "You taught me that move a long time ago."

His eyes widened and he then seemed to realize how close our faces were, I let go of his hands and sat back on my ankles.

He was doing all he could to avoid looking me straight in the eyes. "Evi— Your Highness, it is getting late. You should go prepare for dinner."

He hadn't called me Evie for months, and now he'd done it twice in less than a day; it was a nickname my father had given me, and while we were growing up Lorkin had adopted it too. I nodded begrudgingly, stood up and helped him up. We both dusted ourselves off and walked over to the drinking trough, gulping down water like it was the first time we'd tasted it. Then we walked out of the pits together going our separate ways once we got to the top, me to the east and Lorkin to the west wing where the guards and servants' quarters were. After the day I'd had, I definitely deserved a nap, but after that training session I needed a cold bath first.

The dining hall was on the ground level of the castle, off to the left of the throne room. The ceiling looked like the inside of the hull of a ship, and there were three massive chandeliers hanging over the Ashwood table like glistening sails. Silver candelabras lined the walls, and the centerpiece had been changed to autumn wreaths, red apples, and purple berries. Despite all that, the large room still felt empty. It was big enough to fit four more tables the same size as the lone one sitting in the center of the space. But what would be the point? It was just Mother and I the majority of the time, I wasn't even sure that we had spare tables.

Three places had been set at the far end of the table that could seat more than thirty people, my mother was sitting at the head, she was still wearing her shimmering white dress. I saw her shake her head as I got near.

I bowed. "Your Majesty."

"Evalina, why must you stir?" She sighed.

I held my arms out. "Do you not like my dress? Lord Fallows made it specially for tonight." It was deep blue, our mourning color, fitted at the waist and flowing down to the floor. The neckline rested just on the edges of my shoulders, folding in on itself and bunching between my breasts.

"Of course he did." She leaned forward and pinched the bridge of her nose. "I shall have to have a word with Lord Fallows, I think."

I sat in the chair to my mother's right, grabbed my goblet of wine and slumped down in my seat.

"Really, Evalina, we are trying to repair our relations with Osiria. How do you think the Prince will take you wearing our mourning colors to dinner?"

I shrugged. "To be honest, Mother, I don't think he'd give a damn. And you don't get to be mad at me right now, how long have you been planning this damn ball and why did you not tell me?"

She loosed a breath. "I knew you would say no and try to talk me out of it. Don't you understand that we need this ball? Now that you are named Heir you must meet the dignitaries from the other Kingdoms and find a future husband."

Ah, there it was, the real reason for this ball.

"Mother, I am only two hundred and ten, don't you think I'm a bit young to get married?"

"Of course, but you're also very young to be expected to run a Kingdom alone—a husband will help."

"It's not like it was my choice to be Heir."

She sat back, her expression pained. "I couldn't remarry, Evalina."

I took a big gulp of my wine and placed the goblet back down just as the doors to the hall opened at the other end of the table.

My mother and I stood as Prince Thanatos marched toward us down the left-hand side of the table. He was wearing pretty much the same traveling clothes as he was at tea, but had put on a tan vest with gold buttons and had changed out of his heavy riding boots, now sporting a regular pair.

When he reached us, he bowed deeply to my mother and nodded to me. I graced him with a nod in return.

"Your Majesty, I'm sorry I'm late. I was exploring your grounds, it is not often I have the opportunity to wander freely through a forest."

My mother motioned for us to sit, ignoring the fact that he had been freely exploring our grounds, potentially scouting for weak points in our defenses.

"I also would like to apologize for my early arrival, I miscalculated the time it would take for me to get here from Ravenna."

My mother waved a dismissive hand. "It is no worry, Prince Thanatos, it has been many years since any of your kin has traveled this far south."

Thanatos smiled and dipped his head, when he looked up he studied me for a moment, then said, "Forgive me if I am wrong but is blue not a mourning color here? Have you lost someone, Princess?"

"Only what little freedom I had left," I murmured.

My mother kicked me under the table.

"I mean to say, I am simply mourning the loss of summer, Prince," I said loudly gesturing to the autumn-themed centerpieces. "Tell me, Prince, do you feel the change in seasons in Osiria?"

My mother gave me a subtle but sharp look; if only she knew how the Prince and I had spoken to each other earlier.

"Not really, my Lady, the tundra is slightly less freezing in summer but near the volcanoes is always blistering."

Sounded like a Mother-cursed place to live to me.

"Shall we start dinner?" My mother asked and both the Prince and I nodded.

My mother clapped her hands and servants rushed in from a door that led to the kitchens behind me. Plates of steaming vegetables, boiled fish, roast venison and stewed rabbit were placed on the table before us. Thanatos and I waited for my mother to be served before we dug in to serve ourselves. Thanatos again filled his plate higher than I'd ever seen anyone before, he took a large serving of everything on offer. It made me wonder whether or not they actually fed him in Ravenna.

We ate in silence, my mother finishing her usual meal of just vegetables long before Thanatos and I finished. She patiently waited with her hands folded in her lap, occasionally taking a sip of wine while waiting for one of us to start a conversation; but I had nothing I wanted to say to the Prince and I doubt he did me.

"Prince, I take it your journey was pleasant and uneventful?" my mother asked.

"Yes, Your Majesty, very peaceful. I stopped in Sillessia for a few days to talk trade and such with the Wood-Elves, and then headed straight here through Shinchaku. There really is peace throughout the other kingdoms, it seems only fitting that there be peace between our two kingdoms."

"My thoughts exactly, such a shame your father couldn't make it to discuss things further."

I grinned at the subtle dig from my mother.

"Yes, he sends his sincerest apologies, he had an emergency that needed to be dealt with."

"I see."

The Prince fished around in his coat, pulling out a box; half of the box was white, the other black. It was about the size of the Prince's palm and had the symbol of the Osirian royal family on the lid, two many-pointed stars sat diagonally across from each other divided by two licks of flame.

He placed the box in front of my mother. "A gift from my King." He opened the lid and my mother and I leant forward to inspect the contents. "An obsidian stone from our hottest volcano that will never go cold and ice from our coldest mountain that will never melt." He bowed his head to my mother and gestured for her to touch the two items.

The obsidian stone was carved into a Fire Lily, thin and trumpet-like, and the ice a Hellebore blossom, flat and star-shaped. They were beautifully carved, if I hadn't known better I would have assumed they were real flowers.

My mother hovered her hand over the flowers and smiled. "Most impressive, you must thank your father for me and send my compliments to the craftsman." She twisted the box to face me so I could get a better look and feel for myself.

I hovered my hands above the flowers and sure enough, the obsidian was warm and the ice cold but comfortably so. The carver had put every detail they could into the flowers, from veins in the petals to the tiny filaments and anther caps of the stamens.

"Evalina, they would look beautiful in your chambers, above your fireplace."

I looked at my mother, of course she would palm them off to me, not that I would object. "Yes, Mother, I think they would. Thank you, Prince, for your kind gift, and do send my thanks to your father, too."

The Prince put his hand on his heart and bowed his head to me. "My father will be pleased to know his gift was accepted and appreciated and so will the craftsman."

My mother smiled and motioned for the servants to clear up dinner before rising from her chair. "Forgive me, but I must retire. Do stay and have dessert, it is blackberry pie, I believe—Evalina's favorite."

The Prince and I stood and bowed to my mother as she left through the door behind her. It was not unlike my mother to leave me halfway through dinner or dessert, it was as if she just got tired of being around people.

We took our seats once she had closed the door behind her and looked at each other as if we both saw the other as a sheep and ourselves the wolf.

"Going to throw my father's gift into your fireplace as soon as you enter your chambers?" the Prince questioned with a baiting grin.

"No, actually I do really like them. They'll look great in my privy."

He gave me a one-sided grin and leaned back as the kitchen staff placed our slices of blackberry pie in front of us.

We dug into our dessert in silence. Blackberry pie really was my favorite, when I was a child I had begged my father to let me eat it for every meal and for my birthdays he would—but that tradition had died with him.

"So, Princess, when can we expect the other dignitaries to arrive?" Thanatos had finished his pie and had been watching me slowly munch on mine.

"I would assume the day after next. They don't need a full day to prepare for a ball." I said. After finishing my last mouthful of pie, I wiped my mouth with my napkin and made to rise. "I'm going to retire now, big day and all that."

Thanatos rose with me. "I'll walk with you. I've had a rather big day too."

It was another cool night; I guessed that we had about two months until the snows came, but I wished they would come quicker. I loved the wintertime. The winters were shorter in Isidia than they were everywhere else, so when it did snow here it made it seem like I was in another part of the world and, even though I had my issues with it, sometimes I would pretend I was as far away as Osiria, where the snow never melted. I shivered as a breeze went through the grounds and glanced at the Prince walking beside me, completely unfazed by the chilly gust.

I had the small box containing the two flowers in my left hand. I was tempted to take out the obsidian Fire Lily so I could hold it to my chest and steal some of its warmth but didn't want to give the Prince the satisfaction.

"Your mother is kinder than I expected," the Prince said as we entered the residential wing. "I had heard stories of her being cruel and unaccommodating, but she seemed fine enough during dinner."

"You caught her on a good day," I muttered back.

My mother had been unnaturally civil during dinner, normally when we had guests all they'd get was a greeting and a farewell but she'd actually struck up a conversation with Thanatos. Something good must have happened to her today.

"Losing their Other has driven many to madness, consider yourself lucky she still has her sanity."

"If you call locking her daughter away from the world and never talking to anyone sane, then I worry about what to expect from people at this ball."

"If you think that is insanity then you're more sheltered than I first thought."

I glared at the Prince next to me. "I may be sheltered … Prince," I spat the word, "but at least I have manners and decency."

The Prince, still looking forward, grinned. "Do you call what you did with the Captain in the training pits today decent?"

I straightened. "Were you following me?"

"I was going for a walk and came across the pits." He shrugged. "You just happened to be training. You're a good fighter."

"How is training to fight indecent? Are the women of Osiria not allowed to fight?"

"Of course they are, we encourage it actually. But you two weren't just training. How long have you been sleeping with the Captain?"

We'd come to a stop before my door, thankfully, because I had no interest in pursuing this conversation with the Prince. I swung the door open and stepped inside. "Good night, Prince Thanatos," I said sharply and slammed the door.

Mother damn the Prince. I couldn't wait till he fucked off back to his volcanoes and ice. I threw the little box to the floor and watched with regret as it bounced once and settled with a loud thud before my lounge. I walked over and picked it up, opening it to check the contents were still intact, my breath coming hard and fast. I held my hand over the ice Hellebore and shivered violently, I quickly moved my hand over to the Fire Lily and instantly stopped shaking at all, it was as if a heated blanket had been wrapped around me. I picked the obsidian Fire Lily up. I wondered if this was how the Osirians survived their winters.

Osirians. Were they all arseholes like their Prince? Would I want to wring all their necks as much as I wanted to wring his?

How dare he come to my home, insult me, insult my mother, and question both mine and Lorkin's honor.

Yes, the sooner he was gone the better.

The sooner things got back to normal the better ...

But, did I want that? Normal meant going back to my same routine of waking up before dawn, training, meeting with the council, lunch with my mother, meeting with the guards and mages, training again, dinner with my mother and repeating that until I became Queen.

Queen. Who would want a Queen that knew nothing of the world outside her own kingdom? Who would want a Queen that had never seen the lands of her possible enemies and so couldn't assist at war meetings? Who would want a Queen that couldn't stand up to her mother and accept invitations to the balls she was invited to? I was the last of the High-Elven royal family, I had to produce an heir to keep my bloodline going. How was I going to do that without having met a possible husband? I hadn't ever really thought about having children. The idea was terrifying but I guessed I was too young to think about it seriously, plus I hadn't met any males I cared enough about to think about having kids with them. I didn't even know if what I had with Lorkin was love, lust, or just familiarity.

I placed the little box on my mantle between a vase of Autumn flowers and a pile of books and rang my little bell and asked for my bath to be prepared.

Once my bath was ready, I locked myself in my bathing room, peeled off my dress and slumped into the warm, rose-scented water. I rested my head on the side of the copper tub, letting the warmth seep into my muscles. I soaked for what felt like hours, sometimes sitting and sometimes floating in the pond-sized bathtub.

I sighed as I realized that the day after next, the royal families of the other lands, human and elf, would arrive for the ball. I didn't know too much about the other families but I was excited to see my father's family again.

My cousin Simeon was the same age as me and we shared the same weight of being heir to our Kingdoms, his father, Darius, had been named King not long after my father had died. Many said that it was because of my father's death that the King stood down, but I think my grandfather had just had enough, he was too light-hearted to deal with the responsibilities of being King. Though he had been great, it was obvious that he didn't enjoy it. Had he not had my grandmother, Zephyrine, I think he would have stood down many years ago.

The person I was most excited to see, though, was my Aunt Bellona; personality-wise, she had taken after my grandfather, she was a prankster and a warrior, and one of the only people in the royal family to be born with gills in over ten thousand years. Having gills was a great honor in Carracalla, it made you one step closer to being able to meet their sunken gods. I wanted to show her the progress I had made from my training. We had talked about it in letters but she didn't believe that my mother would let me look at a sword, let alone train with one. I couldn't wait to prove her wrong in the training pits.

I woke well past midday to my stomach protesting at the lack of food, wrapped in only my bathrobe. I went into the living-room and rang the bell for a maid to see if there was anything left from lunch. I flopped down into one of the arm chairs, massaging my tired eyes. I'd slept through morning training—I was surprised that Lorkin hadn't come to find me. I guessed he was busy with ball preparations, the guards' schedules would all have to be redone for the night of the ball and the night leading up, incase of any other early arrivals. While there was peace in the land, you could never be too careful.

I sat back in my chair and rang my bell again. I was so hungry I felt sick now, though I wasn't entirely sure I could put it all down to being hungry. I was worried about the ball, about the safety of our guests, possibly meeting my future husband, and mostly about how my mother would cope surrounded by so many people—and the possible war erupting around us. Most days, my mother couldn't even stand to see *me* twice in one day. How was she going to survive seeing at least two hundred people at once? And what if I did meet my future husband? Would I get to pick or would my mother and his family arrange it?

My stomach growled and I was about to angrily ring my bell again when my chamber door burst open and the maid stumbled in; her short black hair was a mess and she was frantically trying to smooth out her crumpled dress.

She hurried to stand in front of me and gave a quick curtsy. "Sorry for the delay, Your Highness, how may I help you?"

I looked at her with wide eyes, her round cheeks were flushed and her plump lips swollen. Her green eyes were focused on the floor but I saw the guilt and worry in them.

"I would like some food to be bought here for me, just anything leftover from lunch is fine, and do you know if the Prince is in his room?"

Her flush deepened. "Of course, Your Highness, I will bring what I can. And yes, the Prince is in his chamber." She curtsied again.

"Good, I trust you are making our guest feel at home?" I grinned as her whole face went red. It was cruel to tease her.

"Y—ye–yes, your highness."

"Wonderful. You know, just between us, I've heard that Prince Thanatos picked up a sickness on his travels, so while you're down in the kitchen could you please remind the cook to put goldenseal and elderberry in his food and tea."

The maid's face lost all color. "Goldenseal and elderberry, Your Highness?"

"Yes, good for fighting infections commonly caught from paramours. Right away, if you could—I'm starved."

She curtsied and practically ran from the room. While I waited for my lunch, I decided I'd have a word with Prince Thanatos.

I quickly dressed, left my chambers and turned right down the white stone hallway. The carpets on the floor were a deep green with gold speckled through it, and the curtains on all the windows matched. There were paintings of all types lining the walls, most were of my family and the landscapes of Isidia, but sometimes you'd come across a painting of the rice fields of Sillaxing or the jewel mines of Kushyam.

I reached the Prince's room and banged on the white Ashwood door.

In seconds, the Prince answered, topless and tying up his pants. "Linette, I really do—" He looked up from his pants, his eyes widening as he saw that it was me and not the full-lipped maid. "Oh, it's you," he said, leaning against the door frame and crossing his arms over his bare, heavily muscled chest. His whole upper body was covered in gold tattoos, the same color as his eyes.

"Charming. I would appreciate it if you didn't distract the maids when I'm hungry."

He looked me up and down. "Gee, let me guess what you think we were doing." He leaned slightly forward, his snow and ash scent filling the air around me.

"What else am I to think?"

He shrugged. "Perhaps I had your Captain in here with me."

I almost laughed at the thought. Lorkin was much too uptight to sleep with someone he'd just met.

"Is sex always the only thing on your mind?"

"It is when someone else brings it up," he said with a grin.

"Look, just don't fuck the maid on duty. You won't be interrupted and I'll get my food, everybody wins."

"If that's all it takes, deal." He held out his right hand for me to shake as if we had just stuck some formal bargain.

I stretched my hand out to grasp his, the stark white of mine standing out against the purple hue of his. I hadn't noticed it before, but he had a golden tattoo on the back of his hand, a Fire Lily, like the obsidian one his father had gifted us. His hand was warm and calloused and held mine tightly. His eyes searched my face for a long moment before I pulled my hand back. He stepped forward after me and seemed to want to say something but he shook his head and stepped back into his room.

"Enjoy your lunch, Princess," Thanatos said before slamming his door.

Odd, I thought and flexed my hand, still feeling the warmth of his.

CHAPTER FIVE
AFTERNOON LIGHT

The papers on my desk had piled higher than I'd ever let them. Most of them were nothing, my important reports had gotten mixed in with the pointless ones, pathetic disputes over land boundaries and property theft; why they thought these matters needed to be raised to the Queen was beyond me. I'd spent all morning attempting to make some sense of the mess covering my desk.

I'd been so paranoid about the Prince being here that I'd completely neglected my duties outside of protecting the Queen and the future Queen. Even the threat of the Corse had slipped my mind. I rested my head in my hands for a moment, massaging my eyes with my fingertips. I had forgotten all about the attacks and we were about to host hundreds of guests, I wanted to kick myself for the carelessness. If anything happened, it would be my fault.

A knock echoed through my small office.

"Come in, and make it quick!" I ordered. The handle turned and Evalina stepped through the door, a broad grin on her face that only widened as I felt the color drain from my face. "Apologies, Your Highness," I said, quickly, rising to my feet and bowing low. "I was not expecting you, I thought it was the mages again."

She chuckled and waved a hand. "Don't worry about it. Are you too busy to go for a walk?" she asked, glancing down at the mass of papers before me.

I thought it over for half a second before agreeing to leave with her.

We walked through the freshly manicured gardens, they hadn't looked this good since Evie and I were children; both of us had been too busy to even think about ordering them to be maintained throughout the years. Not to mention Islina's tendency to fire staff during one of her episodes.

It was nice to see the garden cleaned up, it took me back to a time when life had been easy and simple. Evalina and I had been happy.

"Have the mages been bugging you?" she asked.

I sighed. "When don't they? They've fixed the wards and now they're studying the creature to see if they can trace the magic. They're not having much luck but still feel the need to give me daily updates."

Evalina let out a breath. "What are we going to do about this Necromancer?" She pinched the bridge of her nose. "I feel as if Mother doesn't care at all."

"Of course she does, Your Highness. Last I spoke to her, she said she had a plan and that she'll reveal it at the meeting with the Kings and Queens after the ball." I sensed Evalina roll her eyes beside me and laughed. "The ball is just as important as our safety—"

"And how do you come to that conclusion?" She interrupted. "At the moment, it just seems to be a distraction from what's really going on. Our people are in danger, Lorkin! How can my mother ignore that?"

"She's not ignoring it," I insisted. "If this is bigger than we think, we may need help from our allies, the ball is the perfect opportunity to strengthen our ties to the other kingdoms." I paused, I hated thinking of the next part but she needed to hear it. "And if you find a suitable husband, we'll have the backing of his family indefinitely."

She groaned.

I don't know when or how, but at some point Evalina seemed to have forgotten that it was part of her duty to marry. She avoided all talk of it but, eventually, she'd have to. She couldn't run a kingdom alone, there were three of us doing it currently and we were struggling.

We entered the forest, the leaves had already begun turning orange and the flowers on smaller bushes were beginning to wilt. Soon the ground would be mostly mud and sludge, I prayed to the Father that war would not happen, at least not during winter.

We walked in silence. I could tell she was thinking of what I'd said, running through her mind what a suitable husband was. Were it up to me, I would insist on screening all suitors prior to her meeting them; but I'd lost that right the day I'd slipped this green tunic over my head and begun commanding her future guards and armies. I again wanted to kick myself. It could have been me, I could have been the suitable husband—but I'd made my choice. I chose the freedom to protect her in ways that a husband, a King, could never. It was times like these that I regretted that decision; when I saw her in the afternoon light, the sun sparkling off her deep blue hair, her green eyes almost brown with the reflected orange leaves.

I sat on a log in the clearing we'd stopped in, gazing above her head but studying her in my periphery. She strolled to the small creek that ran through the grounds and kicked off her shoes, dipping her toes in the water and sighing. Despite all the signs of impending winter, it was warm in the sun.

"Do you remember, Your Highness, the day the tutor came to train you as a lady and she found us playing in the mud? She said 'no Prince will marry a Princess that would rather play in mud like a pig than know how to act properly in court.' And you said, 'I'd rather marry a pig than be a boring hag, like you.' " I laughed and she laughed with me, her deep hearty laugh so like her father's.

It had been a long while since we'd spoken of our shared childhood, and longer still since we'd laughed together.

"Do you remember that time we were playing in my father's office and he had told us not to touch his sword, the one his father had given him, and you decided you wanted to see how heavy it was. I told you not to but you still plucked it off the wall and tried to swing it, it flung out of your hands, hit the wall and broke at the hilt!" She laughed.

I groaned. "That got me in so much trouble."

She laughed harder as I covered my face with my hands. Eevan had caught us trying to place the sword back on its wall hooks in a way that you wouldn't be able to tell that it was broken, but the second the door swung open we both jumped out of our skin and dropped the pieces we were holding. The King had scolded us, then Islina, then my father; it was horrible at the time, but looking back I realized how easy we'd gotten off. I pulled my boots off and joined Evalina in the creek as her fit of laughter continued.

She gasped for air after laughing so hard that she'd stopped breathing. "Oh, the Mother and Father, our parents wouldn't allow us to see each other for a week after that."

I took her hands in mine, stroking the backs with my thumbs. "It was the best punishment our parents could give us and the worst week of my life. After two days, I swore to myself I would never go a day without seeing your face at least once," I said, looking down at our hands, instantly wishing I'd kept that promise to myself.

"What … What happens if I do find a husband at the ball? How will I know if he's suitable?" Evalina asked, her voice small.

I squeezed her hands and took a deep breath. "He should be kind, smart and know what's best for a kingdom." I turned her hands over and began tracing the lines on her palms with my thumbs, not wanting to let go. Savoring the intimacy. This was the closest we'd been in weeks, not including the times we were training in the pits. Since I became Captain, we had been nothing but formal with each other, we'd gone from being best friends and lovers to the future Queen and her Captain of the Guard in mere seconds. "As for what happens, you'll marry, become Queen, and, one day, produce an heir." I hated the words before they'd even left my lips, they burned like sour wine.

She snatched her hands from mine and stepped away, "That's it? That's all I get? Become Queen and then be bred like a prize cow!"

I stepped forward and reached for her but she stepped back further into the creek, the water soaking her skirt. I could already hear Islina chiding her for it.

"I am not a prize cow and I will not sit idly by while some stranger from another land rules my kingdom. I am the last Heir to the Isidian throne, it is my blood rite and I will fight to protect my kingdom."

I stared past her shoulder again, fighting for control of myself. "Then tell them that!" I snapped. "Tell your mother that you wish to be Queen *now*, tell the council you don't wish to marry. You were never one to follow traditions, so why do you just keep letting these things happen if you *don't* want them to?!" She stared at me blankly. I'd never raised my voice to her in this way before, but the last few days had been suffocating.

"What are you talking about? I haven't let them do anything," she challenged.

"You never wanted to be Heir, you never wanted to be Queen! When your mother named you, you said nothing. You just accepted it. You just threw us aside like we were nothing." I looked at everything in the clearing but her, if I looked at her I knew my will would crumble.

"You're one to talk! As soon as they put that crown on my head you shut me out. Even if I didn't want to follow traditions, you forced me to. I tried to talk to you, at every opportunity, but you treated me like a stranger."

"Because we can never be anything more than what we are now! You're going to be the Queen! You can't be with the Captain of the Guard, that's not how this works."

She grabbed my chin and forced me to look her in the eyes. I was breathless from yelling.

"I'll be Queen, I can be with whomever I want."

That had done it. I reached for her without a second thought, grabbed her waist and pulled her into me. Her arms linked around my neck as our lips met in a frenzy.

It felt like it had been an eternity since we had been together like this, I never realized how much I missed the feel of her body against mine. Her fingers tangled in my hair, lightly tugging as my teeth grazed her bottom lip. I stopped kissing her mouth and kissed my way down her cheek to her neck while also undoing the lacing on the front of her blouse so I could kiss lower. She pulled my face back up to hers and desperately kissed me. You don't realize how intimate kissing really is until you haven't done it for a while. I moved my hand from her blouse to the back of her head gripping her soft inky hair between my fingers, she hooked her leg around mine and pulled my knee forward forcing me to lose balance, before I could even register what she was doing. I fell backwards with a splash and she fell with me landing on top of me in the shallow water.

"You are a fast learner," I murmured between kisses.

She grinned against my mouth. "What can I say? I learned from the best."

I chuckled and again began kissing down her neck. She adjusted her legs so that she was straddling me and within seconds I had flipped us so that I was now above her with her legs wrapped around my hips, holding me against her.

We were both completely saturated, we would have to wait in the forest till our clothes dried before heading back to the castle so people wouldn't suspect anything. Though from the snippets of gossip I sometimes overheard from the maids, it sounded like half the castle had been placing bets on how long it would take until we snapped.

We had never hidden our relationship, it would have been impossible considering we'd spent almost every waking hour together practically from birth. I wouldn't be surprised if at least half, if not the whole kingdom, had known about the Princess and the Lord's son.

We were completely lost in each other, my tunic was removed and her blouse was almost completely off. It wasn't until she moved to untie my trousers, our actions finally registering, that I stopped her. Grabbing both her hands and pinning them above her head, we were both completely breathless. She poked my nose with hers and I kissed her deeply one last time before releasing her hands and reluctantly climbing off her. She sat up in the water and watched as I picked up my tunic and laid it flat on the fallen tree to dry. I heard her rise from the water, cursing myself for not helping her stand, and walk over to me. She wrapped her arms around me from behind, her face resting on my bare shoulder. My heart was racing in my chest. I was so confident that I was almost past this. That I could be alone with her and not have to work to restrain myself.

"What's wrong?" She asked as I took a deep breath and squeezed her arms against myself, wishing she'd never let go.

"We can't do this Evie … *I* can't do this." I twisted to face her and wrapped my arms around her, kissed the top of her head and combed her wet hair with my fingers. "Nothing can come of this, and I'm not prepared to become your lover." I added, knowing she would suggest it.

"Surely you can be my lover? Even after I get married." She said it almost nonchalantly, and I wasn't sure if that hurt more or less than if she would have never said it at all.

I kissed her head once more and pulled away from her. "You know that can't happen, I'm not a Lord anymore. If I hadn't become *this*"—I gestured to my Captain's Tunic drying on the Log, regret clouding my mind—"then maybe we could have had something. But you have to marry a Prince. The Heir has to have whole royal blood."

She reached up and stroked my face with the back of her hand, I closed my eyes, savoring the touch. "Why can't I have you? As long as I have one royal heir, the rest doesn't matter. When I'm Queen I can make the rules, I can change the rules! I can make this work." I was surprised at the desperation in her voice, it made it hurt so much more than it already did.

I played with a lock of hair near her face and kissed her gently. "It will never work, Evie, I'm not even supposed to look at you anymore let alone touch you …" I stroked her face and continued down her neck and chest, losing control once again. "Your mother could have me killed for this."

"Indeed, she could."

We jumped apart and I turned to see Prince Thanatos leaning casually against a tree, eating an apple on the other side of the creek. I leaned past Evalina to grab my tunic, pulling the wet fabric over my head, a calm rage settling over me at the Prince's presence.

"You sick bastard, were you watching us?!" Evalina spat.

Thanatos grinned and threw his apple core behind his shoulder. "Sadly, I think I missed the main event—but I did win the bet I had with the cook."

Evie's hands were tight fists at her sides, I was worried she might actually hit the Prince when she questioned, "What are you doing out here?"

"I was just going for a leisurely walk when I heard splashing. Naturally, I thought someone was drowning. As I got closer, I realized it was, ah, something else. Seems you got to him before I could, Princess." He winked one of his yellow eyes at me before leaping over the creek and landing gracefully before Evie with a quiet thud. I ignored the fact that they'd been talking about me and stepped closer to the Princess.

Watching the two of them together, I couldn't help but notice how they complemented each other, how their wit bounced effortlessly off the other's. I felt a pang of jealousy.

"Can I assist you with anything, Your Highness?" I said, stepping forward to stand next to Evalina.

"Yeah, you can tell me what's being kept in the mages tower?"

Evalina's eyes flicked to mine but I ignored them and kept my face neutral. "I don't know what you're talking about—or how it would concern you, Your Highness."

Thanatos raised an eyebrow and looked down at Evie. "Princess Evalina, can you tell me what is being housed in the mages tower? I've heard screams from that direction multiple times."

Evie crossed her arms over her chest. "Am I on trial in my own Queendom, Prince Thanatos?"

He smirked. "Of course not, I just want to know if I, and the other guests, of course, are in danger?"

"It's just a Naeinn, due to be sent to Sillessia after the ball. Nothing to worry about." Evalina snapped.

He looked skeptical, or was it anger that crossed his features?

"What are you doing around there anyway?" Evalina pushed.

"Just … exploring, I suppose," he said while picking his nails. "Anyway, if it *was* just a Naeinn, I guess we would have nothing to worry about. Sorry to have interrupted." He bowed low, dramatically sweeping his arms out. "I'll leave you to … continue your discussion." Thanatos straightened and walked out of the clearing, back toward the castle.

I watched him until he was a speck in the forest. "What an insufferable asshole." Evalina nodded in agreement.

I turned to face her. "Evalina, this can't happen again," I said forcefully. "I can't risk getting caught again, your mother will either exile me or have me killed. And I intend to live at least long enough to see you on the throne."

She nodded and reached for my hand and, even though it pained me, I stepped away.

"I'm sorry, Evie, this is just how it has to be." I looked deep into her eyes one last time, the green more vibrant than usual as she fought to hold in tears, before turning away and walking back through the forest.

It got harder and harder every time, turning away, but I had to. It was my duty. She wasn't entirely wrong when she'd said I had followed tradition over having a relationship with her, but I had to hope that one day she would understand why. That it was a sacrifice I had to make to know that she would always be safe.

CHAPTER SIX
THE WRAITH AND THE BURN

I had a bath. I felt like I was covered in grime from the creek, and I felt dirty and cheap knowing that the Prince had seen us. I wanted to scrub every bit of Lorkin off of me.

Even after sitting in the scolding water for over an hour and scrubbing my skin till it almost bled, I swear I could still faintly smell Lorkin's scent on me. He smelt like the forest after a rainstorm—fresh, piney.

After my bath, I skipped dinner and went straight to bed. With my blankets over my head, Lorkin's scent was all I could smell; my mind flashed through memories of us being together, being happy. Memories of us catching frogs and chasing cats around the castle, to our first kiss and the first time we'd shared a bed. I fell asleep with tears rolling down my face and soaking my mattress.

It was raining heavily in the forest. I was standing in the middle of a small clearing I didn't recognise, couldn't even tell if I was still in Isidia.

A tall, lean figure appeared on the other side of the clearing, their features obscured by the rain.

"Who's there?" I called over the roar of the downpour, to no answer.

The figure was not moving, didn't even seem to be breathing.

"What do you want?"

The figure tilted its head. I stepped toward it and it stepped toward me. I took another step forward and so did the figure, as an experiment I moved one foot backward ... the figure copied.

"Who are you?!"

It just tilted its head to the other side.

I walked forward cautiously and the figure mirrored, I didn't stop until the figure and I were no more than a few steps apart.

As soon as my foot touched the ground, the rain stopped. It didn't clear, it froze in the air—as if time itself had stopped. I looked at the creature in front of me. We were the same height, as far as I could tell it was a she-elf, or rather, it had been a she-elf once. Her white, hip-length hair was mangled and patches were missing from her head, her face was so rotted I could hardly make out her features, her eyes were whited over matching her ragged hair, and her skeletal body was hardly covered by a shredded, beige gown.

I resisted the urge to scream, vomit, run, and instead stood my ground. "What do you want, monster?"

The elf's head fell back a bit as she once again tilted her head to the other side and I noticed that she had a gaping slit across her neck, as if her throat had been cut through to the bone.

Then I heard the most beautiful voice in my head—a deep, soft, female voice, the kind you could fall asleep to.

"Princess Evalina, there is much you must learn about our world before you are made Queen."

The voice paused, as if waiting for me to say something, but I was paralysed. I could hardly breathe, let alone speak.

"You must go on a journey to discover the truth. You will know what I speak of, in time ... . You must go with the one you would not choose, to the land you would not think."

One I would not choose? Land I would not think?

"The task is not an easy one, and you will lose much, but gain much more." The elf reached out to me with her dead, rotted arm, flesh and maggots falling from the bones. "Go to the land you would not think, with the one you would not choose, to complete the task that must be done and reveal the truth to set us free."

Her hand reached for my shoulder and I screamed when it made contact. It felt like my shoulder was on fire. I wanted to beg her to stop, to let go, but I couldn't speak. I could only scream. Her eyes were glowing yellow, her mouth opened and lava spewed out pouring down her chin and back into her body through the slit in her throat.

I screamed until my throat felt raw and I could feel and taste blood sliding down it.

My scream became silent and I fell to my knees.

I woke up screaming and being held down in my bed. I opened my eyes to see Prince Thanatos sitting on the side of my bed and leaning over me with his hands firmly pinning my arms.

"Somebody go and get Captain Norward! NOW!" His hair was wild, like he'd had a rough night.

He was topless and I noticed some scratches on his tattooed chest, thin trails of blood leaking down his abdominals.

"NO!" I shot my hand out to signal the guards. "Let the Captain sleep and do not speak of this. I only had a nightmare. All of you leave my rooms, now."

The guards hesitated but left and the Prince let go of my arms, but didn't move to get off my bed, his thigh resting against my leg radiated warmth.

I took a deep breath and sat up, pushing my sweat drenched hair out of my face. "Didn't you hear me, Prince? It was just a dream."

"I don't think it was just a dream, Your Highness." He was staring at my right shoulder, the one the elf in my dream had grabbed.

I looked down at my shoulder and gasped. On my shoulder was a hand shaped burn, exactly where the elf had grabbed me in my dream. "What the fuck!?" I touched the burn gently and snapped my hand away with a hiss. It was a fresh burn, a real burn. "What in the Mother's pit is going on!?" My heart was racing, I could hardly keep my breath.

The Prince grabbed my arm, held his hand a few inches above the burn on my shoulder and shut his eyes, breathing in and out very slowly. A black mass surrounded my arm and a soothing coolness settled over the burn. The Prince was healing me.

An Isidian would have been better, we were master healers thanks to our life-giving gift, but I didn't want to call the guards in and have them see the burn. If they did, I wouldn't be able to stop them from going to Lorkin. After ten minutes, more than enough time for even an Osirian to heal a burn, the black mass faded away but there was still a bright pink scar.

Thanatos pulled his hand away and shook his head. "That's the best I can do, Your Highness, it won't heal anymore—even if you saw your best Isidian healers."

I gently touched the burn, the skin was raised but smooth, and didn't hurt anymore. "Thank you, Prince Thanatos."

The Prince gently put his hand on my leg and leant forward. "What happened in the dream? What did you see?" He said it so quietly it was almost a whisper.

I thought back to my dream … was it in a forest? No, it was a desert, no. A male spoke to me! No … it was a she-elf … was it raining? I shook my head, the more I tried to remember the more I forgot.

"I can't remember all of it … *'a task that must be done'*—that's all I remember."

He squeezed my thigh a little and searched my eyes, as if he was making sure I wasn't lying. He loosed a breath, running a hand over his face and through his hair. "When I heard the screaming, I thought you were being murdered." His voice shook.

"Worried they'd pin it on you?"

He chuckled. "Well, I would be the obvious choice, wouldn't I?" He removed his hand from my thigh and grasped my hands in his. "As much of an asshole as I can be, you must believe me when I say I want peace between our Kingdoms. Our races are the most powerful in all of Carynthia, it would make sense for there to be peace between us, so that, together, we can keep peace over the Land." He took a deep breath and stood, still holding my hands. "I don't want to see you hurt, Evalina." He hesitated for a second before letting go.

I wanted to reach for him again, to ask him to stay with me for the night, terrified to be left alone. Instead, I laid back down.

"I assume those scratches are from me?" I asked.

He looked down as if he hadn't even noticed they were there and nodded.

"I'm sorry, I can heal them if you want?" I made to sit up again but he held his hand out.

"No, you rest. I'll get one of the guards to do it. Did you want me to send for the mages? It's not a regular thing to get burnt from a dream."

"No, I'm fine. I'll talk to them in the morning."

He nodded and walked over to the door of my bedroom. "Try not to have that dream again, all right?"

I nodded and rolled on to my side

"Goodnight, Princess," he said as the door clicked behind him.

I brought my hand up to feel the scar again. Touching it now I could feel traces of Thanatos' healing magic. Some part of me felt happy at that, and the rest confused. I was grateful that he had come. Had he not woken me up, the Mother and Father know what could have happened.

What had that dream been about? *'A task that must be done'*. What did that mean? The only task I could think of was getting rid of the Necromancer, but I couldn't do that locked up in my castle.

I sighed and rolled onto my back, staring up at my ceiling of stone and ashwood. I wouldn't talk to the mages, they would tell Lorkin, or worse, my mother. I shut my eyes and tried not to think about what just happened. On top of having to now hide my shoulder from everyone in the castle, tomorrow I also had to worry about the hundreds of people arriving for the ball that night, and hope that they all arrived alive.

CHAPTER SEVEN
THE MORNING AFTER

I woke up just after sunrise, later than I normally did but still earlier than the rest of the castle. When I first woke up I'd thought that maybe all of the day before was a dream—that I hadn't been kissing Lorkin in the creek, Thanatos hadn't caught us, I didn't have a strange nightmare, and the Prince hadn't saved me from it and healed my wound. I'd almost started crying all over again when I saw the lumpy pink skin of my shoulder out of the corner of my eye, but there was no time for tears. Ashby had already set up his things in my living room, my dining table was covered with hair brushes and cosmetic powders and creams. A pedestal was set up in the center of the room and a bag with my dress in it was laid on one of the arm chairs by the fireplace.

For the next few hours I was put through a vigorous beauty routine. My hair and face were washed multiple times and all kinds of ointments were added to both.

Ashby began working on my hair just as the sun started to set, the orange light of the setting sun turning the blue parts deep brown. Ashby pulled a section from the center of my head and began coating it in something that felt like beeswax. He then wrapped the hair around a strange looking stuffed piece of fabric, combing and working the hair till it was smooth and then pinning it in place. He added a few pins with little gems on the ends into the shape he'd created on the top of my head until he was happy with how it looked. When he was finished brushing the rest of my hair and smoothing any stray strands I moved over to the floor length mirror in my bedroom to take a good look at what he had created. It wasn't until I saw the whole thing that I realized what he'd done. The shape he had wrapped and smoothed my hair over was the shape of the crown I would normally wear to such events as a ball. It started at the sides of my head, in line with the start of my ears, rounded corners about an inch high joined together in the middle in a two-inch-high rounded peak. The tiny green gems scattered through the 'hair crown' made it look like a real crown. Having my hair styled like this made my face look even more angular than it already was. I had inherited my mother's sharp features but my father's thin, round-tipped nose and large eyes.

"Your highness, we must put your dress on now or you will be late."

"Yes, of course. I'll put it on in here," I said, trying to hide the panic from my voice.

I had forgotten about the burn. I couldn't let anyone see it and risk them telling my mother. Ashby looked confused. It wasn't like me to be self-conscious, especially not in front of Ashby—he had been dressing me since I was a child.

"I want to put the dress on in front of the mirror, get the full effect straight away."

He bobbed. "Of course, my Lady."

Minutes later, I was studying myself in the mirror again, twisting and turning at all possible angles to make sure the dress never showed my new scar. Thank the Mother and Father Ashby had put sleeves on this dress.

It was a gorgeous, wine-red velvet. From the front it looked like a regular ball gown, with a square neckline, velvet sleeves to the elbows where it then became flowing gold silk; the velvet continued down the back and sides of the skirt but the front panel was the same gold silk as the sleeves. The back of the bodice, however, was completely cut away. I had no idea how the dress was staying on— Ashby must have enchanted it somehow. I pulled my long hair over my shoulders to expose my bare back, thanking the Father that the burn was mostly on the front of my shoulder. The cut out of the bodice started midway through my shoulder blades and continued down my back, coming to a point at the base of my spine.

I went back into the living quarters of my room and twirled for Ashby. "I love it Ashby! More conservative than I'm used to from you, but I love it."

Ashby grinned. "Your mother gave me a stern talking to after the last dress so I did make a few changes to keep my head on my shoulders a little bit longer, I'm sure you understand."

"Of course." I grinned and stood on the pedestal so he could adjust anything that needed fixing.

After slipping my feet into a pair of velvet slippers that matched my dress perfectly, and doing some final hair fixes, I was ready to go to the ball.

Lord Ashby and I were silent as he escorted me through the castle to the ball. I wasn't sure if it was due to my nervousness or his. This was my introduction to society, which was long overdue, but it was also a showcase of his skill and creativity, given that he'd dressed most of the Isidians attending. From what I'd read about Isidian balls, I'd gathered that we would be introduced and get to know one another in the ballroom, or our throne room, then move into the dining room for a meal and then back into the ballroom for dancing.

Dancing … that's what I was dreading. I was skilled in the art of drowning out boring conversation, but I couldn't pretend that I knew how to dance. Maybe I could get away with not having to dance with anyone?

The second we stepped outside I thanked the Father that this dress had sleeves, the temperature had dropped drastically from the day before, the path in front of me was obscured by a thin layer of fog, a slight breeze making it almost dance. As we turned the corner and came into the gardens, I was amazed at how the lanterns transformed it; the flames inside had been charmed to glow in different colors. In the fog and breeze, the lanterns in the trees looked like fairies floating around the garden.

I'd never seen a real fairy, they tended to hang around the woods of Sillessia where the Wood-Elves worshiped them as gods, believing that they were the helpers of the Mother and Father. In Isidia, we didn't have any beliefs like that, we simply had the Father of Protection and Strength and the Mother of Love and Vengeance. They were the creators of our world and the Mother and Father of both the human and Elven races. No one knows why they made us all so different, or who they made first, and for thousands of years wars were fought over it, but, eventually, both sides realized that it didn't matter who came first or who was more powerful—in the end, we had to share this world and war was destroying it.

Ashby and I were almost at the door to the throne room when he stopped us and did one last sweep of me, making sure not even one strand of hair was out of place.

He sighed and kissed both my cheeks. "You look perfect, my masterpiece for tonight! I'll go in now, you wait out here for a few minutes. I wouldn't want your grand entrance to be dwarfed by me." He winked and walked to the door of the ballroom where I heard the herald address him to the crowd. He turned back to me before entering. "Deep breaths, and remember, they're all here for *you*. This is *your* night." He gave one last reassuring nod before joining the crowd of attendees.

I took a deep breath and began pacing, my nerves suddenly trying to strangle me. During my last check over in my room, Ashby had told me that once I am announced by the herald, I must walk up to my mother, curtsy and take my place in the throne to her left. The throne on her right was to remain empty in memory of my father. After three minutes, the cold became almost unbearable and was made worse by my sudden nausea. I decided to get it over and done with.

I straightened my back, stuck out my chest and lifted my chin; my princess training was finally getting its time to shine. I clasped my hands together in front of me and strode into the ballroom, stopping just in front of the herald. He smiled at me and bobbed his head, as if asking if I was ready, I nodded in return. He twisted to face the room and tapped his staff loudly on the floor, silencing the chatting crowd of humans and elves.

"Her Highness, Evalina Elsrine Glenon, Crown Princess of Isidia."

CHAPTER EIGHT
LOST IN THE CROWD

The second the herald's staff hit the floor, everyone's heads turned our way and my heart stopped. Once he said my name, the crowd parted down the center, giving me a clear path to my mother and my throne.

I kept my eyes looking straight ahead at my mother. I knew that if I looked to the side and saw all those faces of people I didn't know, I would probably stop breathing and never make it to her.

My mother was wearing green, the color of our house, the same color as High-Elven eyes. Her long, ebony hair was styled neatly in braids and curls pinned to her head, with two long strands hanging down her front. Her gold crown glittered brightly against her hair, the single large emerald in the center catching the light, shining like a beacon. She was smiling proudly, as if she had been waiting for this day, the day I would be forced to act like a lady. A cruel part of me couldn't wait for her to see that the back of my dress was missing, and a sweet part of me, that hid itself very deep within my core, felt bad.

I finally reached my mother, after what felt like centuries of walking; I curtsied, waited for her to nod back, and then took my place next to her on my throne. As I sat, everyone in the room bowed to me and then instantly went back to their conversations. I looked around the room, wondering if I could successfully pick and name anyone out of the crowd. I saw Ashby and his husband, Winton, first, talking to a group of blonde, light-skinned humans, most likely the royal family of Aurali. The Shinchaku royals in their bright robes, deep-skinned Kushyami royals covered in gold and jewels, red-haired Sillessians, tanned and dark featured Minomians, my gray-skinned kin from Carracalla and, at the back of the room, standing alone, a single, white-haired Osirian.

I felt a pang of pity for the Prince. Osiria had good relations with Kushyam and Sillessia, but most other kingdoms didn't trust them. The Dark-Elves had a dark past and many had avoided being involved with them. Kushyam being on their borders, however, had to keep peace with them.—their volcanoes also helped the Kushyami treasure mines. And the Wood-Elves were friendly with everyone.

I turned my attention back to my family. My grandfather and grandmother looked the same, my grandfather still had his large, warrior physique, thick, deep-blue beard and short hair. My grandmother was regal as ever, slim and extremely beautiful, there were rumors that she was half siren. No one had actually met her mother, but her father was a great sea captain and, after one voyage to the far west, he came home with a baby girl, claiming that the mother died during child birth and they'd buried her at sea; but no one could get the crew to confirm that story. Aunt Bellona had her mother's beautiful, slim, high cheek-boned face, but her father's muscular build. She wore pants and a tunic instead of a gown, and had her short hair braided back out of her face, she wore no jewels except a single, ornate hoop earring with a blue stone in the center and carried a sword at her side. My uncles, Darius and Peverell, could be twins, they looked so similar. Darius had shorter hair and wore the King's crown, while Peverell had jaw length hair and looked slightly more like my father.

I took a deep breath, I'd forgotten almost what my father looked like. He'd had more round features in his face, like my grandfather's, while the rest of his siblings had slightly more of their mother's straight and angular features. He'd always worn his hair longer, too.

I was scanning the crowd, trying to find my cousin Simeon, when I spotted Lorkin watching me from his post by my mother's chamber door. He glanced away quickly when he realized I had noticed him, his expression never changing.

I leaned forward slightly in my throne so I could whisper to my mother. "Mother?"

"Yes?" She turned her head slightly to the side to address me.

"Can I … um, leave my throne and talk to people?" I cringed at how childish the sentence sounded, but my mother smiled and nodded.

I rose from my throne and saw a few faces in the crowd turn my way and watch me as I stepped down from the dais and turned to bow to my mother. She smiled and dipped her head, I turned to face the crowd and suddenly panicked. I didn't know how to talk to new people, I'd been surrounded by the same people my whole life. I wanted Lorkin to be with me, to help me navigate through the crowd and conversations. I glanced over to him, he wasn't looking my way, but I saw him give a slight nod and knew it was meant for me. I took a deep breath and was about to enter the mass of strangers when the scent of ash and snow hit me.

"You looked a little lost, so I thought I would assist you," Prince Thanatos said as he came to stand next to me.

Thanatos' white hair was brushed and in his usual half up, half down style. The half that was up was tied back into a braid with other tiny braids laced through it, rather than the normal knot he wore it in. He was wearing a black and gold tunic that had the fireflake sigil of his kingdom on the left side, over the area where his heart would be. The neckline of the tunic was wide enough that it sat just on the edges of his shoulders, the draping front hanging low enough that you could see the upper half of his tattoo covered chest. His pants were black and his boots were black with a gold pattern climbing up them starting at the toe and feathering out at the top of the boot. The pattern resembled the branches of a tree in winter but also a flame ripping through everything in its path.

This would get the crowd talking.

"Where do you propose we start?" I said looking over the crowd, noticing a few surprised glances aimed my way. It had been a very long time since an Isidian and an Osirian were in the same room together and not trying to kill each other.

"I always like to start with the Kushyami. They're the richest kingdom, my strongest ally, but also the most fun people here," he replied with a wink.

The Kushyami had almost the same values as elves and, unlike the other human kingdoms, the women weren't seen as property to be saved and held until they could be sold to the highest paying male.

I nodded to the Prince and began making my way through the crowd toward the deep skinned Kushyami royals. They were definitely the most colorful group in the room, each person covered in gold and multi-coloured jewels. The bright colors contrasted against their deep-brown skin.

The King smiled as we got closer, his large, gold headdress glittering in the light of the ballroom. He was wearing a white, knee-length tunic, gold belt encrusted with all sorts of gems, and gold sandals with buckles all the way to the knee. The Prince was dressed the same as his father, but wore a thin gold band around his head in place of a headdress. The Queen was in a beautiful gold dress that seemed to wrap around her body and be held in place by gems and jewels of all kinds at the waist and shoulders; it hugged her slim body perfectly in the front and flowed out at the back with more jewels speckling their way up the train.

The closer Thanatos and I got, the more jewels I noticed on the three of them. As well as having her dress covered in them, the Queen had small yellow gems speckled up her arms and placed above her eyebrows; both the King and Prince were wearing multiple rings and large, jeweled collars around their necks. The King's collar had the largest ruby I'd ever seen encrusted in the middle of it, with small diamonds circling it. The Queen's cap crown had the same ruby detail at the front, and the hair that was spilling out the end of the cylindrical crown had gold threads woven through the many tiny braids.

"Your Majesties and Highness," Thanatos said as he bowed low in front of the Kushyami royals. "This is Princess Evalina."

I curtsied as Thanatos continued the introductions.

"Princess Evalina, this is His Majesty Keon, King of Kushyam. Her Majesty Anouk, Queen of Kushyam, and their son Hollis, Crown Prince of Kushyam."

Each of the royals bowed or curtsied as they were introduced to me.

"It is an honor to finally meet you, Princess Evalina," King Keon said. "My father was very saddened by the death of your father, Eevan. They were great friends in my father's youth."

I smiled. "The honor is all mine, Your Majesty, I thank you and your family for making the occasion. I hope your son and I can be as good friends and allies as my father and his grandfather were." I bobbed my head toward the Crown Prince, Hollis. He stayed straight faced but nodded his agreement with my statement.

It was clear to me that the Prince, if not all the human royals, were not too sure how to conduct themselves at our court. It had been a lifetime for humans since we'd opened our gates, I thought it was quite understandable.

"I hope the journey here was comfortable?" I asked the group.

Queen Anouk smiled and dipped her head, her braids swinging forward, making the gold strands shine. "It was quite comfortable, Your Highness. The lands are so peaceful that we hardly had any troubles. We followed Thanatos's advice and came down through Sillessia and Nishinoyama. I have a fondness for a certain tea that can only be bought in the markets of Alani. Perhaps, tomorrow morning, you would like to have breakfast with me and try it? It's quite delicious."

The Osirians and Kushyamis must be close for the Queen to get away with addressing Thanatos so casually. It would be good to strengthen our relationship with Kushyam as an extra step to mending the feud between Isidia and Osiria; breakfast with the Queen in the morning would be a good stepping stone in that direction.

"I would be honored, Your Majesty. Here in Isidia we get most of our tea from Aurali, but I'm always open to trying something new. I've read that tea from Shinchaku is supposed to be the best in all the Kingdoms."

"Shall we say an hour post sunrise??"

"That's perfect, I look forward to trying the tea."

The Queen smiled and curtsied. I saw the Prince next to her relax a little, but his face remained serious.

"I'll come back to you later, Hollis, I'm just going to make the rounds with Evalina," Thanatos said, clapping Prince Hollis on the shoulder and leading me away. Prince Hollis simply nodded.

"Well, he's a happy chap," I said to Thanatos as he led me toward the red-haired Wood-Elf Queen.

"Prince Hollis is in the same boat as you, just been named heir and trying to get his foot in the door with new treaties and alliances. He's much more fun in his own Kingdom, when he's not trying to impress anyone."

Part of me believed that, and another part told me to never invite Prince Hollis to a party ever again.

I glanced toward my blue haired kin, laughing and chatting with the pale, light-haired Aurali royals, their closest neighbors and best traders. My cousin was still not with them.

"You'll get to your family, don't worry. It's courteous to greet guests before family, they'll understand."

I took one last look at my family before continuing on toward the Sillessian royalty, their red hair glowing like beacons.

Speaking to the Sillessian Queen was like speaking to a puppy, every now and then we'd have to pull her away from watching leaves fall from the non-existent ceiling—and her sons weren't much better. The Crown Prince Zared was, for lack of a better word, an airhead; and his brother, Soren, one of my possible suitors, while a little more coherent, occasionally spoke in verses. We were stuck with the Wood-Elves for so long we didn't get to talk much to the other guests before a bell rang and the herald announced dinner.

Everyone waited for my mother to rise out of her throne and make her way into the dining hall before even thinking about food.

I was placed at my mother's right hand, the other end of the table, where my father would have sat, remained empty. Prince Thanatos was sat across from me, surprising not only me but every guest at the table.

I scanned down the length of the table and my eyes met Ashby's. He wiggled his eyebrows at me and I shook my head, he was deplorable. Looking past Ashby, I saw that my father's family had been placed down at the end of the table, next to where he would have sat had he been here. I thought it cruel of my mother to seat them so far away from me, but also to have them be reminded of who was missing.

More tables had been set up to accommodate our guests filling the room in a way I'd never seen before. The suits of gold and silver armor that lined the walls had been freshly polished, to the point they almost worked as mirrors. Every single candle in the room had been lit, filling the room with a warm glow and casting us all in yellow-orange light. The new tables had been decorated with wreaths that matched the ones from the night I'd had dinner with the Prince, with the addition of orange and red leaves sprinkled down the center. Golden candelabras lit the faces of everyone in their seats, the candlelight changing their hair and eye colors. I could almost imagine I was in some strange world other than Carynthia but, for once, I didn't want to.

I hadn't noticed Lorkin follow my mother in, but there he was, posted behind her, standing stiff as the decorative suits of armor scattered through the room. My mother cleared her throat and a pageboy rushed over to pull her chair out for her and tuck it in underneath her. Once she was seated, she raised her hands and nodded for everyone to take their seats.

Once seated, I took a little more of my surroundings in, everyone in my nearest vicinity were Isidian courtiers, people I'd known my whole life—boring people. My only choice was to converse with Thanatos and my mother and, with one glance at the Prince, I could tell he'd come to the same conclusion.

Thanatos, my mother, and I were silent as the other guests began chatting with the people around them. Maids and kitchen hands began pouring wine and placing baskets of bread in front of everyone, but, before anyone could reach for a glass or piece of bread, my mother rang a small bell and rose to her feet.

"I would like to thank everyone for being here on this very special occasion. It has been many years since we've had an event like this in Isidia, and I hope you are all enjoying your night so far.

"Tonight, we are celebrating my daughter, Evalina." My mother motioned to me with her hand.

I bowed my head and when I looked back up at her, I saw nothing but pride and happiness, for the first time in many years.

"Being named Heir to the Isidian throne, a title that has been thrust on her late in life, but one she is prepared to bear." She looked away from me and projected her voice louder so that everyone in the room would hear what she was about to say. "In a bid to make Princess Evalina's transition to the throne easier, King Methuzelah and I have decided to finally make peace between our two kingdoms."

Chatter erupted around the table.

Thanatos and I looked at each other, it was obvious something like this was happening but to announce it at a ball, and so soon ...

"Unfortunately, the King himself and most of his kin could not attend this evening. In their stead, we have Prince Thanatos, our honored guest for this evening."

My mother and Thanatos nodded to one another.

"Tomorrow evening, my council and I shall have finished writing a peace treaty that Prince Thanatos will then deliver to his father. Once King Methuzelah signs the treaty, there will, finally, be peace throughout Carynthia."

The table erupted into applause. The Counselor sitting next to Thanatos clapped him on the shoulder with one hand and shook the other. Thanatos was winking down the table at Prince Hollis, who looked like he'd been punched in the gut, unlike his father who was booming and clapping as if this treaty benefited him the most.

I was stunned, this was such a big move for my mother to make, and for me to not know anything about it.

The reason I was so prepared for the throne was that I made all the decisions, every lunch and dinner I had with my mother was nothing but discussions about new laws, treaties and trade routes. Not one decision had been made in the last twenty years without me hearing about it and having my say first. When had my mother thought this up? Surely she wasn't sane enough to do it alone, and the council members were too spineless to even think to bring something like this up with my mother.

A peace treaty with Osiria. It made sense, and it *would* make my job a lot easier, but it was strange for my mother's hatred, a hatred she'd fanned the flames of for more than seventy years now, to just disappear seemingly overnight.

"Now please enjoy your meal!" My mother sat.

I stared at her, still in shock at the announcement.

"Yes, Evalina?"

I fumbled for words. "I just—It's just … it was such a big announcement. Why did I not know anything about it?"

My mother shrugged, taking a sip of her wine. "Am I not still the Queen of this Queendom?"

I leaned back in my seat. "Of course, Mother."

She took another sip. "Can I then not make my own decisions for my Queendom?"

"Of course you can, but this is such a big one and, if I am to be Queen, should I not know about such decisions?"

My mother put her glass down on the table and leant forward leaning on her hands as if to look casual so no one would notice her scolding me. "This decision has been in the works for months, the King and I in communication for longer.

50

We did not tell you or the King's children for fear of revolt, you obviously being the main threat. The King did not want me to announce it tonight, but, after seeing how well you and the Prince got along these last few days, I decided to act now before you could sour the relationship with your stubbornness." She leaned back, grabbing her glass and taking a deep swig.

I couldn't react to those harsh words, not in front of our guests.

My mother turned to Prince Thanatos. "So, Prince, what do you think of the treaty?"

Thanatos looked happy but somewhat skeptical, as if he expected a troupe of guards to come in and lock him away forever. "I'm truly over the moon, Your Majesty. This is exactly why I came here, to promote peace between our lands, and now we shall have it." He raised his glass to my mother and drank a mouthful, then did the same in my direction and watched me over his glass as he drank.

I picked up my glass and took a quick sip then placed it back on the table. Thanatos flashed me a smile which I ignored and instead of conversing with him and my mother I started picking at a piece of bread.

I continued to ignore my mother, Thanatos, and the Councilors seated around me for the remainder of dinner and dessert.

I was itching to talk to my family, to know what they thought about the treaty. I knew nothing about where they stood when it came to Osiria, we never discussed it in our letters. Did they see the execution of the pirates as justice for the death of their son and brother?

I was annoyed at myself, for so quickly accepting Thanatos. The pirates were his subjects, his people, and they killed my father. But, for some reason, I didn't feel like I could be angry at him for that anymore, like I had been before we'd met. I couldn't say that the Prince and I were friends, but he was not at all the 'Demon Prince' I'd expected. Yes, he was a flirt, but he had helped me when I was burned, even though the guards could have easily arrested him on suspicion and I could have easily accused him of burning me.

Assisting me tonight with introductions was also an unnecessary kindness on his behalf. It made me realize there was definitely a soft side to the Prince, as much as he wanted to act like the careless asshole.

I glanced at Lorkin, posted by the door behind my mother. His face seemed graver than it was before, I would have to find a way to talk to him before the night was through; then again, the future Queen conversing with the head of the castle Guard would not be a strange occurrence.

The instant dinner was over, my mother formally left and returned to her throne in the ballroom. I went straight to the end of the hall and waited for the guests to make their way back in, deciding I would talk to Lorkin after I finally spoke to my family. I had still not seen my cousin and was beginning to get worried.

"Look at this little flower."

I swung around and beamed at my Grandfather.

"Though she's not so little anymore."

There was happiness but also sadness in his black eyes. I flung my arms around him and hugged him tight. He smelt exactly as I remembered, and exactly like my father had, like sea salt.

"It's good to see you, Papa, I'm so happy you could make it."

Papa Adalric was stroking my hair softly while I hugged him to me, soaking in as much of his scent as I could before he would leave and I would probably not see him again until my coronation.

"Let me look at you! Bellona says you've been training in the pits," he said as he took a deep breath and pulled away to hold me at arm's length. He gripped my shoulders hard, feeling the muscles, and twisted me left and right as if he could see every muscle on my body. "Ah, yes, you'll make a fine warrior Queen!" He said with a wink.

"We'll see about that tomorrow when we face each other in the pits."

I looked past my Grandfather and saw my aunt Bellona leaning against a pillar with a pint of ale in her hand.

I crossed my arms and sat back on my heels. "Oh, we definitely will, when I kick your ass."

"Tough words for a Flower." Bellona had always scoffed at my grandfather's nickname for me.

The day I was born was the same day the native flower of Carracalla bloomed that year. Only Carracallans knew its true name, but I had seen paintings of it in my father's study. It was a flower only found in the caves on the coastlines of Carracalla; it glowed in the darkness of the caves, the petals were blue in the center and faded to black on the edges, like my hair with its streaks of blue.

"Bellona, leave our poor niece alone."

I looked to my left to see my uncles, Darius and Peverell, and my grandmother, Zephyrine, coming toward us.

My uncle Darius handed me a glass of wine and my grandmother slid her arm around my shoulders and gave me a quick hug.

"It is good to see you, Evalina. You are looking well," she said.

I leaned into the hug and savored it. It was not often my grandmother would show affection, even in her letters she was cool and calculated.

"Thank you, you have no idea how happy it's made me to see you all."

"Us too, Flower," my grandfather said affectionately, running a hand down the side of my face.

While he may look like a fearsome warrior, my grandfather really was just a harmless old seadog.

He straightened as he spotted someone over my shoulder. "We were surprised when we saw that the Osirian Prince was here."

I quickly glanced over my shoulder and saw Thanatos chatting with the very uncomfortable looking Minoman royals, probably discussing new trading between the lands, now that Isidia and Osiria were going to be allies.

"Believe me, I was surprised when I found out he was coming mere minutes before being told of his arrival! But the Prince is, despite his reputation, quite respectful and refined. He has been a pleasant guest."

My family looked skeptical.

"All the Prince has done whilst he's been here is advocate for peace, and I find myself siding with him. It does make sense to put this feud behind us, we are the only kingdoms still at odds with each other, and it's been over two hundred years since the last war. There are other things to be worried about than old feuds that started thousands of years ago."

My grandfather looked proud. "We made peace with the Osirians not long after Eevans death, once those pirates got what they deserved." He took a deep breath. "But it is still hard to see one. Knowing that that white hair and orange eyes were the last thing he saw ... "

I felt a stab of guilt and had to tell myself again, it was pirates that killed my father, not the royal family.

"Will you introduce us?"

My head snapped up. "What?" I looked at my grandfather, confusion clear on my face.

"I would like to be introduced to the son of the man who avenged my son's death when I couldn't."

My whole family had straightened, Bellona was no longer leaning against the pillar and my uncles and grandfather were standing at their full height; while way taller than me, they were still shorter than the prince.

"Of course, Papa." My grandfather gave me a nod and linked my arm in his as we headed over to the Minomian lords and the son of the man who avenged my father's death.

Prince Thanatos shot me a quizzical look once he'd realized that my grandfather and I were headed his way, I simply shrugged and gave a weak encouraging smile. The Minoman Lords noticed the interaction and scuttled away, eager to be free of Thanatos' presence, the King's eyes lingering on me for a moment.

The Prince straightened and squared his shoulders as we reached him, as if he were preparing for a fight. My grandfather stopped in front of the Prince. I cringed as he tilted his head up to look the prince in the eye.

Thanatos spoke first.

"Your Majesty." He bowed as low as he could with my grandfather standing less than a meter in front of him. "It is an honor to finally meet you—my father has told me stories of your adventures on the seas since I was a boy."

My grandfather huffed and smiled. Thanatos relaxed a little and I released the breath I had been holding.

"A pleasure to meet you, too, Prince Thanatos. A shame your father could not be here to meet with me."

Thanatos bowed his head. "Unfortunately, my father had other pressing matters to attend to in Osiria. Could your grandson not make it, either? I did not see Simeon at the feast."

"Ah, yes, Simeon is currently on his first voyage! A very important coming of age tradition in Carracalla."

It saddened me that I was so far removed from my family that I had forgotten one of their most sacred traditions, the first voyage. Simeon's day of birth had been just a few days before the ball, it would have been sacreligious for him to put off his voyage just to come here. He'll be out at sea, all alone, for at least a month, longer if he wanted to show off. All Carracallans did this when they reached adulthood, it was to show their readiness to be at sea and survive under its harsh conditions, but it wasn't just the seas they had to worry about, there were also the many monsters that lurked beneath its depths, monsters that only Sea-Elves could speak to.

Simeon being on his voyage must be stressful on my family, it made me appreciate them being at the ball even more.

"I wish Simeon the best of luck on his voyage," Thanatos said and bowed his head to my grandfather, and then past my shoulder to my Uncle Darius.

"As do I," I said and did the same.

CHAPTER NINE
A LOSING BATTLE

The dinner had gone smoother than I'd expected. Islina had spoken well in front of the large gathering, had sat through the whole dinner and dessert, and delivered life-shattering news without a single falter.

A treaty with the Osirians—it explained the Prince's presence, but when had she had the time and energy to organize that and keep it from both Evalina and I? And, from the reactions around the dining hall, the court and council as well. It made me hope that perhaps she was improving, perhaps she'd never been as bad as we'd thought.

My gaze again locked onto Evie. She had stolen the attention of many people in the room. She seemed to glow from the attention she'd been so starved of, though she'd spent all night with the Dark-Elf at her side. I again couldn't help but notice how well they seemed to fit together. Even in their interactions with others, they seemed to bounce off the other in conversation as if they were always on the same thought.

Seeing him with my King's family enraged me, and part of that rage was aimed at Evalina. At how quickly she seemed to have accepted him, how easily she'd taken his arm and allowed herself to be led by him through the room of guests. It almost seemed like a betrayal of her father's memory. I just had to hope it was all for the treaty, for the safety of her people.

The Carracallans, too, seemed to be at peace with the Prince, which surprised me. Though, I supposed as long as Orrick was dead, they were satisfied that amends had been made.

"Can you believe it?" An Aurali human whispered to a Minoman as they walked by me. "A treaty between Isidia and Osiria, I never thought I'd see the day." Both humans bowed as they passed the throne; Islina paid them little heed.

"I know what you mean," the Minoman replied. "I was shocked when I saw the Deathbringer here, lurking in the back corner."

55

I couldn't stop the smirk that took over my face, they spoke so boldly while the Prince was a hundred feet away, but what would they do if he was right beside them? They certainly would not have the gall to insult him so outwardly.

The murmuring about the Prince continued, many questioned the motive behind the treaty, and many praised it. I just hoped it wouldn't do the opposite of what we wanted, or rather, needed. We needed stronger allies. I prayed that this treaty with the Deathbringers wouldn't scare them away.

My attention snapped back to Islina, I thought I'd heard her murmur something. "Your Majesty?" I stepped closer to her throne. Her hands were clenched in her skirt, the knuckles white. Her shoulders tense and her eyes focused on the back of Thanatos' head. "Islina?" I asked again gently.

"He's dead. He's dead. They killed him. It's not him, he's dead," she murmured to herself.

I glanced around the room, to be sure no one would notice anything wrong with the Queen. Evalina was distracted, guzzling wine down with her aunt.

"Lorkin, where is he?" I froze, staring at my Queen's almost blank expression as she gazed at the throne to her left. "Where is Eevan? He should be here." My stomach sank, she never talked about him.

"He can't miss this," she said sadly. "Look at her, look how beautiful she is." Islina gazed adoringly over the crowd at Evalina, who was now laughing at something the Prince had said, "Where is he, Lorkin? Where is Eevan?"

"Your Majesty, perhaps it is time to retire," I said, attempting to hide the growing concern from my voice. I knew this ball was a bad idea. How could I have thought she could handle it?

She shook her head. "I need to watch Evie with that Osirian, Bell says not to trust them."

Evie, Bell, these were names she hadn't used in decades, but she still recognised me. Time was muddling together, she was no longer here or there but everywhere at once. This was the beginning of it getting worse, the mages had warned me that this would happen. I'd only hoped I'd have more time; I hadn't yet told Evalina of this risk.

"Islina, I think it's time to rest."

Islina tensed and looked as if she was about to leap from her throne, I blocked her and quickly looked to see what had set her off and caught sight of Evalina speaking with her grandfather, his arm around Thanatos' shoulders.

"Islina," I said, my tone more strict than I should have been allowed to use with my Queen. "It's time to retire." This seemed to snap her back to sense.

She nodded and rose from her throne, taking some deep breaths as the herald at the end of the hall slammed his staff into the ground to quiet the crowd. She gave a short speech of thanks and granted everyone permission to continue without her, before excusing herself from the ball. She took my arm as she descended the dias, her finger tips digging in so deep I could feel my skin being punctured by her nails.

"It's all right," I soothed. "Everything will be all right."

56

I was glad it was me that had noticed and not Evalina. Had it been her, had she heard what Islina had said, she would have broken and it would have ruined all chances of a treaty with Osiria.

Once in her rooms, I assisted the Queen with preparing for bed. It was nothing new to me—I had been doing it for years. I took her hair down from its pinned curls and braids and brushed it through before braiding it again; all the while, the Queen still muttered on about Eevan and Osirians. Bellona was mentioned more than once, which struck me as odd. The last time I'd seen them together, it had not been a positive interaction. I placed the crown in its box and was about to lead the Queen to her bed when she bolted for the door. I ran to catch up with her, wrapping my arms around her waist and pulling her away from the door.

"No, no!" She cried. "I have to find Eevan!" She struggled agaisn't me. "Let me go," she ordered, and I had to go against every bit of training I'd had to ignore her order. This was what I hated most about whatever plagued my Queen; the requirement to keep her safe meant going against orders, going against my sworn duty.

"Your Majesty, please!" I grunted. "You can't go out there." I couldn't bring myself to tell her that Eevan was dead, deep down she knew it but, during these episodes of past and present colliding, I was never sure what she knew and saying it could potentially make her worse.

"I'll find him," I said, hoping it would calm her enough to get her into bed. "I'll go and find him, you stay here."

She relaxed for a moment only to elbow me in the face as my arms had begun to loosen. I gripped her tighter, hauling her away from the door.

"Get off of me!" She fought—had she been stronger, she would have broken out of my hold—but she was weak. If only she'd eat. "Traitor!" She slung back at me as I managed to at least get her through the bedchamber doorway. I tried to hide how much the word hurt me, how much I believed it of myself.

"When you have your sense back you'll know I did this for you," I said as I dropped her onto the bed and darted out of the room, slamming and locking the door behind me. She pounded on the wood, begging and yelling for me to get Eevan, to bring him to her, to save Evie from the Osirian, to keep him away from Bellona. I slid to the floor, trying desperately to catch my breath, but memories of Evalina screaming as guards hauled her away filled my mind. How was this any different? How did Islina do this to her daughter?

Eventually, she stopped. When I heard her pad to the bed and collapse onto it, I risked opening the door. She was under the covers, her shoulders shaking with sobs. I crouched by the side of her bed and took her hand in mine.

"Why did he leave me?" She asked, the tears streaming down her face leaving a dark stain on the white pillow.

"To protect you," I whispered, pushing rougue hairs off her face and tucking them behind her ear.

She could never understand how much it pained me to see her like this, to need to care for her the way I did when she was the closest thing I'd had to a mother for so long. I wanted to keep this from Evie, but I couldn't anymore. She had to know.

I opened the top drawer of her side table, removed a small vial of purple liquid and pulled out the cork with my teeth. "Islina, can you drink this for me?"

She looked at me quizzically, I couldn't tell if she even knew who I was. "It'll help you feel better, I promise." I added for good measure.

She took the vial and drank it down, her face screwing up at the sharp taste, before relaxing back into the pillow.

As the elixir took effect, she continued to ramble, she talked about anything and everything. Sometimes she'd speak of my parents, and at those times I liked to close my eyes and imagine the scenario was reversed and she was caring for me, retelling happy times from my childhood to lull me to sleep.

CHAPTER TEN
MERRIMENT AND MISERY

The rest of the ball passed by in a blur. I briefly spoke to other royals and dignitaries from the other kingdoms, was fed wine by my family and danced until my feet felt like bags of broken glass.

Somewhere between my grandfather and Prince Thanatos speaking about the best way to kill a Kraken and my aunt Bellona giving me my sixth or seventh glass of wine, my mother stood, said her farewells to the party and had Lorkin escort her to her chambers. I watched them closely as my mother took Lorkin's arm and he began leading her away; my mother's grip on Lorkin's arm was tight.

My parents had always treated Lorkin like their own son, especially after his parents had died and he began living with us at the castle. Our fathers and his mother had died within a year of each other, but he didn't seem as heartbroken about his parents' deaths as he was about my father's. We had spent weeks crying ourselves to sleep, holding each other until our nursemaid would find one of us missing from our beds and separate us.

After my father had died and my mother was … broken, Lorkin became our mediator, defusing the roaring matches between my mother and I and stopping us from almost killing each other during my teenage years. The more my mother's condition deteriorated, the more Lorkin became more of a carer to her than a son or Captain of her Guard.

From this distance, I could see Lorkin was whispering in my mother's ear but I was too far away to read his lips. Words of soothing by the calmed, yet almost frantic, look on my mother's face. I was surprised she'd stayed as long as she had—I'd half expected her to leave after the first course of dinner.

A wave of pride came over me, for my broken mother, who had managed to sit through the main events of a ball, the first ball she had been to in almost 100 years.

"She did well to last so long."

I turned back to Thanatos, my grandfather had wandered off to talk to the Shinchaku about trade.

"Yes, she did," I agreed.

He gave me a knowing smile and grabbed two goblets of wine off a servant's tray as they walked past, handing one to me and holding his own out for a toast. "To your mother surviving the ball, to Lorkin not killing every male that's looked at you for too long, and to you, Princess, for being the most beautiful being in the room."

I scoffed at the last part but clinked my goblet against his. He grinned at me while he drained his cup.

Once he'd finished his drink and placed the goblet on another passing servant's tray, he bowed dramatically to me and asked, "Would the Princess care to join me for a walk through the garden?"

I smiled but quickly looked back to see if Lorkin had left my mother yet and given that he wasn't standing in front of her chamber doors, I assumed he was still with her, probably soothing her until she fell asleep like a child being soothed by their parents.

I looked back to Thanatos and curtsied dramatically to match his bow and accepted his offer.

The cold air hit me like a black smiths hammer and I instantly regretted agreeing to this walk. I felt the Prince lean in closer to me. "You should have bought the Fire Lily," he whispered in my ear.

"How do you know I kept it? I may have thrown it out my window for all you know."

He laughed. "I spotted the box last night. Your mother was right, it does look good on your mantle."

"Well, I didn't think I was going to be walking around a freezing cold garden all night." I huffed, my breath fogging before me.

"And I thought it would be nice to get away from the fuss, and that the wine would warm you."

"I haven't drunk nearly enough wine for this level of cold."

He laughed again and then we were silent for a while, just walking and admiring the effort that had been put into the gardens.

"I wanted to check on you, make sure you're all right after last night."

And with that short sentence I felt our relationship shift. A part of me still didn't feel totally comfortable being around him but, after last night, I couldn't despise him as I had before I'd met him, before he'd healed me. I knew he would still be a pain, but we could at least respect each other.

"I'm fine, and thank you. I can't remember if I said it last night. Did you have those scratches healed?"

He grinned. "Yes, I did. I told the guard I was with one of the maids, but I wouldn't tell him which one. I think I saved all of them from any unwanted attention from him. My second good deed of the night."

I laughed. "Sorry, again, about that. Did the other guards not see it happen?"

"No, I heard you before they did. You'd already scratched me by the time they came in."

I nodded and we fell silent again.

"You're not going to see the mages, are you?" Thanatos finally asked.

"No, I'm not. Got a problem with that?"

He held his hands up in front of him. "Of course not, it's your decision … though I would like to know why it didn't heal. I know Dark-Elves are meant to be shit healers, but I'm one of the best."

I sighed. "I don't know why, and I don't know if I want to know why. Maybe if I complete "the task that must be done", it'll go away."

The Prince looked at me expectantly. "And what might that task be?"

I shrugged. "I have no idea."

"Well, you'll never complete a task locked up in this castle, unless the task is dusting," he joked, looking up into the trees lining the path. "The lanterns remind me of Sillessia, of the fairies in the trees."

I looked up to the Prince's face; he seemed far away, like he was in a different place … or time. "You've been to Sillessia and seen the fairies?"

His amber eyes warmed as a smile spread across his face. "Yes, it's beautiful. Thick forest, fairies glittering in the night, everyone is so sweet—a little mad, but sweet." He paused, as if debating whether or not he should tell me more. "I like to go there and help with the Naeinn."

So he really had seen crazy, and a level of crazy that well surpassed my mother's, it explained how he knew how to act around her.

"That is surprisingly kind and uncharacteristic of you, Prince."

He stopped walking and faced me. "Is it? How do you know?" he asked, his tone sharp "Because of stories you hear from the maids?"

I was surprised, I hadn't expected this reaction. "I can guarantee that if you told anyone that you helped Naeinn, you would get that reaction. I think your reputation is far worse and more widespread than you know."

He huffed. "I guess so, but maybe that's a good thing."

I looked up at him quizzically. "Why?"

He sighed. "Never mind, shall we continue?" He gestured forward and we continued our walk, in silence, until I spotted a garden bench and begged to sit.

I sighed loudly as I plonked onto the seat and took my shoes off to massage my feet, letting the slightest bit of my healing power seep into the muscles and tiny bones.

The Prince chuckled but threw himself down next to me and let out a long sigh. "Is that not a waste of your gift?"

"This is the most I get to use my gift." I pointed out.

The Prince sat forward watching my hands work on my feet, studying the way I slowly released my power when I found a particularly sore spot. "Have you really been hidden away all this time?"

I paused my massaging and thought about how to respond. Was three days too little time to tell a new 'friend', if I could call him that, my sad little story? I guessed there was no turning back from the night before and the more time I spent with the Prince, the more I began to doubt all the horrible stories I'd heard about him.

"I haven't been past the border walls of this castle since I was a child, and if I ever tried …"—I sighed and pointed straight in front of us—"if I ever tried to leave, my mother would lock me in that tower for weeks, if not months."

The tower was an old watch post from thousands of years before I was born. Before it was my solitary cell, we used it as extra food storage in the winter and it still stunk of salted meat to this day.

"What was the longest time she kept you up there for?"

I tried to think back, to remember a part of my life I longingly wanted to forget. "Three months. I had tried to sneak away and follow Lorkin to his first training camp."

Lorkin had woken before the sun had risen that day, I hadn't slept all night, not trusting him to wake me up before he was to leave me for sixmonths of intensive guard training.

Sure enough, when it was time for him to leave, he did try to sneak out and leave me sleeping. As he leaned over me to quickly brush a kiss on my cheek before walking out the door, I pulled him on top of me and tried to convince him to stay. It had almost worked but Lorkin was as stubborn as me.

The guards in training were about sixty paces past the castle boundaries before I tried to follow them. I had a leather pack filled with food and a dagger in my boot; my plan was to follow a distance behind and, in the dead of night, Lorkin and I would run away and never return to Lonthia.

The mages had alerted my mother and the guards before I'd even made it to the outer edge of the wards. Guards had grabbed me, kicking and screaming, carried me up to the top of the tower and locked the only way out. Food, water and other necessities were pulled up the side of the tower in a bucket making it so I didn't have to leave the tower—for anything.

The Prince hid his wince well, but I saw it in his eyes. He gazed up at the tower, from this distance it seemed small, but to stand under it … it made you feel like an ant.

"Would you leave?"

I twisted my head to face him. "What?"

He leaned toward me and said a little quieter, as if he were worried about people hearing. "Would you leave this place? Forget about being Queen and leave, wander the world and see the fairies of Sillessia?"

It was almost as if he was asking me to leave with him.

"I–I can't just leave my mother as Queen, and Lorkin has sworn an oath to the Kingdom. I couldn't just leave."

"Then take an absence and let one of the Council take over, or leave Loverboy Lorkin in charge." He shrugged, as if it was that easy.

"That is not the kind of Queen I want to be."

"So, instead, you will be a Queen who's never seen past her front gate?"

I gaped at him, he'd hit a nerve he couldn't possibly have known was already raw. "I don't see how it concerns you." I straightened. "If I choose to stay here it is because I want to be here." I lied as I put my shoes back on my still aching feet.

"That's a lie and you know it, I know it! You have a longing for adventure and escape."

I stood and began to storm away.

"Evalina, please, I don't like the idea of you being cooped up here forever."

I felt his fingers wrap around my wrist.

"Who are you to care? You don't know me, I met you three days ago for Mother's sake." I pulled out of his grasp.

"Evalina—"

I turned away and stalked back through the garden.

"Evalina, we need to talk about this!" Thanatos called after me.

I made a foul gesture in his direction and continued walking back to the ball to say my farewells to my guests and go straight to bed.

After addressing the crowd and saying goodnight to my family, I searched for Lorkin to walk me back to my room. Damned if I was going to walk back alone and risk running into one of those creatures again with my feet in the state they were.

I found a guard posted outside the door to my mother's chambers, and he told me that Lorkin had gone down to the kitchens. I groaned, thinking about walking down the stone stairs with my aching feet.

I took the servants' stairs down to our large kitchen rooms, all the cooks and servants were frantically cleaning and preparing for tomorrow morning's breakfast, so busy that none of them noticed me. I spotted Lorkin sitting at the end of a large wooden table with a tankard of what I assumed was ale. He wouldn't be caught dead drinking wine, though I knew he preferred it; he was slouched and resting his head on the rim of his drink.

I quietly walked over and took a seat to his left. "Is everything all right?"

He lifted his head slowly and gazed around, as if making sure no one would hear what he had to say. "She's getting worse, I don't know how much longer we can hide this."

He was talking about my mother.

"But she did so well tonight! I thought it was an improvement." The look in his eyes told me I was wrong, I took a deep breath and stared at the wall in front of me. "How bad was she?"

He sat up, lent back in his chair and took a deep swig from his drink. "It started when you first spoke to your grandfather." He looked into his tankard, avoiding my eyes. "She wasn't speaking directly to me, but I could hear her mumbling under her breath, stuff about your father and King Adalric. The longer you spoke to them, the worse it got. When your grandfather went to meet Prince Thanatos, she almost leapt out of the throne—to do what, I don't know."

I leant forward on the table and let my head rest on my hands, feeling drained.

"I managed to calm her by listening to her rambling, none of it made sense. It was then that she started to ask where your father was … I thought that was a good time to escort her to her chambers."

My head flicked up and I stared at Lorkin. "She asked for my father?"

He nodded, still looking at his drink.

My mother had always been very firm about my father being dead, for her to ask for him …

"It took me an hour to calm her enough to give her a sleeping elixir, the whole time she was asking about Eevan, where he was, why he wasn't with her. It was horrible, Evie." His voice cracked.

I leaned forward and gripped his shoulder. "It will be all right. I'll be on Islina watch tomorrow, you take the day off and get some rest."

He looked up from his tankard guiltily.

"It's fine, Lor, really." I gave his shoulder a squeeze and rose from my chair. "I'll go find someone else to walk me to my room, you just relax." He made a move to stand and follow me, but I held him down firmly by the shoulder. "Relax, I said."

He looked like he was going to protest but thought better of it, taking another swig of his ale instead.

I smiled and walked away. I could feel his eyes following me as I rounded a corner and headed up the stairs.

The whole walk back my head was racing; my mother was getting worse, there was no ignoring it. While she had made it through most of the night, it may have been her breaking point—and, clearly, the ball was Thanatos's breaking point as well. To suggest I just up and leave my Kingdom in the hands of the council or Lorkin!

It was ludicrous.

I would see the world as Queen, I told myself. Being Queen would require me to attend balls and to meet with my allies, but a voice in the back of my head told me that this wasn't what the Prince was talking about. He was talking about adventure, traveling with nothing but food, weapons, and the clothes on my back, slaying monsters and visiting village after village in kingdom after kingdom, perhaps even venturing east to the lands across the sea. I let out a breath and thanked the Guard for walking me to the east wing as we reached the doors.

As soon as I reached the spiral staircase, I slipped off my shoes and walked up barefoot, groaning as my feet seemed to reform into their natural flat state. How Courtiers wore these heeled slippers everyday I would never know.

I woke not long after sunrise the next morning and had to dash to my breakfast with Queen Anouk. The tea she'd wanted me to try truly was exquisite—I sent a servant down to the kitchen straight away to ask for it to be ordered. The Queen told me that the tea could only be bought in person from a stall in the great marketplace of Hanomura and, when I asked how she came by her orders, she told me that Prince Thanatos himself would buy it for her and bring it back to the Nebu Oasis.

"You seem surprised by that, Princess," the Queen said, leaning back and smiling over the edge of her teacup; the sun caught the fine gold powder she had put on the high points of her face making her glow like the Goddess she was believed to embody by her people.

"It seems we only hear unpleasant stories about the Prince in Isidia, every good deed I hear is a story that has not yet reached us."

The Queen frowned a little. "That is a shame. Thanatos is like family to us, my son thinks of him as an uncle and my husband a brother, believe me when I say the good outweighs the bad, whether you have heard of it or not."

I nodded and sipped my tea, savoring the spicy yet soothing flavor.

I did not want to speak of Thanatos after last night, he'd reacted so strangely, so passionately, about something he knew nothing about, someone he knew nothing about. Thanatos had years before he had to worry about taking over the throne from his mother and father, but my mother was unpredictable. She could break at any moment and, in that moment, I must be here to take her place.

After a moment's silence, Queen Anouk and I began discussing trade routes and a possible expansion straight from Nebu to Isidia. Once it got close to mid-morning I excused myself, explaining that I wished to discuss the trade routes with my mother urgently.

Really I just wanted to make sure my mother was sane enough to speak of the Necromancer at the meeting with every foreign leader currently at the palace.

The Queen graciously accepted my excuse and bid me farewell; just as I was about to close the door to her rooms she called from the window. "Princess Evalina, I know relations between Isidia and Osiria have been ... stressed for many years, but give Thanatos a chance to show you his true self. He has more heart than any other I know."

I blinked at her words; not sure of what to say, I curtsied and gently closed the door.

How could it be that one Kingdom could see the Prince so differently than the rest of Carynthia? Many humans feared the Osirians for their ability to kill instantly; though elves knew it was too risky to use that power as freely as what the humans believed, the fear remained.

I headed to my mother's chambers and prepared myself for the worst—for the nonsense speaking that Lorkin had told me of the night before, for my mother to be screaming and rocking on her bed begging to see my father. When I reached the door, I took a deep breath before knocking loudly.

"Enter, if you must!" My mother called over the echo of the knock.

I opened the door and walked down the short, dark hall, she was seated on her green velvet chaise with a stack of papers sitting on her lap, her being awake and dressed was already a promising sign.

When she looked up and saw it was me that had entered, she seemed to almost rush to hide the papers from me. I took a seat in the arm chair opposite her, running my nails over the fibers of the velvet.

"What are those?" I asked as casually as I could.

"Menus from the kitchens and notes for the meeting. Must you know all my business?" She snapped as she slid the papers into the draw of the closest side table.

I sighed, thankful that she was back to her normal, terse self. I knew she was lying about the papers, but I didn't have the energy to argue with her.

"Of course not. How are you feeling today, Mother?"

She rested her head against the back of the chaise, closed her eyes and took a deep breath, as if centring herself. "I feel … fine, foggy but fine. Where is Lorkin? He didn't have breakfast with me this morning." She lifted her head to look me in the eyes, as if waiting for me to confess that Lorkin had been with me.

My mother had supported mine and Lorkin's relationship for a time, though it must have been before the Councillors had informed her that either she needed to remarry and produce a male heir, or I had to marry a Lord, if not a Prince, to follow the laws of succession correctly. Though Lorkin had been a Lord, his desire to be Captain of the Guard had never been a secret. We had just thought we'd have more time.

"He probably just slept in—I gave him the day off." I shrugged. "He deserved it after the last few days."

My mother's eyes narrowed. "Are you two still … ?" She raised an eyebrow.

"No, Mother, but he's still my friend and I can tell when he needs a break."

She held her hands up in surrender. "I just worry that you two haven't accepted that you can never be together."

I kept my face neutral but my breath had stopped and my chest felt as if it were caving in. "Believe me, we've accepted it."

Cruel, that's what my mother was; she loved the fact that I would never be happy—loved that I couldn't be with Lorkin.

Her eyes narrowed once more and she lent back against the chaise. "Prince Thanatos is quite attractive, don't you think?"

I almost laughed before I saw the seriousness in her face. "I–I mean, I guess, he has a nice jawline and his tattoos are—" I stopped myself before I said any more.

My mother raised an eyebrow. "Tattoos?"

"Rethinking your taste in men?"

"Evalina," she chided.

"Don't worry about it. Look, Mother, Thanatos is the Heir to his kingdom. Unless you want to marry again and have another child, there is no chance and I'd rather die alone." I snapped.

"So, you'd be happy with the Sillessian boy that talks to himself?"

"Perhaps, *Soren*, that's his name by the way, will make me happy."

My mother looked almost amused. "I know you came here to see if I've regained my sanity. I really wish you would just come out and say it, Evalina, rather than start an argument with me."

I felt a pang of guilt. "I … I just don't know how to go about it." I lowered my head and stared at the floor; clearly, this was one of the days when my mother remembered her previous episode.

I felt my mother's fingers gently close around the sides of my face and tilt my head so that I was looking directly into her green eyes. "I'm fine. I'll go to the head mage tonight and have him look me over before bed." Sadness and guilt flared in her eyes. "Tell Lorkin I'm sorry about last night … something about seeing Adalric set me off, and when I saw him speak to Thanatos … he just reminded me of your father so much, and when I saw him speak to an Osirian …" She gulped and a tear ran down her face.

I reached up and wiped it away, feeling tears prick at my own eyes.

She smiled and leant to kiss me on the head. "I think it's time we start to come up with a solution." She released my face and walked around my chair to the tea cart behind me.

I twisted to face her. "Solution for what?"

She paused making a pot of tea to look me in the eyes. "A solution for me, you and Lorkin both know you can't hide my … illness forever."

"Mother, please, can we not speak of this?"

She slammed the lid of the teapot down, almost shattering it. "Damn it, Evalina! This is the first time in years I've felt this clear headed, we can't keep putting this conversation off! You, Lorkin, and I all know that I'm getting worse and I don't want the council deciding my fate."

In one of my first training sessions, I had paid a guard a substantial amount of gold to teach me how to fight and to not go easy on me. He decided he would teach me the same way they had taught him when he became a guard. This meant we would start with a sparring match even though I knew nothing about fighting. During that sparring match the guard had managed to kick me in the head, chest, and groin all within the first 3 seconds. That is how I felt in this moment—like I had been kicked in the head, chest and groin by a seasoned warrior.

My mind was blown that my mother felt clear headed, my heart broke that she knew she was getting worse and the groin kick was for the fact that she didn't want the council to decide her fate but was quite happy for them to decide mine.

"Sillessia, with the Naeinn."

I looked at my mother in disbelief.

"It's the most logical option, Evalina. If anything happens, if I hurt anyone or don't … just … send me to Sillessia."

I nodded, not knowing what else I could do.

My mother clenched and unclenched her hands then went back to making tea. I stayed silent, absorbing what she had said.

A knock on the door cut the silence.

"Come in!" My mother called, placing the tea trolley between us and sitting back down on her chaise as a guard strolled up the small dark hallway.

"Your Majesty, Your Highness"—he bowed low—"we have finished gathering the necessary dignitaries for the meeting." Another bow.

"Wonderful. Seems tea shall have to wait." She rose from her chair and brushed non-existent dust off her green gown.

I rose with her and mentally prepared to be involved in the biggest council meeting to be held in Lonthia in at least two hundred and ten years.

CHAPTER ELEVEN
DECIDING OF FATE

I had never seen so many people stuffed into the council room in all my life. The carved, Ashwood-paneled room was full to the brim with lords, ladies, and royalty from every elven kingdom in Carynthia; but no humans.

I was about to mention it to my mother, but she was led away by the guard that had come to her rooms and now sat in her ornately carved chair at the head of the solid, long table.

I was forced forward by the crowd, the lords and ladies pushing to be closer to the royals sitting at the table; relishing the honor of being invited into a Royal Council.

My mother stood to speak and the crowd went silent.

"Majesties, Lords and Ladies, I thank you for taking time out of your day to attend this meeting. You will find yourselves glad that you did. I do not take pleasure in being the bearer of this news but, as far as I am aware, it is so far focused on Lonthia."

The crowd began to stir, the royals around the tables faces were drawn. I caught Thanatos' gaze, he gave me a look as if to say 'I knew you were lying', and I hoped the look I sent back portrayed enough to suggest where I wanted him to stick it.

"Ladies and Gentlemen, I regret to inform you that another Necromancer has risen to power."

The crowd erupted, royal families conversing quickly with each other, the lords and ladies around the table discussing the appropriate solution to deal with the Necromancer; what worked last time and what didn't, some were having to explain to the person next to them what a Necromancer actually was.

My grandfather rose to his feet and the crowd hushed. "Are you sure, Islina?"

My eyes darted from my grandfather to my mother, she took a moment and a deep breath.

"Yes, Adalric, my guards have fought and killed multiple Corse in the last cycle. They also managed to capture one and interrogate it."

A collective gasp ran through the crowd.

"What did the creature say?" Prince Zared asked from my mother's right.

"The Necromancer wishes for Lonthia to fall first, but the ultimate goal is to eradicate all Elf-kind."

The room erupted again, this time with shouts of panic, the guard next to my mother tensed and reached for his sword; ears pricking up to hear anyone take a step too close to his Queen

"So, you invited us all here to die with you?!" A Sillessian she-elf called over the crowd from the opposite side of the room to me.

"Not at all, the ball was already planned before I was informed of this situation, it made sense for me to warn you while you were here and also to plead for your help." The room again went silent, waiting for my mother's next words. "The last time we encountered a Necromancer, we all lost a great many, and now Lonthia, no, the whole of Isidia, is under attack by a force that will not stop until we have met our demise. Once he is done with us, he will move on to another kingdom. I am asking that, in order to save your own kingdoms, you will help me save mine."

Queen Ambrosia now rose and looked around the room. "A Necromancer is a great threat on the whole of Carynthia and, yet, you have not invited any of our human brothers and sisters to this meeting. Why?"

My mother nodded to the Queen of Sillessia. "We do not yet know where the Necromancer is based, nor his reason for targeting elves. I would propose that we keep this between us and send out a scout team to investigate each human land, to see if anyone is harboring any resentment towards us. Until then, I say we trust no human."

My uncle Peverell rose. "Are you suggesting an entire human kingdom is using a Necromancer to attack us?"

My mother's stern face said enough and the crowd once again erupted into shouts.

"The humans love us!" Insisted a Sillessian

"Makes sense, they've always been a selfish race!" Shouted an angry Carracallan.

"Surely we could pressure the creature into telling us the location of the Necromancer?" My grandmother suggested over the shouting of the crowd.

"We have tried, but the Necromancer seems to have blocked our compulsion," my mother explained.

"Get the Osirian to have a go!" Shouted a Sillessia lord from the back of the crowd.

The shouts quietened to a murmur, as if almost everyone was in shock that Prince Thanatos was even there.

Thanatos cleared his throat. "I trust that Isidia's mages have sufficient compulsion abilities to extract the information we need but, if the Queen wishes it, I offer my services." He bowed to my mother and she nodded in return.

"The Corse that we have in custody was Minoman and, being that Minoma is the home of human scholars and mages, I would suggest we start there." My mother suggested.

"This could start a war, Islina," Aunt Bellona said over the crowd, sounding more excited than concerned.

"I am trying to avoid a war by keeping the attacks contained to Isidia and having the scouts find and eliminate the Necromancer before his army can grow too large."

Darius rose from his chair. "It's not how we've done things before, but this could work." He expressed looking around the room. "Islina is right, we don't know how far up this Necromancer is connected, and with which human kingdom." There were a few nods of agreement. "I don't believe it could be one rogue human with a goal to wipe out all elf-kind. A two person scout team should be enough to hunt him down and not alert the humans to our knowledge of the Necromancer. As for Isidia, you have my ships to aid you; we can clear out the villages as the situation worsens and take them to Carracalla."

My mother bowed low. "Thank you, Darius, you do not know what this will mean to my people, or to me."

My grandfather rose again. "Are we all in agreement then? A small scout team will hunt him and the rest of us will fight to protect Isidia until the Necromancer is dealt with?"

A resounding "Aye!" echoed through the room in response and my mother gave a small smile.

"Now we must discuss who shall be on the scout team." My aunt Bellona stated "Two, you say, Darius?"

My uncle nodded. "Two good warriors should be sufficient."

Bellona clapped him on the back with her large hand almost knocking him over. "Well, sign me up!"

"I will need you and your ships to help evacuate the villages."

My aunt looked disappointed but caught my eye and winked.

Discussion sparked about warriors and who was the best to send on the scout mission. My mother was hesitant to send our best warriors, insisting we would need people who knew the forests around Isidia to protect it fully. My Carracallan kin had left their strongest warriors at home, not expecting to be needing them, and Sillessia didn't have much to offer—not that anyone would say it out loud.

Lords and Ladies were suggesting guards from their own houses, scraping at any kind of honor they could take away from this meeting. Some argued that we should wait to hear from the Osirians, saying they had the upper hand against a Necromancer, to which Thanatos argued there was no time.

The room was getting progressively louder and warmer, sweat was beginning to bead on my forehead; Ladies were pulling out their fans, the males standing next to them moving slightly closer just to feel a lick of air.

The discussion quickly turned to arguments between Lords and Ladies of different courts and kingdoms, some claiming they had the best warriors in their land, only to be shut down by another claiming they had beaten them in some battle that may or may not have actually happened. Shouting broke out and guards were called in to restrain certain ladies and lords that couldn't keep to using words.

Suddenly the burn on my shoulder throbbed. *A task that must be done …* was this it? The task … *it must be …* the task from my dream.

I shot forward in the crowd trying to get to the edge. I realized, then—later than I should have—what the wink from my aunt had meant.

"I'll do it."

My mother's eyes darted to me. My aunt and Prince Thanatos grinned.

"What?" My mother asked.

I squared my shoulders and said loud enough for the whole room to hear. "I will go." The room went silent, so silent I wondered if everyone had just dropped dead. "I will hunt down the Necromancer and stop the war before it has a chance to begin."

My mother's eyes seemed to glaze over and she sat down in her chair.

My grandfather cleared his throat and I turned to look at him. "Are you sure, Evalina? You don't have much experience in the world."

His words hit me but I pushed past them.

"I've already fought and captured a Corse, and I'm one of the best warriors we have."

"Lorkin told me he captured the Corse." My mother's eyes narrowed on me.

"He lied to spare you the worry, it attacked me in the woods. This Necromancer is attacking our home, Mother. Let me go, let me protect our Queendom."

She looked to my grandfather, my uncles, my grandmother, anyone that would side with her and shut me down—but no one would. "I don't know, Evalina … it's so risky, you could–could—"

"Who else would you trust if not me? Lorkin? He will need to be here to lead in battle. I don't know the forests outside the walls, what good would I be here? I can do this, Mother, just give me a chance."

Her eyes softened, as if knowing that Lorkin would still be with her gave her more comfort than me staying here.

"Islina, think of it as her first voyage. Eevan would support her. He would want this." My aunt said gently.

A knowing look passed between my aunt and mother, and I knew she was close to agreeing, because Bellona was right.

"Your Majesty, surely you're not considering this?" A Councilman interjected, forcing his way to the front of the crowd. "Evalina is soon to be our Queen, how can we risk her leaving now?"

At his words, something flickered in my mothers' eyes, a defiance I'd never seen.

"Who will go with you?" she asked.

The one you would not choose.

I looked across the table at Thanatos and smiled. "Prince Thanatos will come with me. He knows the lands well and, really, who would pick a fight with an Osirian?"

There was a murmur of agreement through the crowd.

"Now, hang on a moment, do I get a say in this?" Thanatos rose from his chair across from me, towering over almost everyone else in the room.

"Are you really going to say no to an adventure, Prince?" I goaded.

The whole room was staring at the Prince expectantly, waiting for an argument.

"Fine!" The Prince exclaimed. "I'll go with you, in honor of the treaty and because I know you'll need my help."

"There! We have our scouts, should they head to Minoma first?" My grandfather questioned.

"I will need to stop by Osiria to collect my things, we'll take the Mid Road north and then head to Minoma, stopping in Kushyam on the way."

King Adalric nodded. "Then, I'd say this meeting is over. Prince Thanatos and Princess Evalina will scout and, if possible, kill the Necromancer while the Carracallan army—and the Sillessian, if needed—help hold Isidia." And, with that, he hit his fist on the table and the meeting was over.

Slowly people filed out of the room; every second or third person putting their hand on my shoulder and wishing me luck on my journey, none did this to the Prince, until it was just my family, Prince Thanatos, and I left to see to my mother.

I took the empty seat to my mother's left and placed my hand over hers, she stayed silent and still, hardly even breathing. Thanatos and my family moved down the table until we were all sitting at the same end.

Darius leaned forward. "This will be good for her, Islina," he said gently to my mother. "Evalina can't rule the kingdom on book smarts alone." He flicked a quick apologetic look my way. "She needs experience in the real world and to meet the people she'll be ruling over."

My mother sighed and gripped my hand. "I know …"—she sucked in a breath— "I know this is the best thing for Evalina, for the Kingdom, there is no one else I would trust with keeping Isidia safe." She smiled at me and squeezed my hand tighter. "I just *wish* there was someone else …"

As terrible as my relationship was with my mother, I knew that my death would be her breaking point, and hers mine. For the sixty years before my father's death we had had the perfect mother daughter relationship, and, sometimes, we still had our moments.

"Your Majesty, I swear I will protect your daughter to the best of my abilities on our journey. I cannot promise that she will not be injured, but I can assure you, she will not die on my watch."

My mother gave the Prince a grateful smile, as did the rest of my family; I could sense the worry in all of them, and they were right to worry. What if we didn't find the Necromancer in time and Isidia was destroyed? What if the Prince died on the journey and the Osirians start another war—or vice versa? So many things could go wrong, but I had to push those thoughts aside and think of the good coming out of this situation. I was finally leaving the castle.

"When should we leave?" I asked no one in particular.

My grandfather put his hand on my shoulder. "Given the severity of the situation, tonight."

Excitement and dread rose in my chest—tonight was so soon.

"Surely it can wait till morning, Adalric," my mother breathed.

"Tonight all the guests of the ball will be leaving. It will be a mass exodus of carriages and riders, so they will go unnoticed to any Corse that may be lurking by, and any humans that may report it to the Necromancer." My grandfather pressed.

"And only the guests of the ball know what Evalina looks like. As long as we hide her appearance from them, no one will know that the Princess has even left the castle. And with the Prince's reputation it would come as no surprise if he left Lonthia with someone new at his side." Bellona added, shrugging at Thanatos's glare.

"Tonight then," Thanatos agreed. "Will you be ready, Your Highness?"

I gaped at him. It was already past midday, I had a few hours to say goodbye to my loved ones—who I may or may not see again.

I nodded and he rose from the table. "I'll go to the stable and have our horses prepared, we'll meet there at nightfall."

I nodded again and he turned and left.

My family and I sat in silence for a little while, each of us lost in our own thoughts, until a clock chimed two o'clock. Nightfall was around six, and it dawned on me that I only had four hours left here.

My aunt cleared her throat. "I guess we'll have to save our sparring session for when you get back."

I nodded glumly, gripping my mother's hand as tight as I could.

Suddenly, my mother pulled her hand away and rose quickly to her feet. "Come now, Evalina, we must pack your bags."

Everyone at the table looked as surprised as I felt.

"We'll save the goodbyes for later, or else nothing will get done." My mother clapped me on the back and I rose slowly to follow her as she strode from the room.

I looked back at my Carracallan family's confused faces.

"We'll meet you in the stables at half to 6 to say a proper farewell," my uncle Peverell called.

I nodded as I shut the door to the council room and almost jogged to catch up to my mother, already halfway down the corridor.

"Come, Evalina, we have a lot to do."

I fell into step beside her. "Could I not have had a little longer with them? I haven't seen them in decades."

"I know, darling, but you need the time to pack and prepare. You go to your rooms, I'll go to the armory and the kitchens, and meet you back there." And with that she sped off toward the training pits and I was left confused and alone in the hallway.

My mother's mood swings had always been unpredictable, but this was one I'd never experienced before—from seeming too worried to function, she now seemed almost ecstatic to see me go. I couldn't say it was a bad thing, but it was certainly unexpected.

Instead of rushing to my room, I decided to take my time walking through the gardens, breathing in the scent of Lonthia, committing to memory particular scents that I never wanted to forget.

I loved the winter, but I wished I could have seen the castle in spring one last time, the white, stone walls covered in multi-colored blossoms. Sometimes, the crawling plants grew so thick it looked like the castle was built out of them.

I strolled through the gardens and woods until I was standing in front of the tower. The structure loomed over me, but close up it didn't look as huge as I remembered it being. Since I'd stopped trying to run away, the tower had been ignored, crawling plants that had long since died still clung to the stones, and parts of the old thatch roof were scattered across the base of the tower. I pressed my hand against the cool stone; this time, when I left the castle grounds, I wouldn't be dragged up the stairs of the tower, kicking and screaming—I would be free.

My pointed ear twitched at the sound of stomping boots coming my way. I knew by the rhythm of the steps that it was Lorkin, and that he knew I was leaving.

CHAPTER TWELVE
ROLES REVERSED

I halted beside Evalina before the tower, my hands shaking at my sides. "What in the Father's name is going on?!" I panted. "I leave you alone with Islina for one day, and now you're leaving?"

"Who told you?" She whispered, still gazing up at the tower that had been her prison more times than I cared to remember.

"Islina. She practically pranced into my bedroom and said I had three hours till you leave and that I'd better see you. What in the pit happened at the meeting?" I never thought she'd leave without me and now here we were, saying goodbye.

She took a deep breath. "Everyone agreed that in order to discreetly dispose of the Necromancer, a scout team of two people should hunt him down while the majority stay here and protect Isidia."

My mood darkened. Two people. It couldn't be me; she was leaving Isidia for the first time without me. "Was there really no one else that could go in your place?"

She spun to face me, her eyes red-rimmed. "It's my Queendom, Lokin, who else should go, if not me?"

I chewed my cheek. She was right, it was the best outcome for her and the Queendom. She got to leave, to experience the world and show her people what she was capable of. But, for some reason, I still wanted to provoke her. "So, you're just going to drop everything and leave tonight?"

Tears welled in her eyes and I fought to stay where I was. Logically, I knew this was hard for her, but, emotionally, I was betrayed and angry. We'd always been together, save when I was away at training and she … I gazed up at the tower above us.

"I'm sorry," she said. "This could be my only chance."

I nodded, not knowing what to say. Then my head snapped up. Two people. "Two person scout team. Who is the second?"

Evalina stiffened, as if she was preparing to take a hit. "Thanatos has great knowledge of the wor—"

"You're going with him?!" She shrank away from me, my rage plainly displayed on my face, "You couldn't go with one of our own warriors?" I spat.

"Thanatos knows the world better than any of our people, and it's a great opportunity to strengthen the relationship with Osiria."

The words slammed into me as if she'd hit me with them and then my mind raced, before I could try to stop it, sifting through all the times I'd noticed them together, noticed their ease and body language. "How close are you and the Prince?"

Her mouth fell open. "Excuse me?"

I narrowed my eyes at her, searching her face for confirmation. "Every time I've seen you lately, you've been with him or have come from being with him." Her expression was incredulous but I continued, unable to stop myself. "Doesn't it seem strange that he got here so early? Why would he not have just shacked up in the town and waited till the day of the ball to show up like everyone else?"

She squared her shoulders, her hands raising to rest on her hips. "What are you saying, Lorkin?" She demanded.

I could barely see through my rage, her face was tunneled in my vision while my mind was racing through images of her and the Prince, laughing together, walking together, dining together. "It just seems strange to me that the Prince shows up early the same day you're attacked, then he's seen coming out of your bedroom—twice—and last night at the ball—"

"Did you have people watching me!?"

It was my turn to gape at her. "Of course I did! I was worried. Evalina, our enemy was sleeping right next door! Was I supposed to just ignore that fact? As Captain of the Guard, I couldn't, and as someone who cares for you, I couldn't." I couldn't keep the disdain from my voice. "Clearly, I shouldn't have bothered. You can take care of yourself well enough, it seems."

Pain lanced across my face as my head whipped to the side. I hadn't seen her move and even she looked a little shocked as her handprint blossomed across my cheek.

"You seem to forget to whom you speak, Captain," she spat, quickly recovering from the shock. "Perhaps when I return from my journey, you'll have remembered." She spun and stalked back to the castle.

"Fuck." I sighed, slumping against the side of the tower, the ground still damp with the morning dew. My head fell into my shaking hands and stayed there. I was still so angry, but the tightness in my chest and shortness of breath was something else. It felt like I couldn't breathe, would never breathe again.

She's leaving. Evalina is leaving without me. She's leaving with him.

I didn't know what worried or angered me more, that the decision was made completely without me, that I'd been told by Islina, or that Thanatos was involved, and I had no time to work out a plan or to fix things before Evalina left.

Before I knew it, the sun was setting and I was still sitting against the cold stone of the tower. Evalina would be leaving soon and, when she did, I would need to be with Islina.

I rose and dusted myself off; even in a highly emotional state, Islina would chastise me for being covered in dirt. As I straightened, I caught sight of the Dark-Elven Prince coming toward me through the garden. I froze, taking a moment to quash the rage that had risen at the mere sight of his face.

Prince Thanatos was dressed in his traveling clothes and laden with packs overbrimming with supplies. He stopped a short distance from me, eyeing me as if he half expected me to pull a weapon on him.

My hands tightened into fists at my side. "Your Highness," I ground out, not bothering to bow.

"Captain." He said, straightening to his full, hulking height. "I was just consoling the Queen, she's a bit upset about the Princess leaving."

My jaw clenched at the jab. "I'll see to her now. Good luck on your journey." I moved to pass him but he held out an arm to stop me.

I tensed.

"Captain Lorkin." The Prince's yellow eyes bore into mine. "I want you to know, before we leave, that the Princess is safe with me and I will do my best to protect her."

"She better be. Because if anything happens to her, if you do anything to her, the treaty is void and I will go to war."

"If I do anything to her …" the Prince said, more to himself than to me. "Trust is needed from both sides, Captain, and I'm not really feeling it from you, or anyone here. Do you think I strolled into this Queendom thinking I owned the place and nothing could hurt me? No, I was nervous, terrified even, that the second I stepped into any town an army of your soldiers was going to swoop me up and bring me here as a prisoner." He paused, scanning my face. "My people are not the monsters you tell your children they are, but perhaps you are the ones we tell our children about." He looked me up and down, disapproval clear on his face. "Your Queen needs you, and I am needed by your Princess," he said with a grin as he pushed past me and strode toward the stables.

I took another moment to compose myself, to calm the fury coursing through my body and the aching in my chest, before leaving to console the Queen.

CHAPTER THIRTEEN
A WORLD WAITING

When I reached my room, I slammed the door hard enough to make the glass in the windows shake. I stormed through to my bedroom and found a large pack waiting to be filled on my bed. I wasted no time; I pulled all of the training clothes that I could find in my dressing room out and stuffed them into my pack, dressing in some while I was at it. I was halfway through shoving my feet into a pair of worn, brown leather boots when my mother strolled into my room holding a long leather case.

"Are you all right?"

I looked up at her; she still had an air of excitement around her but it had calmed. "Did you have to tell Lorkin?"

"Well, I thought someone had better and you were too busy dancing through the garden."

I finished tying my lace and stood. "I was not dancing. I don't know how long I'm going to be away, I just wanted some time."

She gently laid the case down on my bed and cupped my face. "You'll be back before you know it." She gently kissed my forehead and moved back over to the box. "I take it things didn't go well with Lorkin, then?"

I ignored the pricking behind my eyes and tried to focus on what my mother was doing. "No, he thinks I'm running away with Prince Thanatos."

My mother straightened. "Well that's just silly, but maybe it's just easier for him to let you go on a bad note. You can patch things up when you get back."

I plonked down on the end of the bed, watching my mother as she bent back down to fiddle with the locks on the case. "What if something happens to one of us?"

"Lorkin will be by my side the whole time you're gone, planning battle strategies and protecting his Queen. Unless Isidia falls, he will be completely safe. As for you, I trust Prince Thanatos wholeheartedly, he will protect you and bring you home."

79

"Mother, we hardly know the Prince! For all we know he could have agreed just so he could kill me the second we're outside the castle walls."

The last lock on the case popped open and my mother smiled. "Evalina, I know more about that boy than you ever will. His father and I have been speaking of this treaty for months, do you think our conversations are solely about land and war?" She gestured for me to stand next to her. "Now, I know that at first it didn't look like I was supportive of you going, but you must understand that even though we have our problems—I have problems—I am still your mother and I love you. Were your father alive"—she patted the lid of the box and cleared her throat—"were your father alive, he would want you to go on this journey, and he would want you to take this." She pulled up the lid of the case and revealed my father's emerald and sapphire encrusted longsword; the jewels ran halfway down the length of the blade and covered the hilt almost completely.

I gaped at the blade, it was the exact one Lorkin and I had broken when we were children.

"It was a gift to your father on our wedding day, from Adalric. The sapphires and emeralds signify our two houses. You are born of our two houses, so the sword should be yours."

"Mother … I can't possibly—"

"It is your birthright, Evalina, and it's not doing any good sitting in a dusty old study."

I ran my fingers down the length of the blade, in the case was a simple, brown leather sheath and a whetstone. I lifted the sword from the box, sheathed it and attached it to my belt. I found the weight of it comforting, as if my father were coming on this journey with me. I looked up at my mother and saw tears streaming down her face. I pulled her into a tight hug and cried with her, tears of sadness, fear, and joy; I let them fall freely until I had none left—there would be no time for tears later.

When the crying finally stopped, my mother sat me down and braided my hair back, making sure every bit of it was tucked back and could be hidden by a hood. The only thing that would give me away as the Princess was the blue in my hair. She then unpacked and repacked my bag, pulling out things I wouldn't need and adding essentials I'd missed, scolding me for forgetting them as she went.

Half five was drawing near and I was trying desperately to ignore the tightening in my chest and the bile rising in my throat. My mother had sent out a guard to double check that all the humans had left the castle, so I could easily slip out of my room and get to the stables with no one noticing. The guard returned minutes later and informed us that most of the human visitors had already left Lonthia completely, and that it was safe for me to leave.

My mother pulled me in for a tight embrace. "I'll say goodbye here. I think if I was down there with you, I wouldn't let you go after all." She pulled back to look at my face, tears resting in the corners of her eyes. "You'll be safe, you'll do great, and you will return to me." She kissed me gently on the cheek and stepped away. "I'll talk to Lorkin, try to smooth things over before you return, but it probably is easier for him to let you leave on a sour note."

I nodded in thanks and agreement, silently wishing I could sort things with Lorkin before I left.

I slung my green traveling cloak around my shoulders—it still looked brand new, despite me having it for well over thirty years—pulled my pack on to my shoulders, double checked my father's sword was securely attached to my belt, and finally lifted the hood to cover my hair. I said a final goodbye to my mother, quickly embracing her one last time before sweeping out of my room.

This time, I decided against savoring every last moment of walking through the castle for possibly the last time, and started walking quickly to the stables, stopping only to ask a guard to send Lorkin to my room to see to my mother.

The castle stables were the busiest I'd ever seen them. Six or seven stable boys were mucking out stalls throughout the large wooden structure, and another three or four stable hands were refilling water and food for our own horses, who would have been put second to the guest's and probably hadn't eaten all day.

My brown mare, Faenor, was in her stall munching on some grain, already laden with saddle bags packed to the brim with travel supplies. In the stall next to Feanor was a horse I'd never seen before, white all over except the very tip of its muzzle, which was black. This horse, too, was strapped up with twin saddlebags over-filled with supplies—mainly food, from the looks of them.

Like clockwork, my grandfather, grandmother and aunt stepped through the stable doors right on half five, each one carrying a different sized box.

"We've just said hello, and now it's time for goodbye." My grandfather sighed, looking sadly down at the small box in his large hands. "These are your belated birthday gifts, we were going to give them to you at dinner tonight, but now seems like the last chance." He handed me the small blue box and I thanked him before flipping open the lid.

Inside was a locket on a silver chain; on the front of the locket was a rectangular cut emerald, glowing in the dim light of the stables. I opened the locket and inside were two impossibly small, but very detailed, portraits of my mother and father, and on the silver backing of the locket my initials, E.E.G, were carved in a beautiful, flowing script.

I wished I could have stared at the portraits for longer, the images perfectly captured my parents' likeness. Tears threatened my eyes once again as I gazed at the portrait of my father, his warm eyes staring back at me. His blue hair resting past his shoulders, his nose straight, unlike my crooked and broken one, but every other feature was so similar to mine. How had my mother stood it all those years? Staring at my face that was so similar to his?

I closed the box and handed it back to my grandfather

"I'm sorry I can't take it with me."

He hugged me so tightly I thought I was going to die of oxygen deprivation. "It's fine," he said into my hair. "It will be waiting for you here."

Once I finally weaved out of my grandfather's iron grip, I accepted the gift from my grandmother, a smaller box than the one the locket had come in and, when I opened it, I saw why. Inside the tiny box was a small, delicate looking silver ring with a tiny, rectangular cut sapphire to match the emerald on the locket.

My grandmother smiled at the ring. "You may be Heir to the Isidian throne, but you still have Carracallan blood. We'll keep these safe for you until you return." She stepped forward and placed a kiss on my forehead before making room for my aunt to stand in front of me with her much larger box.

"Your uncles and I bought you something that may actually come in handy on your journey," she said proudly in her booming voice. "They're writing to their Captains, so they couldn't be here, unfortunately." She excitedly yanked open the lid of the box she was holding and I gasped at what lay inside.

Resting on a black, silk cushion were two brown leather leg sheaths with a Sai blade in each, the hilts were wrapped in matching brown leather and the blades and prongs were folded steel. I took out each sheath, strapped them to either leg, and embraced my Aunt.

"Tell Darius and Peverell that I love them, they were always my preferred weapon in training."

My aunt gave me a short squeeze. "We remembered from your letters. Be safe, Flower." Bellona's voice cracked and I squeezed her tighter.

My grandfather came up behind and scooped us both into his large arms, almost squeezing the life out of us, my grandmother only rested a hand on my shoulder.

For a time, all I could smell was leather, sea salt, a hint of fish, and then, slowly, the sharp smell of snow and ash began to join the mix.

My grandfather released us from his bear hug and straightened and my aunt quickly turned away, wiping at her face just as Prince Thanatos strode through the door of the stables. He was dressed in the same traveling clothes as when he'd first arrived only two days ago, with the addition of a black leather vest and traveling cloak, a sword hanging from his hip. Had it really only been three days? My life had gone from routine to chaos in a mere three days?

The Prince bowed to my grandparents and strode off to the white horse, checking the buckles and the bags, he moved over to Feanor and did the same check, he then came over to us and held out his hand to my grandfather. "It was a great honor meeting you, King Adalric. My father will be jealous when I tell him I had the pleasure of sharing a drink with you."

My grandfather chuckled, grasping the Prince's hand tightly in both of his as he shook it. "Tell King Methuzelah, as long as he brings you, he is welcome to my Kingdom anytime."

Thanatos smiled. "He will be overjoyed at that, thank you, Your Majesty." Thanatos moved to my grandmother and held out his hand to her, she placed her hand on top of his but stopped him before he could bring it all the way to his lips.

"You watch her out there, not a second is she to be from your sight."

It was a threat, and the Prince knew it.

"You have my word, Your Majesty. Not a second, even if she has something to say about it." He lowered his face down the rest of the way to her hand and pressed a light kiss to seal the promise.

My aunt was watching from a few feet away where she was leaning against a post, fiddling with her single earring. She turned her head to the side and spat on the ground. "That doesn't mean you watch her while she pisses, perv."

My grandmother groaned. "Bellona, please."

My aunt chuckled and pushed off the post, clapping Thanatos on the shoulder. "Look after her as much as she'll let you, but you over-step, boy, and I'll have your balls hanging from my figurehead till they shrivel into nothing."

The Prince clapped her back. "I believe you."

My aunt huffed and strolled back to her post.

The Prince turned to me. "Are you ready to leave?"

I looked at my family, their faces plastered with encouraging smiles.

My gut twisted, bile began to rise again and breathing was almost impossible. My grandfather reached out and stroked my face, and it again hit me how much my father had looked like him.

'Go, Evalina, Flower. You won't get another chance like this."

I smiled and swallowed down the bile and my tears. I nodded to the Prince and strode to my horse, swung on to her back, made sure my hood was secure and followed the Prince out of the stable.

We trotted through the grounds, first heading south to exit the castle grounds.

Once we'd walked around the servants' quarters and onto the main path that led to the castle gates, I risked a look backward at my chambers, but it wasn't my mother sitting by the window, crying as her only daughter walked away not knowing if she would return; it was Lorkin, staring blankly at me as I left the castle with another man.

It was pitch black and raining by the time we reached the gates of the palace wall. The guards didn't speak to us, didn't check who we were, just opened the gates and waited for us to make our way through before beginning to close them again. I stopped my horse and watched the gates close, watched the guards shout that we were the last ones leaving and to chain the gate.

This time, there was no guard chasing me, no one was dragging me back to lock me in a tower.

This time, I was free.

This time, I was free.

I was glad for the rain, it hid the tears—happy tears—that were sliding silently down my face. I faced forward in my saddle and stared down the road ahead. All I could see in the darkness was Prince Thanatos atop his white horse, cantering steadily into the shadowed world, waiting for me to discover it.

CHAPTER FOURTEEN
FIRST TASTE

It took us two days to reach the Mid Road from Lonthia, two days of silently following behind the Prince, rarely speaking, only stopping to water the horses, relieve ourselves and sleep.

When we finally came upon the Mid Road, Thanatos stopped his horse by mine. "Here we are, Princess, the Mid Road. We follow this all the way up to Nebu, then I'll lead the rest of the way to Ravenna from there."

"Tell me again, Prince, why we're going straight to Ravenna and not Minoma?"

"I need to collect some things from Osiria before we head to Minoma, and you can call me Thanatos while we're on the road."

I squinted down the road, there were a few travelers and vendors selling wares, but not as many people as I'd thought there would be. "What things? You've got clothes and a sword, what else do you need?"

"I just have to go back for a bit, all right?" He said sharply. "We'll walk through the woods, next to the path—keep you out of sight so you can let that hood down."

I nodded in agreement and relief, the last two days had been uncharacteristically humid. I longed to take my cloak off, or at least my hood.

We crossed over to the left side of the wide road and walked through the woods until we found a clearing far enough away from the road that we couldn't hear any vendors yelling about their wares.

We tied the horses and I waited in the clearing while Thanatos scouted the area to make sure it was clear for me to remove my cloak. He returned a few minutes later and gave me a simple nod. I pulled the cloak and hood off with one quick yank, kicked off my boots and collapsed onto the thick damp grass.

"I never want to wear that damn hood again," I huffed as I wiped the sweat off my face with my sleeve, leaving another smudge of dirt on the already filthy fabric.

The Prince laughed and sat on a log nearby to stretch his legs. "I didn't realize you were suffering so much."

"Because, like all males, you were not suffering, so you didn't think I should be."

The Prince scoffed. "You are handling traveling a lot better than I had expected."

"Because I'm a Princess?"

"Because you were held in a very clean, luxurious prison."

I chuckled. "It was very clean compared to this." I thudded the ground next to me, enjoying the feeling of the dirt on my fingers. Had I been at home, my mother would have ordered me to bathe immediately.

"We should have lunch and get moving."

I groaned. "Can't we just rest for a day? I'd like to get the feeling back in my arse."

"I could help you with that," the Prince suggested, laughing when I threw a rock at him. "We'll reach a human village by tomorrow night, if we make good time today. We can have a break there and resupply, but you'll have to put your hood on."

I groaned again but the thought of visiting a human village excited me; actually, the thought of visiting any sort of village excited me.

The Prince had laughed at me on the first day of our journey, when I'd insisted on stopping at every vendor on the road. I hadn't bought anything, but to browse their wares was a luxury to me. In the palace, I'd always had my clothes and jewels made by Ashby, and he always just knew what to make. I'd never picked anything for myself.

I stayed on the ground for a few more seconds, savoring the coolness of the grass, before I pulled myself up to grab lunch from the saddlebags on Serelene, Thanatos' mare. Bread, cheese and apples; it wasn't a terrible lunch, but nothing close to what I was used to. Our dinners so far had been rabbit stew, much to my disgust. Thanatos caught the rabbits himself, and every night I studied his skinning technique so that eventually I could help prepare dinner, or make it myself. I found it so refreshing to do things for myself, for once.

We ate our lunch in silence, then packed up and were back on our way. We stayed in the woods so that I could get away with not wearing my hood, but for safety's sake I kept my cloak on. Thanatos had wanted to ride, but I insisted on giving the horses a break, and my arse. I had never ridden for so long and my legs were raw, aching, and desperate for a stretch.

We walked at a quick pace so as to keep to the Prince's schedule. I could tell there was more waiting for him at home in Osiria than just his weapons and other supplies, but I doubt I would find out what it was before we were walking through the doors of Ravenna Fortress itself.

Ravenna Fortress was the home of the Osirian royal family and its highest ranked courtiers. It sat between two peaks in the Helice mountain range in Osiria, and the mountain range itself was wedged between a volcanic wasteland and an unforgivable icy tundra. All the books I'd read said you needed a guide to find

Ravenna, for monsters and false paths litter both sides of Osiria, as if they had built labyrinths to purposefully deter people.

"Did you not enjoy your lunch?" Thanatos asked. "You looked like you were going to throw up."

"I did! I just don't really eat rabbit," I confessed. "When I was a girl, I saw one caught in a bear trap while I was traveling with my father. It was so small and completely mangled in the trap, it made me feel terrible for ever eating them. My mother doesn't really eat meat, either, so it was easy for me to avoid it."

"Speaking of your mother, she was surprisingly supportive of you leaving."

"Yes, I think she realized that Bellona was right—my father would have wanted this."

"How did my good friend, Lorkin, take the news?"

I stiffened.

"Not well, then?"

I shook my head and concentrated on the ground in front of me. "My mother got to him before I did, and she wasn't as forbearing as she could have been." I kicked a pebble and sent it skittering before us. "He also …" My eyes flicked to the Prince, he was watching me expectantly. "Nevermind."

"He also what? Come on, you can tell me. I promise I won't spread any rumors," he joked.

I sighed. "He got it into his head that we were having some sort of tryst."

The Prince chuckled. "I don't have trysts—I have affairs. I'm almost insulted that he'd think so little of me." He reached over and lightly squeezed my shoulder. "It'll work itself out."

I smiled and nodded, again surprised by his gentleness.

How had the Prince racked up such a bad reputation when, according to Queen Anouk—and based on my own experience—he was a decent male? A scoundrel, yes, but nowhere near what the rumors suggested.

"And what will your family say of this quest, Prince?"

"Thanatos. And I'm hardly ever home to begin with, so it will be nothing new to them."

"You're lucky—to come and go as you please—I can't imagine the things you've seen."

"I can show them to you. Once we've sorted this mess with the Necromancer, we'll take the long way back to Isidia and I'll show you everything."

I laughed. "Let's not get ahead of oursel—"

We both stopped and listened. Somewhere, behind us—footsteps.

I yanked my hood up, tucking my long braid down the back of my cloak and loosely into my belt so it wouldn't swing as I walked. We slowly started walking again, quieter though, our steps hardly making a noise.

The steps behind us were gaining quickly but not running to catch us. I had one hand holding the reins of Faenor and my free hand resting on the hilt of my Sai blade attached to my thigh. I glanced at Thanatos and saw he was positioned the same with his sword. We continued walking at a regular pace, listening to the footsteps get closer and closer, until—

"Thanatos! You bastard!" The voice was little more than a growl.

Thanatos stopped next to me. "Rangkar?"

We both turned to look behind us, I froze.

The creature coming toward us was about human sized, green-skinned with too-broad shoulders that held his too-long arms, large pointed ears sat on either side of his bald head, his yellowed canines were oversized and protruding out of his mouth—an orc. Rare, especially this far south.

Orcs had claimed some land just above Minoma a few thousand years ago, after centuries of having nowhere.

"Rangkar!" Thanatos called happily and strode back down the road to meet the Orc and clap him on the shoulder. "What are you doing in Isidia?"

"Oh you know, this and that," the orc, Rangkar, replied, as he looked at me past Thanatos. "I almost didn't think it was you, I don't think I've ever seen you travel with anyone before. Is that Thra—"

"No, it's a diplomat from Lonthia." Thanatos cut in, shooting Rangkar a warning glare. "Osiria and Isidia have finally signed for peace."

Rangkar burst out laughing and slapped Thanatos on the shoulder. "I'll believe that when I see it!"

"Come, let me introduce you!" Thanatos cried as he led Rangkar toward me.

Rangkar wasn't wearing much, probably due to the horrid heat, just a simple pair of loose woven pants and a belt with weapons, a coin purse and another large sack hanging off it, his chest and arms were decently muscled and, as they got even closer, I noticed his hands bore the calluses of someone who trained with and used weapons frequently. My eyes flicked down to the sack hanging from his belt and, judging by the size, I would have put all my money on it being a head—most likely of a wanted man. Many orcs got jobs as bounty hunters; it was one of the few jobs they could get outside of their lands.

"Rangkar of the Malthu Clan, a pleasure to meet you, milady." Rangkar stretched his hand out.

I grasped it firmly and shook it. "Elsrine, and the pleasure is all mine. I've never met an orc before."

Going by my middle name seemed like the best thing to do, rather than Thanatos and I forgetting a made up one; I doubted anyone outside of Isidia would even know it.

"Not many have come this far south, milady, get a lot of attention down here— not that I mind, of course." He added, winking.

"Elsrine is fine, please. Using titles when we're traveling so casually seems absurd," I said smiling as the orc nodded and kissed the back of my hand.

"So, you're headed to Osiria then? You'll be the first Isidian in millennia to go there not wanting blood. How did this treaty even come about?"

"My Queen wanted to prepare things for her daughter to take the throne. I can only assume she did it almost as a gift to the Princess."

"Ahh, yes, the mysterious Princess no one has ever seen." He waved his hands in front of his face.

"Except everyone that was at the ball four days ago," Thanatos added.

"I heard about that. I assume you went? What's she like then, the next Queen of Isidia?"

"Short tempered."

I shot a glare at the Prince.

Rangkar scoffed. "Probably gets that from the Sea-Elf side. You'll be heading to Oakfell, then, Thanatos?"

"Hoping to get there by tomorrow evening."

"I'll walk with you, if that's all right. I've a bounty to collect."

The Prince glanced my way and I gave a subtle nod—*hood staying on, then.*

"Let's get a move on, then, before we lose the day."

Thanatos said there was a clearing nearby with a creek not too far from it that we could wash in and fill our water flasks, so we kept walking well past sundown and eventually found it. Thanatos and I tied our horses while Rangkar made a fire from wood he'd collected while we walked and listened to stories of his recent hunt. It was, indeed, a head hanging from his belt and it belonged to a thief that had been terrorizing the people of Oakfell. By the sounds of it, he'd been quite difficult to catch and had made it most of the way to Lonthia before Rangkar had caught him.

I listened to more tales from Rangkar as Thanatos washed and then hunted for our dinner. The life of a bounty hunter was the exact opposite of my life as a Princess. He had traveled everywhere in Carynthia, and most places beyond, fighting and killing his way out of all kinds of situations and always collecting the bounty at the end.

"You must be very good at your job."

"He is, but terrible at bets," Thanatos said as he strolled through the trees with four dead rabbits slung over his shoulders; he plucked one off and threw the limp body at me.

"You can do this one yourself, you should have picked it up by now." I caught the rabbit before it hit the ground, it was still warm. I tried to ignore that and the cuteness of its fuzzy ears as I broke the skin at its knees and began preparing it to be stewed.

While Thanatos and Rangkar cooked dinner, I went down to the creek to bathe; my mother had thankfully packed a few bars of soap. As much as I was loving being covered in dirt, I didn't like the slick greasiness of my hair. When I got to the creek, I did a quick scout of the area to make sure there really was no one about. Once I was sure, I peeled off my dirty clothes and slipped into the water. I scrubbed my hair and nails with the soap, and then my shirt, glad that it was too dark to see the color of the water around me.

Once I thought I was sufficiently clean, I dressed in a new shirt, the same leather pants and boots, and braided my hair back before putting my cloak and hood back on. I walked quietly back to camp, not wanting to disturb any creatures living in the nearby woods. As I got closer, I could hear Rangkar's raspy laugh echoing through the trees.

"Goldenseal and elderberry!" He gasped between laughs. "She's a witty one."

"Indeed, she is." I heard the smile in Thanatos' voice.

They were gossiping about me. I found a shrub nearby to crouch behind, Thanatos and Rangkar were sitting by the fire, passing a silver flask between them.

"Witty and tortured."

Rangkars face turned quizzical.

"You've heard the rumors—the tower, the Queen—it's all true."

Rangkars face fell. "Oh, unfortunate."

My gut churned—the world knew.

"Speaking of unfortunate, tell me, have you heard anything worrying?"

Rangkar sat up straight. "You know, I have, for once. I met a bloke in Ulfilas that was spewing some shit about dead people walking about in the woods in Sillessia. Told him it was probably Naeinn, he said no, and it wasn't the fairies either, apparently. Says they were dead, rotted and all."

The Prince's face turned grave. "I may have to take a detour through Sillessia."

"If you believe such things." Rangkar shrugged.

"I do. Be careful out there, friend, dark forces are at work."

Rangkar only nodded and passed the flask back to Thanatos.

I quietly stood and walked back into the clearing. "I hope there's enough in there for me." I said placing my wet shirt on one of the stones surrounding the fire.

"Of course, milady!" Rangkar said as he snatched the flask from Thanatos, who was mid sip, and passed it to me.

"Hey!"

Rangkar kicked the Prince and I winked at him as I took a mouthful of the harsh spirit from the flask.

"What time will we get to Oakfell tomorrow?" I asked Thanatos.

"We made good time today. If we wake at dawn, we should get there by early evening."

I nodded my thanks as I took a bowl of rabbit stew from him and ate it in silence.

The dead were in Sillessia, going after our most vulnerable; perhaps the humans really were trying to wipe us out with their Necromancer.

CHAPTER FIFTEEN
MANORS AND BATHWATER

It had been a miserable morning, not long after we'd packed up camp and got moving, it started raining, and with the rain came a cool wind. Rangkar, still dressed in only his woven pants, insisted he was fine without a cloak—apparently, orcs kept their temperatures well; Thanatos had thrown his thick black cloak over himself to keep himself dry, making him look like some demon traveler with only his amber eyes visible under the hood.

The wind was a blessing to me; after spending so much time stifling under my cloak, I now welcomed the warmth. The rain was too heavy for us to hear each other speak, so we traveled in silence for hours, the time dragging out.

When we did finally arrive in Oakfell, Thanatos led us to a Tavern called the Oak Tree. It was a large building, considering the size of the village, and looked very well maintained compared to the state of the other buildings surrounding it. The streets that led to and from the Oak Tree were not paved and, thanks to the rain, had become nothing but thick sludge; even the horses were struggling to walk in it.

Once we'd got the horses settled in the stables attached to the tavern, Thanatos and I made to move inside.

"Are you not coming with us, Rangkar?"

His eyes skittered over the building and then down at the mud floor before him. "No, Elsrine. I'll find lodging elsewhere and meet with you two tomorrow. I've got to collect my bounty before the sheriff shuts up shop." He nodded to Thanatos and stalked back down the road.

"What was that about?"

Thanatos was staring after Rangkar, his face expressionless. "This Tavern is goblin owned."

Pity for Rangkar hit me right in the chest. Almost all businesses in Carynthia were owned by goblins; I could only imagine how hard it must be for Rangkar to do anything in towns.

91

It was impossible to forget the dark history of orcs, though many, including the orcs themselves, wished to. The bastard offspring of goblins and elves, born from war and abuse and left to fend for themselves after neither race would claim them. Elves didn't pay them much mind, but Goblins were bitter and hated the reminder of losing their homeland all those millenia ago.

"Where will he go?" I asked.

"He'll find somewhere dry to sleep, maybe another inn or someone willing to loan out their stable."

I took one last look down the road where Rangkar was heading, it indeed seemed to be the poorer end of the village, the wooden structures barely holding together.

"Speaking of dry, let's go inside. I could use a few pints of ale."

Thanatos swung the door of the tavern open and the smell of alcohol, urine, and hot food hit me all at once. It reminded me of the few times when Lorkin and I had snuck out to the servants' Solstice celebrations. They held them out in the stables and everyone—guards, maids, butlers—all got stupidly drunk and danced till the sun came up. This place, though, was not as merry. There were people strewn across the large open room, each one looked to be at different stages of inebriation; the paramours of the tavern sat at a table in the corner of the room whispering amongst themselves.

"Ah, Master Thanatos! What a pleasure to see you again." The gravelly voice came from behind the bar built into the middle of the room.

Thanatos and I moved closer

"Oh, an Isidian, don't get many of your lot here—especially not with Osirians."

I leaned over the edge of the bar to get a look at who was talking. The green creature was about the size of a small child, with beady black eyes, a large hooked nose, and pointed ears the size of my hand—a goblin.

He grinned up at me with pointed yellow teeth. "Did you want a room for an hour or the night?" He said with a wink.

"Two rooms, Glik," Thanatos said with a disapproving tone. "And have someone draw baths in both."

"Will you want some entertainment tonight?" Glik nodded toward the table of paramours, none of them looking particularly interested in picking up a client.

"Not this time."

Glik sighed in mock disappointment. "Then I can only offer one room." The goblin grinned mischievously, winking at me as the Prince closed his eyes and pinched the bridge of his nose.

"Fine, one room, but two beds." Thanatos countered, jabbing a finger at Glik.

The goblin grinned, again showing his horrid yellow teeth. "Room six, up three flights and to the left," Glik responded. "Dinner is in an hour and a half." He handed Thanatos the key and winked at me once more before returning to wiping down glasses with a dirty rag.

The stairs at the back of the tavern groaned under the weight of the Prince and he had to duck halfway up each staircase so as not to hit his head on the landing above. It made me wonder if all Dark-Elves were giants, or if it was just him.

We reached room six, the number roughly scratched into the door. Thanatos sighed, sliding the key into the lock on the door, and seemed to hold his breath as he opened it. The room inside was cozy, or, in other words, small. Two cots sat on either side of a small, grime-covered window to the right, and to the left was a small, dusty chest of draws and the door to a bathing room.

Thanatos shrugged off his pack, dumped it at the end of the right side bed and stalked into the bathroom. "There's only one bath," he called back into the room. "We'll have to take turns, or bathe together," he added, poking his head out of the door to wink at me.

I rolled my eyes, slid my pack off my back and hung my cloak on a hook on the back of the room door, amazed at how much lighter I felt. "Taking turns is just fine with me," I called back, slumping on my cot. I barely fit, I couldn't imagine Thanatos having a very comfortable night. I sighed and relaxed into the mattress, it wasn't the softest bed I'd ever slept on, but it was softer, and dryer, than the forest floor.

Instantly, sleep threatened to take me. I was exhausted, both physically and mentally. So much had happened in the last week, so much had changed. My eyes began to flutter closed and I forced myself to sit up; I was not going to miss out on a hot bath and food that hopefully wasn't rabbit stew.

There was a quiet knock on the door and, before I could even think to get up and answer it, Thanatos sped out of the bathroom and threw me my cloak, waiting until I had it on and covering my hair before cautiously opening the door.

"Sorry, my Lord, just the hot water for the bath," the frail maid said as she lifted a steaming bucket, clearly Glik took more care of his paramours than his housekeeping staff. The maid was small and bony, her simple woolen dress hung off her shoulders. I was amazed that she had managed to carry the bucket of water all the way up here from the ground floor. Thanatos nodded and opened the door wider to allow her into the room, the maid looked to me for half a second and quickly looked away, scurrying into the bathroom to fill the bath.

Thanatos sat on his bed across from me and frowned at the length of it. No, it would not be a comfortable night for him.

"She won't have to carry more buckets up will she? She looks like she's going to keel over any second now." I heard the splash of the first bucket being emptied, but the sound continued for much longer than it should have.

The Prince smiled at my confusion. "Do you not have enchanted buckets in Isidia?"

I wanted to groan at my stupidity, but threw a dust covered pillow at the Prince instead. "Not in the palace."

The Prince caught the pillow and fluffed it up before throwing it back to me. "Who will have the first bath, then?"

"You go ahead, I'm starved." I hopped off my bed and stretched, made sure my hood was secure and prepared to leave the room.

"Be careful down there, this inn can get quite rowdy and the locals are often wary of strangers."

I waved off his comment. "Ask the maid to leave the magic bucket will you? We can share a room but I'd rather not share bath water," I threw over my shoulder as I closed the door.

I made my way down the stairs, music floating up from the bar as well as the smell of hot food. I took a seat closest to the fire, hoping to dry my cloak and warm myself after a day of sludging through the rain.

The inn had filled quite a bit in the few minutes the Prince and I had been upstairs, the work day must have ended. A majority of the crowd were dirty and tired from a long day in the rain, too worn out to cook their own meals for the night, and the other few were clearly here for a good time. The few drunks that had been here before had either left when the new crowd arrived or had been joined by others. The paramours were no longer disinterestedly chatting amongst themselves but were now actively trying to pick up clients, sitting on patrons laps and laughing at jokes that were likely not amusing, jokingly stealing someone's drink and squealing when they got caught, making others laugh.

Glik shuffled through the crowd toward me and plonked himself on the chair across from me. "My Lady, how can I be of service?" He grinned, black eyes shining in the fire light.

"A pint of ale and dinner when it's ready, please."

Glik smiled again and snapped his elongated fingers. With a flash and a small popping noise, two pints of ale and two dinner plates came into existence on the table between us. On the plate before me were two large sausages, mashed potato, and steaming vegetables; Glik's plate was covered in berries and two raw, plucked quails. I raised my brows at him.

"I like to treat my honored guests." He shrugged.

"Am I an honored guest?"

"Anyone that shows up with Master Thanatos is an honored guest, he's one of my best customers." I glanced toward the paramours working their magic on the farmers, laughing and slapping away straying hands; they were all surprisingly attractive, considering the size of the town and how secluded it was.

"I don't doubt that."

Glik gave a rasping chuckle. "I own a chain of taverns and Inns across Carynthia, and Master Thanatos is a repeat customer, thanks to his vast amount of traveling, and a dear friend." Glik focused his eyes on me. "I have never seen Thanatos travel with anyone, other than that orc friend of his," he added disdainfully.

"I'm going to Osiria to negotiate a peace treaty." I took a sip of my ale. "I'm a diplomat."

Glik picked a berry off his plate and popped it into his mouth, letting the red juice drip down his green chin. "Diplomats don't often travel one on one and by horse, especially not Isidians."

"It's easier to travel this way, faster." I shrugged. "We thought it best not to draw attention, though it seems we're attracting a lot."

I held back a shudder as Glik began tearing one of the raw birds apart with his sharp teeth, he ate the whole thing, bones included. I picked at my plate, suddenly not as hungry as I was before.

"You can't fool me, you know, I can smell royal blood."

My eyes flicked to Glik's, a smile spread across his face, bits of bird and berries caught between the yellow points of his teeth.

I slowly put down my fork and let my hand rest on the blade strapped to my thigh.

"You have nothing to fear from me, Princess," he whispered, still grinning. "I just don't recall Thanatos telling me he was leaving Isidia with a bride."

I choked on the piece of sausage in my mouth and tried to wash it down with some ale. "I am not his bride," I rasped, pounding my chest trying to dislodge the food still stuck in my throat.

Glik chuckled. "Are you sure? It's not everyday a Prince goes to a ball and leaves with a Princess that isn't." The goblin had a point, but my mother would never organize something like that, not without consulting me first. I hoped. Then again, goblins were known to be tricksters; even if Glik was Thanatos' friend, I would take everything he said with a grain of salt.

"I am certainly sure," I said firmly.

I downed the rest of my pint, thanked Glik for dinner, and excused myself from the table. I cut my way through the thickening crowd and headed back upstairs to our room, ignoring the sounds of men and women that had been successfully picked up by the paramours of the inn.

"That was a quick dinner," Thanatos called from the bathroom as I entered our room.

"Turns out I wasn't as hungry as I thought." I again removed my cloak and hood and plonked down on my cot, pulling my travelling pack up with me.

As I was looking for a clean pair of socks, my hand brushed against a small box at the base of my bag. I frowned and pulled it out. It was the small black and white box containing the two broaches the King had gifted my mother, that she then had passed on to me. My mother must have packed them while I wasn't looking, part of me wished they were back at the castle, safe on my mantle and the other part was annoyed that I wasn't wearing the ice Hellebore the last few days to keep myself cool under my cloak and hood.

"So, you do like them." Prince Thanatos smiled as he exited the bathroom with only a robe on.

I quickly looked back at the box in my hands. "My mother packed them, actually, otherwise I would have been a lot more comfortable these last few days." I ran my hand over the obsidian fire lily and shivered as the warmth spread from my fingertips to the rest of me.

"Well, I'm glad she sees the value in them, then," the Prince said as he pulled his pack onto his bed so he could find his change of clothes. "How was dinner?"

"Enjoyable. Glik knows who I am," I said casually.

The Prince whirled on me, his robe barely staying tied at the suddenness. "How?" He asked, eyes wide.

"He can smell royal blood, apparently." I kept my eyes at face level in case the Prince made any more sudden movements.

Thanatos huffed. "That's a lie."

"Then he put two and two together? I did nothing that would give me away."

He sat down on his bed facing me and rubbed his chin. "Glik can be trusted, I'll make sure of it. What else did he say?"

"He thinks you've spirited me away to be your bride."

A strange look passed over the Prince's features for a second and was quickly replaced with a laugh and smile. "That's preposterous, but definitely something Glik would come up with—ever the romantic."

A tension I hadn't realized I had held seemed to relax, I prayed to the Father that it was just a goblin's romantic imagining, and not reality.

"It's getting late," Thanatos stated firmly. "You should have your bath. We'll wake early and resupply, then head back to the Mid Road."

I nodded and gathered my bathing things.

Once I'd closed the door of the bath room and used the magic bucket to refill the bath, I heard Thanatos leave the room to have his dinner and finally undressed, climbing into the deep tub. The water was a perfect temperature, warm enough to heat my frozen core but not hot enough to make my feet sting. After the day of walking through the rain, I wanted nothing more than to stay in the tub forever. Thanatos could hunt down the Necromancer alone, and I would stay here in the warm water. I pushed back thoughts of what Glik had said at dinner—it made no sense considering both Thanatos and I were to inherit our respective kingdoms. Despite what I'd heard of the Prince, he did not seem the type to marry a girl against her will, or to marry at all.

I scrubbed dirt, sweat and rainwater out of my skin and hair with the soap my mother had packed, the smell of lavender filling the air. Once I was done, I wrung out my hair and tossed it over the edge of the bath to dry as I relaxed into the water. I thought of cutting it and quickly ignored that thought. My hair was the one feminine feature I could stand about myself, I could easily braid it and tuck it out of the way when training and it never caused me issues when I ran; unlike my other feminine features.

I leant my head back against the tub and allowed myself to close my eyes for a moment, and only a moment; they were dry and heavy from exhaustion, aching for me to go to sleep.

I made to stand up but instead of my feet hitting the hard surface of the bath, I seemed to simply float, weightlessly.

Opening my eyes I saw that I was no longer in the bathroom of the inn, but floating in the ruins of a manor house. Patches of the roof were missing, allowing a cast of moon light to illuminate the inside; walls had begun to crumble, and moss covered almost every surface of stone. There was a faint scent of ash in the air, though there was no sign of a fire.

I kicked my legs to make myself twist in the air so I could see more of the room, my hair flowed around me. From the few pieces of destroyed furniture that I could make out, I guessed I was in what would have been a nursery. Floating down to the ground I shivered as my feet rested on the slick, cool floor. I stepped toward what looked like an ornately-carved, wooden bassinet, my hair streaming behind me as if caught in a current; I looked into it and saw a single, white Hellebore blossom. A deep sadness washed over me and tears spilled over my eyes as I held in a sob that desperately wanted to escape. I reached in to touch the flower but, before my finger tips could reach the petals, I saw a movement out of the corner of my eye. I spun to face the figure, my hair followed along at its own sluggish pace.

"You are on the right path." The beautiful voice echoed around me as a figure stepped from the shadows.

"You!" I sucked in a breath.

White, silky hair drifted around the decaying body of the she-elf from my dream—the she-elf that gave me the burn on my shoulder. Her hair was no longer missing patches, and her beige gown seemed in better condition.

"What do you want from me?"

The hole in her throat seemed to open and close as she took a deep breath. "Go to the land you would not think, with the one you would not choose, to complete the task that must be done, and reveal the truth to set us free."

"That's what you said last time."

"You are on the right path." She repeated, her mouth did not open when she spoke.

I threw my arms out, my hair slowly tangling around them like an octopus' tentacles. "On my way to what?"

The she-elf tilted her head to the side, her white hair following in slow motion. "Is the Prince 'the one I would not choose'?"

The corner of her decaying mouth quirked up.

I released a breath. "Good, I got that right, at least."

A cry rose in the distance; the she-elf's small smile faded away. "Go to the land you would not think, to complete the task that must be done, and reveal the truth to set us free," she said more urgently and, just as she'd appeared in my last dream, she disappeared, as did the manor and the ground with her, and I was floating again. But, this time, I was surrounded by nothing but black.

I twisted to see if I could spot anything, a light, anything at all.

Then, beneath me, a pair of eyes opened. I thought to move to them at first, perhaps the person may have been able to help me. When the eyes were fully opened and the irises rolled into view, I saw they were two different colors, one green and the other a murky white—like the eye of a dead thing.

I decided against going toward those eyes, but the second that I tried to move away something latched onto my ankle and pulled me down. I tried to scream and it wasn't until then that I realized I couldn't breathe. My lungs began to burn and I suddenly felt water in my mouth and nose.

I kicked as hard as I could at whatever was holding my ankle, pulling me down toward those half dead eyes, but I couldn't seem to hit whatever it was. As I was pulled closer to the eyes I saw them crinkle at the corners as if the owner was smiling. My lungs were screaming for air, my eyes burning from being open underwater.

I felt a sharp pull on my hair and, without thinking, reached up to try to grab whatever it was snagged on, hoping it was something above the water. Instead of a branch or tree root, I felt my fingers close around another, much bigger, hand and let it pull me up and out of the black water, away from the green and dead eyes.

My body thudded to the floor, my wet hair sticking to my naked form. I tried to suck in air and instead coughed black water into my hands. I reached quickly for the bucket and vomited more black water, sucking in as much air as I could between retches. A warm hand began pounding me on the back, helping me to expel the water from my lungs. Tears streamed down my face as I continued to throw up until the bucket was almost full, and the tears continued to fall as I sobbed at the realization that I had almost drowned.

The pounding became soothing rubs and pats, they only stopped for a second as my hair was gently moved from my back and a blanket draped over my shoulders. Then I was being carried. I knew by the tattooed, lavender hand that it was the Prince.

Prince Thanatos placed me on my bed, hair dripping and covered in nothing but the blanket, he handed me a cup of hot tea and sat down on the end of my bed, watching me carefully as I collected myself.

Once the heaving sobs had subsided I took a long drink of tea, watching the Prince over the edge of my cup—worry and confusion laced his eyes.

"Thank you," I rasped between gulps. "Again."

The Prince sighed. "What happened?" He asked, leaning closer and putting a reassuring hand on my knee.

I placed my cup down on the small side table between our cots. "I guess I fell asleep."

"No, that was something different. That's a decent bath but I almost had to jump in to pull you out."

I looked at the Prince's arm and realized it was dripping wet all the way up to his shoulder.

"I had a dream … again."

The Prince's eyebrows rose. "Can you remember anything? Was it the same as last time?"

I leant my head against the wall behind me and took a deep breath, trying to remember any parts of the dream that I could. My throat and lungs still burned from almost drowning and trying to scream underwater, my eyes felt even more tired than before.

"There was a she-elf, the same one from my last dream; I remember her now. She was dead, but speaking to me, I can't be sure of much else."

"What did she say?"

I racked my brain for the memories of moments ago, flashes of blackness and a nursery came into my mind, the hole where the she-elfs throat should be and, then, the words she'd spoken. *"Go to the land you would not think. Complete the task that must be done, and reveal the truth to set us free."* Those were the words." I looked at the Prince.

He looked deep in thought, but confused.

"She also said that I'm *'on the right path."* I left out the part about the Prince; too much of what she'd said didn't make sense, and I didn't know if being with him was a good or bad thing just yet.

"So, she wants you to hunt down the Necromancer?" Prince Thanatos asked.

I shrugged. "I guess so."

Thanatos reluctantly took his hand off my knee to run it over his face and through his hair, I shivered as the warmth disappeared.

"When you pulled me out, I was being dragged toward these … eyes. One was green and the other white, as if one were alive and the other dead."

"Becoming dead or becoming alive?" Thanatos asked.

"I couldn't say."

The Prince searched my eyes and sighed when he saw most likely nothing but fear and confusion. I pulled the blanket tighter around me, cold and very conscious of the fact that I was naked.

"I can tell this is going to be a much more difficult journey than I'd first thought," Thanatos said with a sigh.

I nodded in agreement.

"Are you all right to dress yourself? I could call one of the maids?" He added quickly.

"I'm fine." I rose slowly from the bed and walked back to the bathroom.

The bath was empty, though I didn't remember hearing it drain, and there was no water on the floor. I looked back at Thanatos sitting on the end of my cot, staring at his hands and deep in thought.

"Thanatos, how did you know to come back?"

He looked up from his hands at me. I couldn't tell if he was surprised that I'd asked or if he wished I hadn't. "I was just coming back from dinner at the right time, I guess."

I nodded and closed the bathroom door to change. I made sure I kept as much distance from the tub as I could while I dressed.

CHAPTER SIXTEEN
A WELCOME DISTRACTION

My fingers tapped anxiously on my desk. It had been almost a week and we'd had no word from Evalina or the Prince. I knew they'd still be within Isidia's borders, but it didn't stop the panic that rose to my throat every few minutes when my mind decided to remind me that she'd left with an Osirian.

I'd read the letter before me three times, and still had no idea what it said. I threw it aside and pushed away from my desk to stand by the window. King Adalric had taken over the night Evalina had left. The transition of power had met with little resistance, given that he'd done this in the past—had helped Islina when she needed it most. It was a nice reprieve from how things had been previously, issues being double and sometimes triple handled between the royals and I. All of us tried to maintain the facade that Islina was still running the Queendom, while Evie and I did most of the actual running—and, even then, there was so much I kept from Evie.

Now, Adalric had taken almost all of it on board and I was left with only my Captain's duties. I was so used to having endless amounts of work to do that now I had a regular amount, I was bored. I found myself allowing distractions, given that I had so little pressure on me now. Even Islina had calmed since Adalric had taken over, her episodes few and far between; though the presence of Bellona seemed to either calm her or agitate her without warning. Evalina's aunt didn't seem fussed by it outwardly but, sometimes, I caught a glimpse of emotion in her eyes that she never let out.

I stared out over the yard; we'd been training the guards harder in recent days, preparing them for the battle that was most likely heading our way. Adalric had been impressed with the condition of our current guard, given that we'd never had a war during my term, but I still insisted they train harder. The pits were constantly full of guards training, the rotation of watches shortened so that they could train more and to prevent tiredness. I would not risk the safety of Lonthia for the comfort of a few soldiers.

Hemfain had assured me that the wards were Corse-proof, but I was hesitant to trust him. He had been a mage of Lonthia for so long, it would be disrespectful of me to fire him—but he was old, his mind forgetful, and the younger apprentices and assistants were at his mercy. It was only a matter of time before Adalric saw to them and, while I knew he would chide me for not doing it sooner, I was glad that it didn't have to be me.

We'd gotten word from Darius and Peverell's fleets; they were making their way over after taking the time to stock up on whatever supplies they could afford to bring, in case the trade routes were disrupted by the Corse.

It had been a shock to realize how much a battle, let alone a war, could affect the lives of civilians. I'd been so focused on the Queen's safety and supplies for my soldiers, that I'd completely forgotten to consider the lives of the villagers and townsfolk. Adalric had alerted me to my miscalculation almost immediately, firmly and fairly—as was always his way.

We'd organized for scouts to travel to and from the towns and villages daily to report any Corse activity; so far, there'd been a few sightings in some of the northern towns, but nothing else. They'd been dispatched quickly and efficiently, the families warned and told to relocate if possible.

Rain pattered against the window, the droplets obscuring my view of the training guards running laps as Bellona yelled at them and occasionally motivated them to run faster by throwing knives at their heels. It was unconventional, but it worked, and I didn't want to risk my own safety to ask her to stop. My eyes focused on the gray clouds above—would Evie be traveling today? Or would she insist on finding somewhere to wait out the storm? I almost laughed at the thought; of course she wouldn't. If she had it her way, she'd be stripped almost bare and dancing down the road, letting the rain soak into her skin.

I trusted that she knew what she was doing, that she could handle herself, but the Prince was a different matter. He'd assured her safety, but what did that mean? Safe, alive? Safe, but a prisoner? I trusted nothing that came from his mouth, despite what my Queen insisted, and wouldn't until Evalina strode back through the gates and told me herself. If I was there to see that. I couldn't know how the inevitable battle would fare, though I hoped we'd all make it out alive.

Adalric burst through the door of my office. The Carracallans didn't seem to know about knocking.

"Lorkin! I was wondering if you had some free time?" Evalina's grandfather asked, bounding over and slamming a hand into my shoulder, almost lurching me through the window. They also didn't seem to know their own strength—or they liked to flaunt it.

"I suppose I do," I said with a glance back at the unread papers on my desk.

"Excellent!" The old King exclaimed, once again slapping my shoulder. "Join me for a sparring session, I think we could both use the distraction," he said, giving my shoulder a gentle squeeze.

I nodded, making a mental note to better hide my emotions. With everything else going on, I didn't need people feeling like they needed to mind my moods.

The rain had dulled to a drizzle as we entered the pit, the ground muddy beneath our feet. Adalric insisted on using wooden training swords; at first, I thought he didn't want to risk actual injury, forgetting that he was in a castle full of Carynthia's best healers. But, after sparring with him for a few turns, I realized it was so he didn't kill me. The old King was substantially larger than me, and, like all Sea-Elfs, much broader-shouldered from swimming and working the lines on ships. So, when his sword came down, it came down hard and fast.

The King didn't hold back as he swung the wooden sword at my head, giving me barely enough time to duck. I then leapt to the side as he slashed down, skidding a little on the wet earth. He swiftly blocked my swipe at his legs and forced my blade up toward my face, I twisted my blade around his to force it away from my body.

I was so concentrated on the sword play, I didn't notice his leg until it connected with my stomach; as I lurched forward at the force, his head purposefully and forcefully connected with mine with a sharp crack. I crumpled to my knees, the mud soaking my pants, blinded by the pain. But he didn't stop there. A whoosh of air told me he was going to strike again.

I waited for any sound that would give him away. A boot shifted to my right, an intake of breath. I raised my sword in a second and blocked his next attempted strike to my head. Then pushed up from my knees, our swords still engaged, knocking him slightly off balance. I took the opportunity and tripped him with my foot but, as he fell, he hooked our blades and pulled me down with him.

"And we both die," he said, laughing deeply as I crashed down on top of him into the muddy ground, each other's swords against the others' necks. "The best outcome a warrior could ask for."

I rolled off the King, unable to stand, my head still thumping and foggy from the hit. He must have felt the same because he didn't move either. Rain and mud soaked our clothes, neither of us had bothered to change into fighting gear.

I moved my hand to my face and began healing, the glow lighting up the backs of my eyelids. My head cleared in an instant.

"You respond well to dirty fighting," Adalric said, sitting up. "I was worried you'd only be trained in pretty swordplay."

"I trained with your granddaughter," I joked. "There was no way I could have gotten away with only pretty swordplay."

The King boomed and slapped my shoulder. "Takes after her father does she?" He was smiling when he said it but his eyes were pained that he'd even had to ask.

"Definitely, if not her aunt," I said, nodding to the top of the pit where Bellona was still throwing objects at my soldiers, having run out of knives.

"Bellona!" The king bellowed. His daughter paused, looking down at us. "Take it easy," the King called. The Princess's shoulders sank and she dropped the cannon ball she was going to throw next. "Hopefully, we'll have an army left after she's done with them." I offered my hand to heal the King but he brushed me off. "I'll wear the pain a little longer," he said, rising to his feet and pulling me up with him. "Thank you for this. I really needed to get that out, and I hope it did something for you as well," he added, concern again flickering in his eyes.

A nod was all I offered back and the conversation quickly diverted back to guard training and supply route protections. Soon, we'd have two armies to feed and we had to be certain we had enough food for them and the civilians.

CHAPTER SEVENTEEN
HIDDEN STARES

The sun was high in the sky when I woke up the next day. My chest burnt with every breath, my throat was dry, and my eyes stung. I pulled myself out of bed. Thanatos' packs were gone and there was a note on his bed.

'Getting supplies in the village,

Find me when you're ready.'

I got ready and pulled my pack onto my shoulders to head down stairs. I stopped at the bathroom door on my way out of the room, and glanced into the tub from the doorway. I saw nothing but the smooth, off-white base of the tub and left the room without a second thought.

The stairs creaked at my weight as I tried to creep down. I was aiming to avoid any more awkward conversations with Glik the goblin, but as I began to creep and creak down the last set of stairs, I heard him shuffling about behind the bar at the base. I sighed and prayed to the Father that he would just ignore me.

"Good morning, Your Highness." Glik's gravelly voice called from behind the wooden bar.

I stopped dead in my tracks and glanced around the tavern.

"No need to worry, there's no one here," the goblin rasped.

I walked to the bar and peered over the edge, Glik was digging around in a crate full of glass bottles of amber liquid.

"Morning," I managed to force out—my voice sounded hoarse and raw.

"Tough night I hear," Glik stated, grinning at me over the crate.

I narrowed my eyes at the little green creature. Thanatos had said he could be trusted but something in the goblins eyes told me that I could trust him as much as I could trust an angry troll. "What else did you hear?" I asked cautiously.

Glik dusted his hands on the already very dirty cream apron he was wearing and climbed up to a small platform on the opposite side of the bar to me, making him about the same height as a human, but still a good few inches out of my eyeline.

"I know more than you might think about this kind of magic. I know my folk don't tend to delve into it much, but I am a learned goblin. Show me the burn on your shoulder."

My mind screamed at me not to do it, but something else, a feeling, told me that I should trust the Prince, and if he said the goblin could be trusted, then he could be trusted.

I cast a glance over the dim room to make sure we truly were alone, then flicked my cloak over my shoulder, exposing my braid and my identity. I unbuttoned my leather jacket, and pulled it and my shirt to the side to show Glick the pink hand print burned into my shoulder. The goblin sucked in a breath and pulled a monocle out from the pocket on his apron. He then climbed onto the bench and inspected my burn through the seeing glass, tutting and muttering under his breath. He poked the angry pink skin and, when I didn't react, he touched and examined it further, even sniffing it at one point.

Finally, after what felt like an hour, he pulled away.

"You'd need to have it confirmed by a mage, but I suspect it's a type of blood oath."

I gaped at the goblin. "I've made no oaths."

Glik gave me a sad smile, it transformed his face into something almost loveable. "It seems this one was forced on you. Perhaps, inherited?"

Inherited? My mother certainly would never make a blood oath, but my father … "My father didn't have a burn like this."

"The mark is not the same for everyone who carries the oath, his mark may have been a small scar on his hand, but it definitely smells and acts like a blood oath, and a powerful one."

My father was a sailor and a warrior, he was covered in scars, it would be impossible to pinpoint when he might have received a certain one, most of them he got before I was even born.

"Can they simply be forced?"

Glik sighed and took a moment to think. "It's not common, but I have read of such things happening. Some spirits have the power to come back to stop history repeating itself. If a particularly powerful one has latched itself to you, then it could have forced the oath. A mage would help you more, Your Highness. You and Thanatos must hurry to Osiria."

I stared at nothing for a long moment, thinking. The she-elf from my nightmares—she must have attached herself to me, but why? She said I was on the right track, so I had to continue with the Prince. I didn't know much about blood oaths, but I knew that if I didn't do whatever it was that the elf wanted me to do, then my life would have to pay the debt. My family line would end with me and Isidia would lose its only heir.

"What does Thanatos know?"

"He only told me what he suspected and I now agree with his suspicions. He wants to help you."

"Thank you, Glik."

The goblin bowed his head to me and I left without another word.

I took my time wandering the streets, though I knew I shouldn't, before actively seeking out the Prince. The ground was still mostly mud from the rain the day before, but it hadn't stopped the villagers from setting up their stalls. Each stall was slightly different from the next and you could tell which ones made more money by how well it was put together. Most of them carried handmade crafts; knitted socks and scarves for the fast approaching winter, delicate and extremely detailed wooden figures of creatures from around the land, clay pottery and carved wooden furniture.

I made my way further through the town, sticking to the main road and inspecting every stall I came across. It was a perfect distraction from the thoughts and memories of the last twenty four hours that kept creeping in. I was angry that the Prince had had suspicions of what the burn and the dreams were and hadn't told me, and that he'd seemingly blabbed everything he could about our journey to Glik.

Why had I been chosen for this blood oath, and who was the she-elf in my dreams? I had too many questions and not enough answers. I thought of the riddle, *'Go to the land you would not think, complete the task that must be done, and reveal the truth to set us free.'* Us—who else was I to set free? And set them free from what? How was I meant to do that and hunt and kill a Necromancer? I began to feel panicky, and thought it best to push these thoughts aside and find the Prince. It was late in the day, and time was becoming more and more precious to me.

It wasn't hard to spot Thanatos in the town, his head sat above the edge of most of the thatch roofs and his white hair shone like a beacon. I found him leaning against the wall of the blacksmiths shop, one of the few double story structures in the village.

He straightened when he spotted me. "Elsrine, how are you feeling?" He asked, his voice laced with worry.

"All right," I croaked, despite all the talking I'd done with the villagers and the water I'd drunk, my throat was still dry. "I might stay away from large pools of water for a while, though."

The Prince nodded. "As long as you don't start stinking." I gave him a light punch on the arm and he chuckled. "I'm buying a few knives, just in case."

I nodded, grateful that I had my Sai blades and my father's sword—not that they did me any favors last night. "Glik spoke to me on my way out, do you plan to tell our business to every friend we meet on the road?"

The Prince glared down the road toward the inn. "I told him in confidence, and only after he'd already figured out who you were. Glik can be trusted, I've known him for years."

"And I'm just supposed to trust your judgment?"

"Isn't that what you agreed to when you decided to drag me along?"

"I agreed that this was to be kept secret, only high-ranking elves were meant to know."

The Prince leaned toward me. "He can be trusted, Princess, and so can I."

I took a step back, letting him win this round.

He was about to say something else when the blacksmith reluctantly came over with two freshly sharpened knives. I used this distraction to turn around and head back to the inn. I would get the horses ready so we could leave before I had any more run-ins with the goblin.

The streets were quieter on my way back through the village, the stalls were still open but everyone seemed to be hiding out back and there were no curious travelers perusing their wares.

As I got closer to the inn I spotted Rangkar and realized with a pang of sadness that he was the reason everyone was hiding away. Glik must've had the town wrapped around his long clawed fingers; humans didn't appreciate orcs very much, but most would still gladly accept their gold.

"Rangkar!" I called, he looked up from the whittler's stall and beamed at me, nothing seemed able to break his spirit.

"Ah, my Lady! I was wondering if you two were still here."

"I slept in." I shrugged. "Did you collect your bounty?"

"Three hundred gold pieces for a notorious horse thief." Rangkar patted his fat leather purse, the coins inside jingling loudly.

"Will you join us for a while on the road?" I asked, hopeful that he might. I liked Rangkar and would've much rather traveled with him than the Prince.

"Maybe I'll meet you somewhere along the way, I've just accepted another bounty," he replied apologetically.

"Perhaps. Thanatos is at the blacksmith. Good luck with your bounty, Rangkar. I hope to see you again soon."

"Same to you and your journey." We clasped each other's forearm in farewell and, with a last smile to me, Rangkar strolled down the main street toward the blacksmith. As he passed I noticed some of the stall owner's comeback out of hiding.

I rolled my eyes at them and continued making my way back to the inn's stable. They would most likely do the same thing once the Prince came back through town, as if even the sight of him could kill them on the spot.

I was glad to see Oakfell fade away behind us as we raced up the Mid Road, especially the Oak Tree tavern. We rode hard for hours, not stopping to eat or relieve ourselves, we had to make up for the time we'd lost while I had slept in that morning. While the Prince had *let* me sleep in. After he'd saved my life the night before. After he'd already saved me from my last nightmare.

That made two life debts I owed Prince Thanatos, whether or not I could actually die in the dreams. It certainly felt like I could, and he saved me. I felt an ache swell in my chest and some part of me seemed to know that being nearer to the Prince would help ease it. I nudged with my foot and Faenor sped up to match Serelene's pace.

I glanced over to Thanatos, he was staring ahead but not focusing his gaze on anything in particular. "I'm sorry about what I said at the blacksmith," I called over the rush of air and the pounding of hooves.

The Prince snapped out of whatever deep thought he was in the middle of and blinked at me. "What?" He asked, surprised.

"I do trust your judgment."

Our horses slowed as if sensing that we were no longer paying attention to the road ahead. We were face to face now; his golden eyes reflected the sunset behind me, his hair orange in the light.

"I wouldn't have asked you to come with me if I didn't trust you. I don't know why I trust you, I barely know you!"

Thanatos' mouth quirked up at the corners.

"But I do. Glik just caught me off guard when I was already feeling defenseless."

I regretted telling him my true feelings the second the words left my lips, but it was the right thing to do, if we were to trust each other we had to be honest with each other. And our journey, our quest, definitely required trust.

Thanatos' eyes softened and he reached out and laid a hand on my arm, a rush of warmth and comfort washed over me. I wanted to lean into him, to have his arms wrapped around me. "You are never defenseless when I am around. I made a deal with your family, remember? And I've seen you fight, you are anything but defenseless."

I smiled sheepishly. The only person to ever compliment me was Lorkin; it felt nice to hear praise from someone else. The Prince's hand lingered on my arm, his thumb stroking back and forth along my radius. His eyes never left mine, nor mine his.

Who was the male before me? He was nothing like the stuck up, lecherous Prince I had met little more than a week prior.

The Prince's gaze turned searching, as if he were looking for something in my eyes. "Let's find somewhere to rest for the night. I feel like we have a few more things to talk about."

I nodded and he slowly removed his hand from my forearm and guided Serelene into the woods beside the path. Faenor and I followed until we found a small clearing and set up camp. Thanatos cooked a beef stew using meat he'd bought from a butcher in Oakfell. I was glad it was anything but rabbit. He also pulled out a bottle of spirits to share.

We ate dinner fast and in silence, neither of us having had anything to eat since breakfast. The hot stew was soothing on my raw throat, each swallow a massage along the tender tissue. The spirits, however, did not help my sore throat one bit, but I felt like I deserved to enjoy a drink.

We passed the bottle between the two of us, each taking a deep swig—as if trying to drink away the awkward air between us.

"I'm sorry I didn't tell you my suspicions," the Prince said as he passed me the bottle across the fire. "I didn't want to keep anything from you, I just wasn't sure I was right."

I took the bottle and drank deeply. I had almost forgotten the real reason I had been angry with the Prince earlier that day. "I would have preferred to have an idea of what it could be, even if it turned out to be wrong." I passed the bottle back and the Prince held it for a while before drinking, swirling it in his hand considering what to say next.

"Blood oaths are dark magic, the mages in Osiria will know more about them." He took a mouth full of the amber liquid.

"Even more reason to get there as soon as possible."

Thanatos nodded in agreement. "I want to stop by Avars before we head to Nebu, Rangkar told me there have been reports of dead things walking through the woods. I'd like to investigate."

I'd had a feeling we were going to end up stopping in Sillessia, whether he was going to tell me about it first I wasn't sure. "You don't think the Sillessians have anything to do with the Necromancer, do you?"

The Sillessians did have a close relationship with the humans, but surely they wouldn't turn on their own race? In every war they had remained neutral.

"I doubt it, but it would be a great place to hide if you were the Necromancer. No one would consider Sillessia as an evil lair."

"How long will it take to get there?" I asked.

"From where we are now … four days' ride, with no breaks. In the long run, it will save us time. It's almost directly south of Nebu, if we go through the forest and up through the desert. It should cut our journey down by three days."

I took a few mouthfuls from the bottle, the liquid making the back of my throat burn even more. Four days to Avars, another, if not two, to Nebu then another week to Ravenna.

Hopefully, in Ravenna I could learn more about the blood oath that had been forced onto me and the spirit that had given it to me. I could only pray to the Father that the Necromancer was in Sillessia and that this whole hunt would come to an end in four days' time.

The Prince studied me with his gold eyes as he reached for the bottle. I passed it to him and laid down in my spot next to the fire. We had drunk more than half of the bottle between us and I was starting to feel its effects. My mind kept drifting away from what Thanatos and I were actually discussing, and the world seemed to be slowly spinning around me.

"What do your tattoos mean?" I asked. It was the first solid question that came to my head, that steered the conversation away from things that I didn't want to think about.

The Prince chuckled and pulled up his sleeves, revealing his tattooed forearms. He held up his hands, showing me the backs. On his right hand was a Fire Lily and, on the left, a Hellebore. "If you stand facing south in Ravenna, the left side is the tundra and the right, volcanic, hence Fire Lily for volcanic and Hellebore for Tundra." He held his forearms into the light so I could see. The gold ink was vibrant on his lavender skin. "I get a tattoo each time I visit a place in Carynthia. If I visit the same place twice I either add to the last tattoo or get a new one to symbolize that particular visit." He pulled his sleeves back down and took another swig of liquid. "My chest tattoos are all things that have special meaning to me—Osiria, my family, my work in Sillessia."

I nodded, not knowing what else to do. I had forgotten about his good deeds in Sillessia, helping the Naeinn. The worry he must've felt, knowing that the Corse were so close to the elves he worked hard to help.

I thought back to the night he had told me of his work in Sillessia, the night of the ball. The same night he'd asked me to run away with him. I chuckled at the memory, how stupid of the Prince to think I would leave with a man I'd just met, and how stupid of me to do that very thing a mere twenty four hours later.

Thanatos glanced at me quizzically. "What's so funny?" He asked with a smile.

"I was just thinking about how hypocritical I've been."

"Oh?"

"Isn't this what you said you wanted, at the ball?" I gestured at the forest around us, the sky above us. "I'm out in the world, with you, on my way to Sillessia."

The Prince considered me for a moment, then set the almost empty bottle of spirits aside and laid down opposite the fire to me. "It's what I wanted for you, yes. Everyone should see the world at least once. Seeing it with me is just a bonus."

I rolled my eyes at him and turned my face to the sky. The stars were bright, and seemed somehow different to the ones in Isidia. The clouds from yesterday had passed and, from the smell of the air around me, weren't returning any time soon.

"Do you regret leaving with me?"

I thought about it for a moment. Did I regret leaving with the Prince? Who else could I have left with? Lorkin had to stay with my mother, no one else could handle her like he could—not even me—and I couldn't trust anyone other than him to keep Isidia safe. Thanatos knew the world in a way no one in Isidia could, and I felt that traveling with him deterred a lot of unsavory attention. Yes, the people that knew him knew the Prince was relatively harmless, but many still feared Dark-Elves.

"No." I felt his eyes on me, studying my face. "Though, it is still only the beginning."

We were silent after that. Sleep claimed the Prince before me. I listened to his deep breathing as I stared at the stars above me, trying to make out constellations shown to me by my father.

Sleep eventually claimed me too and, for once, I dreamed of my father. His soft, kind face was almost identical to my uncle's. He was standing on the forecastle of a ship, his shoulder-length, blue hair flowing in the sea breeze.

I walked forward to stand next to him; he smiled down at me and rested a hand on my shoulder. In my dream, I must have been a child. He bent down to my height, his black eyes glittering in the warm sun, and gestured for me to look ahead. I followed his pointed finger with my eyes and saw the red and white land ahead of us. Panic rose in my chest, but my father just pulled me into a tight hug and that feeling disappeared. Even though it was a dream, I could smell the scent of my father—sea salt and Shinchaku spices.

I looked over my father's shoulder at Osiria, half volcanic waste and half icy tundra. The panic was gone; instead, a comfortable warmth bloomed in my chest.

The dream changed and I was back in my room in Lonthia, preparing for bed. I had just slipped my nightgown over my head, the fabric slipping down just past my knees, when I felt two large arms circle around me. I closed my eyes and leant into them, enjoying the warmth emanating from the body behind me.

I giggled as I was spun around to face the owner of the arms, and was shocked when I opened my eyes and realized it was Thanatos. He was shirtless, his gold tattoos glittering against his skin, his eyes shone with love and lust. He smiled at me and bent his head down toward my face. I felt my cheeks burn and angled my head up so that our mouths would meet halfway, my hands running up his defined abdomen to lace around his neck.

I forced myself to wake before the dream went any further. My cheeks felt warm, my hands clammy. I turned away from facing the Prince, still sleeping soundly on the opposite side of the fire. I tried to think back on the dream of my father, to distract myself from the last half, when movement in the woods nearby caught my attention.

I tried to focus my eyes, but the fire behind me made the darkness between the trees seem even darker. I caught a glint of large yellow eyes slowly moving between the trees and my hands instantly went to the blades still strapped to my thighs. I slowly rolled onto my back, keeping the eyes in the woods in my peripherals.

"Thanatos," I hissed across the fire, the Prince did not stir. "Thanatos!" I hissed more urgently—still nothing.

A low rumble sounded through the clearing. Keeping the creature in my sights, I slowly rose from my place on the ground and got into a fighting stance, my hands hovering over my steel Sai blades. The beast took this as an invitation and slowly prowled out of the darkness toward me. The wolvane's face was almost level with mine, its paws the size of my head. Saliva dripped from the giant canine's mouth. I took a steady step back, inching toward the fire and the sleeping Prince. The wolvane let out a low growl.

"Thanatos, wake up, damn you!" I spat and kicked back with my leg, hitting the sleeping Prince's shoulder, in the same moment the giant wolf lunged.

I had enough time to draw my blades and catch them crossed in the wolvane's mouth, the thin blades wedging between the beast's massive teeth.

It took all my strength and weight to hold the creature back from the Prince's vulnerable figure. Thick saliva and blood oozed down my blades and onto my hands, the creature growled and tried to snap down on my blades but only made them cut further into its gums.

The Prince finally rose, cursing and rushing for his daggers. The horses were whinnying and thrashing against their reins, desperately wanting to get far away from the beast I was wrestling with.

I cried out as the wolvane began pushing its weight down on me, hard enough that I lost my footing and fell to one knee. My arms were shaking under the weight of the creature, it's muzzle mere centimeters away from my face, it's hot breath rolling over me.

I saw a flash of movement to my left and suddenly the Prince was straddling the beast, driving daggers into the monster's neck. The creature reared back, my blades slipped out of my slob and blood covered hands and clattered to the ground beneath the beast. I rolled backwards and darted over to Faenor to collect my father's sword.

The Prince was still clinging to the creature's back, his whole being covered in red blood, stabbing with his knives as the wolvane flung its head, trying to snap at him, creating the perfect distraction.

I wiped as much of the blood and slob off my hands as I could before drawing my sword and plunging back into the battle, barely considering the possible outcome of death. My blood was rushing through my veins, my mind speeding through my training sessions with Lorkin and the other castle guards about how best to kill monsters. The hound was desperately trying to shake the Prince off his back, but Thanatos was going nowhere. Blood was pouring off the beast, mother knew how many times Thanatos had managed to stab it before having to hold on for dear life, but the creature continued to fight.

While the beast was rearing and shaking its head in a fruitless attempt to dislodge the Prince, I ran up behind it, slid between its long hind legs, and drove my sword up under its rib cage through its belly.

The beast whined and slumped a little but still stood.

I twisted beneath the massive creature and raked my sword from its ribcage to the end of its belly, its entrails spilling out behind me as I went.

With one last snarl, the beast finally collapsed.

I pulled myself out from under its large hind leg, partially winded from the creature collapsing on top of me. I slowly dragged myself around to it's head. Despite being disembowelled, the beast still lived. Its eyes were looking around frantically when I finally got to its face, low whines rising from its slack mouth.

I looked the creature in the eyes as I drove my dagger into its head, stabbing the brain and finally ending its life. I saw the light leave his eyes and felt his last breath on my face. I then turned away from the wolf and threw up whatever was left in my stomach from dinner. I was still heaving when the Prince came over to me after pulling himself out from under the wolvane's corpse. He sat beside me and rubbed my back until the heaving subsided. Adrenalin was still coursing through my body, causing me to shake and remain out of breath.

"Not a bad beast for your first kill on the road," he said almost proudly, still running his hand over my back.

"You sleep like the dead!" I snapped. "And speaking of, what the fuck was that?! You could have taken that thing out in a second with your powers."

"That wolvane was a lot closer to civilization than they normally dare to go." the Prince said. "And they usually only attack lone travelers. This beast was quite daring for his kind. And, in regards to my powers, I hope you don't plan to rely on me using them because you'll be sorely mistaken if that's the case." He snapped, taking his hand from my back.

I looked back at the huge corpse, I wouldn't have thought him too big for Osirian magic. But perhaps he was. I didn't know the limits of the Prince's powers. The wolvane could have easily killed us both and the horses within seconds had I not been awake, had it not been for the dream of Thanatos. I felt my face redden.

"Are you all right, Evalina?"

I snapped back to reality. "Yes, I'm fine." I heaved myself up off the ground and stared at the large corpse with my hands on my hips. "Just thinking about the best way to get my weapons back without getting covered in blood and organs."

CHAPTER EIGHTEEN
DEAD WOOD

There was no easy way to retrieve my weapons. By the time Thanatos had calmed the horses and packed up the campsite, and I had dug my weapons out from under the gore of the wolvane, we were both completely covered in blood and sweat and the sun had risen. We desperately needed to find somewhere to bathe and wash our clothes before the stench of blood drew more unwanted attention from other dark creatures. We walked for two hours before finding a small lake.

We made sure to fill our skins and let the horses drink their fill before we both dove in and defiled the water.

"You go first, you're more covered than I am," the Prince offered, looking at my blood speckled face.

I lightly toed the water, having already taken my boots off, and looked over the lake. The water was calm, not another creature in sight, and it didn't look to get too deep in the center—but neither did a bathtub.

Panic rose in my stomach, a panic I would have expected to experience when fighting the wolvane but did not; and, yet, this calm, quiet body of water induced such a feeling.

I took a step away from the gently lapping edge. "You go first. I can wait."

The Prince studied my face. "Are you afraid?"

I looked down at the water, the memory of nearly drowning springing into my head. I made to turn away from the lake and the Prince, but Thanatos grabbed my hand. I didn't remember seeing him take his boots off but he was now barefoot and gently guiding me into the water.

"What are you doing?" I tried to pull out of his grasp but he held firm and tugged lightly on my arm, forcing my feet to move toward him and the water.

"Let's go for a swim," he said with a dazzling smile.

"We're fully clothed!" I argued.

The Prince simply shrugged and, using more force, pulled me into the cool lake. "They need a wash, anyway."

114

We were almost knee deep into the lake when my body began to freeze and my legs refused to move any further.

Thanatos stepped in front of me and took both of my hands in his, holding them against his warm chest. "It's all right," he soothed, "I won't let anything happen to you, I promise." He began walking backwards, leading me like a skittish horse, never taking his eyes off my face.

We were almost in the middle of the lake when the Prince finally stopped, the water sat just under my chest. I could tell the water was cold but couldn't feel it, all I felt was the warmth emanating from the Prince's body, the warmth that disappeared when he let go of my hands and began removing his shirt.

"What are you doing?!" I exclaimed, stepping away from the prince but not wanting to be too far.

"Washing my shirt." He shrugged. "Might as well, since we're out here."

"Oh, so this was all a ploy to see me naked." I crossed my arms over my chest and cursed myself for not thinking of the white linen that was practically see through.

"It was a ploy to get you to wash and stop smelling like wolvane intestines. The rest is just a bonus." He winked.

He set to work scrubbing the blood out of his shirt, the water around us turning an even murkier brown. I sighed and ducked in the water so that my chest was submerged before removing my own shirt and giving it a good scrub.

We continued this process until we were both entirely naked under the water, our clothes scrubbed clean and thrown to the shore of the lake for us to eventually lay out to dry.

"There, was that so hard?" The Prince mocked as he swam laps around me, his freshly washed hair shining in the mid-morning sun.

"I'm surprised you know how to swim," I jeered

"I'm surprised at how little you know about Osiria." He rolled onto his back and continued his laps in a backstroke. I focused all my attention on his face, avoiding the urge to look any lower than his chest. "Ravenna is built in the mountains between the volcanic and icy lands—there are hot springs all over the place. The palace itself has a bath house the size of this lake. I'll show it to you when we get there."

"How much time are you expecting to spend in Ravenna? Our journey has already been delayed enough."

The Prince stopped his laps and stood in front of me. "I would like to be able to say goodbye to my family, just in case."

We paused for a moment; as much as we liked to ignore the fact that it was a deadly mission we were on, it was. The Necromancer could be stronger than both of us, his army larger than we could ever know.

"Why did you never get that fixed?" Thanatos asked, tapping on the crooked part of my nose.

I ran my fingers along the bridge of my nose and felt the bulge halfway up. "I guess I wanted something to make me stick out."

"Cause the blue wasn't enough?" He asked, running his fingers through a length of my hair, the blue glittering against the black.

"I guess it was more to show my people that I was capable—that I could take a hit, as it were."

"I don't think you needed a crooked nose to show them that."

"Does my imperfect nose offend you, Prince?"

Thanatos laughed. "Not at all, Princess, I find it quite charming," he said quietly as he ran the back of his hand down the side of my face.

My body wanted to lean into him, to feel his warmth again, to kiss him like I almost had in my dream.

"Speaking of delay," I said, probably a little too loudly, "we should be on our way—we've already added another day onto our journey." I stepped away from the Prince and made my way back to the shore, not caring what state he saw me in, after all he *had* already seen me naked, which we had both seemed to have forgotten.

My wet hair was plastered to my body as I left the water, thankfully long enough to hide everything from the prince as I walked over to the horses to grab my new set of dry, clean clothes. I wandered over to a nearby shrub and changed in private. I heard the Prince's footsteps coming up the shore and waited a little while longer behind the bush to give him adequate time to dress.

We rode hard into the night, trying to make up for the time we had lost. By the time we'd set up camp for the night, we were too tired to even think about eating and instead went straight to sleep. We did the same the next day. That night, though, we did stop just as the sun was setting.

The horses were tired and refused to go any further, and I didn't blame them. The closer we got to the Sillessian capital, the thicker the forest around us got—slowing our journey even more.

"You must stay close the further we get into Sillessia. The forest only gets thicker and harder to navigate," Thanatos warned.

I nodded, my mouth full of bread.

"You must also ignore any fairies you see. Because we're not taking the main road, they may see us as a threat and try to lead us astray."

I gulped down my bread. "They do that?"

"Anything to protect the weak."

The weak. Thanatos was not only speaking of the Naeinn, but also of the Wood-Elves.

While the Sillessians did have power, they were without doubt the weaker of the elven races, focusing their powers mainly on crop growth.

"Do you think we'll run into any Corse?" I asked for the sake of conversation, we hadn't spoken to one another since the lake.

"Perhaps. Rangkar did say there were reports of them in the forest. I'd say they've tried to get to Avars and the fairies have led them away. We'll have to be on our guard."

Not that we hadn't been. Since the attack, both the Prince and I had got in the habit of sleeping with our swords next to us, just in case.

The trees were getting thicker and thicker as we went, the forest darker and darker. Eyes glowed in the distance at every turn—the eyes of forest dwellers. They kept their distance, though, and I was glad for it. After the previous night, I was not interested in having any interactions with beasts, no matter how small or innocent.

The smell hit us before we heard or saw them, the smell of rotten flesh and old blood. We stopped dead in our tracks.

"Corse," I whispered.

"For the smell to be that strong, there must be hundreds of them."

We backtracked to a small creek we'd passed earlier, tied off the horses, and stalked quietly back through the forest on foot.

"You must stay close to me, we fight back to back if it calls for it."

I nodded.

We unsheathed our swords as quietly as we could and continued through the dense forest, the smell getting more and more unbearable.

It was a while before we encountered our first Corse. It was stumbling clumsily through the thick wood, bouncing off trees as it went and not sticking to one set direction. We let it pass and crept forward once it was out of our vision. We stayed out of sight, keeping behind trees or bushes when one came too close.

"They don't seem to be going anywhere in particular," Thanatos observed as a Corse bounced off the tree we were crouched behind and back tracked the way it came. "They're just blindly walking."

"How will we get past them?"

"Fight our way through?"

I shook my head. "They're stronger than they look and there's too many, even for us."

The Prince considered my words for a moment. "Maybe we coul—"

A shriek from behind us filled the forest.

The Prince and I spun around and spotted a Corse a few feet away, mouth open and screaming, a dead rotted finger pointing straight at me.

"Isidian!" The corpse growled.

I grasped a Sai blade in my spare hand and prepared to lunge, but the Prince held me back. I glared at him but he was too busy looking elsewhere to see.

I followed his gaze.

Corse were popping up everywhere in my field of view—there must have been hundreds just scattered before us. I didn't want to consider what was going on on the other side of the tree.

"What do we do now?" I asked quietly, trying to keep the panic out of my voice.

"Run."

We rounded the tree and bolted, but it wasn't long before we almost slammed into a wall of corpses.

"They're herding us," I puffed, no longer able to hide my panic; the Prince sheathed his sword and grabbed my hand as he led us east. The lines of Corse on either side began to close in.

"Faster!" Thanatos urged.

My legs were already screaming at me to stop, the uneven forest floor not doing my knees and ankles any favors, but I pushed them harder, keeping right on the Prince's heels. The thundering of the hoard of dead behind us only grew louder the further we ran, as if seeing others with a purpose snapped the lost ones out of their daze.

The Prince began to weave through the trees, until I wasn't sure what direction we were heading in anymore. If I lost track of him now, I would never find my way out of the forest. I gripped his hand tighter and savored the small amount of comfort it gave me.

We burst into a clearing through a line of trees and again stopped dead in our tracks.

Not ten paces before us was a camp of at least fifteen Corse.

Thanatos' hand shot out in front of him, a black mist surrounding his fingertips. I stared at the Corse as the Prince pulled his hand upward palm to the sky, his fingers slightly clenched, as if he had a hold of something. I saw the same mist that surrounded the Prince's hand begin to fall out of the dead things' mouths and eyes, as if it were being pulled out of their bodies by Thanatos. Some choked and fell to their knees, others just froze.

The Prince let out a grunt, his hand falling back to his side. "My power won't work on them." He growled, unsheathing his sword.

He gave my hand one last squeeze before releasing it and gripping the hilt of his weapon. I followed his lead and gripped my sword with both hands, turning to face the trees behind us; the rumble of the hoard of dead things was growing and so were the whispers of 'Isidian' from the crowd before the Prince.

Before either of us could move, the ground beneath our feet began to shift. Giant thorned roots shot out of the ground around the clearing closing us in like a cage, I heard cries and growls of pain from the Corse that had been stumbling through the forest toward us.

The Prince slipped his arm around my waist and pulled me against his front, his sword held steady before us in his other hand, our backs against the wall of thorns and both of us now facing the camp.

One of the less decayed Corse snickered. "Now we'll have you, Isidian," it spat, its tongue almost poking through a hole in its cheek as it spoke.

All the Corse were in the same state, with torn and dirty clothes, shoes that were falling apart—if any—and bodies covered in gaping wounds and other signs of decay. The reek of them could not be described, being as close as we were was enough to make me gag.

"All this over one Isidian?" Thanatos jeered. "Surely there are other things to worry about."

"We'll get to you in time Deathbringer, our master has given us strict instruction to kill any and all High-Elves on sight."

"Why?" Thanatos asked in a bored tone but, rather than answer, the corpse began to charge us.

We tensed; the Prince held me tight and close. I tried to step quickly out of his grasp but he held firm. There was a rumble from below us and, just before the creature got within a few paces of Thanatos' sword, a root shot out of the ground and pierced it though. There was no explosion of blood and gore, only a black goo covered the top of the root poking through the skull of the creature.

"That's not you doing that is it?" The Prince muttered to me.

"No, but clearly they're on our side, whoever they are." As the words left my lips, the rest of the Corse across from us were caged up in a series of thorned roots popping through the ground beneath them, they growled and clawed at the roots like caged beasts.

To my left, a path formed, walled on either side by the roots to keep any dead things from getting to us. I looked up to the Prince, he simply nodded and led us through the path still keeping a tight grip around my waist.

We followed the path for what felt like hours but it was impossible to know for sure how much time had really passed. The Prince had told me that we were back heading north; how he could tell, I did not know.

As we walked down the path, the Prince eventually relaxed his grip on me and sheathed his weapon. I focused my attention on the path ahead, trying to ignore the walls of thorns imprisoning us on either side.

"Do you think they're leading us to Avars?" I asked, unable to bear the silence any longer.

"Perhaps. We're still at least two days—if not three, now—away from the capital. I can't imagine anyone having the patience to lead us all the way there."

"Well, I hope we get somewhere soon."

Thanatos flashed me a sympathetic look and continued leading the way through the maze of thorny roots.

We walked for what could have been another hour before the walls around us ended and we stood on the doorstep of a small, wooden cottage built into the base of a giant tree. The mucky windows glowed with light from within and the air around it was full of the smell of spices and herbs, a welcome change to the stink of Corse that had filled the forest. The cottage was surrounded by vegetable gardens and an assortment of wild flowers, some I'd never seen before that glowed as if they were filled with magic. The tree the cottage was built into felt alive, as if somewhere beneath it's bark a heart was beating. Thanatos took one last step toward the door, glancing back at me, before knocking on the sturdy wood.

The door swung open before the Prince's hand had made it back to his side; in the doorway stood a woman. She was chest height to me; her face was beautiful— large blue eyes, soft rounded nose, plump lips, a spattering of freckles covering her pale skin, and bright red hair framed the right side of her heart shaped face. The left, however, was framed by flowers and leaves sprouting from her pale scalp. Green veins were visible under her almost transparent skin, spider webbing their way down her face. The lower left side of her head, starting from where her ear should have been, and her shoulder looked to be made of tree bark.

"Your Highnesses! Please come in."

Thanatos and I glanced at each other and cautiously ducked through the doorway. Thankfully, the ceiling inside was at a safe height, even for oversized elves like Thanatos.

"I am Sevah, Protector of the Father tree. You are Prince Thanatos Helice of Osiria and Princess Evalina Elsrine Glenon of Isidia, on a mission from the Elven royals to hunt down the Necromancer responsible for attacking Lonthia."

I raised my eyebrows at the witch. "Nice to meet you?" I offered, pulling down my hood since she already knew my true identity.

"Thought I'd get all that out of the way." Sevah shrugged. "The Father tree has told me everything, so there's no point hiding who you are and what your journey is."

"You speak to the tree?"

Sevah smiled and motioned for us to sit in a set of armchairs in the middle of the messy room.

Books and parchment rolls were strewn throughout the open cottage, herbs and flowers hung drying from the high ceiling, and shelves of jars, seemingly placed at random, filled with all kinds of ingredients lined every wall. At the back of the house sat a large, open fireplace, various sized cauldrons both clean and dirty were stacked messily on either side. A small bed sat in the back corner of the room, the books and empty jars piled on top of it showed that it wasn't used very often, if at all.

I didn't see where she got it from but, as Thanatos and I took our seats, Sevah set down a tea tray before us, poured us all a steaming cup and took a seat on the work stool before us.

"The Father speaks to me through the tree. Our gods take many forms, for the Carracallans they take the form of fish creatures, for the Osirians ice and fire birds; the Sillessians believe them to be trees, one for the mother and one for the father. I protect the Father tree and the royal family guard the Mother Tree."

I took a cup of the fragrant tea and sat back in my chair. I thought I would feel something—I didn't know what, but something—being so close to a god, but I felt nothing.

All Carynthians believed in the Mother and Father; what forms and lore they believed depended on where they came from. Isidians believed the Mother was the molten core of the world and the Father was the rain that cooled her surface and allowed our land to blossom.

"The Corse have been in these woods for this last week. At first, I could keep the numbers down by myself but, over time, more and more of them showed up. The fairies have protected Avars well, but in doing so have left them to gather close to the tree; and, though they don't seem to have any interest in it, I am worried," the witch continued.

"Do you have any idea where they've come from?" I asked.

"I have seen mostly Kushyami and Minoman humans."

"Then we're on the right track," Thanatos added, also not drinking his tea.

"I have prayed to the Father many times for answers, but he is … unresponsive." Sevah sighed, staring up at the roots that made up the ceiling of her house.

"Is there a witch at the Mother Tree?" I queried.

"No, the Mother is much more tolerant of elves, she would not take well to a human caring for her. The Sillessians don't have much to do with her, they are too easily swayed by her darkness, but Thanatos may be able to get answers from her." She nodded to the Prince. "The Mother regards Queen Omisha highly."

Thanatos' eyes narrowed. "We shall see—I do not hold the same values as my mother."

I glanced quizzically at the Prince. What values could his mother have that he would not?

"Even so, the blood relation may be enough to sway her," Sevah said.

"And how do you propose we get to Avars without getting mobbed by Corse?" Thanatos asked.

"Now, that will be tricky. I can't use magic to get you all the way there, or I'll lose myself entirely." Sevah replied, pushing some stray leaves over her left shoulder. "Our best bet is asking the fairies. You'll have to stay here for the night." Sevah waved her hand and the tea set in front of us turned into a small cauldron of soup, a plate of bread, and two bowls. As she used her magic, I noticed a small sprig of tiny blue flowers sprout from her head. "Eat up. I'll be back at dawn with your horses and, hopefully, an answer from the fairies." The witch waved her hand once more and the bed cleared of all its mess and another one appeared next to it. She then hurried through the door and left us.

Thanatos and I looked at each other.

"Well, that was interesting." I offered.

"I suppose we have no choice but to trust her." Thanatos shrugged as he reached for a bowl and served himself some steaming soup.

"Do we not?"

"Well, we can either sit here and wait for Sevah and the fairies, or we can go back into the forest and be killed by a swarm of Corse." He blinked at me over his bowl of soup.

I sighed.

The Prince sniffed his soup and after a moment of consideration gulped down the murky liquid and reached for a chunk of bread. I waited a moment to see if he had any reaction before reaching for my own bowl of soup.

We ate dinner in silence, both of us gazing around the room. There was so much mess and clutter in the tiny house that I wondered how Sevah managed anything.

After soup and bread, I rose from my chair and strolled through the piles of books and scrolls and jars of dried herbs and insects.

Thanatos lounged in his armchair, resting his feet up on the coffee table, and surveyed my strolling.

"Was she telling the truth about the tree?" I ask Thanatos as I skimmed a scroll about how to properly harvest Belladonna.

"Yes, this tree is believed to be the physical embodiment of the almighty Father." Thanatos said, raising his hands to the roots above us. "Do I believe it? No."

"You believe they're birds, fire and ice?"

He laughed. "No, I don't believe that either. I believe the Mother and Father live in their own world, if they even exist, and we live in ours. I do not believe in prayers, blessings and sacrifice."

"Then you won't speak with the Mother tree?"

"I will. To prove either that they don't exist or that they don't care." Sorrow glinted in the Prince's gold eyes.

"Why?"

His eyes flicked to mine and quickly away. "You will see soon enough," he almost whispered.

I looked away from the Prince and my eyes locked onto a book. It was large and caked in dust, its black leather cover cracked and worn, you could barely read the title—*Nekros Librorum*. I recognised the word *Nekros*, old Minoman for dead body, and *Librorum* I could only assume was a book. I flicked through the pages and gasped, almost dropping the book. Inside were detailed drawings and diagrams of bodies and rituals, rituals for what I could only guess were to bring the dead back to life.

"Hey," I called to Thanatos, "look at this."

The Prince made his way through the piles of clutter and looked over my shoulder at the *Nekros Librorum*. I flicked through a few pages, showing diagrams of dissected creatures and twisted runes for ritual sacrifice.

I spotted a few words I knew on random pages as I flicked through, but nothing to solidly tell me what the book was really about. "Can you read any of it?"

Thanatos shook his head. "It must be about Necromancy, though. Look at that." He pressed his finger to a page showing a person standing before a large group, their arms outstretched, behind them a lone person with a dagger. The Prince turned the page—revealing the next part of the story. The lone person had stabbed the other standing at the front of the crowd and, in the last drawing, everyone except the killer had fallen.

We were silent for a moment.

"Do you ... do you think the fallen one is the Necromancer and, if he dies, his creations die with him?" I spun to face the Prince. "What if we only have to kill him, just the one man, and every Corse he's created, his army will fall with him?"

Thanatos' eyebrows rose. "It would certainly make our lives easier," he said as he gently took the book from my hands and studied the drawings and text more closely. "We must take this book with us to Minoma and have it translated."

I gestured around the room. "I don't think Sevah will notice." The Prince smiled, and I said, "I wonder why she'd have a book like that."

Thanatos shrugged. "Researching the creatures invading her home?"

"Perhaps." I plucked the book from his hands and placed it under the pillow of one of the beds in the corner of the room.

"Do you not trust her?" Thanatos asked.

"I just think it's strange that she's out here, surrounded by those creatures, and yet Queen Ambrosia was surprised to hear that there was a Necromancer. Would Sevah not have told the Queen she serves that the dead were strolling around in the woods?"

Thanatos considered this, his lips settling into a pout as he thought. "Perhaps she didn't want to alarm Avars if the fairies were already protecting it. Were you alerted the first time they showed up on your doorstep?"

I squared my shoulders, preparing for this to become an all-out argument. "No, I was not, but I was the second it became obvious the attacks were not stopping."

"She said they'd been here for a week, yes?"

"Yes."

"A week ago, the Sillessian royals would have been leaving Isidia after attending your ball."

I gaped at him. "So, it's my fault they're here?" I challenged.

"That's not what I'm saying but, now that you bring it up, they have been ordered to kill all High-Elves they come across, so, clearly, your people have done something to piss off this Necromancer."

I stormed across the room, stopping an arm's length from the Prince. "My people haven't done anything," I hissed, "but with words like that, how can I trust that the Necromancer isn't a Dark-Elf on some revenge mission? How can I trust that your father really did kill those pirates? Maybe it's them, hunting down the rest of Eevan Glenon's family." My voice cracked as I said the last sentence. The Prince's eyes softened. I silently cursed my mother for using that story to keep me in the castle.

When my father's murder was still fresh in my mind, my mother had told me to stay in the castle or the fearsome Captain Orrick Abram would kill me as he had killed my father. It had worked until Lorkin had heard some Councilmen speaking of the execution of the pirate Captain and his last remaining crew in Osiria.

"Orrick is dead, Evalina." The Prince gently placed his hand under my chin and tilted my face so he could look me in the eyes. "I was there, at the execution. I saw him die with my own eyes. He is dead, they're all dead, I promise you." His eyes shone with truth, not a hint of a lie. I was starting to believe that the Prince was not capable of lying. Not sharing information, yes, but lying, no.

"Nothing happens in Isidia without me knowing, there is nothing we could have done that would make someone want to destroy us," I said definitively.

"I know," Thanatos almost whispered.

His hand was still on my chin, his thumb gently stroking the side of my jaw.

Without even thinking, I leant into his touch, his hand spreading to cup my face, his ash scent flooding the air around me. I closed my eyes and breathed it in. The Prince's other hand brushed up the other side of my face, from jaw to temple, before continuing into my hair and gently running along my scalp, sending shivers down my spine. I felt his breath hot on my face and part of me ached to feel that breath on other parts of my body.

Lorkin's face flashed in my mind; I opened my eyes and stepped back, out of the Prince's reach. A look of confusion flashed across his face, as if even he had not realized what he was doing.

My heart was racing, something inside me longed for the Prince, but my rational mind shut down those thoughts. It was too soon, we'd just met, and Lorkin had just ended things.

"We should rest while we can," I spluttered. "Sevah could return at any moment and expect us to leave." I turned away and crawled into the cot against the wall.

I heard Thanatos sigh and extinguish a few of the candles around the room before crawling into the other cot himself. I could have sworn I could feel his eyes on my back, studying me, so I stayed facing the wall and fell asleep to the crackling of the fire.

Chapter Nineteen
Ghosts of the Past

Corse attacks were on the rise; in the last four days, there had been seven attacks. Tension around the palace had risen to an all time high as concern for the Princess's welfare spread throughout the council. They'd been quiet on the matter, but we still hadn't heard from her—had no proof that she was still alive. Even the Carracallans were becoming concerned.

"King Adalric, of course we trust Queen Islina, and we want nothing more than the treaty with Osiria, but we still have not heard anything. We believe a party must be sent out to track Princess Evalina and the Osirian Prince down, if only to check on her well being." Councilman Brooks suggested with a hint of hesitation; no one wanted to be the one to speak against the Queen's orders.

"I understand, Brooks, but we must have faith in Evalina. This is her chance to prove herself and, I believe, if she felt the need to inform us of something she would have by now. If anything, no news is good news," Adalric lied. I knew he was as stressed as I was about the lack of communication from Evie—our sparring matches could attest to that.

"With all due respect, Your Majesty, the first voyage is *your* tradition, not our own, and Princess Evalina is the last of her line—"

"She is also half Carracallan. It's her tradition as much as my own. Have you forgotten your King so soon?" Adalric interrupted, his shoulders squaring.

"Of course not! We only mean—It's just, well—" Councilman Frind stammered.

"We'll give the Princess a little longer. If we don't hear anything soon, we'll send Lorkin out for her."

I straightened at the sound of my name. If we heard nothing, I would be sent out. The Council bristled.

"Send Lorkin?" Brooks questioned. "I don't think that would be a good idea."

"If a battle breaks out, Bellona and I can handle it. If you've got a problem with that, you can take it up with the Queen who, though you seem to have forgotten, has left me in charge."

The councilmen shrunk in their seats. They weren't used to being spoken to so bluntly by someone that wasn't Evalina. She had a way of putting them in their place, and it was clear now who she'd got that from. The more time I spent with Eevans family, the more I realized how much like him she really was. It made the distance between her and her mother make so much sense.

"This meeting is over," Adalric declared. "Lorkin, with me."

I nodded and followed the King out of the council room. I had expected him to lead us to the training pits, but we instead made our way behind the servants quarters and barracks to the armory. I'd spent much of my time there recently, double and triple checking our stock of weapons, making sure people in the know weren't stealing them to arm their families. I gave Adalric a quick tour, showing the layout and how everything was stored and cataloged, informed him of my recent counts and when I planned to do another. He was silent throughout, a slight nod was all he offered in response.

"Lorkin," he finally said after I'd begun to lead him out of the dim space; there were no windows to make it harder for thieves to get in or out without notice. "You're an honest lad?" He asked, his voice quiet.

"I like to think so, Your Majesty."

"So when I ask you to tell me what life was really like for my Flower, you'll tell me the truth." His eyes bore into mine. I resisted the urge to look away.

"Your Majesty," I paused, my mind racing, "I can tell you if you would like but … you will not like what I tell you."

Pain was already spreading across the King's features. "I've heard stories but"— he took a shuddering breath—"I need to hear the truth."

I nodded and began, recounting the sad life Evalina had led and Islina's slow descent into whatever afflicted her now. It had started as a deep sadness, as was expected, but it had never passed. She pushed everyone away, including her daughter, fired staff that had worked at the palace while Eevan had lived there, and receded into herself. The Council ran the Queendom for many years, manipulating Islina until Evalina and I had stepped up, until we became the manipulators.

Islina had refused to remarry despite the many suitors, but also would not name Evalina—for what reason, I didn't know. All the while she did her best to snuff any trace of Eevan out of her daughter. Any playfulness, rebellion, coarseness, she would punish and drill out of her. Evalina's princess training had almost been more militant than my guard training, her punishments more severe. I told him of the tower, her solitary cell within the prison she lived in, and his face turned almost murderous. I wished I could show more emotion, to show him that I didn't support the treatment of her, but I was so numb to the events that I couldn't even muster a frown. It had been my life, too, the only life I had known; while I didn't enjoy a lot of it, I didn't know any better. It had been improving in recent years, but the improvements came at the cost of Islina's health; the more she deteriorated, the more quality of life for Evalina and I improved.

I wanted the best for Evalina, after so many years of watching her suffer in forced silence. It was why I had taken the position as Captain, to be able to take the work load from her without anyone noticing, without anyone thinking it strange that I was always with the Queen. I was her Captain, her guard, her confidant, her scribe. All things I couldn't be had I stayed a Lord.

Tears had rolled down the King's face as I'd told our story. I stood silently before him staring at the ground, fiddling with my fingers behind my back, now struggling to control my own emotions.

"I'd known it was bad but ..." He trailed off as another wave of emotion hit him, he collapsed onto a bench, his head in his hands. "Eevan, I'm sorry," he whispered. "I've failed you and your daughter."

My own eyes pricked as Eevans warm smile flashed into my mind. He would despise what we had become, how we had lived, but I was also furious with him. If he hadn't left, hadn't gotten himself killed, life for us could have been so different. I clenched my jaw and turned my sadness into anger. "There was nothing you could have done." I said sharply, the King's wet eyes flicked up to mine. "Islina forced you out, remember? She would have started a war to remove you had you not left." I stated.

"I'm surprised you remember that, you were so young."

"I don't remember much, but I remember that day."

Evalina and I had huddled together behind a pillar in the throne room. We'd known something was wrong for days; Islina's temper had been unusually short and then she'd requested the whole family meet in the throne room. Evalina and I knew that was it. The second that everyone arrived, Islina had gone ballistic and told them all to leave. The only one that had stayed was Bellona, but after a few more weeks even she was sent away by the Queen.

"I wish we'd done more." The King reflected.

"What's done is done, there's no point wishing it now," I said a little too harshly, judging by the King's flinch. "All we can do now is aim to make Evalina's life as Queen as easy as possible."

Adalric nodded, rose from the bench and gave my shoulder a light squeeze before leaving me alone in the armory. I leant my head against the cool stone of the walls and breathed deeply, thoughts of the past and fears for the present clouding my mind. No matter how hard I tried, the image of Evie being dragged away into the tower could not be erased. But the land around her wasn't Isidia— but a land of snow and volcanoes.

CHAPTER TWENTY
LIKE WILDFIRE

The Prince and I sprung up in our beds, daggers raised as the door to the cottage flung open loudly.

Sevah stumbled through the door lugging both of our full packs behind her. Thanatos jumped out of bed to assist the witch in her struggle.

"Thank you, Your Highness. So, the good news is the fairies will help us. The bad news, they'll only help us for the last leg of the journey—but I found someone else that can offer some assistance."

Thanatos dropped both packs onto his bed, pulling out an apple as he turned to face the witch. "The last leg?"

"We'll travel from here to the Miriana River, from there the fairies will guide us and conceal the Princess's identity." Sevah bowed to me.

"And if we don't make it to the river?" I asked.

Sevah smiled at me. "We will, Your Highness."

"And what of the Father tree?" Thanatos asked, his mouth full of apple.

"The fairies have assured me that the Corse have no interest in it, but will protect it in my absence nonetheless." Sevah waved her hand and a large empty pack appeared on the workbench.

As the witch was busy tottering about the cottage, filling her bag with supplies, I slipped the *Nekros Librorum* out from under my pillow and into my pack.

Within the half-hour, we were ready to leave the Father tree. We found Faenor and Serelene happily grazing on the garden beds of the cottage; both seemed to sigh as they caught sight of the Prince and I coming through the door. I paused, wide-eyed, as a hulking figure rounded a tree by the horses, his yellow eyes landed on me and Rangkars mouth fell open, "Your Highness?" He said questioningly.

I gave a sly shrug.

"Rangkar, what are you doing here?" Thanatos asked, his tone slightly panicked.

"Well, I was on my way back from Shinchaku and thought I'd check out the claims for myself and ended up getting lost in the woods. Sevah found me last night, fighting off some of the creatures. She saved me, to be completely honest, I was getting my ars—uh, they were winning." He chuckled sheepishly, glancing at Sevah and I. "She said she was leading some others to Avars, and I thought I'd tag along. I knew it was you guys the second I saw the horses. She filled me in on what happened. It must have been terrifying for you, Princess, worse than traveling with this fiend," he said, taking my hand bringing it to his fanged mouth. I laughed at Thanatos' outraged expression.

"Yes, traveling with Thanatos is worse than any undead beast I could face."

"Now you're just being rude." Thanatos said as he pushed past us to load the pack onto the horses.

I took the spare moment to fill Rangkar in on the plan and explained why I had to protect my identity.

"Hmm, very troublesome. Well, it is a pleasure to officially meet you, Your Highness."

"Please, just call me Evalina on the road."

The orc nodded and bounded off to join Thanatos with the horses. Moments later, we were ready to leave.

Thanatos turned to the witch. "How do you plan on protecting Evalina?" he asked firmly.

"Well, in my experience with the Corse, I've found they're not too fond of fire." On the last word, Sevah's hands swept to the sky and a ring of fire erupted around me.

I froze and Thanatos tensed.

"What in the pit do you think you're doing, witch?" The Prince spat, reaching for his sword. Rangkar gripped his arms, holding him back from Sevah.

I slowly moved my hand toward the fire. I felt no heat radiating off it, the flames licked at my hand but I felt no pain. "It's an illusion, I feel nothing," I said to Thanatos in an attempt to calm him.

"Then why can I feel heat?" He demanded.

"I'm protecting her Highness, of course. The flames will not burn you, Princess Evalina, but they will do anything, or anyone, that tries to touch you." She raised her eyebrow at the Prince.

Thanatos was watching me intently, Rangkar with an air of wonder. I shrugged and he and the orc relaxed.

"Shall we get moving?" The witch smiled and gestured to a path leading into the woods.

Thanatos stormed ahead before us, leading Serelene behind him. I glanced at Faenor.

"I'll lead her, you stay in between the Prince and I," Sevah said.

"And I'll stay with you, my Lady," Rangkar purred to the witch, receiving a blush in return.

I nodded and fell into step behind the Prince and Serelene, the witch, orc, and Faenor following at the rear.

We walked in silence for a while, each of us straining to hear any sound that would alert us to the Corse presence.

After a few hours, I fell into step with Sevah; Rangkar had ventured forward and was having what looked like a very terse conversation with Thanatos.

"How did you come to protect the Father tree?" I asked the witch.

She smiled at the question. "My grandmother was a Wood-Elf, hence the red hair. That means I have more of an affinity for magic than regular humans, but because I'm mostly human and using natural magic, not mage magic, I still have to pay the price." Her free hand absently ran along the bark that coated her neck. "I ended up at the Father tree because the elves saw how gifted I was, more gifted than them, some would say, and I prefer it to living in Avars."

"What about your family?"

"I see them every now and then, they live in Avars."

"I don't mean to be rude, but does it hurt?" I gestured to the bark and flowers that covered one half of her head.

"Sometimes, it depends what I've used the magic for. Usually it just happens without me even realizing." Sevah toyed with a tendril of leaves resting on her shoulder. "I am luckier than most witches, the Father has blessed me with beauty." She winked at me. "Other witches' transformations are grotesque and ugly."

Those were the witches I'd heard of in stories—ugly, deformed humans that sap the life out of plants and animals to use it as magic. The more they use their magic, the more they transform into whatever it is they've chosen to sap life from. Sevah's transformation was beautiful; the colors of the flowers contrasted beautifully with the red of her natural hair while also bringing out her blue eyes.

"I'm sorry I cannot help you with your blood oath."

I frowned. "How do you know of it?"

She raised her hands above her head and looked to the sky. "The Father knows all, and is a bit of a gossip. He said it is the matter of Elves and Humans, as is the Necromancer."

"And the Mother?"

She shrugged. "The Mother is unpredictable, like fire—it can keep you warm and alive, or burn you to ashes."

I shuddered and kept my hands tightly at my sides as the flames of the ring around me flickered. "How long will it take for us to get to the river?"

"We should get there by nightfall, then it's another day's travel to Avars."

"How could we be so close? Thanatos said it would be four days?"

The witch smiled. "If you were following the usual paths, it would. Even the shortcuts through the woods the Prince takes are paths created by the fairies. They're everywhere, though you may not see them, always playing tricks. The woods are nowhere near as big as they are on maps, it's all a clever trick."

I chuckled, even Thanatos had been tricked by the fairies and the woods he thought he knew so well. I glanced up at the Prince stalking ahead of us, were it not for his white hair he would have been almost invisible in the dark forest; his purple skin blended seamlessly into the shadows.

"He cares for you."

I sighed. "So I've been told."

Confusion spread across Sevah's face. "You do not want him to?"

"It's not that, I just … we've just met. We hardly know each other, and it seems like everyone is forcing us together."

"Maybe we see what you do not."

I rolled my eyes at the witch and quickened my pace to catch up to Thanatos and Rangkar. "Sevah says we're only two days away from Avars." The Prince's eyebrows rose in question and I shrugged. "Fairy magic."

"Well good, I want to get out of these woods." His face softened. "Are you all right?" He tensed again as I waved my hand through the flames that surrounded me and held my unmarked hand out for him to inspect.

"Never been better." I grinned. "Though I do find it suspicious that we haven't run into any Corse."

"I was just thinking the same thing. It's too quiet in these woods," Rangkar said, peering suspiciously through the trees.

"If we're as close to Avars as the witch says, then it doesn't surprise me. The fairies wouldn't let them get too close to the town."

I nodded and fell back into my space between the two parties and let silence fall between us.

I thought of home, something I had been trying to avoid doing. I wondered how they were going, my family. I wondered if my uncles' fleets had arrived, if Bellona had whipped the soldiers into shape, how my grandparents were fairing dealing with my mother.

My mother, was she well? She had known where I was every day of my life up until a week ago—now she had no idea. I could be dead already, for all she knew. Lorkin—my chest tightened as I thought of him—he was so angry the day I left, so hurt. Would he take me back when I got home? Did I want him to?

Time dragged as we walked, all of us tensing at every noise that came from the woods, only to find out it was just a rabbit, deer, or bird. We didn't stop for lunch when the sun reached the middle of the sky—just kept walking.

I slowed for a moment to pull a carrot out of my bag when, all of a sudden, the fire around me flared and engulfed a spear that aimed for my head.

I unsheathed my blades and scanned the woods for my attacker, I heard Thanatos and Rangkar do the same, Sevah was still. Another spear came flying toward me and was turned to ash by the fire before it could reach me.

"Behind!" Sevah yelled, spinning to face the other direction.

"It's an ambush," Thanatos growled, his sword in one hand and a dagger in the other.

"I knew it was too quiet," Rangkar ground out.

I scanned the woods again and spotted figures in the distance, slowly becoming visible in the darkness. I rolled my shoulders and got into a fighting stance. I would not run this time—this time, I would fight.

CHAPTER TWENTY ONE
BLAZE AND BLADES

The fighting began slowly, the Corse stumbling out of the forest almost one by one. Most of them headed straight to me and were either dispatched by the flames or by my blades.

Before the battle had begun, Sevah had whispered to the horses and they'd bounded off ahead of us. "They'll meet us at the river," she'd said quickly before taking up her position beside me on the opposite side to Thanatos, Rangkar covering my back as I continued up the path. "Decapitation!" Sevah called over the fighting "It's the only way to keep them down other than burning."

We heeded her advice and soon heads were rolling over the forest floor, leaving black sludge as they went.

"We must keep moving forward!" Thanatos grunted as he dueled with two Corse.

I moved to help him, my fire flicking towards any Corse that got too close and lighting them up with a screech; the few out of my fire's reach had their heads lopped off by my blades. I came up behind the creatures attacking the Prince and cut one's head off just as the Prince managed to dispose of the other.

Thanatos reached for my hand without thinking and snapped it back as the fire leapt for him. I shrugged and began to run north through the forest. I could hear the Prince trailing behind me, dodging the flaming Corse I left in my wake, the scent of their charred flesh following us through the forest. The compulsion on them was strong, so strong they had no sense of self preservation and walked straight into the ring of fire.

I glanced behind me to make sure Sevah was following. She was flinging fireballs and slicing with a dagger as she went. Rangkar was sticking close to her, hacking through necks with his shining blade. There was no form to his combat, it was savage and brutal, the desperate fight for life of someone used to one on one skirmishes.

We ran for what felt like an eternity, cutting and burning our way through the Corse to reach the river. We were covered head to toe in black, sticky blood, nauseous from the overbearing smell of the dead.

Our pace began to slow, the continuous fighting and running beginning to take its toll on us. The fire protecting me had begun flickering in and out of existence, I looked behind me at the witch. She and Rangkar had fallen behind, the witch only using her dagger to fight off the Corse that were still attacking, the orc covering her back.

"Thanatos, Sevah and Rankgar need help!" I called.

I still had doubts about the witch but she had kept me safe thus far. The Prince skidded to a halt and made to turn back, I raced back toward the struggling duo, helping Sevah dispose of the Corse surrounding her as Rangkar caught up to us.

"I'm sorry, Princess, I can't keep the flame up any longer," she huffed, her voice thick with exhaustion and small, purple flowers beginning to bloom along her hairline that weren't there this morning.

"We can't keep up with you elves," Rangkar puffed.

"It's fine, let it down and use this." I unsheathed my father's blade and passed it to the witch, her eyes widened as she beheld it. "It will do a lot more damage than that dagger."

She nodded and grasped the blade as the flames around me flickered out of existence for good.

Another wave of Corse streamed out of the woods toward us. We engaged without hesitation, our movements noticeably slower than they had been.

"We're almost at the river," Sevah called over the fray.

Relief flooded me, I was exhausted.

The four of us took out as many of the monsters as we could, ducking and hacking as needed and assisting each other when we could. I almost wished I could stop fighting and just watch the Prince, he moved so smoothly and effortlessly— as if he were dancing. It was beautiful, in a way. I watched in awe as he dropped to one knee, dodging an attack from one Corse, then spun and cut the legs off another, in another swift movement he'd decapitated them both and moved on to the next opponent.

Behind me, Sevah was struggling with the weight of my father's sword but holding her own against the onslaught; Rangkar was close by her, dispatching a horde of his own.

My Sai blades were drenched in black blood, my hands cramping from holding them as tightly as I possibly could.

I was fighting off three Corse, jumping and rolling backwards to dodge their attacks, when I backed into a tree.

One of the creatures smiled cruelly. "You're ours now, Isidian."

Panic was rising in my chest, the calm of battle fading as the three monsters edged closer. My mind frantically thought of escape routes, of fighting techniques that could help in this situation.

I risked a glance at the others, all were preoccupied with their own enemies. I had height and reach on my side, but my blades were too blunt to quickly dispose of all three. I sheathed my weapons and waited.

The female Corse on my left moved first, swiping at me with a dirty knife. I grabbed her wrist and twisted until she cried out in pain and dropped the small blade. I then used her body to knock the Corse in front of me off his feet and again to balance myself as I kicked the last Corse in the head, knocking him to the ground. Before the first male could right himself, I twisted my leg around the female's, causing her to fall on top of him, then grabbed a chunk of her hair and smashed her head into the males with a sickening crunch. The male and female now laid on the floor, unconscious, as the third Corse charged toward me, I moved at just the right moment to grab his shirt and throw him hard, head first into the tree behind me. I couldn't tell if the loud crack had come from his neck or the top of his head as he slumped to the ground.

Despite the fighting still going on before me, I felt victorious after having taken down that many enemies at once.

I looked up to see the Prince coming toward me, no doubt to decapitate the fallen Corse.

The pride shining in his eyes turned to worry.

"Evalina, look out!" He called breaking into a run.

I whirled, behind me was a Corse the size of a bear, his deep skin made him almost invisible in the dark of the forest. There was nothing I could do as he swung a huge club right at my head.

CHAPTER TWENTY TWO
FADING LIGHT

Evalina slumped to the ground; a panic like I'd never felt before filled my chest.

I pushed my legs to move faster, the Kushyami Corse had already raised his club, about to bring it down once again on Evalina's head, when I quickly reached for my knives and threw one. It planted right between the hulking figure's eyes, stunning it for a moment.

It was enough time for me to reach it.

Despite the surprising size of the creature, I was still bigger.

I rammed him, knocking him off balance, and, with one more quick movement, had him disarmed.

The Corse roared in frustration as I dodged his clumsy attacks, doing my best to stay close to the Princess, crumpled and vulnerable on the floor. Black blood leaked down the Kushyami's face and into his eyes as he tried to wipe it away, blinding himself temporarily. I used this moment to slip behind him, reach over and yank my knife out of his head. Blood spewed from the wound and the dead man roared once again, his hands flying to the space between his eyes. I grabbed a bunch of his hair and pulled him away from Evalina before cutting his head off.

It was not easy, his neck was thick and my blade blunt. I had to use both hands to pull my sword all the way through, giving myself a deep slice on my right hand.

Once the head toppled from the body, I spun quickly back to Evalina and, without a moment's hesitation, threw her over my shoulder and began running north. I heard the witch and Rangkar following behind, the Corse not far behind them. I knew I should have slowed to be sure the witch was safe, to relieve her of the weight of Evalina's sword that was much too big for her, but Rangkar was with her and all I could think about was getting Evalina out of the forest, getting her safe.

My legs were barking at me, wanting to collapse under the added weight of Evalina slumped over my shoulder, but I pushed forward. I held firmly onto Evalina's legs despite the bite from the slice on my hand; when she woke, the Princess would no doubt scold me for getting blood on her boots.

"Sevah! Are we almost to the river?!" I yelled over my shoulder.

"Yes! We're almost there," the witch huffed; she sounded distant.

I slowed to look at her.

"No, just keep going! They only want the Princess," Rangkar called back, sounding as distant as the witch.

I squared my shoulders, readjusted my hold on the unconscious Princess and forced my legs to run faster.

The sun had almost completely set when we came over a hill and finally saw the river.

The Corse were beginning to gain on us—it was a miracle we'd managed to out run them as long as what we had.

"Almost there," Sevah breathed, more to herself than to Rangkar and I.

We rounded the hill and began our descent.

My shoulder was aching from holding the Princess and my mind was filled with worry that she still hadn't woken up. I had to heal her.

Something soared past my head, narrowly missing my ear, we paused to inspect what had planted itself in the ground before us.

"An arrow—run!" I tightened my grip on Evalina again, flinching at the stinging from my hand and ran full pelt, again.

Arrows continued to fly past us, we ran listening to the patter of them hitting the ground. There had to have been about five hundred paces between us and the river when I noticed the glimmer of a magic ward and sent a desperate prayer, to the gods I didn't believe in, that it was one made to protect us.

Pain shot through my shoulder as a cheer sounded from the hoard behind us.

I clenched my teeth and powered through as another arrow embedded itself in my back, dangerously close to the limp Princess's head.

Close—we were so close.

We couldn't die now.

Not mere paces away from that shimmering wall of magic, not when Evalina was so close to seeing the fairies.

I stumbled as the pain traced its way over my body, the whole of me aching.

I only assumed Sevah and Rangkar were still behind me, I could hear nothing over the pounding of my heart and my own ragged breath.

My pace was slowing more and more by the second, it was by miracle alone that I was still able to carry the Princess's weight. Vibrations from the approaching horde rattled me through the soles of my shoes. My survival instincts told me to throw the Princess to the Corse and be done with it—but another, stronger, side of me insisted on protecting the Princess till my dying breath.

And so I would.

I cursed as another arrow hit me, this time in the leg, and another round of cheers sounded through the host of monsters. They were so loud, so close, and I was so close to the river, less than a hundred meters. Limping heavily and straining to keep myself conscious, I kept moving forward, pushing through the pain.

"Drop the High-Elf, Deathbringer," a low, gravelly voice called from behind me. "We have no qualm with your kind … yet."

Just a few more steps.

"You can be free of this mess."

I was in too much pain to come up with a witty reply, too busy focusing on the last few steps toward the barrier, so I just limped on.

"Have it your way." A quick, sharp whistle sounded. "Kill him," the voice ordered and low, thudding footsteps followed.

They couldn't have been more than a few paces away from me and I was only a few steps away from the wards, but they were gaining on me faster than I was getting to the barrier. I limped faster, the thundering footsteps speeding up too, gaining on me until I could feel their hulking presence mere steps behind me.

"Farewell, Deathbringer," came an even lower voice.

I was surprised I couldn't feel the creature's breath on the back of my neck with how close he sounded. I clenched my jaw and grunted as I once again pushed myself to move faster, barely breaking into a run. I heard the Corse roar, steel slice through the air, and waited for the impact, for the pain.

But it never came.

The world around me was quiet, I dared to stop moving and look behind me.

Corse, more than I had seen in the last two days put together, were running, swinging weapons and clawing at the mostly invisible ward before me.

I stood in surprised silence for a moment and watched, completely forgetting about my injuries, the Princess, and the witch. How powerful the fairies must be, to create a ward like this—to block out sound.

I slowly, painfully, adjusted the Princess so that she was cradled in my arms instead of slung over my shoulder. Her pale skin glowed in the light of the moon.

I tried to walk a step and cried out in pain, my knees buckled and hit the floor.

I could move no further.

I laid the Princess gently on the ground before me, pushed a few strands of hair out of my face and, ignoring the pain from my injuries, began healing her.

I placed my hands on either side of her head and pushed my magic into her. The familiar black mist formed around my hands, the darkness masking the blue in her hair, the blue that I liked so much.

"Thanatos!" I heard Sevah's steps behind me. "You need help."

"I'm fine," I grunted, barely keeping my eyes open. I needed to save her, needed to see her eyes open, to know that she was all right.

"You have three arrows sticking out of you, you are anything but fine," Rangkar chided.

"I need to save her."

Sevah pleaded, "You need to be saved first, I can get the fairies—"

"No. I can do it, I can save her," I breathed.

My hands were shaking, sweat pouring down my face.

My wounds had gone numb and the world around me began to spin as the Princess's eyes fluttered open.

CHAPTER TWENTY THREE
FEINT GLIMMER

My body ached and my mind was cloudy as I slowly opened my eyes.

For a moment, all I could see was black mist; as it cleared, the Prince's face came into view. Thanatos' eyes warmed for a moment before they rolled back into his head and he collapsed on top of me, forcing the air from my lungs.

"Thanatos!" I exclaimed, breathless.

Rangkar rushed forward to help pull the Prince off of me. "Don't roll him on his back," the orc warned.

Confused, I looked him over and discovered why. Three arrows—one in his shoulder, mid back, and the last one in his calf. I thought back to the battle in the woods, trying to figure out when it could have happened. It must have been after I'd gotten hit. Then I noticed the world around me.

"Where are we? What happened?" I asked.

Rangkar and I gently laid the prince down; I was amazed that we could lift him at all.

"We're at the river. You got knocked unconscious and the Prince carried you here." Sevah answered as Rangkar knelt down beside the Prince and checked his breathing, holding a green hand before Thanatos' mouth.

All the way to the river.

I looked down at the Prince—his breathing was ragged, his features laced with pain.

I knelt down beside him and rubbed my hands together. I had never healed injuries this substantial before, but I had to try—to repay him.

I leaned into the Prince's face; his mouth was taut with pain, his eyes scrunched tight.

I concentrated my magic, felt it rise from my chest and into my mouth. As the Prince was about to suck in air, I gently blew my magic onto his face. I watched and made sure he breathed in every bit of the glimmering white mist, hoping that I'd put enough numbing magic into it.

His face relaxed and his breathing fell into its usual sleeping rhythm.

I motioned for Sevah to join me and she squatted on the opposite side of Thanatos to me. "Help me remove the arrows. I've numbed him, but he may still fight us. Rangkar, help her hold him down."

The witch nodded, exhaustion was plastered all over her face but determination shone in her eyes as she held down Thanatos' torso. Rangkar gripped his friend's ankles, and waited for me to pull the arrow from his shoulder. I rested a shaking hand on his back, before counting to three and yanking on the arrow, tearing his flesh more in the process. Thanatos' breathing only halted a second before resuming, it was his only sign of pain through the whole process of removing the arrows.

Blood trickled from each wound, spreading over the Prince's light coloured clothing.

I held my unsteady hands over each wound, focusing on only one at a time, and willed my magic into my hands. The glimmering mist flowed down from my palms and into the wound itself. I could almost see the progress in my mind, the mist clotting the blood and working with the cells of the body to speed up the creation of new tissue.

As I finished healing the last wound, the Prince stirred and relief flooded through me.

"I will go talk to the fairies, let them know we're here," Sevah announced with a smile, and strode toward the wooden bridge a few paces behind us.

Thanatos moved to sit up.

"Careful." I reached to help him, he grunted in thanks. "Take it slow, I'm not too confident in my healing abilities."

The Prince smiled. "Well you should be, I feel great." He flinched as he put his right hand down to steady himself.

"I guess I forgot one." I reached for his hand.

"It's fine, I can do it"

I shushed him and grabbed his wrist. I twisted his hand so that the palm was facing up and began healing it.

"Well, I'm glad you're still alive, brother," Rangkar said, rising from his spot by Thanatos' feet. "But I'm going to check on the witch." He winked at the Prince before following Sevah.

Thanatos marveled at the mist of my power, barely registering the orc's words. "I've never seen an Isidian heal before, not in a way I could study, anyway. It's beautiful." He summoned his power with his left hand, watched the black mist swirl around his fingertips. "Not like Osirian magic."

He was right, in a way. His magic seemed to suck the light out of the space around it, as if nothing could thrive in its presence.

"At least your power can be used in battle."

"Not this battle," he countered.

"No, you'll just have to fight dirty like the rest of us."

The Prince chuckled.

His hand had finished healing but I continued to hold it, savoring the feeling of comfort after the hard few days we'd had. I laid my other hand atop the Prince's. "Thank you for saving me—again. I don't mean to be such a burden."

His face softened. "You are anything but. If you hadn't been here to save me, I would have died just now. You are the target of a deranged lunatic, I think that gives you a few burden rights." Thanatos gently lifted my chin with his free hand, making me look him in the eyes. We were sitting so close I could see little specks of black in the gold of his irises. "Thank *you* for saving *me*."

We stared into each other's eyes, our faces so close together we could feel each other's steady breath. I was tempted to lean in further, to press my lips to his.

I heard footsteps behind us and slowly pulled away from Thanatos. His fingers grazed my jaw as I went and I reluctantly released my other hand from mine.

I got to my feet and helped Thanatos to his. He moved slowly, testing. When he was upright and I was sure he could carry his own weight, I turned my attention to the approaching footsteps.

Sevah was coming toward us, Rangkar behind her, leading Feanor and Serelene by their reigns. "I kept them restrained for as long as I could but they were desperate to see their friends." The witch smiled as Rangkar handed us the reins.

Feanor nuzzled my neck and huffed happily as I stroked her neck, of all the horses we had at Lonthia she had always been my favorite. The Prince was holding Serelene's face gently and whispering into her ear. I wondered if, during his time with the Wood-Elves, he had learnt the language of beasts.

Wood-Elves were gifted linguists, they could talk to all manner of life and, for many reasons, that was why they had always been neutral.

"Are the fairies ready to see us?" Thanatos asked the witch.

"Yes, come this way." Sevah motioned for us to follow.

I glanced at the Prince as he began trailing after Sevah, making sure he was walking normally, breathing regularly. Rangkar almost clung to his side, his arms braced and ready to catch in case the Prince fell. I didn't take it personally, orcs had always been wary of elf magic—all magic, really—as they had none. And I was so rusty when it came to my magic; soothing pain and healing scrapes and bruises was easy work, but bringing someone back from the brink was tricky, and my head was still a little woozy. I was glad there was someone else to catch him if he did fall.

The Prince had been close to death, I could feel it as my magic moved through his body; it had felt like a cool darkness had settled through him and my light, warming magic had had to peel it away. It made me even more grateful towards him, that he would let himself get so close to dying and not even think to leave me to save himself.

Warmth spread through my chest as I thought about the sacrifice Thanatos had made for me, as if a fire had been lit within me. I smiled as my eyes fell to the back of the Prince's head, his white hair glowing almost blue in the bright moonlight. He had taken me to Sillessia after all, and, now, we were going to see the fairies.

My excitement was rising the closer we got to the end of the bridge. I could see a single, green glow floating about the space as if it were pacing. Thanatos and I tied the horses to the end of the bridge and waited behind Sevah.

My eyes followed the pacing fairy, trying to spot the tiny figure that existed somewhere in that bright glow.

"Your Highnesses, this is Maioc." Sevah explained. "She has been charged with helping us by the Grand Fairy."

Maioc halted her pacing. I tried my hardest not to gape at her; while I couldn't see her true form, she was beautiful.

A soft voice echoed through my mind. "You have done well to make it this far, Princess, given your lack of worldly experience."

I was taken aback by the backhanded compliment. "Thank you?" I felt a pang of disappointment.

Sevah shot me an apologetic look. "It has been a hard journey Maioc. What assistance can you offer us?"

Maioc ignored Sevah's question and zipped through the air to the Prince. "Prince Thanatos, how odd for you to involve yourself in a game like this."

The Prince's eyes narrowed at the fairy, but she simply flitted away.

"And an orc," Maioc said with a tone of disapproval. "Interesting company you keep, Sevah."

"Please Maioc, how do you intend to help us? We must get to Avars as soon as we can," Sevah pushed.

"How unfair it is that I should not be allowed to play with you before I send you off, but we fairies do understand how serious this threat is. The dead things are strong and fast when they want to be, and they are getting ever closer to our dear Naeinn. I thought about simply changing the Princess's features, but the temptation to leave them changed is too strong." I raised a brow at the fairy and somehow, in my mind, felt her shrug. "I have another way, you must hold your breath, though."

I was about to ask why, had just sucked in enough air to form the words when a loud clap sounded and suddenly the world was rushing past me.

I held in the tiny bit of air I had and watched as thousands of colors and textures flew past my eyes in a blur. Air was rushing past me so fast and strong that I was frightened that if I was to breathe my insides would be sucked out through my mouth.

There was a splash and suddenly I was submerged.

Panic filled me.

Beneath my feet was nothing but the black depths and around me nothing but open water, until Thanatos was suddenly before me, looking as surprised as I was. I clawed my way through the water toward him, still holding on to the tiny breath I'd managed to take before Maioc had sent us speeding through the world.

I clung to the Prince once I'd reached him. Thanatos wrapped an arm around my waist and began kicking and guiding us to the surface. I tried to help, pushed as much as I could with my arms but my head was beginning to lull, my lungs scream. I wished I'd inherited gills like my aunt Bellona, that I could breathe underwater and never fear drowning, but I didn't and I was.

My last nightmare began to flash before my eyes, the ruins and the Wraith, the eyes—those eyes.

I tried to focus on what was really happening around me, on the Prince I was holding onto, the Prince that was saving me once again.

I tightened my grip on Thanatos.

I looked above us and, sure enough, I could see the surface of the water but my lungs couldn't hold out any longer. Before I could stop myself I gasped and my mouth flooded with water. I spasmed as my lungs began to fill and expel water simultaneously. My grip on the prince began to loosen as black spots fluttered into view. My throat fought against itself, taking in and then instantly expelling the water that was filling my lungs in a vicious cycle, the muscles searing with pain.

I felt the Prince grip me harder and force his legs to kick faster, propelling us to the surface of the water.

When we broke the surface, I was barely conscious as the Prince forced his fingers into my mouth and down my throat, causing me to gag. I coughed and threw up water and bile—not as much as after my nightmare, but enough to know that my throat would again be sore for days.

"Are you all right?" Thanatos asked desperately.

"Yes," I replied hoarsely. It was painful to talk, to swallow, to breathe.

"Damn fairies!" He cursed. "She couldn't magic us into the palace, it had to be the lake." He took a deep breath, through his nose and out through his mouth, and rested both his hands on either side of my face. "Are you all right?" He asked again, softer this time, his voice laced with worry.

"I'll be better once we get out of this damn water," I croaked, wincing as my throat burned with each word.

Thanatos nodded. "Can you swim?"

Though my body felt the weakest it ever had, I nodded and he pointed to the shore. It was a good distance away, not much of a feat for elves; but for elves who had recently been healed and almost drowned, it would be a long, slow swim.

Boats littered the shoreline of the lake, barely visible in the moonlight; this must've been the main body of water for Avars. At least Maioc had delivered on her promise of getting us there—the execution could have been better but, all in all, she'd saved us a lot of time and a little trouble.

We crawled out of the water and collapsed on the shore, weighed down by our wet clothes. I let out a long painful sigh and laid next to the Prince on the beach in silence for a while, letting my body catch up.

"I never want to see a large body of water again," I said once I felt a little better.

"I'm inclined to agree with you." He chuckled.

I rolled onto my side to face the Prince, only to find him already gazing at me. A flutter ran through my body. "Avars must be close."

"Just past those trees. If I could stand, I'd carry you there."

I smiled. "Let's save that for the next time I get knocked out."

Something passed over the Prince's eyes at my words. I reached out for his hand and held it to my chest, hoping the feel of my heartbeat would calm him.

"I'm sorry your first experience with a fairy wasn't great," he whispered.

I shrugged. "I kind of expected it, I know they're all tricksters."

Thanatos offered me a sad smile. "Not all of them are like Maioc, you'll see once we get to the palace."

"If we can ever stand up."

The Prince laughed.

"Thanatos?"

"Yes, Evalina?" The fluttering feeling sparked through me at the sound of my name.

"I'm sorry about how I acted at the ball, in the garden." I clarified at his look of confusion. "You were right, I did want to leave. I had wanted to leave since the day my father died. Even now, I sometimes think about not going back, or at least taking the longest way back." I smiled sadly at the Prince's stunned expression. "My mother has always said I'm more like my father, I guess that included his lust for adventure. Don't get me wrong, I love Isidia, it will always be my home and, one day, I will be its Queen—but I needed this." I gestured around us, my eyes lingering on the unfamiliar stars above me. "So, you were right and I apologize."

Thanatos' face softened. "You were also right that night. It was presumptuous of me to practically ask you to run away with me, but the offer is still there and will be—always."

My chest felt as though a million butterflies were trying to explode out of it. I wanted to move closer to the Prince, to have his whole body touch the whole of mine, but the sensible side of me told me this was not the time and definitely not the place. Something in his eyes told me that the Prince felt the same, something had shifted between us, but now was not the moment to act on it.

So, instead of acting on whatever urges were trying to take hold of us, we rose from the shore and Thanatos led us through the woods surrounding the lake into the Sillessian capital.

CHAPTER TWENTY FOUR
HOME SWEET SECOND HOME

Avars was more beautiful than I could have ever imagined.

The town was made up of a group of giant trees, each one had a carved staircase spiraling up the trunk leading to homes and stores that were also carved into the thick trunks. The ground beneath the vertical town was covered with various garden patches, each patch overflowing with abnormally large produce.

The palace sat in the very center of the town, carved from the stump of one of the impossibly huge trees. Rounded balconies jutted out of the structure seemingly at random making the palace closely resemble a clump of overgrown fungi.

Littered around the town and the palace were actual fungi, large glowing mushrooms that illuminated the whole of Avars with a steady, blue-green ambience. The Prince and I trudged slowly through the gardens toward the gates of the palace, when it occurred to me that Sevah and the horses had not landed in the lake with us.

As if he could sense my thoughts, the Prince stopped in his tracks. "I hope Maioc sent Sevah, Rangkar and the horses as well."

"Where else would she have sent them, if not with us?"

"The palace perhaps, or the town stables."

I shrugged, they were safe with any of those options, as long as I wasn't with them.

There were no guards when we reached the palace gates; Thanatos didn't seem worried and continued to stroll through the palace as if he lived there. I nervously trailed behind him as he led us to a stairwell lit, like the rest of Avars, by small clumps of glowing mushrooms.

"Shouldn't we tell someone we're here before we get arrested?" I asked.

The Prince waved me off. "The palace is rarely guarded. Everyone loves the Wood-Elves, remember? And, anyway, I have my own rooms."

I was surprised. Yes, the Sillessians were loved by all but to leave their royals unguarded, especially now, seemed incredibly irresponsible.

Thanatos having his own rooms was almost as surprising, even if he did spend as much time here as he had led me to believe; to offer a foreign royal a permanent room in your palace was a pretty big statement.

Inside the palace was just as beautiful as the outside. Every hallway and room that I saw on our way to Thanatos' quarters was beautifully carved, there were no sharp edges, every surface was soft and rounded. From the wooded ceiling hung fabrics of all different colors and textures, draped this way and that, rippling softly in the light breeze. There was no glass in any of the windows we passed, just more fabric drapings.

"Here we are," Thanatos announced. "Home sweet second home," he said with a grin. The door before us was ornately carved with a scene of what I could only imagine was Osiria. A mountain sat in the center, split in half by the opening of the door; on the left side were volcanoes with rivers of lava flowing down the mountain range at the base of the door, the right side was covered in ice caves and frozen lakes. In the sky on each side were carved two birds, one of fire and one of ice, flying toward each other to meet at the top of the mountain range in the center. Thanatos pushed the doors open and gestured me into his rooms. I hesitated for a moment, we'd shared a room and slept by fires before, but something about being invited into his space felt different.

I stepped through the door and walked into the sitting room. There were no arm chairs or lounges, but large cushions and low tables scattered around the room. In the center of the room was a large fire pit. A balcony straight ahead of me looked out onto the hollowed out center of the palace. I made my way through the embroidered drapes and looked over the edge. At the bottom there was a garden with an ornate water fountain in the center. It looked to be made of marble but, from the height of the Prince's balcony, I couldn't tell for sure. I sensed, more than heard, the Prince coming to stand beside me.

"It's beautiful," I said in awe. "More beautiful than I ever imagined."

"I'm very lucky to have it as a home away from home." I could hear the smile in his voice.

"Should we not tell someone we're here?"

"They'll find out. Nothing is secret when fairies are around."

"Where are all the fairies?" I had expected to see them everywhere in the main town, but there had been none.

"They can be a bit skittish around strangers, and at night they tend to stay with the Naeinn."

I nodded, still gazing at the many balconies scattered throughout the tree trunk palace. I had never realized just how different the world could be from Isidia.

"So, do you want food or sleep? The sun will be rising soon."

The question struck me out of my daze. I was exhausted. "Definitely sleep."

The Prince grinned. "You can sleep in my bed." I raised my brows and he held his hands up. "I'll sleep in the living room"

I again nodded, too exhausted to form words now that he'd mentioned sleep.

Thanatos led me to the bedroom. In the center of the room sat an intricately carved, four post bed with sheer netting draped over it; more cushions and small tables were scattered throughout the room and a large, carved wardrobe sat in the back corner. The Prince went to the wardrobe to grab some fresh clothing and offered me some as well, since our packs were somewhere with the horses.

I thanked him and said good night.

Once I'd changed into the clothes the Prince had given me, a much too large pair of flowy pants and an even larger tunic, I collapsed onto the bed. The mattress was incredibly soft, the blanket warm; it was not difficult to fall asleep.

I woke in my bedroom in Isidia. The mattress was hard, my nightgown tangled around my body uncomfortably, and my stomach was filled with dread. I climbed out of bed slowly, taking in my surroundings. I could have sworn I was somewhere else when I fell asleep.

I left my bedroom and wandered into my living room. Lorkin was sitting in the armchair by the fire, sipping a cup of tea.

"Good morning, my love," he said, standing to plant a kiss on my cheek. He was confused when I didn't return the kiss. "Are you all right?"

I looked around the room in confusion. "I ... I'm a little lost. How did I get here?"

Worry spread across Lorkin's face as he guided me to a chair. I took a seat and accepted the tea cup he thrust in my hands. "Where is Prince Thanatos?"

"In Osiria I assume, and hopefully staying there," Lorkin said with a tone of annoyance.

"But ... we were hunting the Necromancer? We'd just made it to Sillessia."

Lorkin's face softened as he took a deep breath. "We've been over this, love. You never went anywhere with the Prince." I stared at Lorkin, shocked. His green eyes shone with worry. "There was no Necromancer, and you've never left Isidia."

I gaped at him. He was wrong. "That's not true. Why are you lying to me?" I placed the tea cup on the side table and stood.

Lorkin placed his hand on my shoulder. "I'm not lying, Evie. After the ball, Thanatos left, and your mother ... she asked to be sent to Sillessia."

"But the dead things, the Corse! What about them?"

"There never were any, you read about them in one of your books and became obsessed."

I tried to step out of his reach but he grabbed me by the shoulders. "Let go of me! You're lying to me! My mother is here, I need to defeat the Necromancer."

"This all started after your coming of age, you became obsessed with leaving, created thousands of stories—any excuse—you tried to convince Thanatos that we were keeping you prisoner at the ball so he'd help you leave. You can't leave your people, Evalina, you have a duty as Queen."

I froze. "Queen?"

Lorkin smiled. "Yes, Evie, Queen Evalina and King Lorkin. That's us." He rubbed my arms. "We've been married for months. Do you remember the ceremony?"

I didn't.

"This is a lie."

Lorkin sighed and looked at me with sad eyes. "I didn't want to do this, Evie, but you leave me no choice."

Panic rose in my chest—I tried to pull out of his grip but he held firm.

"Guards!" Lorkin twisted me and wrapped his arms around my torso tightly, holding me so close I could barely move. "I love you, Evalina."

I struggled harder as the guards burst through the doors, kicking at Lorkin's legs with my heels but he didn't seem to feel it.

"Take her to the tower to clear her head."

I struggled harder still, begging Lorkin, tears streaming down my face.

I fought the guards as hard as I could, kicking and headbutting, going limp, but still they dragged or carried me through the gardens and up the tower steps. I had panicked and cried so much that I had made myself vomit somewhere along the way, the smell surrounded me making me feel even more nauseous. The guards threw me to the floor of the tower and locked the door. I screamed and pounded the door as their retreating footsteps echoed through the tower. I threw what little furniture there was in the tower against the wall and shattered every piece, I didn't stop my rampage until my hands were bleeding, swollen and full of splitters, I then curled in a ball and sobbed.

I bolted upright in Thanatos' bed in Sillessia, tears running down my face and my chest heaving with panic.

I tried to calm myself as best I could, taking deep breaths in through my nose and out my mouth, but couldn't settle. I climbed out of the comfortable bed and opened the bedroom door as quietly as I could. Thanatos was fast asleep on the pile of cushions in the center of the living room. I tiptoed past to go to the bathing room on the other side of his chambers.

There was a mirror on the wall above the jug and basin; I dared a glance and was shocked by what I saw. My face was blotchy from crying in my sleep and dark circles lined my eyes. My hair desperately needed a good brush and everything was covered in blood and dirt. I poured some water into the basin and splashed my face, scrubbing the dirt and specks of Thanatos' blood away. I took a long drink of water straight from the jug and made my way back to the bedroom. I was just about to turn the door handle when Thanatos' hoarse voice called out to me.

"Evalina? Are you all right?"

I mustn't have been as quiet as I thought I had. "I'm fine, go back to sleep."

Thanatos sat up and patted the cushion next to him. "Come talk about it."

I sighed and let go of the handle and made my way over to the Prince. I sat on the cushion beside Thanatos, close enough that our thighs were almost touching and reluctantly recounted my dream, noticing the same glint of annoyance when I'd mentioned Lorkin as the latter had had in my dream when I mentioned him.

"What do you think it means?" The Prince asked when I'd finished.

I shrugged. "Perhaps it's a mix of a fear of commitment and turning into my mother, or it could mean nothing and simply be a nightmare."

Thanatos searched my eyes and sighed. "At least it was a normal nightmare, as real as it may have felt at the time."

I nodded in agreement. I wondered when my next dream of the she-elf would come, and if I would be more prepared next time. I had a feeling she was somehow involved with the Necromancer but I couldn't think of how.

I intended to question her more the next time she decided to invade my subconscious.

The thought of going back to the bedroom and to sleep frightened me, especially the thought of being alone.

I thought back to my dream and how cruel Lorkin had been. I knew he would never be like that in real life—would never dismiss me like that. Then again, he had, when he accused me of having relations with the Prince and the argument we'd had at the creek. He'd made it very clear that things between us were over.

I looked at the Prince, his face soft in the light of the rising sun.

"Will you come to bed with me? I don't want to be alone," I added quickly at his shocked expression.

He nodded and we went into the bedroom.

Thanatos laid down on the left side of the bed and I took my place on the right. I couldn't tell how long we both laid there staring at the ceiling before Thanatos fell asleep, but it felt like an eternity.

I rolled onto my side to face him; he was sleeping so peacefully, you'd never have imagined that mere hours before he had almost died.

I gently coiled my arms around his and nuzzled into his neck, savoring the scent of him and the rightness of touching him.

CHAPTER TWENTY FIVE
NO SIGN OF LIFE

I rolled to the side, dodging the Corse's blade by a hair; they were becoming more and more competent with each skirmish. The mages suspected it was because the Necromancer was improving.

The blade whizzed over my head. I kicked my leg out to knock the creature off balance but it dodged my leg. I blocked its next attack with my sword, quickly rising to my feet to meet it face to face. Another came up behind me but I heard it before it could get a jump on me, moving my torso only slightly to the side so the blade of the Corse behind me pierced the one in front. I used the moment of confusion in both creatures to lop their heads off, the blood splattering across my face.

Bellona crashed into my back, almost throwing me off balance. "Come on, pretty boy, there's more fighting to be done," she said before pushing off me and charging back into battle, her blades cutting the air before her. She wielded two cutlasses and fought more fiercely than I'd ever witnessed. Despite her size, she was quick and as strong as her father. We'd been fighting for a while. My blades were already beginning to blunten, making removing heads difficult—but Bellona ... she made it look effortless.

We disposed of the remaining Corse quickly before examining the bodies for any potential information we could gather. Poking and prodding at clothes and weapons, trying to distinguish where they'd come from. Most that we encountered were Minoman, but every now and then we'd have run-ins with Kushyami and Aurali Corse. The weapons this lot had, though, didn't look familiar to me; they looked old, older than anything I'd seen before. The blades had designs imprinted in them, something that sword makers hadn't done in millenia, not outside Shinchaku, anyway—but these were not Shinchaku blades. Vines creeped up the length of one blade, flowers on another, they almost looked ceremonial, rather than made for war.

150

"Nothing." Bellona sighed, stepping away from the last body. "There's no information to be plucked from these chickens," she added, pulling out a pipe from her coat and packing the bowl.

"Nothing from the blades?" I asked, knocking one with my foot.

Bellona shook her head, puffing on her pipe trying to light it. "I don't recognise them. They could be Minoman, they could be ancient elven." She shrugged.

"Would Peverell know?"

"Perhaps," she said smoke from her pipe obscuring her face as she spoke. "We can bring them to him, then melt them down and make a better blade from them."

"We'd better head back," I said, gazing at the sky, orange peaking over the horizon. "Queen Islina will be worried."

Bellona nodded and helped me gather the weapons before we walked back through the field to our horses.

We had been inspecting a farm on the outskirts of Lonthia, following reports that the family had not been seen in town, and they were one of the closest sources of grain. When we arrived at the house it was clear why.

The bodies of the family had been mutilated, arms and legs cut off, stomachs ripped open, their innards scattered on the ground around them. From a tree hung their heads, all four tied to the branches by their hair, their unblinking eyes staring toward the palace. It had been a message, and we had received it.

The Corse had been camped out in the field, no doubt waiting for the cover of night to return to their main host.

Bellona and I took the time to bury the bodies, saving the gruesome task from falling on someone else. We both had seen our fair share of bloodshed and horrors, this was just another to add to the list.

We returned to the castle covered in blood and exhausted. We'd asked a guard to go ahead and request that Adalric, Darius and Peverell meet us in the council room as we'd entered the gates. We were just finishing up in the stables when Islina burst through the doors.

Shit.

"Lorkin! Bellona!" She exclaimed, rushing to our sides.

"Your Majesty, we're both fine." I soothed as she halted before us reaching her hands out but not touching our blood-caked bodies.

"All that blood—"

"It's not ours," I said quickly, seeing the blankness spread across her face.

"You shouldn't be the ones going out, it shouldn't be you." She faced Bellona now, her hands shaking, still raised before her. "Stay here. Don't leave me," she whispered. "Don't leave me. Don't leave me." She repeated again and again, tears filling her eyes and pain coating her features.

"Islina—" I started toward her but, before I could reach her, Bellona had pulled her into her arms.

"I've got her," Bellona said to me quietly. "Speak to my father, I'll mind the Queen," she added in a delicate tone, softer than I'd ever heard from Bellona.

I did my best to hide my surprise, but knew it was still clear on my face. Sometimes, I found it hard to believe Bellona and Eevan were brother and sister but, in this softer moment, she became the Eevan I remembered. When her face was relaxed, her features softened until you would have thought they had been twins. After hesitating for a moment, I left the stables, the sound of Bellona's soothing words trailing out behind me into the night.

Adalric's fist slammed down on the table with a loud thud. "The children as well?"

I nodded. I'd just finished informing him of the afternoon's events, the two Kings' and the Prince's faces had been grave throughout the tale; Peverell's had almost turned completely green as I'd described every detail of the macabre discovery.

"This Necromancer is beyond mad," Adalric spat.

"Do you think this means a larger host is close?" Darius asked.

"I don't know what else it could mean," I said bluntly.

Peverell scratched his chin, his thin form hunched over one of the blades Bellona and I had bought back with us. He'd been studying it since I'd given it to him, before I'd begun my tale, every now and then jotting something down in a notebook. "This sword is indeed thousands of years old, but it's not of Minoman make." He leaned back in his chair, pinching his nose. "I could be wrong, but I'm almost certain it's Osirian."

Everyone in the room tensed.

"I could be wrong," Peverell insisted with his hands raised.

My heart was pounding against my ribs, I could hear my blood rushing through my ears. "I should go to her. He can't be trusted," I said, rising from my chair, hands shaking on the table.

"No. She needs more time," Adalric insisted.

"Your Majesty, I can't just leave her out there with him," I argued.

"She will contact us if she needs help."

"Your Majesty," I said more sharply. "You have to see that something is wrong. The Prince arrived early, so soon after the palace was first attacked, and he took every opportunity he could to be with Evalina—"

"As I said in the council meeting," Adlric said, silencing me with his raised hand. "We will send you out when I see fit, and I do not—yet. As for your obsession with the Prince—"

"I am not obsessed," I snapped, and the childishness of it slapped me.

"Let it go," Adalric said. "As Peverell said, he cannot confirm that the blade is Osirian and, even if it is, it's thousands of years old. Why would the Osirians send an army of the dead with thousand year old ceremonial blades?" He paused, allowing me time to ruminate on my stupidity. "Now, what this really means is that we need to train a bigger army. Darius, how close are your fleets?"

Evalina's uncle straightened. "A week at most."

"That may be too late," Peverell said matter of factly.

"We need to start training civilians," I said, adding it to my mental list.

"I was hoping it wouldn't come to that." Adalric sighed.

"It always comes to that," Darius concluded.

"I'll organize a proclamation to go through the town tomorrow," I said. "Any able-bodied person, to train here?"

Adalric thought on this for a moment. "That might upset Islina. We'll open a camp outside the castle walls—training will be done out there from now on."

We all nodded agreement. And so the discussion of the training camp began, and as the father and sons discussed the details of it, I found myself unable to concentrate. I should have, it was my home they were discussing, my people they were working to train and protect, but my mind was on the road with Evalina and the Prince.

And, as the worry started to build up again, the so far unjustified hatred of the Prince bubbling to the surface, two flowers popped into existence on the table before the King. Everyone in the room fell silent. One of the flowers was white and star-shaped, a Hellebore, and the other ... I rose from my chair and walked closer to the King, who had picked up the flower gently, as if it would turn to ash in his grasp. It glowed dimly in the candle light, blue in the center, its petals fading out to black at the edges. It was a flower I'd seen many times despite it being native to only Carracalla.

"She's safe." Was all the King said, tears lining his eyes.

CHAPTER TWENTY-SIX
HOLLOW FIT FOR A QUEEN

I woke to the afternoon sun shining onto my face and my bladder aching to be emptied.

Thanatos was still sleeping heavily behind me, our legs tangled together under the blanket, his arm draped over my waist, and his chest slowly rising and falling against my back. I slowly detangled myself and climbed out of bed without waking him up before quietly leaving the room.

Soap and wash things had been laid out in the bathing room by some incredibly quiet castle staff. Thanatos had said the fairies would pass on the news of our arrival and thank the Father they had—I was in desperate need of a wash.

The thought of using the bathtub filled me with dread, so I resorted to using the cold water in the jug and basin with a washcloth to bathe. I brushed through my hair and clumsily rebraided it before getting dressed into the same clothes the Prince had given me the night before.

It felt good to be clean.

I left the bathroom and found food and tea laid out on a table on the balcony. I took a seat on one of the cushions and poured myself a cup of tea.

The teapot was the only thing on the table not made of wood, even the cutlery was carved wood. The platters were piled high with fresh fruit and pastries, I took a single sip of tea before I dove into the food.

I was most of the way through my breakfast when Thanatos joined me; I found it hard to look him in the eye, suddenly feeling very self-conscious about not being able to sleep alone.

"Did you sleep all right?" He asked, piling his plate high with mostly fruit, where mine was mostly pastries.

"I did," I said between sips of fruity tea and the Prince smiled. "I guess you were right about them knowing we're here. Will the Queen want to speak with us?"

"Not unless we seek her out, which we'll have to do if we want to see the Mother tree."

I could tell by his tone that it wasn't something he really wanted to do. "Why do you hate the gods?"

Thanatos sighed "I wouldn't say I hate them, but I'm skeptical of their existence." He paused for a moment. "They've never done me or my family any favors, let's say that."

I wanted to know more but didn't want to push. "You don't have to do it if you don't want to."

He looked at me with grateful eyes. "I will, just in case there's a chance it could help us."

I reached across the table and took his hand in mine. "Thank you. Do you know where the Queen may be?"

"She'll be in the town, most likely in the vegetable gardens." He smiled at my shocked expression. " Not all royals keep to their palaces."

"I can see that." I winked at him before turning away and heading for the door.

The hallways of the palace were still empty, not a guard, servant, or courtier in sight; but, looking through the open windows, I could see the bustle of the town below.

I hadn't bothered to cover my telltale hair before leaving the room. If my mother was right about the Necromancer, I should be safe around other elves.

The town was softly lit by small shafts of sunlight, peeking through gaps in the dense branches above, and the glowing mushrooms, giving the town a greenish hue.

Despite the Wood-Elves all having the same coloring, varying shades of red hair and green skin, the town was a sea of colors. Never in my life had I seen such colorful clothing. The males wore long, brightly-colored tunics with light trousers underneath; some wore a coloured sash around their waists and others a small round cap on their heads. The females wore long, flowing skirts with multiple different colored layers, a short top that showed their midsections, and a sash that wrapped around the skirt and draped over one shoulder; each garment was embroidered with gold or silver thread that glittered in the dim light.

I strolled through the gardens, looking for Queen Ambrosia and admiring the size of the produce. I had never been through farmland before—the Mid Road that Thanatos and I had traveled on so far had been lined by thick woods—and found the orderliness of it comforting after the chaos of the previous days.

There didn't seem to be one dedicated farmer for the land, rather everyone maintained and tended the gardens in return for produce instead of money payment. Every elf I passed was covered in dirt up to their elbows, and all were happy—

as if nothing was or could ever be wrong in the world. Perhaps it was why the Naeinn chose to come here.

I was halfway through a pumpkin patch when I finally found the Queen; she was elbow deep in dirt trying to pull something from the ground. Her gown was no different from the common elves around her, the only difference in appearance was the wooden crown resting atop her head. Her red hair had been messily piled on top of her head, pinned in place by the crown and what looked like a regular stick, her green skin was so similar in color to that of humans that, were it not for her pointed ears, you might have thought her to be one.

"Your Majesty."

"Ah, Evalina, I was wondering when you would seek me out," she said, not using any formal titles or even rising from the ground.

"Can I assist you?" I offered after a failed tug of whatever she was trying to extract.

"No, no. Just a stubborn rabbit, perhaps I should leave him here." She rose with a smile, dusting her hands off on her cobalt and silver skirt. "Maioc told me of your arrival late last night, or would it have been early this morning?" She considered this for a moment and shrugged. "She also told me of the trials you and Thanatos have faced. I am surprised you didn't sleep for longer." She linked her arm through mine and began guiding us back to the center of town through the pumpkin patch.

"Unfortunately, Your Majesty—"

"Please, Ambrosia, we are all equals here."

"Ambrosia," I corrected with a nod, "time is not on our side and resting will have to wait—"

"I wonder if the rabbit would rather parsnips than pumpkins? Perhaps I can simply relocate him."

I blinked at the Queen. "Um, perhaps. Ambrosia, I must ask you something rather important."

"Of course," she replied with a smile.

"Thanatos and I have reason to believe that speaking to The Mother may help speed our efforts—"

"So you wish to see the mother tree?"

"Yes." I dared a glance sideways when she did not answer immediately and, to my surprise, the Queen was not offended at our request to visit their sacred tree but was intently watching a ladybug climb the length of her finger and fly away once it reached the top. "Your Majesty?"

"Ambrosia, please. I don't see an issue with that. It will have to be after dark and no Wood-Elf can go with you. The Mother has a way of twisting the mind and my people are very weak minded."

I gaped at the Queen's words. Everyone knew them to be true, but to hear the Queen speak it of her own people was unexpected.

"We do not shy from the truth here, Evalina. We know what we are and what we can handle, and speaking with The Mother is not something any Wood-Elf can handle," she noted with a smile.

156

"Tonight, then. Thank you."

Ambrosia patted my arm with her free hand and gazed ahead. "Let's get you some new clothes. I take it you are heading to Kushyam when you leave here?"

"I believe that's Thanatos' plan, yes."

"The traveling clothes of Isidians are too heavy for the desert and you'll need something for dinner tonight."

"I will need to go back to the palace to retrieve my purse."

Ambrosia waved her hand dismissively. "We do not trade in gold here, we trade in kindness and work."

I couldn't wrap my mind around it, a society without money and worry—it was too perfect.

The Queen led me through the town to different stores, some halfway up the giant trees and some burrowed under ground. She picked out traveling clothes fit for the deserts of Kushyam, including a head scarf to cover my hair and a veil to stop sand from getting into my mouth and nose, and appropriate attire of green and gold for dinner that night at the palace. I carried the parcels back toward the palace alone, leaving the Queen to decide if she would relocate the rabbit or leave him with his pumpkins.

I was halfway through the markets, admiring the peaceful trade of goods for other goods, so different from the squabble of bartering over coin, when I spotted Thanatos.

"Leave you alone for an hour and you end up shopping," Thanatos said with a grin.

"The Queen insisted, actually. Traveling clothes for Kushyam and a dress for dinner tonight."

Thanatos nodded and held out a letter to me. "Reports from Isidia."

I gaped at him and snatched the letter he passed me. It was addressed to both of us, from my Grandfather.

Evalina and Prince Thanatos,

Isidia remains safe and in our hands. Darius and Peverell's fleets have arrived sooner than we expected. The Father has blessed the winds.

Guards have been set along the borders of the kingdom and so far no Corse have tried to enter, but we are ready for when they do.

All is well.

We will send this letter to all Elven kingdoms in the hopes it reaches you.

Flower,
your mother is fine. Most days she's herself and when she's not, Lorkin is by her side.

He's a good lad.

I let out a sigh of relief and relaxed my suddenly tense shoulders. Not knowing what was going on in my Queendom these last few weeks had been gnawing on my mind; to know that everything was well and that my uncles and their fleets had arrived safely and speedily was welcome news.

"If it had been bad news I would have found you immediately," Thanatos said.

"I know. I would have liked to have had the good news sooner though."

"Noted," he said with a smile.

"The Queen said we can go to the Mother Tree after dinner."

Thanatos' expression stiffened. "I was hoping she'd say no," he said with a sigh. "I've been looking for Sevah and Rangkar. Have you seen them?"

I blanched. Sevah, Rangkar, the horses, I had completely forgotten them; my father's sword was with them too.

"They won't be far, there's still a few places I haven't searched."

"I'll go with you."

The Prince led us back through the town and asked a few elves he must know from his times here if they'd seen the horses and a witch; others kept their distance.

We had no luck in the main town.

"There's one other place they could be," Thanatos said, looking to the edge of the town.

We began walking out of town, heading out toward the lake that was covered in boats, fishing from the look of it, but I saw no fish in the nets. We walked around the edge of the lake and came upon another, smaller, village.

I felt the air around me change as we stepped through the trees; it felt warm and comforting and right.

I stopped dead in my tracks as I beheld what was in front of me.

It was a small village of wooden houses and two large buildings in the center, small vegetable patches and multiple flower beds. All of that was normal, it was what lit the village that made me stall. Other than a few gaps in the canopy of branches above, there were hundreds of small, colored orbs lazily floating through the air, making it look as if the town were built at the end of a rainbow.

Fairies.

It was more beautiful than my mind could ever have pictured, everything seemed to glow with an ethereal light. I completely understood, now, why the Naeinn called this place home. I'd felt instantly calm, as if any worries I had in my life had simply floated away with the fairies.

"This is the main area they keep the Naeinn, if the horses aren't in the town they'll be here," Thanatos said.

I was in a complete daze as the Prince led me through the Naeinn village. I couldn't take my eyes off the fairies flitting through the air. It blew my mind that the most powerful creatures in Carynthia were so small and so beautiful.

Fairies had access to any magic they wanted; they could kill, heal, move, and grow anything, grant anyone they wished any power they wanted, or destroy anything and everything if they wanted, but where would the fun be in that? They're tricksters after all, only doing what they find amusing

I would have thought the village deserted, had it not been for the laughter and chatter I heard in the distance. The houses we passed, as far as I could tell, were empty and the two buildings in the middle, I assumed were reserved for the worse off Naeinn, were also quiet. I'm not sure what I was expecting but it definitely wasn't the peaceful settlement I had been led to.

Laughing and talking grew louder the closer we got to the end of the long center buildings and we soon found out why.

Seated on the floor of a large courtyard, being fed platters of fresh fruit and vegetables and being meticulously groomed by elves of all races, and a few humans, were Faenor and Serelene. I sighed with relief as my eyes rested on my mount, mouth full of apples as an Aurali human braided her mane.

I spotted Sevah leaning against a building a bit away from the crowd, our packs and my sword resting at her feet, and made my way over to her while Thanatos continued on to the horses.

"Lucky you two came to find us, the horses wouldn't listen to me. Where did Maioc send you?" the witch asked.

"The middle of the lake. We swam to shore and went straight to the palace," I replied.

The witch nodded. "We popped up here and it's been like this ever since." She gestured to the two lazing horses being doted on. "Is Rangkar with you?"

"They deserve it. We were actually hoping he was with you," I said, smiling at the mares. "You keep your distance?"

"He'll show up somewhere close by." The witch shifted on her feet. "My appearance can sometimes agitate the Naeinn." Sevah toyed with a strand of leafy vines hanging over her shoulder and the many flowers that made up the left side of her head almost seemed to droop. "Though sometimes I come and show the young ones sleight of hand tricks."

I stiffened at the term 'young ones'; it was a term used for elves that hadn't reached adulthood yet. It was rare for young ones to become Naeinn but some elves just couldn't control their powers.

My eyes drifted to the Prince. He was speaking in hushed tones to a Sillessian Elf on the other side of the lounging horses and Naeinn. I patted Sevah on the shoulder and made my way over to him.

A few of the High-Elves in the group gaped at my hair as I strode passed; it saddened me that my own people only recognised me by my hair. I had to change that.

Thanatos halted his conversation to introduce me to Zohar, the head carer of the Naeinn. He was slender in build, his hair almost burgundy, and skin a deeper green than the Queen's. His face was beautiful as all elf faces are, but plain in comparison.

"I was just telling Thanatos how our village has fared since he left," Zohar said to me, his eyes never leaving Thanatos' face.

"And how's that?" I asked, glancing back at the horses and villagers still gorging on fruit and vegetables.

"Well, but many miss the Prince when he is gone, though they understand he has other responsibilities."

Thanatos smiled knowingly and bowed his head to the Wood-Elf. "Send the horses to the palace stables when the others are finished with them? Evalina and I have dinner with Ambrosia soon, but I want to show her around the village a little more before we leave."

A flash of emotion passed over Zohar's features. "You'll be leaving soon?"

"Tomorrow, if all goes to plan."

Zohar did not hide the hurt and disappointment this time. Thanatos, to my surprise, gave him an almost stern look, one I had received many times ... from Lorkin. The Prince held out his arm to Zohar and they gripped each other's wrists in farewell; Zohar's hand lingered on the Prince's arm before he nodded farewell to me and strode to sit with the horses and Naeinn.

Thanatos guided me down a path through some of the bigger houses in the village and away from the crowd doting on the horses.

"No Rangkar?" He asked after, looking about for the orc.

I shook my head.

He nodded and continued on. "I wanted to show you the village. It's rare that we get a royal visitor." The Prince winked at me.

"I wanted to see it." I took a deep breath. "My mother has decided she would like to come here, once everything is sorted." Everything being Thanatos and I going up against a crazed man with dark magic trying to end the world, or at least my world.

"I think she'll like it here. Fresh fruit and vegetables for every meal, calm, good looking attendants, and no annoying daughters."

I slapped the Prince's shoulder as he grinned and led me to the biggest house in the small village. "Speaking of good looking"—I glaced sidelong at the prince—"Zohar ..."

Thanatos sighed deeply. "You picked up on that?"

I gave him an incredulous look. "A blind elf could have picked up on that."

The Prince laughed. "We had a relationship a long time ago. Zohar has never managed to get over it."

"But you did?"

Thanatos glanced quizzically at me. "Yes. Once the relationship began interfering with our work, it had to be ended. I was coming and going all the time, never here for more than a few weeks at a time. Zohar never minded, but I did."

"Lorkin and I were like that while he was training to be a guard." It pained me to speak of Lorkin; it brought back the memories of my recent nightmare and of waking to the Prince coiled around me.

"Is Lorkin the only one you've been with?"

I almost blushed at the question, my mind having recalled another dream that involved the Prince. "No," I scoffed.

Elves lived such long lives it was almost impossible to find one person to spend it with. Even humans, their lives so much shorter than ours, tended to bed at least two people over the course of their lives.

"Lorkin and I were never truly courting, not officially. We could do whatever we wanted. I guess it came with the familiarity—we always knew we'd end up back with each other. But that's not to say we never got jealous." I didn't know why I was telling the Prince those things, why I couldn't stop, but I couldn't. I told him stories of jealousy and rage, heartache and forgiveness, happiness and sorrow, all while walking through gardens and streets filled with fairies bobbing in the air. It felt good to tell him, as if a weight I didn't know I had been lugging was lifted off my shoulders.

I finally stopped blabbing about my complicated relationship with my childhood friend and lover when we reached the largest house in the village.

The house was built into the hollow of a giant fallen tree and looked almost exactly like a smaller version of the palace.

"This would be where your mother would live if she came here. A hollow fit for a Queen," Thanatos announced.

I stared at the log, tears pricking my eyes as I pictured my mother standing in the doorway, alone and so very far away from home.

"Let me show you inside." The Prince gently took my hand and led me through the front door.

The inside was almost exactly like the palace, but with proper glass in the windows rather than just curtains and far more grand furniture, almost as if it had been built specially for my mother. I gasped as the smell of home hit me as I stepped over the threshold, and felt instantly homesick.

"A fairy spell, to help the Naeinn feel comfortable."

"It does not make me feel comfortable," I stated, my stomach turning.

"It works better on the weak minded and those that have accepted that they cannot go home."

The Prince showed me every room in the house, all more than suitable for my mother to live out her days—half were better than the rooms she had in Lonthia.

Thanatos explained to me how the village worked. Everyone in the village had a choice of how they lived, either with someone or alone. Meals were taken in the large hall and everyone was required to cook and work the fields for produce. The Sillessian and volunteer carers only helped when required and acted as counsel for elves and humans like my mother, touched by madness that was not caused by magic.

I didn't think my mother would enjoy getting her hands dirty, not when she'd lived her whole life as a Princess and Queen with everything done for her, not to mention she could barely stand the sight of me being dirty, let alone herself.

After the tour of the house, Thanatos showed me the gardens and dining hall and the barrier that the fairies had put in place to keep the Naeinn and others safe within the village before we had to return to the palace for dinner.

We walked back to the palace with Sevah in tow after inviting her to dinner as well. It was only fair to have her enjoy a hot meal at the palace after all she had done for us; were it not for her, we would never have known about the sacred trees and certainly would not have lasted in the forest. I only wished that Rangkar was with us to enjoy it, too. The Prince and witch assured me that he would show up at some point but Maioc hadn't seemed too pleased by his presence in the first place. I was worried.

Sevah came to Thanatos' rooms with us and assisted with getting me dressed for dinner. There were no servants in the halls to ask and I had no idea how to properly lay the drape; to me, there looked to be too much fabric, but after Sevah had finished pleating and draping the green and gold garment fit perfectly.

It was strange to have my midriff showing, my mother certainly would not have approved, but I liked the freedom of movement it offered—much more comfortable than a corset. I wore my hair down for the first time in weeks; it had a wave to it from being braided for so long and was long enough that I had to worry about sitting on it.

Sevah wore her traveling clothes, despite me offering some of the new clothes that I had picked up, though she did take special time and even a bit of magic to really clean herself up. The too-big white blouse no longer had dirt and blood stains on it and her layered skirts and belts were almost completely different colors to what they were before, they were so clean. She seemed almost self-conscious of the fact.

"Had my mother not been so strict growing up, I would always be covered in dirt," I said to the witch, smiling at her reflection in the mirror.

She gave a small smile and fussed with her hair. "It's been so long since I've dined with the Queen, or anyone for that matter. I don't know what to do with my hair."

"Your hair looks beautiful! I wish I had hair such an amazing color as yours." I frowned at my own plain black and blue hair. I supposed I had it better than most High-Elves, with the touches of blue, but it was still dark and boring; not like Sevah's red, curly mane.

"Do you think Thanatos is prepared to see the tree?" Sevah asked.

"I'm not sure, he has some grudge against the gods so we'll see if he can even summon her."

Sevah looked at me quizzically and I shrugged in answer to her silent question. Thanatos had said I would find out soon why he hated the gods but when that would be I did not know, though I longed to.

"The Prince is kinder than I thought an Osirian could be." The comment took me by surprise, but I understood how Sevah had come to think that.

There were so many rumors of the Prince, more than I knew, terrible rumors of brutality and sordidness.

I glanced at the witch, she was staring dazedly at her reflection in the mirror, off in her own world. "I've found that, too, but was beginning to think it was just Isidian prejudice."

Sevah smiled. "I'm glad we've been proven wrong in our prejudices—and I think the Prince is too." She grinned at my reflection and declared that we were ready.

Thanatos had dressed out in the living room while Sevah and I dressed in the bedroom. He was wearing a knee length white tunic with silver embroidery around the edges with black flowing pants. His eyes lingered on me before he smiled at the witch and gestured for us to leave the room and head down to dinner.

CHAPTER TWENTY SEVEN
STONY SILENCE

It baffled me how the Prince could find his way around the Sillessian palace, every room and hall looked the same to me and, thanks to the cylindrical build of the palace, I simply felt as though we were walking in circles.

Once we got to the dinning hall I was completely disorientated, I would never have been able to find my way back to our room alone.

The dining hall was smaller than I thought it would be. There was a lone, low table carved into the center of the room, surrounded by cushions for us to sit on. Candles were scattered throughout, casting a warm light over the space, and incense filled the room with a thick, stuffy floral scent.

The Queen and two Princes had already taken their seats at the head of the table and did not rise to greet us, but the male sitting with them did.

"Rangkar! We were looking everywhere for you," Thanatos called.

The orc made his way toward us with open arms. He wore new clothes; brown, flowing pants with intricate patterns dyed into the fabric and a matching vest. I was half tempted to ask him if he just didn't like shirts when I realized that the sleeves would all be made too short for his arms.

He greeted Thanatos first with a quick one-armed hug and a clap on the back, then Sevah and I each with a kiss to the backs of our hands.

"Where did the fairy send you?" Sevah asked, her eyes locked with Rangkar's.

"North of the village, into a thorn bush."

It was then that I noticed the tiny scratches that littered his green body.

"Perfect excuse to buy new clothes," he said, spreading his arm. "My others were shredded. It took me a while to get through the thorns, I arrived here not long after mid morning."

"I'm sorry she did that to you," Sevah said, resting a hand on the orc's arm.

"You know, it *was* very painful," Rangkar continued.

Thanatos rolled his eyes and strode to the end of the table to sit by the royal family and Rangkar led Sevah to sit with him on the opposite side, continuing his harrowing tale of escaping the thornbush, mentioning more than once that no plant near it was as beautiful as the blooms that covered half of the witches head.

I was unsure of what to do, this whole situation was the opposite of what I had been taught to expect from a formal royal dinner, but nothing in Sillessia had been formal.

I made my way over to Thanatos and sat cross legged on the cushion beside his. I would follow his lead.

"Good evening, Evalina," Crown Prince Zared chimed from the other side of Thanatos. "I heard of your arrival late today, my apologies for not greeting you sooner."

"We arrived early this morning very unceremoniously, I don't blame you for not knowing we were here."

"We're all a bit busy during the day here," Ambrosia added. "We like to be involved actively with the harvest. It's not normal royal protocol but it keeps life balanced."

"It's truly amazing how things work around here, nowhere else could survive like this."

The Queen smiled and nodded her thanks. She was clean of any dirt from her day in the fields and had traded her blue ensemble for purple. My eyes moved from the Queen to her son on her right. Soren, one of my suitors, and the only royal one other than my cousin Simeon. I'd tried to speak to him briefly at the ball but he barely spoke, and when he did it was in riddles and verses. Soren was oblivious to my gaze, studying something past his brother's shoulder, though I couldn't see anything worth holding his attention. His mother placed a hand over his and gave a small squeeze; it was enough to snap his attention away from whatever he had been distracted by.

"Apologies, the Father had something he wished for me to see, though I can't quite figure out the importance."

"You're a seer, Prince Soren?"

Soren's eyes snapped to me, as if he hadn't noticed I was there until I spoke. "I am, though not a good one. I often have trouble deciphering what I'm being shown, much like yourself."

I smiled softly at the Prince. "I am not a seer," I said gently.

The Prince studied me, his gaze intense enough to make me shift uncomfortably. "No..." he said, but did not take his eyes off me.

Zared and Ambrosia were discussing the fate of the rabbit in the pumpkin patch, occasionally darting to other topics, at a pace I could not keep up with and Rangkar and Sevah were besotted with each other, leaving me only Thanatos and Soren to speak with.

I chose to keep quiet. Thanatos had been quiet since we'd sat down and did not look to be in the mood for small talk. I could tell he was focussing on what awaited us after dinner.

Even after the food had been set before us and eating had begun, Soren did not take his eyes off me. I tried my best to ignore him and the sullen Prince on my left but it was proving difficult. I focussed my attention on whatever was happening between Rangkar and Sevah as I toyed with my bowl of leafy greens and nuts; meat, it seemed, was not on the menu in Sillessia.

Throughout the whole dinner, the orc and witch did not take their eyes off each other—Rangkar asked question after question and Sevah obliged each with an answer.

Dinner ended faster than it had begun, I hadn't even noticed until Thanatos nudged me in the side with his elbow. The Queen had risen to her feet, we followed suit and thanked her for the meal.

"I suppose you would like to go to the Mother Tree now," the Queen stated.

"Yes, and then we'll be on our way in the morning. I would like to thank you on behalf of all Isidia for your help, Ambrosia."

The Queen took my hands in hers and squeezed gently. "I just hope she has something to offer. The Mother can be quite troublesome." The Queen glanced at Thanatos, he only nodded. "Let's be on our way."

The Queen led us through the maze of the palace and down so many flights of stairs that I lost count.

Sevah decided against coming down with us, fearing that she would be corrupted by The Mother. Rangkar, on the other hand, was very interested in coming with us. He seemed to be as doubtful of the gods' existence as the Prince. Thanatos said nothing the whole journey down; I could not read his expression but Rangkar stayed close to him.

At some point our surroundings changed from the carved wood of the tree hollow to ancient-looking stone.

The deeper we went, the thicker the air became. Sweat was trickling down my face and my thighs were beginning to sting from rubbing together. I wished I'd thought to wear pants under my skirt. I almost groaned with relief when the Queen announced that we were close—until I saw the guards.

There had been no guards anywhere in Sillessia so far, not even any weapons that I'd seen, but here, deep under the palace, were ten or more armed guards with stern faces. The guards stood before a large stone archway, armed with swords, daggers, and fierce looking halberds. Beyond the archway was a long hallway with a large wooden door at the end. I knew the tree was behind those doors, could feel it in the phantom breeze that washed over us.

Ambrosia stopped to speak in hushed tones with one of the guards before walking us to the archway.

"This is as far as I can go." I could see the anxiety in her eyes, it was the same look my mother would get before one of her episodes. "The Tree is through that door, my guards can help if anything happens but only if you can make it to this archway."

I nodded, unable to speak. The air was so heavy I could barely breathe.

"How am I to communicate with her?" Thanatos asked.

It was the first time I'd heard him speak since dinner.

Ambrosia placed a hand on his cheek, a gentle, maternal touch. "I'm not sure, but I hope that you can. Perhaps meditation?" With one last smile and well wish, the Queen left.

Thanatos took a deep breath and pressed on through the archway toward the large door at the end. Rangkar and I followed closely behind.

When we reached the door, Thanatos couldn't seem to bring himself to open it, as if he were afraid to see what was on the other side. Rangkar and I waited a moment before stepping around him and pushing the door open.

Cold air burst from behind the door—I'd have been worried had it not been such a relief. We all entered the room cautiously, hands on our weapons, but there was nothing to fear. The room was empty, save a leafless, charred tree in the center. The space was cold and, despite the emptiness, I felt eyes on me, thousands of eyes. The sooner we could leave, the better. From the matched expressions on their faces, I could tell Thanatos and Rangkar felt the same.

Rangkar gave a slight shiver before turning to the Prince. "Right, let's do this and get out of here."

"Easy for you to say, I don't know what I'm meant to do." Thanatos walked up to the tree and studied it closely. "What if it's just a dead tree?"

"Then all of this time will have been wasted. Maybe try meditation like the Queen suggested," I offered.

"The Queen suggests meditation for everything." Thanatos circled the tree, his footsteps echoing off the stone walls and floor, being careful not to touch it, and sighed. "Okay, I'll try meditation." He plopped down in front of the tree and took a deep breath. Rangkar and I watched on expectantly, waiting for something, anything to happen.

"I can feel you watching me," Thanatos murmured.

Rangkar sighed and turned away to face the wall. I took one last look at the Prince sitting cross legged before a dead tree and did the same.

The instant my eyes were on the wall the cold air in the room disappeared and became hot and moist, Rangkar and I turned to each other and as we did we heard a loud thud echoing through the room.

We spun to find the Prince sprawled on the floor beneath the tree. We rushed to his side, I instantly called on my power, I could sense nothing wrong but he was cold to the touch, so cold I had to pull my hand away.

"What is it?" Rangkar asked desperately.

"I don't know," I said. Thanatos's face was calm, he simply looked as if he were asleep. "Perhaps it's the Mother, he's made it through to her."

CHAPTER TWENTY EIGHT
GREEN GARRISON

Islina sat next to me on the chaise in her living quarters, the Carracallan men sitting across from us, Bellona pacing behind them, even Zephrine had joined us. I hadn't seen the Carracallan Queen since the day Evalina had left. She was a very private person and had kept her distance from everyone in the palace, though I had been told she was spending most of her time in Eevan's office and had routinely been checking in on Islina.

The two flowers sent from the fairies sat before us in a vase, the white resting against the blue and black bloom.

"Are we surprised at their survival?" Islina asked sarcastically.

Adalric had been eager to show the Queen proof of her daughter's life, had thought that maybe it would improve her mood; we hadn't expected her to be so indifferent.

"Not at all, just thought we would share the good news. We haven't heard anything since the two of them left after all," he said, his grin broad across his face.

"Adalric, have you forgotten how unforthcoming your children are? I was not expecting to hear from her as I never expected to hear from them," she said with a glance at Bellona. "And she is in the presence of the Prince, she could not be safer." At these words she placed a hand on my knee and gave a pat, as if she knew how much I had been worrying, despite my best efforts of hiding it from her. "Evalina will contact us when she sees fit. Until then, let her have her time. As you all said before she left, this is what Eevan would have wanted, so we should let her do it the way she wishes."

It almost felt as if this whole conversation were directed at me and my worry for Evalina, and while I took comfort in some of it, my worry did not subside. I was at least glad that Islina seemed to be coping with the lack of knowledge regarding Evalina's whereabouts, but in some ways it concerned me also. She was too trusting when it came to the Prince. She may think she knew him from

168

her communications with the King, but we didn't even know if we could trust him. It was all very suspect.

"I am curious as to the reason for their presence in Sillessia, of all places, though," Zephyrine added, her voice like silk, eyes focused on my Queen.

"I wondered at that, too," Adalric said, leaning forward to study the flowers more. "If only the fairies weren't so cryptic."

Bellona paused her pacing. "Surely it's because of the Corse, why else would they bother?"

I glanced at Islina but kept my mouth shut. It wasn't my place to tell her news, but, based on how tightly she pressed her lips together, I doubted she was going to tell them anytime soon. Bellona's head cocked to the side as she noticed the same thing, her eyes narrowing at the Queen but her own mouth staying firmly shut.

"Again!" I called over the crowd of training people. I couldn't call them soldiers, because that's not what they were. They were farmers, shop owners, regular people that should be free to live their lives. The recruits swung their swords at wooden pells, hacking the wood into splinters as they practiced various fighting maneuvers.

The mornings were getting colder, the dew not completely clearing until almost midday, and even then the recruits were slipping on the grass or muddying the ground. They weren't terrible, but they weren't good either.

There was one she-elf that fought fiercely, a butcher's daughter I'd been told, not one to shy from blades and blood. She reminded me of Evie—her hair was almost as long, flowing down her back, but missing the tinge of blue that made Evie stand out. Watching her train always made my mind travel back to a time when Evalina had barely been able to hold her own against even the weakest of our guards, but she'd trained harder than most until she could face anyone. She'd worked hard and it pained me that I had forgotten that, that it had taken a butcher's daughter to remind me of how capable she was.

Wherever she was, whoever she was with, she would be fine. The fairy conjured flowers had told us that she and the Prince were at least still alive and somewhere in Sillessia.

Had they moved on from there? What were they doing there in the first place? We hadn't heard anything from Queen Ambrosia, though there was no surprise there. Even if Avars itself was under attack we would hear from the fairies before the Queen. Clearly, whatever they were facing they could face it alone.

Perhaps it was Corse that had drawn the duo in. Or perhaps Evalina had wanted to use the opportunity to inspect the land Islina wished to relocate to.

After Evie had left, Islina had told me of her wishes, of the house she'd organized to be built for her. How she did it without Evalina and I noticing, I wasn't to know, but she had. Had we truly been so busy that we hadn't noticed all her scheming?

"That was better!" I called over the assembled recruits. "Tonight Captain Glenon will lead training." The crowd looked at me quizzically, I'd forgotten there were four captain Glenons here currently. "Captain *Bellona* Glenon."

A collective groan rose from the crowd, but the butcher's daughter only grinned. "Rest up," I said before turning away. We trained every morning, a warm up incase of an attack during the day, and then again in the afternoon for the same reason. The last thing we needed was unprepared soldiers getting cramps and stitches while fighting.

I made it halfway through the camp before I felt a tap on my shoulder.

"Apologies Captain," the she-elf huffed. "I called out but I don't think you heard me."

"What can I do for you?" I asked the butcher's daughter. Up close, I saw how different her features actually were to Evalina's; her eyes were smaller and duller, her nose straight and sloped at the end, her lips plumper.

"I was wondering," she answered, tucking a loose hair behind her ear, "if there was any chance I could get extra training, perhaps one on one?"

I raised a brow, this wasn't the first time I'd been asked this same thing, though usually it was in the cover of night.

"Not like that," the girl rushed to get out, her eyes wide as she realized how her words had sounded. "Actual training," she stressed. "I've wanted to be a guard all my life but my father wanted me to take over the shop. I was hoping if I trained with you, you would see how good I am and request me."

"What's your name?"

"Roana, Captain."

"Roana, I unfortunately don't have time to train you myself." Her face fell. "But, I can pass on your request to the others or even Bellona. They'll find you if they can take you."

"Thank you Captain!" She exclaimed and turned back to the recruit tents, and, for a moment, I let myself believe she was Evalina, running through the camps to study everyone and everything.

I continued my way through the rest of the camp, the paths most frequently used reduced to muddy tracks, the lush grass that usually coated the ground unable to withstand the constant abuse of soldiers' boots. The tents surrounding me got more and more grand the closer I got to the palace. Despite the grim circumstances, Evalina would have loved to see this, would have loved to see this many people so close to the palace, to feel the excitement in the air.

I thought that knowing her whereabouts would have calmed me, but I found myself only worrying more, missing her more, and nothing could fill the void. I wanted her home, even if it was only so I could apologize for my outburst the day she left.

"Recruits are looking good," Bellona said, coming up beside me.

"There's one that wants one-on-one training, do you have time?" I asked, before I'd forget.

Bellona scratched her chin. "Possibly. Is it the butcher girl? She's been eyeing me off for weeks, thought she wanted to fuck me." She joked, knocking my shoulder with hers.

"Just training. She wants to join the guard."

"I'll tell one of the other guards to take her and see if I can squeeze in a few sessions here and there. Islina is requiring more attention of late," she said softly. "The war tents remind her of a time she wishes she could forget."

"I can handle Islina," I offered.

"No, no, it's fine." Bellona smoothed her short hair back away from her face. "I'm going to see her now actually, any messages?"

I shook my head and watched Bellona leave and head to the Queen's quarters, a bounce in her step that hadn't been there when she'd first arrived.

I should have been grateful to Bellona for taking on most of the work required to keep Islina at ease but it felt like one more thing that had been snatched away from me, as if they didn't think I could handle it despite the fact it had been left with me the day she'd kicked them out of the palace all those years ago. And I couldn't ignore the nagging in the back of my mind that told me to keep an eye on Bellona and Islina's relationship. Something was going on there and it would only end badly, for the both of them.

CHAPTER TWENTY NINE
ALONE TOGETHER

The cold intensified, it was nothing to an Osirian, we're used to low temperatures but something about it felt wrong.

"Did you guys feel that?" I got no answer. "Rangkar? Evalina?" I opened my eyes, Evalina was sitting across from me, she seemed different—her eyes a bit brighter, her hair more blue.

"Feel what?" She asked.

I looked around the room. "Where's Rangkar?"

"He left to find Sevah—wanted to ask her if we were doing this right." She lent back on her hands and studied me. "What should we do while we wait?" I gaped at her suggestive tone, she smiled and leant toward me until she was on her hands and knees in front of me, close enough that I could feel her breath on my face. "He could be gone for hours, Father knows how far she's gotten from the palace."

"Evalina, are you all right?"

"I'm fine, better than fine." She moved closer forcing me to almost flatten completely to the ground with her above me. "I've been longing to be alone with you for days." The Princess ran her hands up my chest and nuzzled her face into my neck.

It took all of my self control to keep my hands away, to stop them from doing what they've wanted to do for weeks. This was wrong, this was not Evalina.

"Evalina, please …"

She ran her lips up the side of my neck, grazing her teeth lightly along the sensitive skin. Gods, how long had it been since I'd laid with someone? Every part of my body was screaming for this, screaming for her, but I knew it was wrong.

"Stop!" I pushed her away and rose to my feet. "What is going on here?"

Faster than I could follow, Evalina was standing before me, almost five paces away.

I blinked, confused.

"I'm sorry," she whispered "Would you prefer me like this?"

With a blink her clothes vanished, leaving her bare before me, my treacherous eyes scanned the body I'd pulled out of an impossibly deep bath tub. Her skin was so pale I could see the delicate blue veins clear as day tracing through her. She sauntered toward me, her long black and blue hair swishing slightly as she walked, the muscles in her abdomen shifting with each step, her generous chest held my attention for too long.

She was upon me before I could notice that her burn was missing. The burn from the dreams, the blood oath. I lifted my hand and gently ran my hand over her shoulder, her skin was impossibly warm for how cold it was in the room. I ran my hand up the side of her neck brushing her face with the backs of my fingers and tucking her hair behind her ear, before grabbing a fistful and holding tightly.

"That is cruel, Mother," I growled.

The fake Evalina laughed. It was a cruel laugh, not at all like the real Princess's. "I would have taken a different approach had I known you liked it rough." The woman snapped at me with her fanged teeth and I yanked her away by the hair.

She cackled and morphed into a new figure. Lean and tall, almost as tall as me, Long white hair tumbled out of her scalp and her skin turned a deeper shade of purple than mine.

"You wouldn't hurt your mother would you darling?"

I let go of the fistful of hair and stepped away. My mother's gold eyes followed me as I paced before her and the tree.

"You're real then?" My mother, The Mother, only smiled. "You know why I'm here."

"You're on the right path." Her voice sounded like thousands of voices speaking at once.

"Can you give me any more than that?"

"Your female should listen to the wraith." The Goddess mimicked my mother's cruel smile perfectly.

"That's it? Follow the wraith?" I pinched the bridge of my nose and sighed deeply, the warm air forming a cloud before being swallowed by the cold. "What a waste of time. I knew you'd be no help if you were real."

The Mother tisked. "Now that's not fair, if I gave you all the answers life would be pretty dull, wouldn't it?"

"Would you rather all life be wiped out?"

"So dramatic," she chided. "My husband would never let that happen to his precious children." She spat the word as if it was beneath her to consider us as anything but play things.

"And what about everything else?"

She grinned, cruel and toothy. She knew exactly what I was talking about, had been waiting for me to ask. "My children gifted your kind the ability to deal with that." Her voices echoed off the chamber walls making me feel as though

I was surrounded in the empty space. "Use it. Rid yourself of your weakness to become who you need to be."

Dread flickered in my chest at her implications. "How do I get out of here? I'm finished with you."

The Goddess's face morphed once again into the Princess as she coiled herself around me and pouted. If the real Evalina ever looked at me that way, I would give her everything.

"Why so dull?" She teased as she ran her body over mine. "Don't you want to know what she feels like?"

I fixed her with a glare. "I'd prefer the real Evalina."

"Oh, I know that, I can feel it all over you. You reek of High-Elf magic." She lightly touched the areas on my back that Evalina had healed, then grazed her fingers down my arm and across my palm. "Your mother would be very disappointed."

I pulled my hand from her grip and was about to question her when, in a blink, the real Evalina was staring down at me with worried eyes.

CHAPTER THIRTY
SHROUDED SECRETS

Thanatos blinked up at me, confusion written across his features.

"Are you all right?" I asked.

He studied me for a moment before taking my outstretched hand and hauling himself to his feet. He swayed and Rangkar dashed over to catch him as he collapsed again.

"What in the pit!" I exclaimed, assisting the orc with the limp Prince.

"He's covered in blood."

"What?" I angled myself to check the Prince over and sure enough the back of his white tunic was stained burgundy with blood.

My mind went blank.

This was my fault, I hadn't healed him properly. His wounds must've opened from the inside out.

"We have to get him out of here."

"Can't you heal him?" Rangkar asked desperately.

I shook my head and began hauling Thanatos to the door.

Once through the door we called for the Sillessian guards to send for a healer as we dragged the prince down the long hallway, leaving a trail of his blood behind us.

By the time we'd reached the end of the hallway Thanatos' skin had turned ashy, his breathing ragged. Panic clawed its way through my chest. I couldn't figure out what I'd done wrong. By the time the healers reached us I was nearly sick with worry, I heard them speaking with Rangkar but couldn't muster any words myself.

I was disappointed in myself, almost more than I was worried for Thanatos. It had been my one chance to save the Prince, to make up for all he had done for me, and, somehow, I had screwed it up. As a High-Elf, the one thing I should be good at naturally is healing magic, but maybe that's not true for half-breeds. Perhaps I had taken after my father's side in more ways than I thought.

Rangkar and I helped the healers to move the Prince back up into the main part of the palace, after they'd sealed the wounds.

It wasn't easy and the journey was harder and sweatier than it had been the first time. The Sillessian healers didn't seem to think it strange that they had been summoned despite me being there, or, if they did, they didn't make it known.

I stayed by Thanatos' side as he was healed, studied the way the healers used their magic, and still couldn't find what I had done wrong; but after the healers left I couldn't leave his side. The guilt I felt pinned me to my chair.

I should have been able to heal him but I also should have taken my healing lessons more seriously when I was younger. Never did I think that I would one day leave the castle and need that knowledge. I thought I would be stuck there forever, but then this Dark Prince came and whisked me away. It was the thing of fairy tales, something every young one dreamed of at least once.

I smiled at the Prince's resting form and took his hand in mine, he didn't wake. He'd lost so much blood. I felt tears prick my eyes, it was all my fault, he wouldn't have even suffered those wounds if he hadn't been protecting me.

I had to be better, I couldn't let this happen again.

I woke to the feeling of someone stroking my hair. At first, I lost all sense of time and thought it was my mother. I pictured us lounging on the chaise in her rooms, my head resting on her thigh as she read me a book about pirates and treasure, pirates like the ones my father was out hunting in his effort to make the seas safe for all. But he would never come home from his journey, would never see what a failure I've become.

I was still in the same chair as yesterday but at some point I had laid my head on the soft mattress and fallen asleep, still holding the Prince's hand. I gave it a soft squeeze to let him know I was awake.

He ceased his stroking. "I should get injured more often if I get to wake up to this," he jested. I turned my head to face him and smiled as he tucked my hair behind my ear.

"I'm sorry," I said as the smile fell from my face.

"For what?"

"I should have had you looked over by the healers when we got here, it's all my fault." I squeezed his hand as tears slid down my face. I hated feeling weak and, since leaving the palace, I had felt nothing but.

"What happened is not your fault," Thanatos said sternly, his fingers tightening around mine. "It was that demon we worship as a God," he spat. "She views this as a game, gave me little to no help and then did this." He gestured to his wrappings; they were unnecessary but I had insisted on them, just in case. "She's toying with us, with you, trying to tear down your confidence for her sick entertainment."

"She didn't help at all?"

He shook his head. "She said to listen to the wraith."

I sat up. "Then my dreams are the answer. This whole time I thought they were something else, but if the she-elf can help us, then maybe we have a chance."

"I just don't understand how it all ties in together. What does the wraith have to do with the Necromancer?"

"Perhaps she was resurrected by him and wants to return to the deadlands."

The Prince considered for a moment. "What do you remember from your dreams?"

I racked my brain to remember things I desperately wanted to forget. The wraith, the words, the smells and sounds and feelings of each nightmare. "*'Go to the land you would not think, with the one you would not choose.'* Those are the words she spoke to me. The she-elf was too decayed for me to gauge how old or where she was from, but her throat was slit." I held my head in my hands trying to focus on remembering any details I could. "Ash and snow, a baby crying … the eyes—dead and green, that's all."

Thanatos put his hand on my shoulder. "It's all right. After your last one, you said she'd told you you were on the right path, so heading to Minoma is right, and I guess I'm the one you would not choose." I smiled and shrugged sheepishly at the Prince. "Maybe she was burned after they slit her throat and she was killed in winter?"

"It doesn't snow in Minoma in winter."

"Fine, well maybe she wasn't killed in Minoma but was killed by a Minoman or brought to life by a Minoman. I know the last thing you want to do is have those dreams, but we really need you to have one of those dreams."

I sighed. Knowing that the dreams were, in fact, helping us was reassuring but I still longed for them to stop. "Are you well enough to travel?"

"Yes, I feel fine. Some breakfast wouldn't hurt, though."

I smiled and assisted the Prince to his feet, making sure he could hold himself up without assistance, before following him out into the living space. We made our way onto the balcony where we found Sevah and Rangkar enjoying breakfast.

"Thanatos! You're alive." Rangkar rose to his feet and greeted the Prince with a slap on the shoulder.

"Thanks to you and Evalina."

"You spoke to her, then?" Sevah asked after briefly embracing me.

"I did. Turns out, Evalina's been the key this whole time."

We sat at the table and shared breakfast with the orc and witch as we explained my dreams and what the Mother had said about them.

"Why didn't you ask me about these dreams?" Sevah questioned.

"I didn't know if you could be trusted," I replied apologetically. "I found a book in your house that made me suspicious."

"Ah, yes, The *Nekros Librorum*, I wondered where that went."

"How could you possibly have known it was missing?"

"My house may be a mess but I know where everything is. You should have spoken to me about your dreams, I could have helped."

"I know that now. Will you both come with us?" I asked.

Sevah and Rangkar looked at each other and away very quickly.

"I must go back to the Father Tree, I may have more books and scrolls that can help you, now that I know more about the blood oath." She glanced at my shoulder and I felt a slight prickle.

"I have a bounty in Shinchaku."

I nodded and glanced suspiciously at Sevah. Shinchaku was south of Sillessia; the fastest way for Rangkar to get there would be by going past Sevah's house, and the Father Tree.

"Be careful, there are Corse everywhere in those woods," I warned.

"I can handle them, your highness, I have faced much worse in my travels." The orc declared with a swooping bow.

"And the book, do you want it back?" I asked the witch.

"No. If you believe it can help you, then keep it. I've never been able to fully translate it myself."

I nodded my thanks.

We finished our breakfast hurriedly. Thanatos and I were keen to be back on the road, as were Sevah and Rangkar.

The Prince and I bathed and dressed before heading down to the stables where Zohar had the horses moved to. We were surprised to find Queen Ambrosia, Prince Soren and Maioc waiting for us.

"It is not safe for you to travel through the forest looking the way you do," Maioc's voice announced in my head. I scrunched my face at the fairy. I knew she had not meant it as an insult but surely she could have worded it better.

"Maioc is right," Ambrosia agreed. "We will need to hide the fact that you're an Isidian all together, at least until you get through to Kushyam."

"Can't you just magic us there like you did before?" I asked the fairy.

"I could, but this is easier." I fought myself to keep my mouth shut, arguing with the fairy would get us nowhere.

"What do you plan to do, then?" Thanatos asked.

"We will disguise her, she already has Sillessian clothes, it's as simple as changing her coloring," Ambrosia said, gesturing to my new travel attire.

Appearance altering magic was popular among humans, they loved to change the color of their hair or their eyes; none of it was permanent and would only last a few weeks if performed by a skilled mage—and that could be quite expensive.

I touched my hair, suddenly cursing myself for wishing it was more exciting than the licks of blue, given to me by my father.

"It will not last long," Ambrosia said, placing a gentle hand on my shoulder.

I nodded.

Maioc flew over me and showered me in shimmering dust; as it landed on my hair and skin, they began to change colors. My hair bloomed red and my skin turned a light shade of green. It was strange to see my hands have a color other than paper white, unnerving even, as if someone else's hands had been cut off and attached to my wrists. Thanatos seemed to feel the same way.

"How do I look?" I dared to ask.

"Different," was all the Prince said.

"Like a Sillessian," said Ambrosia with a grin. "I hope it keeps you safe, both of you. I wish you well travels." The Queen left with Maioc after hugging both of us and insisting we return on our way back to Isidia, as if she expected the Prince and I to continue traveling together even after our quest was completed.

"Princess, if I may have a word." I had almost forgotten that Soren was even there until he spoke.

I nodded and Thanatos left us to see to the horses.

"Your Highness, I have had visions, many visions, and I wish to warn you." The words caught me off guard, I'd never heard the Prince talk so much let alone talk in such serious tones. "Believe me when I say I am not trying to come between you and Thanatos but … I see blood and death in your future. I know what your mission entails, but this is seperate from that, be wary."

Weeks ago I would have believed Soren, no questions asked. But now I found it hard to believe that I should be wary of Thanatos. Perhaps it was jealousy that I was spending so much time with a male that was not a suitor, but I didn't think the Sillessian Prince much cared about all that.

"Prince Soren, at dinner last night you mentioned that I had trouble deciphering my own visions, what did you mean?"

The Prince smiled. "You know now that the dreams of the she-elf are visions, messages from her to you, but so too are your other dreams. Remember them all and put the pieces together."

"But I'm not a seer," I argued. "I never have been."

"You don't need to be a seer to have visions, they can be sent by others, living or dead; consciously or subconsciously."

I sighed, realizing that now I had to pick apart every dream I've had in the last two months. The Prince put his hand on my shoulder and gave it a reassuring squeeze.

My head was spinning as I made my way further into the stables, toward Thanatos and the horses. I had so much to think about and so many pieces to put together. I didn't tell Thanatos about what the Prince said; if he was really planning something malicious, I wanted him to keep thinking I had no idea, though I was worried.

Once the horses were ready, we left, speeding through the town to make up for lost time. We were still days away from Osiria, and even further away from our main destination, Minoma. I sent a prayer to the Father begging him for guidance and protection and one to the Mother, that she keep her rage and stay the hand of the Necromancer.

We saw no Corse as we burst into the woods, there was no formal path to follow but the Prince seemed to know where he was going.

We traveled for hours undisturbed by the dead, my now red hair billowing behind me. I was enjoying being able to have my hair down and my face unhidden, to feel the wind kiss my skin.

It wasn't until we stopped for the night that we encountered any Corse. We'd just tied the horses and laid out our bedding when three reeking figures stumbled through the trees, filling the small clearing with the smell of rotting flesh and old blood. My hand hovered over my blades as Thanatos stepped forward and addressed the figures.

"Evening, sirs!" He called across the way. "On your way to Avars?"

One of the figures grunted. "Just passing through, Death-bringer," the dead man spat.

The Prince didn't react to the slur at all, no doubt he was used to it. Rage flared in my gut at the thought.

"We're looking for a Dark-Elf traveling with a High-Elf, you wouldn't happen to know anything about that would you?"

The Prince paused in mock thought. "You know, I think I did see a fellow with an Isidian. Wouldn't travel with one myself, too prim and proper those wraiths. Sillessian, on the other hand, very handy travel companions, can never run out of food!" He reached back and slapped me on the shoulder, bringing me closer to him so the Corse could view me properly. My hair glowed a deep auburn in the low light from the setting sun.

I said nothing.

"Can I ask what you require from my kin? Perhaps it is something I can help with," Thanatos continued.

"Unless you can tell us where they're headed, we have no more to discuss."

"Then I bid you farewell and safe travels gentlemen." The three men stared skeptically at the Prince for a long moment before limping and dragging themselves out of the clearing.

Thanatos and I released a collective sigh once the footsteps had grown silent. "Let's hope they're the only ones we run into."

I doubted that would be the case. "We should eat and sleep quickly, we may not have long to do so."

Thanatos nodded and we did just that.

We didn't stay up any later than we needed to that night, we had too much distance to cover. So, the second our bellies were full we speedily packed away the remains of our dinner and prepared to settle into our bed rolls. Thanatos paused before getting into his own and gave me an unsure glance.

"Evalina, should you need anything in the night do not hesitate to—to—"

"I won't." I cut him off with a smile. "Thank you."

His face relaxed into an almost hopeful smile before he slid into his covers and turned away from me.

I smiled, happy that my relationship with the Prince was at such a good place. Whatever Soren had seen had to be wrong, just like everything else I'd heard about the Prince.

I fell asleep thinking of the first day we'd met, how rude I'd been based on hearsay. I blushed remembering him catching Lorkin and I in the creek, then in the memory it wasn't Lorkin that I was kissing.

The air was heavy and stunk of fire. Light, powdery ash floated in the air before me. Statues of elves were scattered about the well-groomed yard, separated by ornately sculpted pots containing flowers and shrubs.

On one side of the small courtyard stood Lorkin, his pale skin almost glowing in the moonlight, his hair so black it disappeared into the trees behind him. Opposite from Lorkin stood Thanatos, his eyes and hair shining. Each held a hand out to me with a welcoming smile. I looked between them, unsure of which to go to. In that time, the wraith appeared before me.

The one piece of advice the Mother had given to Thanatos was to trust the wraith. I looked into her dead, white eyes, though her face seemed plumper, almost alive, and her skin had its color back.

"You're a Dark-Elf?"

Her mouth turned up at the corners in something that was not quite a smile.

"Why are you helping me?"

She considered this for a moment, glancing up at the night sky, the stars twinkling brightly, then to Lorkin and Thanatos both of them still with their hands outstretched to me, then sadly around the garden as if it were from a terrible memory.

"The world is still so full of hate, despite the peace, I believe you can change that." Her voice sounded in my head, though the wound on her throat spewed black gunk as she swallowed out of reflex. "But first, you need to choose."

I glanced between the Captain and the Prince. "Let me guess which one you want me to choose."

She shrugged and offered me a small smile. "You bought them here, not me, it seems you need to be the one that makes the choice, though it seems clear to me which one you want." She strolled over to Thanatos and stood behind him, her hands on his shoulders.

With the two of them standing together I could almost see similarity in their features, the Prince and the wraith shared the same hairline, similar cat-like eyes, and nose; but her face was softer, more rounded. "Change is not to be feared," she added, sensing my hesitation.

"In my life all change has done is cause problems. Life would be simpler if everything stayed the same."

A sad look crossed the wraith's face and she looked over to Lorkin. "Sometimes change is for the better. Keeping things the same isn't always the best choice, and, anyway, life would be boring if there were no problems."

"Why do I need to make this choice? How does it affect my journey?"

The wraith sighed. "I was once presented with a choice very similar to this"— she gestured between Lorkin and Thanatos—"and I made the wrong choice. I was selfish. I thought I was doing what was best for me and my family, but I was wrong. I don't want you to make the same selfish mistake that I did—the treaty between our two peoples must be enforced."

"The treaty has already been signed, there is peace."

The wraith shook her head, her hands tightening on Thanatos' shoulders, but he did not react. He still stood frozen, reaching out to me. "It's not enough for your people or for mine."

I turned away from the wraith, fueled with rage that this dead Osirian would dare try to dictate what I should do in my life, who I should be with.

I walked over to Lorkin; he didn't react, as if he too were frozen in time his eyes still gazed hopefully at the spot I had just vacated. I tucked a stray hair behind his pointed ear and breathed in his scent, he smelled of home and it made my heart ache. My hand paused on his cheek, it was cool where I touched him and, despite what my mind said, my body seemed almost content with that touch as if that's all I needed. The frantic lust that I'd thought was love for so long, was gone.

When I turned to face the wraith and the Prince, warmth bloomed within me and faded instantly as I noticed the pair of eyes watching us from behind them, one green and one dead like the wraith's own eyes.

I bolted upright in my sleeping roll and scanned the edges of the clearing for eyes, any eyes.

I saw none.

I sighed and looked over to where the Prince was sleeping soundly, his breathing deep and slow. The thought to join him crossed my mind for a second but instead I laid back down and stared up at the stars, barely visible through the trees above us.

In my dream I had said I wanted a simple life that I wished things had stayed the same, but that couldn't be farther from the truth.

Yes, I would return home to be Queen, but things would be different. I would have freedom and, in the end, that's all I really wanted.

I gave the Prince vague details of the dream the next morning while packing our bags to leave, I avoided the main subject the wraith and I had discussed and gave him only the important details.

"Okay let me get this straight, she's a Dark-Elf, she doesn't want you to repeat her mistakes and she wants the treaty between Osirians and Isidians?"

I nodded avoiding his eyes. I was going to ask the wraith how she expected the Prince and I to be together when we were both the only heirs to our thrones, but the eyes ... .

"What does she mean by 'her mistakes'?"

I shrugged as I hauled my saddle onto Faenor's back and gave her a quick pet as she let out a disgruntled huff. "Has there ever been an alliance between our people before? Maybe she stopped a treaty and regrets it."

"I don't know of one, if there has been—we'll have to ask my father. What could the treaty have to do with the Necromancer?"

"Well, he is trying to wipe out all High-Elves, so maybe he's against the treaty." The Prince fell silent. I stopped buckling my saddle bags to look at him, his expression was a mix of irritation and sadness. "You think it's Osirian, don't you?" He said.

I had thought so, for a second, but it was impossible. Even if it was a Dark-Elf trained in the highest level of Necromancy, it would be impossible. we couldn't just go against the will of our magic. A Dark-Elf couldn't use magic to bring anyone back to life the same as a High-Elf couldn't use magic to kill.

"Don't be silly, that would be impossible. It'll be some human either with a grudge or trying to show off their power."

Thanatos nodded but didn't seem to believe me, and I'm not so sure I believed myself.

Magic was a tricky thing, sometimes it was so straight forward and unmoving but other times it could be easily manipulated and, while it would be difficult, extremely difficult, I couldn't completely rule it out. Prince Soren had said I had to keep an eye out for the Prince and, while I honestly couldn't imagine Thanatos doing anything like it, I couldn't completely ignore the warning I'd been given.

We left the clearing not long after the sun had risen and rode all day until after it had set. We stopped only a couple of times; when we'd run into a few Corse and when we'd needed to relieve ourselves.

The Corse were completely thrown off by my fairy disguise and the Prince and I were grateful that it had lasted as long as it had. I'd half expected my hair to be black again when I'd woken that morning.

The horses were not happy with the change of terrain that entering Kushyam brought, their hooves unsteady and sinking into the yellow desert sand. To offer Faenor a small amount of comfort I'd pinned the Osirian Hellebore brooch to her saddle to keep her cool in the hot sun.

The air had seemed to change almost instantly from humid to dry heat and I was even more thankful that the Queen had insisted I buy new traveling clothes.

The Prince and I barely spoke, purely because the air was too dry and we had to conserve water.

"We'll be in Nebu by midday tomorrow," Thanatos said over the small fire separating us, too small to keep anyone warm in the cool desert night but big enough to light both our figures. "We'll have to try to avoid the palace or King Keon will force us to stay for a feast. The Kushyami love to show off their gold, though they don't realize they're doing it most of the time."

"You're very close with all of them," I stated, remembering how they'd acted at the ball in Isidia.

"They're like a second family, I have to pass through Nebu every time I leave Osiria and they've always been gracious enough to host me for the night, or a couple," he said with a smile.

"You leave Osiria a lot."

"I have the freedom to, I can't let that go to waste, many others don't have the luxury."

"Are you always so cryptic?"

"Maybe," he added with mock seriousness. I lent over the fire and made to smack his shoulder with my hand but he grabbed my wrist and gazed down at my white palm, tinted slightly orange from the fire light. "I guess the fairy magic is finally wearing off."

"I'm surprised, but glad it lasted so long."

The Prince's eyes flicked to mine. "I would have liked it to fade faster, Wood-Elf doesn't suit you."

I blushed despite my attempt not to.

Thanatos reached forward with his other hand and lightly brushed it down a length of my hair. He was so close I could see the reflection of the fire dancing in his gold eyes. "I missed the blue."

"So did I," I said not knowing what else to say, my head was in shambles, my stomach performing summersaults.

I was desperately resisting the urge to move away. It was time to move on, the wraith was right; this was what I wanted.

I held my position, frozen and waiting, waiting to see how far the Prince would take it, if he would make the first move.

We sat for a moment, him still playing with my hair and me studying his face, our breaths mingling in the air between us. Then his hand gently released my wrist and slowly traced its way up my arm, around my shoulder, and down my back, so lightly it made me shiver. The corners of the Prince's mouth curled upward in a half-grin. Thanatos' other hand fell from my hair and grazed up my leg starting from my knee and ending on my hip.

His eyes flicked to mine; I raised my eyebrow and he took that as answer enough. Within seconds our lips were pressed against each other and warmth exploded within me. My hands shot to either side of Thanatos' face, holding it in place as I deepened the kiss. The Prince's grip on my hip tightened, his hand on my back moved back up to between my shoulders and pulled me lightly toward him.

Our mouths fought for dominance, our hands gripped and pulled at each other as if we couldn't touch enough of the other with the only two hands the Mother and Father had cursed us with. All I could smell was his snow and ash scent, his mouth tasted sweet like the Sillessian fruit we'd had for dinner and his hair and skin was smooth and warm, smoother than I would expect of a traveler but his hands were as rough and calloused as I'd imagined. He let out a hiss and pulled away as I nipped at his bottom lip.

"I'm sorry—" I breathed, it felt as if the air had been sucked from my lungs. I could barely focus my eyes on Thanatos' face.

"No, it wasn't you." He was sitting up and rubbing a spot on his shin. "I lent too close to the fire and burnt my leg," he said with a sheepish grin.

I fought not to laugh as I moved to the other side of the fire so I could heal the Prince's leg for him. I held my hands over the small burn and watched as my white power slowly welled in my palms, the glow almost brighter than the small fire. I focused on the burn, willing myself not to look at the Prince's face. A blush burned my cheeks as I thought of his hands on my body, my hands on his.

As the healing finished up, the Prince lifted my face to his with a finger gently pressed under my chin and placed a kiss on my lips. "Thank you," he whispered before turning my head to the side and lightly kissing along my jaw.

I sighed and fell into his touch.

We kissed until we physically couldn't keep ourselves or each other awake any longer and fell asleep in each other's arms. Words could not describe the way it felt when he kissed me, the fire that burned under my skin fuelled with longing.

CHAPTER THIRTY ONE
TROUBLE IN PARADISE

I woke the next morning to Thanatos tracing circles lightly on my bare shoulder. I rolled over to face him and traced one of the tattoos on his chest with my finger.

"What's this one for?" It was one of the larger of the tattoos that littered the Prince's chest, a heart on fire and stabbed through with what looked like an ice spear.

"It's to remind me of where my heart truly lies, in the center of fire and ice." For someone who left his home so much, he truly did love it. "Though I would appreciate somewhere a little more green. I know you're probably sick of it, but Isidia really is beautiful."

He wasn't wrong, the landscape of the castle grounds and my lands were burnt into my memory in such a way that I thought, if someone were to keep me away for the rest of my life, in my dying moments I would still be able to recount what it looked like. The exact position of the town and every farm outside of it, the harbor in the distance; I could tell them the usual amount of ships that docked at the port everyday and how many wagons traveled between there and the town.

"You should see it in spring, when the woods are full of flowers and blooms cover the castle."

Thanatos smiled. "I'll take that as an invitation."

I returned my gaze to the many tattoos on his chest, he had everything; animals, flowers, names, even ancient Osirian hieroglyphics.

My eyes paused on one that stood out as odd. Most of them were quite stylized, you could tell the artist had taken their time designing the letters or creatures they were tattooing on the Prince, but right over his heart was a crude, shakey tattoo of his initials, T.H. I ran my fingers lightly over the letters, my eyes darting to Thanatos' as he sucked in a quick breath.

"We should get moving," he said, his tone shifting from carefree to all of a sudden very serious, as if I had reminded him of something important he had to do.

I suddenly felt unsure of what happened between the Prince and I the night before and dreaded the day to come and the awkwardness that had settled over us.

The sun was just beginning to sneak its way above the distant horizon and already I could feel its heat. Sweating on the back of a horse was the last thing I wanted to do. I thought of wearing the Hellebore brooch but removing it from Faenor seemed almost cruel.

We left not long after we woke and rode in silence for most of the morning. It was unbearably hot, even in the thin traveling clothes. It only got worse once Nebu appeared in our sights, half the Oasis obscured from our vision by a large wall, and I had to cover my hair. Sweat trickled down my face and between my shoulders and breasts, tickling irritatingly and only adding to my foul mood.

The sun was at its highest point when we finally reached the outskirts of the city. Thanatos rode ahead to speak with the guards at the gates, trying to pay them off to keep their mouths shut about us entering the city. I hung back, waiting for him to signal me to move forward. I could not see a single drop of sweat on the Prince, no patches on his clothes and not a bead on his face. I dreaded the thought of entering Osiria if even this did not disturb him. My mouth was dry and lips cracked as I took a swig of the last of my water while nudging Faenor with my heels to urge her forward.

Once we were through the gates I was able to admire the contrast between the dry dead desert and the lush green Oasis. Flowers bloomed in all colors of the rainbow and green foliage littered the ground around the water's edge, while large palm trees formed a canopy above. The water flowed through grates built into the base of the city wall, keeping out the large animals that called the Oasis waters home.

The city had been built predominantly out of sandstone; small, flat-roofed houses lined the streets, growing in size the closer you got to the Alabaster and gold palace in the center. The locals wore thin, light-coloured clothing, highlighting their darker features and keeping them cool in the hot sun. I couldn't help but notice how similar it was to how Thanatos dressed and wondered who inspired who. Thanatos had wrapped a linen cloth around his head, partially covering his face and hair. He said it was to keep him hidden from the guards that would likely report his presence to the royal family.

"We just need to fill our food packs and water skins and get out of here," Thanatos stated.

I was only half listening to the Prince, distracted by the small children running through the markets; the colorful hand woven rugs hanging from the front of a building that I assumed was the house of the maker; and jewelry stands that glinted in the sun, showcasing the finest gems I'd ever seen. All along the strip, sellers called out about their wares and they weren't shy to get in your face and almost drag you to their stands—I loved it.

I watched a woman haggle with a man about the price of a tall, skinny, gold teapot, both sides so passionate about the item—the man willing to fight for its worth and woman not willing to leave without it. It was a dance of words. A part of me wanted to applaud when the woman got her way and ended up paying four silvers less than it was worth.

"Are you listening to me?" Thanatos snapped.

"What? Sorry." I grinned sheepishly.

"I said, there's a fountain in the food market a few streets over, we'll go there to get everything and water the horses. We should leave before nightfall."

I nodded but couldn't hide my disappointment.

I would have loved to stay in Nebu for a few days, taste the exotic fruits and buy jewels for my mother; but we had a job to do and we were already pushing our time.

I longed to hear from my family again, but I probably wouldn't get anything until we arrived in Ravenna. This realization made me just as eager as the Prince to reach his home.

The food market was even more colorful than the last with fruits of all shapes, sizes, and colors neatly displayed on market stall shelves, some cut into halves and quarters for people to buy and eat as they walked.

Thanatos led us through the market, the crowd parting for him, stopping to purchase various fruits and vegetables as we went. We watered the horses at one of the communal animal fountains in the center of the street and filled our skins at another to the side.

"What do you think you are doing?" Said a stern voice behind us.

We turned to find a guard, Khopesh in hand, glaring at us, her deep Kushyami skin completely clear of any sweat despite the gold plates on her shoulders, wrist and shins. A gold whip was strapped to her hip, the sheath for her blade strapped to her back providing easy access to both weapons with her single arm.

"Filling my water flask. What does it look like?" The Prince snapped playfully.

The guard clicked her tongue in frustration. "Why are you paying off my guards?" Her brown eyes narrowed on me and I caught a slight hint of surprise before she trained them back on the Prince.

"Because I'm just passing through, I don't have time for a banquet."

"You travel with an Isidian?" She flicked her chin to me.

"Finalizing the treaty."

The guard slowly lowered her blade, not taking her eyes off us for a second. "Where will you stay tonight?"

I raised my eyebrows at the guard, I'd already met one of Thanatos' lovers on this journey, was I about to meet another?

"Most likely at Glik's place. Don't tell them I'm here, please Soraya. I just want to get home."

Soraya nodded. "I'll give an order to leave you be, but it will get back to them eventually and they will not be happy."

"I know. Thank you." Soraya only nodded before turning and striding away down the busy market street.

"What was that about?" I asked the Prince, who'd gone back to filling his flask without another word.

"She's the royal family's personal guard. I guess I should have paid the sentries more to keep their mouths shut. At least they only told her and didn't go straight to Keon."

"They'll be that upset that you didn't stop to see them?"

"Oh, yes. Much like Sillessia this is a second home to me." The small smile disappeared from his face and he seemed to drift into his own world for a moment before going back to what he was doing before I interrupted him.

We finalized our business at the markets and made our way to a tavern on the outskirts of the city, almost as far away from the palace as we could get without leaving the city walls altogether.

The tavern was a complete replica of the palace but on a much smaller scale, Sandstone was painted to look like Alabaster and what I assumed was real gold detailing on the actual palace was just more painted sandstone; and wood for the more intricately detailed areas on the mock palace. As we pushed the doors to the tavern open we were greeted by a familiar, gravel-like voice.

"Ah, Master Thanatos and Mistress ... Elsrine was it?" The goblin smiled, flashing his yellow teeth. "Two rooms?"

An awkwardness bloomed between the Prince and I. I fiddled with a loose string on my pack as I waited for Thanatos to answer the goblin and my heart sank as the Prince replied, "Two rooms."

I plucked the key to my room from Glik's hand and without looking back at the Prince stomped up the stairs to the third floor and firmly shut the door behind me.

The room was small, barely big enough for the bed squished in the corner; there was no door leading to a bathroom, meaning there was most likely a communal one somewhere in the inn.

I dropped my bag onto the floor and flopped onto the bed. My whole body was covered in sweat and sand and my calves ached from pulling my feet through the desert. I longed for a bath but couldn't stand to face the Prince after our terrible morning. I was sick of being kept in the dark but we were close to Osiria, it wouldn't be long before I got at least a few answers.

I sat up and dug through my bag as my stomach growled. Thanatos had most of the food in his pack but I managed to find an apple and some dried meat at the bottom of mine.

I gnawed on the meat as my mind raced through everything going on in my life; my family back in Isidia preparing for an attack that could come at any moment, my mother's deteriorating mental state, and the Necromancer I was responsible for hunting down and killing.

My chest began to feel tight the more I thought. It was a lot to deal with— but being Queen comes with a lot of responsibilities, I would have to get used to it. I took deep, measured breaths between chews, trying to calm the racing of my heart and the tightness in my chest. I told myself that if anything truly bad had happened, my grandfather would have found a way to let me know.

I thought of my cousin, Simeon, somewhere out in the middle of the ocean, with no knowledge of what's happening here on land. Part of me wished we could switch places.

I held back tears that threatened to fall, thinking instead of the positives of this journey; I was out of Isidia, out of the castle grounds, I'd seen the fairies of Sillessia and was now in the Nebu Oasis, and, soon, I would go where no Isidian had been for thousands of years.

I wondered how the Osirians would greet me. Would I be welcome after all the years of unrest? I liked to think of myself as being well read and educated on our history, and I couldn't remember reading about any sort of peace between our people before now.

I used a small amount of magic to massage and soothe the aching in my calves, letting my power collect in my palms and running them along my legs, kneading areas that felt particularly sore. A shadow passed my door; by the rhythm of the steps I knew it was Thanatos. He paused for a moment and so did my heart. I hoped he would knock but he simply continued down the hall. I resisted the urge to throw my boot at the door and scream into the soft pillow like a lovelorn teenager and decided, instead, that I would dare to leave my room and ask Glik to send up my dinner when it was time. I would then find the bathing room.

I managed to avoid running into Thanatos as I darted down stairs to speak with the goblin owner of the inn. Glik was wearing a smug smile as I approached him; he'd no doubt put two and two together and I once again regretted my actions, wishing I could control my emotions better.

"Trouble in paradise?" He goaded, his long ears twitching.

"I would like my dinner sent to my room, please," I said, and made to go back up the stairs.

"You are not the only one with family issues, Lady Elsrine."

I glanced back at Glik, the expression on his face no longer one of jest. Confused, I simply continued up the stairs and roamed the inn till I found the bathing room for my floor.

There were no baths in the large room, only a cluster of small stalls, each one containing a bucket, two towels and a chamber pot. I thanked the Father for this small blessing. I doubted I would ever be able to bathe in a bath alone after what happened in Oakfell.

I sat naked on the floor of the stall pouring water over myself from the enchanted bucket. The water was cool and refreshing on my skin, making me feel instantly better.

As I scrubbed the dirt of the day away, I thought about what Glik had said. It was clear to me that Thanatos wasn't close with his mother, but he and his father seemed to get along fine and he seemed more eager than hesitant to return home. I began to feel even more annoyed at the Prince. He knew so much about my life and I knew nothing of his—the world knew nothing—and he didn't seem interested in changing that at all.

Apart from Sillessia, and Kushyam it seemed, Carynthia viewed the Osirians in a very negative light. Thanatos could change that, if he only shared his good deeds, but he seemed content with the world hating him and his people.

I stopped thinking and concentrated on scrubbing myself until I no longer felt grimey, then sat on the cool, tiled floor for a while before heading back to my room.

I sighed as I looked out the window at the late afternoon sun still sitting comfortably in the sky, it was going to be a long night.

CHAPTER THIRTY TWO
A RIGHT MESS

I'd just worked up the courage to go to her room.

I was going to knock on her door, kiss her the second she opened it and apologize for being such an ass all day—but when I stepped out my door and saw her coming up the stairs … I froze.

Her green eyes were troubled, her face flustered; this heat was too much for her. I'd noticed the brooch on her horse's saddle and knew that telling her to use it for herself would only result in an argument, so I'd ignored it.

I hated myself for making her feel whatever emotion had given her that expression, but I couldn't bring myself to tell her … not yet.

I waited for her to be clear of the stairs, but instead of going into her room she went into the bathing room. I thought for a second of following her in but it seemed too forward. Then again, after the night before, maybe it wasn't. I let out a breath and forced my feet to move, forced my mind to stop thinking of my hands on her body, touching her in ways I'd longed to do since I'd first met her.

I trudged down the stairs and into the bar area, taking a seat in the far corner of the room with a perfect view of the stairs. I flagged down one of the barmaids and ordered a drink before resting my head in my folded arms.

I wished Rangkar was with me. He would have been sensible and told me to get over it and go talk to her like he always did, forgetting that I'm Osirian, that the world hated me and my people even more than they hated his.

Perhaps the night before was a mistake, maybe I could take it all back and we could start again, or maybe I should have asked for one room, should have followed her up the stairs and knocked on her door like I'd wanted to. Glik had said as much.

I thanked the barmaid as she placed my tankard in front of me and lightly gave my shoulder a squeeze. She'd worked for Glik for a while now, lasting longer than most, I remembered helping her a couple of times with drunk patrons and unwanted advances.

I knocked back half of my drink before Glik could take the seat across from me and glare from the otherside of the table.

"What?" I demanded, not in the mood for one of his lectures.

"Nothing." He shrugged. "I just think she has a right to know."

"She'll find out soon enough." I took another deep swig and signaled to the maid for another. She gave me a reluctant smile but turned to fill another tankard anyway.

"She should know before you get there and she should hear it from you."

I ran my hands over my face, massaging my dry eyes with my finger tips. "I know, I just … can't. It would change everything and after last night … she'd think the worst of me."

Glik tapped a talon impatiently on the table. "You don't think she'd think the worst of you hearing about it from your parents, or worse, her mother?"

"I could play dumb, pretend I didn't know about it."

The goblin sighed. "Has she had any more nightmares?"

"Yes, only a couple and none very clear." I tapped my cup on the table. "I spoke to Her." Glik stared at me, confused. "*Her*" I enunciated, flicking my eyes to the ground.

He gaped. "They're really real?"

I nodded and the goblin stood on his chair so he could lay his hand comfortingly over mine. "Then there is hope?"

I shrugged. "She didn't give me much to go off, just said I had been gifted the ability to handle it."

Glik considered this for a moment, his eyes dark. "You need to tell her," he insisted.

"I will, when the time is right." I knew I wouldn't, I would leave it till the last minute as I always did.

"She's asked to have her dinner in her room." The goblin raised an eyebrow. "You could take it to her."

"I don't think she wants to see me right now." The ale was beginning to make my head spin, I was drinking too fast.

"Not like this, she doesn't," he said, cocking his chin toward my drink.

"I've had a hard couple of weeks, give me a break," I snapped.

Glik raised his hands in surrender and retreated back behind the bar. I instantly felt guilty but, instead of rising to apologize, I simply ordered another drink.

I wished for the lull of drunkenness, to forget, if only for a moment, the horror of the past weeks. I wished to unsee the living dead, to unfeel the weakness of my power not working, forget the panic I felt whenever I had to help Evalina.

I eyed the table of paramours. Kushyami men and women dressed in simple white garments, the fabric so thin you could almost see through it, fake gold chains laced around their bodies and through the braids in their hair. They glittered in the afternoon sun. I admired their beauty but wanted nothing more from them, as usual.

The inn's bar was starting to fill up as the sun got closer to setting, the noise level rising. I sighed and wondered if these hard working people would be as jolly if they knew what was going on outside of the city. I hated that we hadn't told the humans of the threat but wished I shared their ignorance. I hoped we found the Necromancer sooner rather than later.

I stayed down in the bar until dinner was served, roast potatoes with pork sausages and thick gravy. I hadn't realized how drunk I was until I attempted to feed myself, my fork swayed before my mouth, dripping gravy over the table. It would have been a humorous sight but no one dared laugh at a Dark-Elf—even in Kushyam, the one place in Carynthia where we were almost accepted.

After eating a majority of my meal I decided it was time to retire. Unsteady on my feet, I began to weave my way through the crowd. A couple turned to protest as I grabbed shoulders, elbows and heads to pull myself along to the stairs, but quietened the second they saw my face.

Whispers rose through the crowd, "Osirian ..."

"Death-bringer ..."

"Friend of the King ..."

"Drunkard."

I was used to the insults, it came with being what I am, but part of me still resented every one of them.

I made it to the stairs and gripped the banister with both hands to help navigate myself up. By the time I got to the third floor, I was breathless and my head spun uncomfortably as I eyed the Princess's door. There was no light coming from underneath, despite the early hour. I walked up to the door, hand raised and ready to knock, but, once again, I froze. I couldn't let her see me like this; I could feel myself swaying though I was trying my hardest to stand tall and still. I instead returned to my room and fumbled with the door until I finally unlocked it and crashed to the floor.

I laughed at myself for a moment but then tears of laughter turned into tears of something else. I wept on the floor of my room, finally having a moment to myself to process the fact that I'd been close to death twice in the last few days. I could recall the moments I felt my life slipping away, the wetness of the blood that had trickled from my wounds. There had been no sweet memories replaying in my head nor the saving grace of black unconsciousness. Evalina's panicked voice echoed in my head as I tried to calm my heaving sobs. I thought of who I would have left behind and how it would affect them. I had to make it home, I couldn't leave them without saying goodbye first, without retelling this last adventure.

I don't know how I'd gotten into bed or when I'd stopped crying, but my chest still felt heavy with emotion when I was woken up in the early hours of the morning by someone yelling my name.

My heart pounded and my head felt fuzzy as I opened my eyes to find Soraya standing over me.

I sat up, too fast, and the room somersaulted around me as Soraya attempted to tell me something. "Slow down," I said while grabbing either side of my head in an effort to stop it from spinning. "What are you doing in my room?"

She glared at me, taking a deep breath before relaying whatever she had tried to say to me before. "The city is under attack, the dead climb the walls."

I was instantly sobered, leaping out of bed, swaying only a bit, to attach my sword to my belt and prepare to help. "Have they gotten over yet?" I asked while relacing my boots and inserting some daggers down the sides of my ankles

"Not yet, but they are close. Have you encountered them before?"

"Yes, decapitation or burning is the only way." I tied my hair out of my face as quickly as I could and did a quick run through my mind of everything I would need to fight with. "Why are you not with the King and his family?" I asked, panic rising in my throat.

"They sent me to get you! We must hurry."

I finished running through my mental checklist and left the room with Soraya, not pausing for even a second before pounding on Evalina's door.

CHAPTER THIRTY THREE
THE HOLLOW HORDE

Angry, gray clouds tumbled across the sky above me as I stood in the center of a large snowfield, thick falling snow limiting my vision to mere steps ahead.

Nestled in the snow before me was a carved bassinet, thick white blankets tumbling over the sides. A maternal part of me panicked and forced my feet toward the cradle. Surely no one would leave their baby out in this weather? Though even I felt no chill. I peered into the bassinet, not knowing what to expect. My pounding heart eased as I saw no babe in the crib, just empty blankets. I picked one up and ran it through my hands pausing as I reached a symbol embroidered into the corner. It was the crest of the Osirian royal family: two licks of flame one above the other with two many-pointed stars on either side. The gold thread of the embroidery glinted as I ran it through my fingers. I felt heat ebbing from my burn.

"Why are you showing me this?" I asked, sensing the familiar presence of the Osirian wraith.

"This is what I lost, what many will lose."

I turned to her, tears littered her face. "If we don't kill the Necromancer?" I pushed.

Her wet amber eyes flicked to mine, no longer dead and white.

"Do you know where he is? Who he is?"

The wraith's lower lip trembled and her eyes pleaded.

I grabbed her shoulders. "Who is he?" I demanded.

I woke with a gasp as a loud knock echoed through my small tavern room.

"*Shit.*" I whispered to myself and quickly dressed. I'd fallen asleep not long after I'd come back from the bathing room, not even bothering to dress because it was cooler in the Kushyami heat. "I'm coming!" I yelled as the urgent knocking continued. I was almost tempted to answer the door naked, hoping it was Thanatos wanting to apologize for his attitude today, but thought I'd better not risk it. I had just finished buckling my sword belt when the knocking became pounding.

"What?!" I yelled as I swung the door open and came face to face with Thanatos and the Guard from the market.

"The city is under attack, we must get to the gate." Thanatos didn't wait for me to answer before turning away and dashing down the stairs, the Kushyami Guard following closely behind, her single hand resting on the handle of her fierce-looking whip.

Flabbergasted, I tagged along behind Soraya, my heart pounding. I'd never been part of a siege before, had no idea what to expect, and I knew very little about the Kushyami way of fighting.

Our horses were prepared for us outside of the inn, saddled and ready to leap into action. A cluster of soldiers stood waiting for Soraya to give them orders, clad in armor identical to hers; gold plates on shoulders, wrists and shins, and densely beaded vests protected their chests and backs.

Everything was a blur, time seemed to speed up the second we stepped into the street. Soraya barked orders to her soldiers telling them how to kill the Corse correctly and to pass the message on to other guards and civilians alike.

I don't remember getting on my horse but I do remember following Thanatos on his through the streets, the pang of jealousy that sat in my gut as Soraya rode with him, and the guilt that came with watching the innocent people of Kushyam board up their houses.

It was my fault the Corse were here. They must have tracked us somehow, or the fairy disguise hadn't worked as well as we'd hoped.

We galloped through the city until we reached the gate, the wood groaning at the weight of the hoard pressing against it. I followed Thanatos' lead and dismounted Feanor, following him and Soraya up to the battlements of the walls and surveyed the city from the new height.

Fires, some that had only just been extinguished, were being lit all over the city in large braziers turning the night sky scarlet. The top of the walls were in a state of organized chaos; archers and spearmen lined the parapets, prepping their stations for the battle, many wrapping oil-soaked cloths around the ends of their arrows and spears.

In the courtyard before the gate, soldiers stood in orderly formations receiving orders from their commanders, while others marched through the streets barking at people to return to their homes and be ready for invasion.

I gagged as we neared the far edge of the wall, the smell of decaying flesh wafting from the Corse host below. I dared a peek over the stone edge and instantly regretted it.

Hundreds and thousands of living corpses clawed at the base of the wall and gate, some hacked with weapons, desperate to gain entry to the city.

I could sense Thanatos' panic more than see it on his stern face. These humans were just as precious to him as his own people, and they were now in grave danger.

I jumped out of the way as a line of men rolling barrels darted down the center of the battlements, placing the barrels along the wall and cracking open the lids.

"Where do you need us?" Thanatos asked Soraya.

"The Palace is secure as are the walls at the back of the city, but the gate ... well, you can see." She motioned down to the hoard. A group of Corse had cut down a palm tree to use as a battering ram, the crowd before the gate parted to allow them to proceed.

Thanatos answered instantly before I could even take in a breath to answer myself. "Then I'll help on the frontlines." He said confidently, with a hint of desperation and, maybe, guilt. He turned to me. "You should head to the palace and help the healers."

"No. I'm staying with you."

His stare hardened. "Go to the palace. Soraya, the soldiers and I can handle things down here."

I squared my shoulders. "I'm staying with you," I said defiantly, over-enunciating each word. I couldn't let him face this alone. We stared each other down for a moment before he let out an exasperated sigh and motioned for me to follow the Kushyami Captain.

We followed her along the battlement until we stood over the struggling gate facing the tense Kushyami soldiers.

"The enemy beyond this gate is like nothing we've faced before but that does not mean we will not succeed." Soraya projected her voice over the clamoring dead to her army. "The Prince has informed me that decapitation and burning is the only way to kill these creatures, so I hope for your sakes that your blades are sharp." A few soldiers tested their weapons with their fingers, most grinned but others frowned. "We will attack head-on, our goal is to keep them out of the city and away from civilians. Archers!" She turned to face the soldiers lining the tops of the walls. "Pick from the middle, create a gap in their force to aid those of us on the ground." The gate below creaked and moaned, it wouldn't be long before it splintered and broke apart at the weight. "Be ready," Soraya said, walking back to the steps and leading Thanatos and I to the head of the army.

The gate groaned again.

"Ready!"

Thanatos and I unsheathed our weapons, glancing one last time at each other. Thanatos offered a slight nod of encouragement and I recalled the promise he'd made to my mother, to my family; he would protect me, as much as I would let him.

"Ready!" Soraya called again, now brandishing her weapon of choice, a long barbed golden whip with a curved blade on the tail end of the handle, the perfect weapon for a single-armed wielder. "Open the gate!" She called.

In the blink of an eye, we went from staring at buckled wood to fighting enraged corpses. The captain caught them with her whip, pulled them into herself and sliced through their necks with the blade as easily as if they were made of butter. We gave the dead a small berth into the city, if only to give ourselves room to spread out and fight more easily. The Kushyami soldiers were formidable, taller—and broader—than a majority of the Corse, their weapons in better condition, and their training impeccable. They fought united as one, vicious force, almost synchronized in their slashes and beheadings.

The Prince stayed close by my side, while still giving me enough room to swing my father's sword. I hated using it to kill these creatures but I liked to think my father was with me in the battle, guiding me, in a way.

It wasn't long before red blood joined the black staining the sand beneath our feet as the corpses of Kushyami soldiers joined those of the enemy on the battleground. With each fallen Kushyami, I saw Thanatos grow less form-based and more savage with his killing, simply hacking through as many necks at a time as he could. He grew further and further away from me as he seemed to be blinded with rage. I tried to keep close to him, to protect the back he was leaving open for attack, but Soraya was there before I could dispose of the dual-wielding Corse before me, it's two short swords getting much too close to my midsection. I pulled one of my Sai blades out and used it to block their second blade from piercing through my ribs as my sword blocked the first from slashing my face. I hooked the first sword with my crossguard and twisted it from the Corse's hand. After doing the same with the other blade, I crossed the blades on either side of the creature's neck and sliced them through, its head bouncing by my feet as I engaged a new attacker. I made quick work of it, dipping quickly to slice the knees and then the neck.

There was a break in the battle, the archers having picked off more Corse than I could have imagined possible in the short amount of time between now and the start of the battle. The Kushyami speedily moved to separate their dead and injured from the enemy corpses on the battlefield, clearing the way for the second battle to begin. I could hear the hoard thundering toward us over the sands, could see glimpses of them through the gate. I rushed to catch up to Thanatos and Soraya, the two of them speaking in quick hushed tones.

"If we go through the gate we lower the risk of them getting past us and into the city." Thanatos was saying to the captain as I approached them.

"But then we run the risk of getting backed against the walls, that is not a good position to be in. At least in here we can use the city to our advantage, an open battlefield is not optimal." The Captain challenged.

"I don't understand why they're attacking here." Thanatos expressed, then sighed. "I'm going out there," he said to the Captain. "I'm going to capture one and question it. I need to know what's going on."

"What *is* going on?" Soraya asked, her eyes flicking between Thanatos and I. I reached up and tugged my headscarf down a little more, fearful that she'd discovered my identity. "You come here with a High-Elf and then we're attacked by the dead."

Guilt flashed across Thanatos' face. "Soraya," he said gently, gentler than I'd ever heard him speak to anyone, "after the battle, I'll tell you—and Keon—everything."

I nodded, not that his words were directed to me. "I agree with Thanatos, we must interrogate one and discover why they are attacking. Is there any way we can buy some time to let us do this?"

Soraya thought for a moment, her eyes darting across the battlements. "We'll use oil and fire. Let a few in and then release oil over the walls," she said.

"Will it put the city at risk?" I asked, the information surely wasn't worth risking the lives of the civilians.

"Not if we're careful."

I nodded. Thanatos looked hesitant, as if he'd forgotten there were others in the city that we were protecting. Soraya darted up the battlements and relayed the plan to the archers, shouting a warning to those of us still on the ground that the hoard was growing closer and we needed to prepare. I turned to Thanatos, he was tense and breathing heavily despite the moments of quiet we'd had.

"Are you all right?" I asked, searching his angry amber eyes.

"I just—I don't understand. They're attacking humans now? I just can't make sense of it." Thanatos ran his bloody hand through his hair, staining the white a wine color.

"We'll figure it out, don't worry." I rested a dirty hand on his shoulder, his breathing had calmed but was still rapid. He was worried, I was worried. This changed what we previously believed of the Necromancer's goal. Isidia had no bad blood with the Kushyami but we weren't particularly close, not like the Osirians. And had they only been targeting wealthy kingdoms, they would have attacked here first; no one, except maybe the Osirians, was richer than Kushyami.

"Positions!" Soraya called as she reached the bottom of the battlement steps. Her soldiers, Thanatos, and I all fell into a formation that felt natural—the elves and Captain at the front and everyone else behind.

My heart raced, each beat hitting at the same rhythm as the steps of the approaching Corse hoard. I took some last-minute deep breaths telling myself to control my breathing, keep my form, and injure the enemy, not myself, as they began to spill through the city gates

Thanatos rushed forward to meet them with a blindingly fast swipe of his sword and echoing warcry; the rest of us followed.

The terrain had changed drastically since the start of the battle and was becoming increasingly more difficult to navigate. Blood had soaked through the sand and created cakes that cracked and caused you to sink further into the shifting grains than normal, meaning I had to monitor my foot placement more than I would have liked. My legs were tiring, it wouldn't be long before I was relying entirely on the rush of battle to keep me going.

Soraya's whip cracked against the stone wall and was followed by shouts trailing down its length. Sweeping up with my sword to remove its head, I dispatched the Corse in front of me, almost losing my footing completely as a sand cake crumbled beneath my boot, shifting my weight backwards, forcing me to pause and watch as the ground shook and flames exploded over the outside edges of the wall. I heard the screams of the Corse that had been close enough to get covered in the oil as it was poured and then lit by the arrows. No doubt some of the screams belonged to Kushyami soldiers that were too confident in their distance from the edges. The few Corse that remained inside the walls were a mix of severely decomposed and almost fresh. Soraya's whip lashed out at one of the fresh ones and caught it around the waist, she pulled it toward herself but instead of beheading it, she dragged it away from the others, none of them caring. I ran to catch up to Soraya and Thanatos as they dragged the creature away from its comrades, keeping my eye out for any that may follow, but none did.

Confusion clouded my mind. I'd thought they were attacking because I was there but they showed no interest in me in particular.

When I reached Soraya and Thanatos, Soraya was holding the Corse tightly in a chokehold as it raged against her, desperately trying to maim any part of her. Its body was whole but bloated and discolored from death, reeking already; the style of robe it wore marked it as Minoman.

"Right," Thanatos said as I skidded to a stop in the sand before them. "Let's do this. You've got him?"

Soraya nodded, tightening her grip just a little.

Thanatos stepped closer to the Captain and the creature, keeping enough distance to be out of clawing range. "Who sent you?" He asked, the dead man simply squirmed. "Who is the Necromancer?" Again, the creature only wrestled to get free of Soraya's grip. Thanatos sighed and raised his hands to either side of the man's head, collecting his black power in his palms and releasing it into the Corse's temples. Instantly, the creature stilled. "Who sent you?" he asked again. "Answer me."

"Necromancer," the creature rasped.

"What is their name? Answer." He demanded, compelling the creature to give us what we wanted.

"Necromancer." Was all it said, in a voice that lacked even the slightest of emotion.

"What are your orders? Answer."

"Get into the city."

"And after that?" The creature said nothing. "Answer damn you!" The Prince's anger surprised me; he almost seemed offended that they had dared attack this city.

"Get into the city." It repeated.

My eyes flicked to the gate, the soldiers there were readying themselves for the next wave, "Thanatos, quickly," I urged.

"Were you ordered to attack Isidia? Answer."

Soraya's head snapped up at that; her eyes flicked to me.

"Get into the city."

Thanatos groaned frustratedly. "What is going on here?!" He asked no one in particular, moving his hands away from the creature's temples and turning away in frustration; black mist still surrounding them. The Corse began to cough and choke, black mist identical to the Prince's began pouring out of its mouth and nose before it went limp in the captain's arms. She dropped him to the ground.

There was no time for me to register what had happened—in seconds, Thanatos, not even looking at the creature, had used his powers to pull its life from its body.

The Prince began storming back toward the battle, darkness surrounding him. "This is a waste of time."

The Captain and I shared a look and kept our distance. Looking back at the gate, I could see that the battle was almost over, the fires had wiped out a large portion of the Corse horde, piles of charred remains littered the ground outside the city gate. There had to be at least fifteen hundred Corse left, it would take us no time to dispose of them.

Just as we were preparing to get back into the fray, Thanatos motioned for us to stop, black mist still covering his body; it seemed to absorb what little light there was around us.

In the same moment, all the remaining Corse attempting to enter the city halted and fell to their knees, choking on the same black mist that now blocked out the Prince's form completely. I held my breath, witnessing for the first time what an Osirian was truly capable of.

My heart thundered at the thought of being on the other end of that power, having my life pulled from my chest, clawing at my throat as it betrayed me and let it happen, as the Corse before me were. It made me almost glad that this was not how my father had died.

Chaos flared on the walls and around us as Kushyami soldiers were affected by the Prince's power. I made to move closer to the black cloud surrounding Thanatos, to stop him before he killed them, but Soraya pulled me back shaking her head. She'd seen him like this before, I could see it haunting her gaze, so I allowed her to pull me back and stood with her.

I waited until the last Corse fell, black smoke pouring from its eyes and mouth as it collapsed to the ground. The cloud surrounding the Prince vanished and I darted to his side, my heart in my throat, fearing he'd used too much of his power. I grabbed his shoulders and stared into his eyes, holding in my gasp as I stared, not at the amber I was expecting, but solid black.

"Thanatos?" I could hear my heart pounding in my ears, my hands tightened on his shoulders. He blinked and when his eyes opened they were back to their usual whites, amber iris and black pupils.

"I'm fine," he whispered and pulled me into a hug, knocking the scarf off my hair in the process.

"What the pit is going on here?!" Soraya demanded.

The Prince and I pulled apart.

Soraya was staring at me, her eyes wide with surprise.

CHAPTER THIRTY FOUR
A TEMPORARY ESCAPE

I will never forget the looks on Soraya and Evalina's faces, the fear in their eyes. I'd promised Soraya that she'd never see me like that again, and now I had to add that to the ever-growing list of broken promises. What if it had been one of them? What if they'd gotten caught in the grips of my power? Had I had enough control to have stopped if that happened?

My mood only darkened further the closer we got to the palace, the one place I'd been avoiding. As we made our way through the town, I saw the damage and the true extent of what my power had done. Corse had gotten over the walls but they hadn't made it far before the guards had killed them or my powers had reached them, but also scattered between the rotted remains were the bodies of unharmed Kushyami. Seeing their limp forms made me want to rip myself to shreds. I didn't flinch as the soldiers scrambled away from me as I walked with the Princess and Soraya. I expected it, deserved it. I had just shown them that I was exactly what they feared.

Evalina had left her scarf down; her blue hair glinted in the early morning light as we trailed up the stairs of the palace, leaving the guards to gawk at her. I didn't know if she was aware how notorious she was in Carynthia. Everyone had heard stories of her and her mother, the mad Queen that had locked her daughter away. I certainly didn't have the heart to make her aware of it if she wasn't.

I watched Evalina from the corner of my eye as she took in the grandeur of the palace. Her eyes lingered on every colorful, alabaster wall as she studied the painted carvings that coated them from floor to ceiling. She chewed her cheek as she desperately tried to piece together the story it told of past Kings and Queens of Kushyam and other histories of Carynthia, still so eager for anything new and different to the life she'd known so far. It made me wish even more that we were visiting in better circumstances, that I could experience her quiet awe without the dread of what was to come.

A cool breeze blew through the open palace, blowing the floor-length sheer curtains in with it. I sucked it down, trying to calm the frantic beating of my heart. I stared at the light shining in through the windows to stop the tears that desperately wanted to flow.

We came to a halt before the King's three-level dias, each step leading to the top was plated with ornately detailed gold pieces that matched the gold of the statues that lined the walls, giving the room a warm glow as the dawn sun bounced off them. Keon sat atop his gold-plated throne, so high up I had to crane my neck to see him. He didn't wear his gold headdress, his black locs freely resting against his head. His face was grave and stressed as he watched us approach. Everyone bowed as he rose.

"What a night!" He projected. "It has been so long since my people have had to suffer through an attack. Though this one was not long, they still suffered." He slowly descended the dais, his gold sandals clacking against the bottoms of his feet as he went, the sound echoing through the room. "How surprised I was to find out that, as well as my dear Thanatos," I flinched with guilt at his open affection, "the Princess of Isidia was on the battlefield fighting for my people." He stopped before Evalina; she was still bent in a bow, her eyes focused on the floor. "I am grateful to you both." Despite his warm tone, my heart sank. *Protecting* his people? I had killed them. "However," he continued, his voice switching to a dark tone, "we were only attacked after you arrived in the city *and* you wanted to keep your presence hidden from me." He paced before us, the tension in the room growing. I felt the eyes of the guards lining the walls on me, their hands hovering over their weapons as if they expected me to turn on my friend at any moment. Evalina's breath was coming as quick and short as my own. "You can see how this would come across as suspicious, yes?" He came to a halt before me. "What are they and what do they want?" His voice was stern, but I caught the worried undertone, could see the sadness for me in his deep eyes and the betrayal that I rightly deserved. "Rise, Princess," he added to Evalina. "You have shown enough respect to us this night."

"I apologize, Keon, we didn't think we were followed," I said regretfully. We shouldn't have come here. I flicked my eyes to Evalina's, seeking permission to tell Keon everything; she gave a slight nod and I took a deep breath before continuing. I told Keon everything we knew of the Corse and their creator, the King's face growing graver with each word, the guards reaching for their weapons, waiting for the order to arrest us for our betrayal. I told my friend of our quest, how the Corse had first attacked Isidia and his gaze on the Princess softened with sympathy for a moment before it was replaced with confusion as I cleared up the details of how, when and where. Anger once again flaring as I mentioned the meeting of the elves.

"And us humans were left out, to fall prey to the Necromancer," Soraya interjected, her tone harsh and laced with betrayal, it hurt me more than she could ever know to hear that tone directed at me.

"Evalina and I both tried to have you included, but the Queen insisted we keep it between the elves as it's most likely a human responsible."

Chatter rose between the soldiers.

"How do we know it's not just the Isidians trying to start another war?" A soldier called from behind us.

"Our powers would not create creatures like the ones from last night and our magic is limited, anyone that tried to raise that many would have failed and become Neainn," Evalina defended.

"And the other Elven races?" The King asked, genuinely curious; the sternness gone from his voice.

"Impossible for Osirians, as it goes completely against their natural powers, the Carracallans are my own kin, and the Sillessians are not strong enough," Evalina further answered.

"I have a feeling, though, that these were not the same Corse we've faced before. All the ones we've met previously have been more alive, have had a sense of purpose. The Corse last night were … different. And my power worked on them, that has not been the case previously," I added.

"You think maybe there are two of these madmen?" King Keon suggested.

My gut sank. Evalina and I looked at each other, dread plastered on both our faces. Gods, I hoped he was wrong.

"If that is the case, then we must leave, Keon, as soon as possible. We cannot let this second Necromancer gain any more power." The desperation in my own voice caught me off guard. Keon and I shared a look, him catching the true reason for my stress.

"I will not force you to stay. You return to Osiria?" I nodded. "Then I will have camels prepared and sent to the inn, they will travel faster in the desert. We will let your horses rest and send them up with the next delivery of goods." The King clapped a hand on my shoulder and we pressed our foreheads together. "Travel well my brother."

"Keon, I—" I began but was silenced by the King with a squeeze of my shoulder. "It was a battle, Thanatos, they would have died fighting for their city either way. Do not let it haunt you." He turned to the Princess and held out his hand, she took it. "I wish the Father's blessings on you, that you may keep your home safe as you have kept mine. Thank you, I hope that next time you come to Kushyam you can enjoy it the way it should be enjoyed."

She smiled at the King and bowed once more before we were led out of the palace by the guards. Soraya staying back to inform the king of the details of the battle. I caught her eye as we exited, there was concern but also fear in them.

We were escorted back to Glik's. I kept my eyes focused on the ground before me, not wanting to look up and see the mess I'd created. I was tired, both from using my magic and from fighting. My shoulders ached, my head pounded, and my heart hadn't stopped beating frantically since Soraya had woken me up only a few hours ago. I was ready to collapse into bed, but as we got to the inn I noticed Evalina glance my way and shudder before quickly looking away again. I almost broke right there on the street.

The guards that led us back to the inn left after Evalina had thanked them and headed toward the city gates to begin removing the corpses. They would be buried in mass graves outside the city, left for the desert animals to pick at until there was nothing left but bones.

Glik hurried out of his office to meet us as we entered, his eyes fixed on me. I could already feel the wetness of tears resting in the corners of my eyes. He flicked his hand motioning for Evalina to go upstairs. Part of me wished she would stay, that she'd let her stubbornness take over, but she followed his instruction and made her way up the stairs as Glik led me into his back office.

He sat me down in an armchair made for someone his height, my legs stretched out almost flat before me. Already steaming on his desk were two cups of tea and tankard of ale. My hands twitched for the tankard but the goblin reached for the tea and brought it to me. The worry in his large eyes sickened me, how could he be worried for me? I was a monster. He handed me the tea and I took a little comfort in the fact that he didn't flinch away or snatch his hand back.

Glik sighed. "Master Thanatos, try not to stress yourself."

"Glik," I croaked, "I killed people, innocent people." My voice cracked and with it tears fell.

"Is anyone really innocent?" The goblin said, offering a sad smile. "What did the King say?" He asked after I didn't respond.

"He said they would have died either way," I breathed. "But they wouldn't have. If I had better control, they would have lived." The guilt had settled itself somewhere deep in my shoulders. I wanted to crumple beneath it and let it eat away at me until there was nothing left. There was a reason Dark Elves didn't use their powers and this was it. We had no control, we didn't know the limits to learn it and to learn the limits was not worth it, it would never be worth it. "Soraya was with me, she saw everything, and Evalina …" I couldn't finish, sobs threatened to take over.

Glik sipped his tea, deep in thought. "Soraya will be fine. She's a big girl now and she deals with tougher brutes than you almost every day." As he said it, my mind wandered to the day I first met Soraya. She'd been tiny, no older than six or eight and too skinny. Her tightly coiled hair had been matted from lack of care and her arm had already been cut off to the elbow, the wound scabbed and festering. She'd tried to pickpocket me; she was so desperate for food and so out of touch with the world that she had no idea how dangerous I could be. I caught her, healed her arm and did my best to brush her hair through. There was no way I was going to let that brave little girl die or be maltreated further. I'd done my best to organize care for her, I couldn't stay in the town forever, but when I returned next she'd lost the remainder of her arm and her hair had been all but ripped out by the people that caught her stealing. She'd lived on the streets so long that she didn't understand what it was to have a place to live and food to eat that she didn't need to steal. That was the last time I'd used my powers.

She'd taken me, at my request, to the stall who'd ordered her punishment and when I'd seen their faces, their pride in what they'd done, I'd killed them all. I would have killed the whole city had Soraya not stood in my way and snapped me out of it. That's what I'd seen today, as my powers had taken hold again, the trembling starving girl with the matted hair, not the strong captain that she's become.

"And the Princess," Glik continued, pulling me from my memories, "you underestimate her and how much she can handle."

"It's not about what she can handle, it's what she's had to handle and she doesn't deserve to have to deal with this." I gestured to myself and Glik looked as if he were about to leap over the desk and slap me.

"You did what you had to, and she will understand. Think how many live because of you. Do you think the few who died are worth more than the many that survived?" I silently shook my head. "Right. Now I want you to buck up and go and talk to her. She has also been through a battle. You need each other right now."

"I should seek out Soraya—"

Glik held up a hand to stop me. "I will check on her, though I can assure you she is fine."

"Thank you, Glik."

The goblin nodded and I rose from the armchair, placing the teacup on the saucer beside the tankard, my fingers still itching for the handle but I ignored it.

As I climbed the stairs to Evalina's room, I prepared what I wanted to say, how I was to say it. But as I stood before the door my mind emptied until all that was left was her terrified face and the image of her shuddering after looking at me. Just do it, I told myself.

I knocked gently after stealing myself, in case she was asleep, and moments later the door swung open. She was wrapped only in a sheet, her hair backlit by the window behind her making it look as if she had a blue aura surrounding her. I began to back away, looking toward my room rather than gawking at her.

"It's fine," she said quickly. "You've seen me in a worse state of undress." She stepped aside to let me enter.

I did my best to keep my face neutral, though, from her concerned expression, knew I was failing. She motioned for me to sit on the bed and I did, waiting to speak until she sat across from me. "I wanted to apologize," I croaked, again holding in emotion.

"For what?" She asked, confused.

I fidgeted, wishing I'd had a drink to calm my nerves before coming up here. "Using my powers like that … I don't—I mean, usually I have more control. I didn't mean to frighten you." I shifted my gaze to the window, not wanting to see her reaction, not trusting it to be an accepting one.

She reached over and placed a hand on my cheek pulling my face to look at her. "You don't need to apologize for anything except putting yourself in danger." I felt my expresion soften, the tightness in my shoulders relax as she reached her other hand up to cup the other cheek. "You saved a land that you love, people that you love. How could you need to apologize for that?"

"Your father—"

"My father was burnt to death," she interrupted. "You and what happened last night had nothing to do with it."

"Thank you," I said gently, leaning into her hands. "For understanding."

She smiled and brushed a tear from my cheek with her thumb. "We've been through so much together already, it would be stupid of us to assume the other wouldn't."

Guilt once again struck me, and it must have shown on my face because Evalina's smile faltered, only for a moment but it was enough. "We should rest." I said, gently gripping her wrists to remove them from my face. "Glik will come to us when the camels arrive."

Evalina held fast. "Stay here," she blurted, her face turning slightly pink. "With me." She added, as if she felt I needed the clarification. I hated that she thought I did.

I nodded and pulled her hands lightly away from my face, kissing each palm before releasing her wrists and moving to lay my head on the pillow. My heart was thundering in my chest again, this time for different reasons. She joined me at the other end of the bed and lay across from me, her green eyes staring into mine. I fought not to reach across for her, to pull her toward me. It was all I wanted to do in that moment; but then her eyes fluttered and she was asleep, her tired mind, I hoped, offering her a temporary escape from the troubling times erupting around us.

CHAPTER THIRTY FIVE
SANCTUARY

The meeting room was tense, as was everyone in it. Corse attacks had increased significantly and we'd already lost people to battle, not many but enough.

At the table sat the Carracallans, Islina, the Council, and I. We were meant to be speaking of battle but it had turned into the Council complaining about the arrival of the Carracallan troops and their camps within the castle grounds.

"Our own are out in the fields while the Carracallans camp safely within our walls and wards." The Councilman shook his head. "Doesn't seem right at all."

"The Carracallans did not have to come here, Councilman Brooks, they offered to help us. They are our guests and will be treated as such," Islina said calmly.

"While I understand the sentiment, and of course am grateful for their assistance, think of how it looks to our people," Brooks continued.

"*Our* people haven't said anything about it," I cut in, sick of his bullshit. "We're lucky to have them here to help us, and our people know that. You seem to be the only ones seeing an issue."

"The Carracallans stay where they are. That's an order and I'll hear no more about it," Islina decreed curtly. "Now on to the true purpose of this meeting. Peverell, if you'd please."

Evalina's thin uncle nodded and pulled a detailed map of Isidia onto the table before us. "The Corse we've dealt with so far have come from the north, quite centrally, so we can't pinpoint where they could be coming from or where their real target is. Given the incident at the farm, I would say they'll target the palace first, which means they'll most likely come down in a south-westerly direction." He pointed at the map with a thin cane. "This general area," he said circling the spot on the map, "is mainly made up of farmland—wheat fields mostly. There's not much cover but the land is flat. I propose this area be the battle ground. If they get further south, the land becomes hilly and we're at risk of, quite literally, facing an uphill battle."

"What about cover?" Adalric asked, his brow creased as he looked over the map.

"The best there is out there would be buildings and the wheat fields. We just have to get there before the Corse and take what we can," I said.

"Or get there early and build battlements," Bellona chimed in from the window where she was smoking her pipe.

Adalric shook his head. "I wouldn't want to waste the resources, any spare wood is going to the villages and towns to board up and protect the people left."

"Is it a waste if it's to protect the armies fighting against the Corse?" Islina questioned.

"I would rather it be used to protect civilians, but it's up to you, Your Majesty," Adalric conceded.

"Perhaps we could create one designated area for civilians, somewhere they can go and shelter together incase of attack. They would require much less of the resources that way," I suggested.

"And where do you propose this sanctuary be?" Councilman Frind asked.

I thought it over, my mind running through buildings in the city that could be big enough to house everyone—taverns, inns, some of the larger houses of rich families, none of them seemed large enough in my mind. "The temple," I said. "It's the only place large enough and, if the situation gets really dire, they can retreat into the catacombs."

"The catacombs?" Bellona said quizzically.

"The catacombs lead to old goblin tunnels that run under the whole city," I said.

"Captain Norward! This is not something you tell people from other Kingdoms," Councilman Wynleth cut in.

"They are the future Queen's family, I doubt very much that they're looking to attack us anytime soon," I said dismissively.

"You can never know in times such as these," Brooks said.

"You realize we're right here, yes?" Bellona asked from the window, smoke clouding her face, her black eyes locked onto the Councilmen.

"I would never attack a Queendom run by my own family," Darius stated firmly, joining his sister in staring down the council members.

"I'm in agreement with Captain Norward," Islina said. "The temple can easily be refitted as a refuge for the people left behind in the towns and villages. A quarter of our current building materials should be sufficient."

"Your Majesty—" Wynleth interjected but was silenced by the Queen's raised hand.

"No. This is decided by me," she said and sat back in her chair, waving a hand for Adalric to continue the meeting.

"All right, the temple will be refitted using one quarter of available supplies," he said as he noted it down. "The rest will be used to build battlements at the farms. We'll have to stock up and ship out pretty soon, going off the recent rise in attacks. Now, do we keep the recruits here and training, or send them out?"

"They still need more training. They'd be virtually useless out there," I said bluntly.

"My crews can go," King Darius said.

"And mine, if needed," Bellona added.

Adalric thought it over for a moment, his eyes darting across the map and meeting once with Islina's. "Darius's crews should be enough for now. I want to save Bellona's for when we're really desperate."

Bellona's crews were known for their skill and unpredictability in battle. After her brother had died, Bellona had taken his mission for her own. Her crews were so used to fighting pirates and outlaws that they had almost become them themselves.

The doors to the Council room burst open, two of my scouts rushing in breathless. They didn't stop to bow or honor the people within the room, just came to a stop by my side.

"Corse, a whole army, north of the border," one of them huffed.

"How close?" I asked, my heart rate increasing rapidly with each second.

"Three days—if that—before they reach it," the other struggled to breathe out.

"We do this now, then," Adalric ordered, and the room became a flurry of movement.

The Glenons leapt into action; the Council encompassed the Queen, whispering desperately into her ear about parts of the plan they didn't agree with. Bellona snuffed her pipe and went to my Queen's rescue, practically pouring ash on them to get them away. And I stood stunned for a long moment.

War had come to Isidia.

The last time this had happened, Islina had lost her whole family. Her eyes met mine across the table as Bellona began to escort her out of the room—they were wide and fearful. Her hands clasped her gown so tightly I thought it a miracle the fabric didn't tear. I wanted to go to her, to comfort her, but Bellona shook her head as she caught my eye. I nodded, catching her meaning.

I needed to be with my soldiers now, they needed to hear the orders from me, not one of Evalina's uncles or her grandfather, even though no one would think that odd. I was their Captain. It was my duty to break the news that they would be facing battle, that they may not return to their homes and families.

I let out a long breath before squaring my shoulders and storming out to the Isidian camp.

CHAPTER THIRTY SIX
A SHADOW OF A DOUBT

I woke in the late afternoon to the Prince gazing at me, his face soft and relaxed in the afternoon heat. I could feel the damp from my sweat all over me, especially between my breasts and the backs of my knees. I yawned and stretched, the muscles I'd been healing before the Prince had come into my room felt great, but the ones I'd missed burnt with each movement.

The Prince chuckled. "Slept well did we?" he asked.

"We did," I replied before yawning deeply once again. "Though not enough it seems."

"You could always sleep more, Glik hasn't been round yet."

I shook my head, stifling yet another yawn. "I'd like to have food before we go and maybe wash. How are you feeling?" I asked, turning to face him.

"Better," he replied, plucking a stray hair from my face. "And you?"

I thought for a moment. "Sore and sweaty."

He laughed. "That will change soon. When we enter Osiria you'll be wishing for Kushyami sun! I can't believe we'll be home so soon, it feels like a lifetime since I've been back."

"A lot has happened, it's been a very eventful first outing," I joked, trying to keep the moment light.

Despite my efforts, Thanatos' face fell. "I'm sorry about yesterday. I didn't want to seem too forward and there's things I have to tell you—" He was speaking so fast his chest was heaving to keep up, but his sentences were scattered nonsense.

I placed my fingers over his mouth to quiet him. "It's all right. Whatever it is, it can wait." I sensed that this was not the case, that it was something I should know, but I didn't want to force it—not if he wasn't ready. "Let's just enjoy the calm while we have it."

He settled but the tension lingered between us. I wanted to know, Mother and Father did I want to know, but it wasn't worth the stress.

"Just promise me"—he took a deep breath—"promise me you won't be mad when you find out."

"Whatever it is, I promise I won't be mad." I could feel the skepticism pouring off him and didn't blame him, he knew me well enough now to know that I'm quick to anger. "So what's the deal with Soraya?" I asked, changing the subject.

"Jealous are we?" Thanatos quipped, raising his arms and resting his hands behind his head.

I jabbed him in the ribs. "No, just curious."

"She's been the Captain of Keons' personal guard for years. She was an urchin when I first met her; tried to steal from me." He chuckled at the memory. "Her parents had worked in the mines, they died in a collapse when she was a baby, and then her grandmother passed when she was a child, leaving her with nothing. The arm she lost because of stealing. The Kushyami don't believe in completely maiming thieves, they will cut off one hand and work their way up that same arm, rather than cut off the other. I remember when I first met her, someone made the remark that, even with one hand, she'd do good in a paramour house when she got older. I couldn't let that happen to that fierce, little thief, who was so hungry she had the guts to rob an Osirian. So I pulled some strings and had her trained by Kushyam's best fighter. The rest she did on her own." The Prince laughed at my expression. I could tell by his own that there was more to his story with the Captain, but left it for him to tell me at a later time. "Sorry, does that not fit my narrative?"

"How could the world have gotten you so wrong?"

His eyes softened. "People believe what they want to believe. I could do all the good in the world and everyone would still just see me as a Dark-Elf hanging around other dregs, there's nothing to be done about it. The Mother sullied our image when she cursed us with this power." My heart ached for Thanatos, to be treated so harshly for something he had no control over, that his people had no control over.

"We have the treaty now. Once word spreads about that, maybe the view of Osirians will change."

He smiled. "Thank you for thinking that," he whispered and gently kissed my cheek. As he pulled away, our eyes locked and something stirred within me. I was just about to grab his face, to plant my lips on his and straddle his hips, when a knock echoed through the room. I pursed my lips to hold myself back from yelling at who was at the door, from telling them to leave—or at least give us another hour.

Thanatos climbed out of bed and answered the door.

"Oh, Prince Thanatos!" Came a surprised female voice. "I was expecting the Princess, I must have gotten the wrong room. The camels from the King are here, Your Highness. I shall go wake the Princess."

"No need, this is her room. Thank you, we'll be down soon. Could breakfast be prepared please?"

"Of course!" The servant girl rushed away, most likely headed straight for the kitchen to gossip.

"You could have said you'd go wake me." I said as Thanatos closed the door. "Now the whole city will be spreading rumors."

"Does it matter if there's no truth to them?"

"Is there not?"

The Prince paused.

I paused.

We stood in silence for a long moment, staring at each other.

I cleared my throat and rose from the bed. "I'm going to bathe, I'll meet you downstairs after." I gently nudged my way past him to get to the door. He grabbed my hand.

"Evalina ..."

I smiled at him. "We'll talk about it later," I said and left him in the doorway, not even thinking about the fact that I was only wrapped in a sheet as I walked through the inn to the bathing room.

I dressed in the clothes Ambrosia had insisted I get, light-coloured, thin, flowing pants and top with long loose sleeves. I had a scarf, too, to wrap around my head and mouth to stop sand from getting in; for now, I draped it over my shoulders. Since everyone in the city knew who I was, anyway, there was no point hiding my hair.

I made my way downstairs and found the Prince sitting at a table by a window, two plates of breakfast in front of him. I took a deep breath and made my way over to join him. He was lost in thought, gazing out the window as if it could give him answers to whatever questions he asked.

"You all right?" I asked as I sat down across from him.

He snapped out of his trance and smiled at me. "Fine. I like seeing your hair out."

I ran my hand down my long braid. "Well, everyone knows who I am now anyway, there's no point trying to hide it." I thought for a moment. "I should write to my family, let them know my identity's been exposed and inform them of the battle."

Thanatos waved down the goblin and requested a piece of parchment and writing materials so I could write as I ate.

King Adalric,

Prince Thanatos and I are this morning leaving Kushyam. We're on the last leg to Osiria and from there will continue on to Minoma.

While in Kushyam, we experienced a siege, an army of Corse attempted to take the city—for what reason, we do not know. The army was dispatched speedily, thanks to the Prince.

These Corse were not like the ones we have faced previously, leading us to believe there may be a second Necromancer, one not as skilled as the original.

I would also report that my identity is no longer hidden. This may make a bigger target of us but, I assure you, we will be fine.

Thank you for the update on mother, I pray she is still well, as well as the rest of you.

Thank you Grandfather, I hope to see you all soon.

There was so much more I wanted to write, wanted to ask, but we didn't have the time. I gave the letter to Glik who assured me it would be sent by the fastest raven he owned, and left the city with the Prince on camelback.

Riding a camel was a different experience to riding a horse. Riding a horse, you bop along with their movements, with camels, you sway. It took me three nauseating hours to get used to it and once I was feeling a little more confident in the saddle the Prince leaned over to me.

"Lets speed up," he said with a playful grin. "I'll race you to the fourth dune!" He called, already speeding ahead.

"Hey!" I called after him, gently nudging my camel with my heels, signaling for it to increase its speed.

We caught up quickly; our camels were neck and neck as they pounded through the sand. I lost count of how many dunes we'd crossed but kept racing, enjoying the thrill of the race and the comfort of the saddle over a horse's. The camels trekked up a particularly large dune, every now and then sliding down a small ways before regaining their footing and pushing on up the sand hill.

The camels stopped when we reached the top, huffing from exertion. I gave my camel a pat on the head and scratch behind the ear, wishing I knew it's name so I could properly thank it. We'd been in such a rush to get out of the city that we hadn't even been introduced to the poor creatures before we climbed on their backs and instructed them to walk.

My eyes drifted up from my camel's large head to the horizon and my body froze, despite the raging heat of the desert.

Before me, hovering in the sky above the horizon, sat thick, black clouds and a sinister mountain range cutting through the top quarter of the continent. Even from this distance, I could see the flashes of lightning on the volcanic side, bright blasts of white light shooting through the black angry clouds.

Part of me began to panic. It was one thing to think of Osiria and another to physically see it. I was not surprised in the slightest that most avoided the land; even from a great distance it looked threatening and dangerous, as if the very ground itself could somehow kill you.

I told myself that I'd known, I'd known this whole time that I would end up here, almost at the doorstep, but it still felt like a punch to the gut. Had I truly gotten over my prejudice toward the Osirian people or was it just the Prince?

How would they treat me? I felt almost insulted on their behalf that I'd even considered stepping foot on their land. I'd heard the way people spoke of the Prince, even in Kushyam; 'Deathbringer, scoundrel, sot.' I wondered what the common folk had to deal with.

Though, when I thought about it, I realized that we hadn't seen any other Osirians on the road. Did none of them travel because of the preconceptions of others? I was once again hit with a wash of guilt, the insults and slurs I'd used in the past circled my mind, haunting me.

"What do you think?" Thanatos asked me.

I jumped, having not noticed he was nearby. "I'm very far from home," I joked.

"It is a bit … foreboding, but you'll love the people," he offered with a smile his voice, laced with excitement.

But … would they love me?

We rode well into the night, led by the moon. The sleep we'd had in the afternoon and the thrill of seeing the next stop in our journey had kept us going longer than I thought we would after the battle.

The moon was mid-sky before we stopped to set up our tent, the Prince throwing one of the camel's blankets over the top to block out the morning sun.

"It would be better for us to travel at night and sleep during the day, to avoid the heat," Thanatos said.

I nodded in agreement, taking a large bite of the green melon he'd handed me. It was warm from being in the pack on the side of his camel all day, but the moisture was well welcome.

The King had kindly given us water skins almost the same size as the camels' humps, so we were not lacking, but the air was so hot and dry that my lips were still cracked. I rubbed the melon along them sighing with relief before taking another large bite.

"Dry lips?" The Prince asked. "Try this." He rummaged through his pack and tossed me a small, wooden box filled with a thick salve. "Smear it on your lips, it stops them cracking in the heat."

"Thanks." I tucked the box away in a pocket in my pants. "How far off are we from Ravenna?"

"I'd say about four days, but we'll be in Osiria in two."

I nodded, staring at the flesh of my fruit.

"Are you worried?" He asked.

"A little," I confessed. "I'm sure you can understand why."

He leant forward and rested a hand on my knee. "Of course I can, but it'll be fine; you'll see." He grinned. "How are you finding the heat?"

"It's horrid but not too bad, I'm sure it'll be worse closer to the volcanoes," I joked.

"Well, I managed to get this back." Thanatos pulled out my small ice Hellebore brooch. "I thought you could use it more than the horse, though I'm sure she appreciated it."

I took it from him and attached it to my shirt, instantly feeling cooler. "Thank you, I do feel bad for Faenor though."

"I'm sure she'll be fine, the Kushyami will look after her."

I nodded, fiddling with the brooch.

I was finding it hard to look Thanatos in the eye. We'd both apologized for recent transgressions, but unspoken feelings still hung between us. I wanted to discuss it before we were in a situation that wasn't just the two of us again but I couldn't get the words to form in my mind, let alone tumble out of my mouth.

We fell into an awkward silence, both of us quietly eating our fruit.

I couldn't take the silence anymore and asked the first question that popped into my head. "Will you tell me about your parents?"

He seemed confused but nodded while trying to quickly swallow a mouthful of nectarine. "My father, King Methuzelah, was an only child and he still acts like it," Thanatos said with a smile. "He's a formidable warrior but really a child at heart, he grew up on stories of your grandfather, the Great Sea Adventurer, so expect that to be a huge topic of conversation. My mother, Omisha, is a mother through and through. She was brought up in an orphanage run by the Phoenix Priestesses, strong worshippers of the Mother." His tone darkened, "She's not a big supporter of humans having magic, or humans in general, thanks to the teachings of the Priestesses. So expect that to be a topic of conversation as well."

"You do not agree with her beliefs?"

"Father, no! I've been around humans, I've seen their magic for what it is and it's nothing compared to what we can do. They can barely enchant things, let alone use it for war. The Priestesses are convinced one day the humans will rise up against elves and use magic to destroy us."

"Is that not what the Necromancer is doing?"

"I guess, we'll have to wait and see. So far he seems to be on some kind of revenge mission."

"Against elves."

Thanatos took a deep breath. "Only Isidian—not that that means anything yet," Thanatos defended. "But we can't just assume that he's trying to kill us all, and he's also attacked humans now."

"If that was the same Necromancer," I interjected.

"I feel like this is turning into an argument." Thanatos said warily, holding eye contact with me.

"I–I just don't know." I shrugged. "I haven't been around humans as much as you, so I'm almost inclined to agree with your mother's views." I held my hands up defensively at the Prince's scowl. "Only because that's how the situation is playing out. I'd be more than happy to be proven wrong."

Thanatos calmed with a grunt.

"I am surprised, though, that you take their side so wholeheartedly, given how they treat you."

"There are good ones, and it's always the ones you least expect," he said.

"I hope you can show me that, then, change my mind for the better," I said with a smile, before a yawn escaped. The first light of dawn had begun to pierce the night sky.

"We should probably turn in for the day," Thanatos said after catching my yawn. "I'll feed the camels our leftover fruit, it'll be spoiled by noon."

I nodded my agreement and yawned once again as he left the tent, arms full of half eaten fruit. I layed down as the tent flaps closed behind him, my eyes closing not long after.

The smell of smoke filled my nostrils and panic rose in my chest, The baby.
What baby?
I have to find the baby.
I ran down the dark hallway, the walls lined with gold drapings, the floor black and white marble.
It was all unfamiliar to me and yet I knew where I was going, down the hall, to the left and then the second room on the right. The smell of smoke hadn't quite made it to this room yet, this room of white; white curtains, a white rocking chair, a white crib.
Crib. I darted to the side and peered over the edge. No baby lay inside, resting while the world was in chaos.
My blood rushed through my veins.
Where? Where is the baby?
I darted around the room, checking behind curtains and in the wardrobe. A cry cut through the pulsing of blood in my ears; it sounded distant but desperate.
I followed the cry, running through the manor as smoke began to fill it. I started coughing, my eyes watering at the assault.
The crying grew louder the closer I got to the drawing room, relief that I was close to her flooded me. I would hold her soon, comfort her and soothe her crying, take her away from this place and be safe.
The crying suddenly stopped and so did my heart.
I skidded into the room, dark figures stood around the edges but I ignored them, I focused on the small shape in the middle of the floor.
Tears already streamed down my face as I took the last few clumsy steps until I too crumpled to the floor. I picked her up, already knowing she was dead and held her to my chest, her blood warm on my hands, her head falling backward, exposing the gaping wound on her neck. There was so much for such a tiny body.
I barely flinched as the cool blade slid across my throat, my blood now mixing with that of my daughters.
I only tried to scream once the flames engulfed us, but nothing came out, I just choked on my own blood.

I bolted up in my bed roll, tears streaking my face. My heart pounded and the burn mark on my shoulder throbbed painfully. Thanatos was still sleeping peacefully across the tent, the mid-morning sun casting a yellow glow through the canvas. I tried to take a few deep breaths and calm myself but the tears kept falling, the sobs heaving through me. I crawled across to the Prince and tried to get close to him without waking him up but failed.

"What's wrong? What happened?" He asked urgently as he wrapped his arms around me and pulled me in close, causing me to cry even harder.

It took me a long while of being comforted by Thanatos before I was calm enough to retell the nightmare I'd had.

"I'm sorry," he soothed. "I'm so sorry you had to see that." He stroked my hair and pulled me tighter into himself.

"I didn't just see it … I felt it." I put my hand to my throat, checking for the sixth time that it was still intact.

Flashes of the dream streamed past my vision and I broke down again. Thanatos held me even tighter as I sobbed, my mind clouded with visions of the corpse of the baby girl. She couldn't have been more than a few years old, still an infant in elven years.

My sweat no longer felt cool, it felt hot and sticky like blood. I pushed the Prince away from me and grabbed my thin blanket and began scrubbing at myself, trying to get rid of the wet feeling. I scrubbed until my skin was raw, but the sweat kept coming back. It was too hot in the tent but I knew it would be even hotter out of it.

"Evalina, stop," Thanatos said gently.

I ignored him and continued my scrubbing.

"Evalina … Evalina, stop!" He grabbed my shoulders. "Stop," he said once again, tears now shining in his eyes. He stared pleadingly into mine. "I can help you if you want. I can make the memory go away."

"How?" I croaked between gasps.

"I … I can compel them away, if you want." A tear slid down his cheek. I was beginning to realize how much he hated using his powers, that he only used them when the situation really called for it. I thought about it for a moment. I'd never been compelled before, it was difficult for races other than Dark-Elves to compel other elves, they seemed to have a knack for it.

I slowly shook my head.

"Are you sure?" Thanatos asked, squeezing my shoulders.

I nodded.

He pulled me into another tight hug. I felt his tear pattering on the top of my head. "I'm so sorry. I'm sorry you have to deal with this. I wish it were me."

I gave him a squeeze. "Thank you, but I need to remember this, it must have something to do with the wraith." I took a deep breath and concentrated on calming my mind. Taking deep breaths and savoring my close proximity to Thanatos. "I'm sorry I upset you."

"No, don't be sorry about that. I wish there was something more I could do."

I nuzzled my face into his chest, taking one more deep breath before releasing him. "Can we keep moving? I know we haven't been resting long, but … I want to get out of this place."

He leant down and planted a kiss on my cheek. "Of course. I'll get the camels ready, you take your time."

I nodded and proceeded to fold up the blankets, lost in thought, thinking of the background details of the dream and avoiding the death.

The layout of the manor had seemed almost familiar. I tried to picture the dark figures that had surrounded the room but no defining features stood out to me. Who had they been? Why and how could they kill a mother and child? What did this all mean with the rest of my dreams?

By the time Thanatos came to pack up the tent, I had mindlessly folded all the bedding and piled it by the flaps ready to be packed onto the camels. We left not long after, speeding through the desert as fast as the camels would take us.

After the first day of riding them I was feeling more confident and less nauseous swaying on the hump of mine. She was a sweet old girl, but she didn't much care for her companion and every now and then would give her a nip on her hind, making her dash a little bit further ahead and causing Thanatos to shout in surprise each time. I didn't know if the camel could sense my dark mood but she was successfully pulling me out of it, even if she wasn't trying to.

As the day went on, Osiria grew closer and closer until the mountain range that divided it from the rest of Carynthia was looming over us. I wasn't sure if it was residual feelings from my nightmare or if the dread was coming from being so close to a land that I had feared for so long.

It wasn't long into the day before my eyelids started drooping and the lack of sleep from the morning hit me like a war hammer. I struggled to keep hold of my reins, to keep myself upright in my saddle. I could see the Prince struggling, too. Every now and then he would sway a little too far to the side and jolt upright, shaking his head as if it could expel the tiredness. I knew that we should have stopped, should have rested longer, but I couldn't suggest it. I wanted to be out of this desert, as if leaving the space I'd had it would somehow distance me from the horrible dream.

So, we pushed on, heads lolling and eyes barely open until we reached the base of the mountain range and the mouth of a huge cave.

The entrance to Osiria.

CHAPTER THIRTY SEVEN
STOPPED COLD

Thanatos seemed to be filled with new energy as we dismounted the camels and set up the tent. Too tired for either of us to cook, we had stale bread and dried meat for dinner. The ground beneath us was, thank the Mother and Father, solid. I prayed that it would be a while before we once again had to trek through the desert, my memory of the exotic land now tainted.

"We'll be at a village in one more day's time, we can bathe and eat a good meal there," he said, tearing off a bite of his dried venison, his eyes bright. "You'll want to switch flowers." He added nodding toward the Hellebore brooch pinned to my scarf. "We'll start feeling the cold tonight and as we travel through Ajal tunnel. Once we're in the snowfields, we'll have to look out for Frost Trolls and other monsters," he added nonchalantly.

I nodded, pushing all thoughts of monsters out of my head—being in the tunnel would be stressful enough without that added worry—and dug through my bag for the little black and white box the Prince had given me a month ago ... or was it only a few weeks? I had no idea, my sense of time was completely lost. I opened the small box and delicately placed the icy Hellebore brooch in, the temperature around me barely shifting. I admired the obsidian Fire Lily for a moment before plucking it from the box and setting it next to my bedroll. The ends of the small carved petals were so thin they were almost translucent.

I smiled at the small flower, thinking back to when Thanatos and I had first met, how rude we'd been to each other, and where we were now. What you'd call us, I didn't know, but it was definitely something more than friends.

"What is it?" Thanatos asked, noticing my smile.

"Nothing," I said. "I was just thinking about how much of an asshole you were when we met."

He laughed. "I'll have to be one more often if it makes you smile like that," he jested. "And you weren't exactly the regal, well-mannered Princess I was promised."

"Promised?"

221

"On your ball invite," he added quickly. "It said something along the lines of *'You are cordially invited to celebrate the coming of age of Isidia's most regal Princess, Evalina Elsrine Glenon.'*" I had to hide a blush as he recited the invite, my insides fluttering at the sound of my whole name on his lips. "Well mannered was implied, I feel, with regal."

"Are you saying I'm not regal?" I poked.

"Regal when you want to be, perhaps."

I feigned shock, pressing my hand to my heart.

"How are you feeling tonight?"

I wasn't ready for the question and took a moment to search my feelings. Anxious was at the top of my list, confused, frightened, tired.

"Fine," I said with a smile. Thanatos narrowed his eyes at me skeptically. "I'm fine, really I am," I tried. "But … would it be all right … if I slept with you tonight?"

"You can sleep with me any night." The color drained from his face. "I mean if you need to, you know, if you feel it would help."

I laughed at his awkwardness and shifted on to his bedroll, breathing in his comforting scent; would everyone in Osiria smell like him? I hoped not.

I laid down and patted the space next to me which he willingly took. "Are you excited to be home?"

"More than you could believe," he said truthfully. I enjoyed the Prince's truthfulness. "I can't wait to show you everything. We don't get many outsiders in Osiria, mainly orcs and a few daring humans—you may be swarmed in the villages."

I felt suddenly self-conscious, I was sure to stick out like a sore thumb in the Osirian villages purely as a High-Elf. I hoped the news of the treaty would be good news.

"We should get to sleep. So we can actually ride the camels tomorrow," I joked.

Thanatos nodded and yawned.

We lay facing each other but it wasn't long before Thanatos fell asleep.

I gazed at his sleeping face, his eyes twitching and shifting behind his eyelids. I wondered what he was dreaming about, if anything. Were they pleasant dreams? Did he dream of home now that we were on the border? Did he dream of me? My eyes fluttered closed as I continued with my speculations, imagining Thanatos' dreams and what they could consist of before slipping into my own dream of him.

The next morning was a rush and flurry of movements. Thanatos had packed the whole campsite up before I'd had a chance fully to wake and we were up on our camels and making our way up through the tunnel—which was more of a giant, enclosed staircase than an actual tunnel—without pausing to eat anything.

My stomach growled and I yawned deeply as the tunnel grew darker and darker around us, the end nowhere in sight. My levels of anxiety were slowly rising the longer we were climbing, the footsteps of the camels echoing around us, being dragged further through the tunnel by the cold wind from the Osirian end. I told myself it wouldn't be for long, we would be out soon, but it didn't stop the dread from rising within me.

There was a flash ahead of me and, for a moment, I was blinded by the new light source, until my eyes adjusted and I spotted a flame glowing above Thanatos' head turning his hair orange.

The light transformed the cave. Once dark and foreboding, it now glittered gold around me, the glow from the torch reflecting off shining particles on the cave walls. It didn't change the level of my discomfort, but it certainly made me feel less anxious to be able to see the walls and ceiling and know that they're not closing in around me.

We were silent for most of the morning, with only the camels and the whistling wind making any noise. I didn't know if I needed to be, but I was fearful of waking strange creatures that maybe slumbering nearby. Trolls tended to like ambushing people in caves; it was best to be quiet and let them sleep.

Light shone at the top of the tunnel after what could have been a few days, but I knew was only a few hours; it was hard to tell time when our only light source for most of the journey was artificial.

Thanatos slowed to walk beside me. "How are you doing?" He asked, not hiding the beaming smile on his face.

"I'm fine, eager to be free of this." I gestured around us. "But, thankful for this." I flicked the Fire lily brooch; I had been wearing it since the middle of the night before after waking up shivering from the cold.

"I'm happy you're wearing it and not the camel," he joked.

"She will be safe in the cold right?"

"Yes, she'll be fine. Camels are very resilient." He leaned forward and gave his a scratch on the head. "Once we get through the cave, it'll be another two days to Ravennna, but we'll be on a path, so we can switch to horses and possibly cut down that time. We'll have to keep time in villages to a minimum." He said it like it would be a hard thing, but whether it would be hard for him or the villagers was yet to be seen.

Blinding light flared as we exited the cave, the bright sun bouncing off the pure white snow on the ground.

Snow.

I resisted the urge to collapse into it or scoop it up and throw it in the air above me, but the temptation was there. The snow was freshly fallen, soft and thick and so purely white.

"The camels took longer than I thought getting through the tunnel," Thanatos said, eyeing the sun's position in the sky. "We'll have to camp here for the night, and at least by morning we'll have the horses back."

"We can't continue on?"

"It'll be dark soon. Day doesn't last very long here. And the wind in the fields is too strong to risk traveling through at night." Thanatos was already unpacking his camel.

We settled down for the night, snacking on dried meats rather than eating a full meal. We were both still so tired from our sleepless journey through the desert that it took no time for us to fall asleep and, this time, rather than have the brooch poking me all night I discarded it and moved in close to the Prince's side, waking the next morning with his arm wrapped across my waist.

The horses arrived with a Kushyami handler not long after Thanatos and I had finished eating. I practically sprinted to my horse the second I spotted them come through the opening of the cave. I hugged her large brown face as she whinnied and nudged me. I imagined she was recounting all the details of her travels from Kushyam without me. Complaining about the sand and snow perhaps. I hadn't realized how much I'd missed her until that moment, she'd always been my favorite horse but, after being on this journey together, I felt a new connection with her. I'd thought they would have been delivering more than just the horses, but the only other thing the Kushyami woman gave the Prince was a small satchel of herbs before she was ready to leave again and take the camels with her. I ran my hand down the neck and back of my camel; she gave a small grunt, as if acknowledging that this was goodbye. I said a small thank you to her and wished her well, wishing I could really speak to her like the Sillessians.

Once the horses were packed and the camels had been led away, we started our journey through the snowfields.

We were silent on the road. The wind was strong, as Thanatos had said it would be, and snow had begun to fall. I tied a scarf around my face to keep myself from breathing the cold air, wishing I could do the same, or just anything, for Faenor to make her more comfortable; but she didn't complain, just kept pushing through the harsh wind and snow.

The threat of trolls and other monsters lingered in the forefront of my mind. It had been a few hours since we'd left the campsite by the cave and we hadn't seen a soul since. Thanatos had told me there were villages at the base of the mountains, we would stop at some before making the trek up the rocky steps to Ravenna. I hoped we would get there soon, but the wind only got stronger, the horses slower.

I began to see movement in my peripherals, though I couldn't tell if it was a trick of the falling snow or something living. I pushed Faenor to catch up to Serelene. Thanatos' horse was almost impossible to spot, her white coat blending in almost completely with the snow. Were it not for Thanatos' purple skin—and her black nose—I would have lost them.

"Thanatos!" I called over the wind. "I don't think we're alone."

He nodded. "I don't think it's trolls," he called back.

And as the words came out of his mouth, a large, horned beast stumbled before us. We pulled back on the horses' reins, both steeds coming to a halt before the hulking creature. It's body was covered in long, scraggly fur, its back almost the same height as me, even seated on the back of a horse, and on its small face sat two vicious-looking horns. I wanted to pull Faenor away, fear clouding my mind, but the Prince rested a hand on mine and held me still.

"It won't hurt us, just stay still and quiet," he said.

I watched the beast cautiously. It dug at the snow with its horn, tearing at the ground beneath, looking for food no doubt. Thanatos slowly reached back into his pack and pulled out a carrot, he gently leant forward and tossed it to the ground. I watched it roll and knock the creature's snout. I cringed waiting for the horned beast to snap into a rage and tear through me with its horn but it simply snorted at the carrot and began munching it down.

I'd never seen a beast so large, except the Wolvane—but that was lupine. The creature in the snow was pure bulk, its shoulders alone were double the size of the giant wolf.

"Right, while it's distracted, we'll walk around it," Thanatos said. Just as we were about to take the first step, the horses reared back and a growl cut through the wind. A large white shape leapt onto the back of the beast, digging its claws and teeth into the hulking creature. Blood sprayed the snow around us as Thanatos and I frantically tried to manage the horses reeling from the two monsters tearing each other apart before us.

"Run!" Thanatos yelled over the fray and gave Serelene a kick, guiding her forward with the reins.

I sped after him, guiding Faenor around the two giant creatures as blood covered horns, claws and teeth flew in all directions. My heart was beating out of my chest. I was expecting trolls, stupid creatures we could have distracted by throwing a rock in the opposite direction, not giant monsters with killer horns and teeth. Part of me wanted to see how their battle would end, would it be the bear or the other creature? Horn or teeth? I risked a look back. The horned beast had the bear speared but the bear was still able to dig its claws into its adversary.

I looked forward and my heart stopped.

Where was Serelene? Where was Thanatos?

Panic filled my gut, my breakfast threatening to resurface.

I searched the space before me but it was a whiteout, I could barely see Faenor's head. I called his name and heard nothing back, the wind carrying my voice in different directions. I should have kept my eyes forward—should have kept him in my sights.

My hands tightened on the reins. I could still hear the battle raging behind me and I prayed they would not catch up with me.

I kicked Faenor, urging her to go faster, to at least get away from the killer beasts.

I called Thanatos' name again. Screamed it until my throat felt raw. I hoped I was still heading north, but soon I would have to go west and I had no way of telling which was the right direction, the sun completely blocked by the blizzard. Tears pricked my eyes, I forced them away, they would only freeze on my cheeks.

I could only run and pray that the blizzard would pass soon.

CHAPTER THIRTY EIGHT
RELIEVED FROM DUTY

The field was coated in blood, both red and black. Cries from the living and the dead echoed through the air. I hacked through the neck of the Corse before me and threw my blunt blade to the side, swiping a new one from a corpse nearby. I'd barely had enough time to straighten and grip my new blade when a club connected weakly with my ribs.

The skeletal Corse raised its weapon to strike again but, before it could bring the club down a second time, I swung and removed its head in a second. The creature crumpled to the ground in a pile of bones, and I moved on to the next. This one had more flesh on its bones but its movements were just as sloppy, its armor so old I couldn't place its origin.

Each battle with the Necromancer's forces was a chance to try to locate him, to discern what it was he could want, who we had possibly offended. But with each new battle came a new host of soldiers, each one different to the next. We'd fought Minomans, Kushyami and Aurali, all in varying states of decay, and all with aged armor and weapons. I prayed we would never face any Shinchaku, the sharpness of their blades, even old, uncared for blades, could never be matched—nor could their skill with them.

While the Corse armies were easy enough to cut through, it didn't stop us from losing many of our own, to exhaustion, clumsiness, and lack of skill. Beneath my feet, Isidians dead or dying lay covered in dirt and blood, the dying groaning as they were trampled. It was noble of the few who stopped to try to save them but it usually resulted in their own deaths. Better to leave them lie and hope they survive till the end of the battle when the bodies are collected, the dead burned in mass pyres, the living healed to the best that they could be. High-Elves can heal and reattach parts but we can't regrow limbs, and trying to find a lost limb on the battlefield that matches the body is more effort than it's worth.

I disposed of three more Corse, their bodies barely holding together. In this particular horde, even the ones with flesh were weak, and almost falling apart, clumsy and practically blind. They were so different to the ones we'd faced before that I was almost worried there was another threat. Surely these stumbling creatures were not the same as the one that Evalina fought before she'd left, or the ones that Bellona and I had fought. But perhaps the Necromancer was getting lazy, his delusional goal thrown away once he realized we would fight back with everything we had.

The battlefield was growing quiet, the last few Corse being dispatched, the wounded being led away to be healed and the dead being collected. A row of soldiers stalked through the field finding any Corse still living, if you could call it that, and decapitated them swiftly. Their bodies too would be burnt, on the same pyre as our fallen comrades, and the smell would stay in the air for days and haunt us for years to come. It tainted everything. Even the taste and smell of cooked meat had been ruined by the smell of burning corpses.

I checked the area by my feet for living Isidians but there were none, only blank, green eyes staring up at me, their faces frozen in expressions of pain, mouths gaping open in a never ending scream. I stared at their faces for longer than I should have allowed myself, imprinting them in my mind and taking them back to the camp with me so they, too, could haunt my dreams, joining the heads of the murdered farmers hanging by their hair from a tree.

"Any number on the dead?" I called to no one in particular as I entered the camp.

"Not yet, Captain," someone called back, "but it will be tallied as soon as possible."

I nodded, walking past a group of Sea-Elf soldiers huddled in a healing tent. Some with their heads bowed in mourning and others clutching limps they hoped to have reattached, their faces white with shock as they stared at the detached limbs, their pain dulled by High-Elven magic. I dumped my stolen sword with the armorer and headed toward my lodgings within the hastily built fort.

My lodgings had been set up in one of the abandoned farm houses that we'd built the fort around, the other two houses were used as food and weapons stores, guarded and locked at all times to discourage deserters, if one wanted to desert they could do so without a weapon or food and see how well they did. Once in the farm house, I removed my leather armor, wincing as the shirt beneath peeled off with it, separating from my leaking wounds. None of my injuries were bad, but they stung. I set to work healing them using the light from my magic to read documents that had been placed on my desk. It had once been the dining table of a family. The children had carved their names into the legs and measured the height of their dog on them. I wondered if it was a family that had survived, or if they had too been killed by a small force that had snuck through the countryside.

A stock of weapons were due to arrive tomorrow, more food was being sent in three days time, wine to thank the soldiers was being gifted by the Queen and was set to arrive after the food. The soldiers would enjoy that treat, if they lived to see it. More troops would be sent in five days, Sea-Elves arriving on the last lot of ships due in.

Under all the short notes was an envelope with the royal seal on it, an Ashwood tree stamped into a pool of green wax. I stood to fetch a tinder box and lit some candles in the room. I needed more light to read this letter clearly.

Captain Lorkin.

We have had word from the Princess.

My breath caught in my throat. She'd written. She was alive.

Princess Evalina and Prince Thanatos were recently involved in a siege of Kushyam by a Corse army.

My hands shook reading the words. Kushyam had been attacked and Evalina had been there. Why?

The army was defeated, the Kushyami victorious and the Princess and Prince unharmed, but the Princess's identity was revealed. They are now enroute to Osiria, after which they will venture south to Minoma.

Queen Islina is pleased at this news but, even still, Bellona is close by her side to offer comfort.

I would also add that construction on the temple is well underway, and request that you return from battle to inspect that it is to your standard. With the arrival of this letter also comes the arrival of Quartermaster Baldulf to lead in your stead. He comes with recommendations and regards from King Darius.

Peverell

Postscript, Evalina also mentioned in her letter that the Corse she faced in Kushyam were different to past encounters. She fears there may be a second Necromancer.

I dropped the letter and sucked in a much needed breath, my mind swirling with the new information. Evalina was alive—and the Prince. The Kushyami were not involved with the Necromancer, that much was certain, but there could be two, and there was nothing to say the Kushaymi hadn't organized the attack themselves to try to prove a false innocence. No, they wouldn't do that, especially not with their closeness to the Osirians and Thanatos present during the attack. I rested my head in my hands, exhaustion threatening to take me over.

A second Necromancer. One was causing enough trouble, what would two be capable of? I was glad to have had my theory confirmed so quickly, though I wished it had been wrong.

One question I did want answered was why Evie and the Prince were making so many stops on their journey, and why wasn't Evalina putting it in her letters?

Could it all come down to the presence of Corse? And, if so, why were we not aiding those kingdoms?

It was moments like these that made me realize how young I was, how unfit for my position I was, but there was no one else I could trust to do it. When I returned to the palace, I would speak with Adalric and get his perspective on the matter. Though we don't tend to agree on every matter, his input is still helpful.

"Enter!" I called as a knock sounded from the door of the farm house.

"Captain Lorkin," the unfamiliar Carracallan said, stopping before my desk, "I am Baldulf. King Darius directed me to come here to replace you."

Baldulf was lean but broad shouldered, like all Sea-Elves—from their time both in the water and on the ships—taller than most, and wore his hair short, but grew his beard, it sat neatly trimmed at the center of his throat.

"You're the King's quartermaster?" I asked

"I am. I replaced my father a decade ago from the same position. While land battle may be new to me, I know how to direct crews and maintain order."

"I assume you do know how to use a sword," I challenged.

"Trained by the King himself, Captain," he said with a grin. "I've just finished a tour of the fort, made myself aware of weapons locations and such, and received word of the final loss count from the battle today—three hundred."

I sighed and jotted the number down. We were almost at a thousand in total already. "More troops are arriving in a few days," I informed Baldulf. "Until then, we should only send out skilled fighters, the recruits are getting slaughtered out there." Baldulf nodded. "And make sure all weapons are turned into the armorer for sharpening before being sent out again, they're beginning to blunten."

"Of course, Captain. I've had a horse prepared for you. Captain Peverell asked for you to return as soon as possible."

"Yes," I said, checking the office for anything I would need to take with me, though I knew there was nothing. It felt odd to leave my people in the hands of someone I didn't know, as if I were a mother that had hired a new nursemaid for her children. "'Spose I'd better be off then."

With a few more unnecessary parting instructions, I took the horse that Baldulf had prepared and left the fort.

Chapter Thirty Nine
Adrift

I glanced behind me to be sure Evalina was following—but she was gone. I pulled on Serelene's reins, forcing her to halt, and scanned the snowfield behind me. I called her name and cursed myself. I should have tied the horses together. I didn't travel with people often, so the thought of losing her in a blizzard hadn't even crossed my mind.

The panic I'd felt at the snow bear's appearance was now compounded with the fear that she may have gotten caught up in the fight between the two beasts. Tunbeests were harmless, unless startled, but snow bears would kill for the sake of killing.

I called her name again, but heard nothing in return. I thanked the Father that she had the brooch—at least she would not freeze to death—but I had all the food. My mind was racing through scenarios of what had or could happen; she was killed, she had killed, I would find her dead once the storm cleared, or she would be fine and we'd meet at the next village. She knew where to go, I'd given her the directions, but she wouldn't find her way in the storm. I couldn't track her, the wind blowing strong enough that it covered any hoof prints instantly. I could only hope, hope that she would find her way, that she'd think to head west and follow the mountains.

I called out for her a few more times, each time sounding more desperate than the last. My chest was aching with worry, but the best thing I could do was continue on, head west toward the mountains, hope she would do the same thing, and maybe the storm would clear and we'd find each other.

—·—·—▸—✦—◂—·—·—

I pulled Serelene to keep her going, I'd tied a scarf around her eyes and was leading her by the reins. The storm had gotten stronger, the snow blasting her face with enough force to leave her blinded were it not for the protection of the scarf. I was thankful that she trusted me enough to allow me to guide her blindly through the blizzard.

Serelene had been on most of my adventures with me, we'd built quite the bond. I patted her neck to let her know things were going well and continued on through the storm.

Every now and then I'd call out for Evalina, just in case she was close by and would hear me, but I got no response, just wailing wind.

The blizzard began to slow, but it had been hours and I still had no way of knowing whether or not Evalina was out there. I hoped she had just kept running, that she had gotten away from the snarling beasts. My mind had shown me sick visions of the Princess being torn apart over the hours, sometimes by tunbeests, sometimes trolls, and other times by the Mother herself. I tried to shake the visions away but I was sick with worry and it was all I could think about.

I called her name again, for maybe the last time, when my voice echoed back at me and I realized I'd reached the mountain range.

I waited for a moment, my heart pausing its beating, as if it was waiting, too. I was met with silence. Just as I was going to call out again, Faenor burst through the blanket of snow toward me.

I climbed down from Serelene, my heart pounding in my chest. "Evalina!" I yelled and cringed at the desperation that echoed back.

The horse came to halt before me.

But there was no Princess in her saddle, only the small Fire ily.

"Fuck, Evalina," I groaned.

The horse nipped at my clothes, flicking her head toward the saddle. I gave her neck a quick pat before swinging onto her back.

The mare turned and darted back through the snow. She knew exactly where she was going, not faltering once as she pounded through the storm.

I could barely breathe, barely think.

New visions of Evalina half buried in snow filled my mind, her porcelain skin blue in the freezing temperatures.

I gripped the reins tightier and scanned the snowy ground flashing beneath me, looking for any sign of Evalina, a flick of blue-black hair.

"Evalina!" I called once again, unable to hold it in any longer, I had to do something.

The horse began to slow, her steps less sure, as if the Princess had moved from where she'd left her. "Evalina!" I screamed, my voice hoarse; I hoped the wind would carry it to her.

I heard a noise to my left, barely a whisper floating on the wind.

"Evie!" I called.

"Than …"

I rushed to dismount the horse, falling into the snow beneath me. I strained my eyes to see through the wall of frost pelting my face. "Evie!"

"Thanatos."

It was louder, this time, but still barely a croak. I spun and ran in the direction the voice was coming from, pulling my feet through the deep snow. I called out again, trying to gauge how close we were to each other. Her voice came back louder, I was getting closer. I pushed myself to run harder, faster, through the snow, my legs aching, lungs burning. I had to get to her. I had to know she was all right. I could still barely see. The storm had calmed, but not completely.

"Evalina!" I called again, hoping to be even closer than the last time.

"Than, I'm here," her weak voice answered back.

And there she was, huddled and shivering violently in the snow, her skin the blue that I had pictured, her eyes frozen shut with tears of fear and lost hope. I collapsed next to her, pulled her from the snow and held her to me. My breathing was rapid, not just from the running, and tears lined my eyes. I had been so scared, so terrified that she'd been killed, or would be lost forever. She leaned heavily against me and I knew she felt the same. I pulled the scarf down from her face and kissed her urgently. I needed to feel her lips on mine, to know it was real. I broke off the kiss and pulled her head to my chest again holding her tighter than I ever had, wishing I never had to let her go. I fixed the Fire Lily to her front and waited until her trembling had reduced before relaxing my hold on her.

"Can we please get out of this storm?" She said, her voice cracking slightly.

I nodded and kissed her hair, still reluctant to let go.

"Let's go."

I helped her climb onto Faenor's back and I led them through the snow to the base of the mountains. I hoped Serelene was waiting for me, after everything that had just happened I felt stupid for leaving her.

We reached Serelene in no time and I didn't hesitate before tying Faenor's reigns to hers.

We would not be separated again.

We continued the rest of the journey, following along with the base of the mountain; by the time we reached the first village we were exhausted. With the storm still raging, we didn't receive the reception we usually would but it didn't matter to us. Evalina and I were just desperate to be together and to sleep.

We gave the horses a good brush down and made sure they were warm and had lots of food before retiring to the inn. Evalina barely registered the Osirian behind the counter, could barely look up from her shaking hands. I booked a room and ordered food to be sent up as quickly as possible. Evalina and I collapsed onto the bed once we got up to the room, our bodies tired and aching.

"Are you all right?" I asked, I still just wanted to hold her and never let go.

"I'm all right now, but I was so scared out there." Her voice shook.

I pulled her into my arms and held her as she calmed herself.

"I looked away for a second and then you were gone."

"I know," I soothed, stroking her hair and kissing her head lightly. "I'm sorry, I should have tied the horses together. It's my fault." Guilt, that's what I felt.

I'd put her through another dangerous and terrifying situation all because of my selfish excitement to go home.

"No," she said softly, angling her head up to look me in the eyes. "It's on both of us. We should have been more cautious, we both knew the dangers." Her mouth met mine, gently, but before any more could happen there was a knock at the door.

Evalina shot out of bed. "Food!" She exclaimed as she rushed for the door.

I hadn't realized how hungry I was until that moment; we hadn't eaten since breakfast.

The food smelled and tasted amazing. We scoffed it down and, once we were full, Evalina fell asleep. I gazed at her sleeping face. The color had faded, her cheeks returning to their stark white. I toyed with a lock of her blue-black hair, glad that I would not be searching for it in the snow once the storm cleared. Her face was relaxed in sleep, as if the horrors of the day had never happened—but they had.

We both would add it to the list of events that would haunt us for the rest of our days. I wanted to be angry at her for her recklessness, but of course Evalina would sacrifice herself for the horse, just as she had already sacrificed herself for her people.

We slept all night tangled in each other's limbs, neither of us wanting to release the other.

CHAPTER FORTY
SEA OF WHITE

I woke the next morning with the events of the day before rushing through my mind. I hugged the Prince tighter than I already had been as the memory of him finding me lost in the snow replayed in my head, his relieved face visible in my mind's eye.

I would never forget that face.

The wind was no longer howling through the slated roof of the inn. I guessed the storm had passed overnight. Detangling myself from the Prince, I dashed to the small window, shivering the second my body left the warmth of the bed covers. From the window, I could finally see the extent of the snowfields; they stretched for miles—pure, white, glittering snow. It was foriegn to me to see such an expanse of land and there be no trees or foliage of any kind, it made me wonder how the Osirians had food at all. I wanted to open the window and smell the snow, have a moment to just enjoy it, but I knew if I opened the window I would freeze.

Once Thanatos woke, it was another rush to leave and reach our next destination and, though he didn't want to admit it, I knew it was because he feared another storm hitting. We'd woken before the rest of the town—even the innkeeper was still asleep—leaving no one to make us a hot meal, so we ate what we had on hand and left.

We traveled with our horses tied together and, even though there was no sign of a storm, or even a breeze across the fields, we stuck to the side of the mountain range, hugging the wall as closely as we could. I longed to get down from my horse and actually enjoy the snow, now that it wasn't trying to kill me, but Thanatos seemed determined to get out of it as soon as possible. It wasn't until a new village loomed over the horizon that Thanatos slowed the horses' pace and eventually got down from Serelene's back. Excitement overtook me; I lept off Faenor's back and landed in the soft, freshly fallen snow, sinking only to my ankles. I loved snow. It snowed in Isidia but never for very long; here, it was always snowing.

With the brooch on, I didn't feel much of the cold but my nose still burnt as I smelled the crisp air. I scooped up some of the powdery snow and ran it through my fingers, watching it pile up on itself as it fell back to the ground again. Thanatos came to stand beside me, still dressed in light clothing.

"Do you feel nothing?" I asked jokingly but genuinely curious.

He laughed. "Yes, I do. I'm just used to it, I guess." He kicked at the snow, accidentally spraying me—I took it as a challenge.

"Let's see just how much you can feel," I said as I scooped a large handful of snow and shaped it into a ball.

Thanatos began backing away. "Now, now, Princess, non—"

I threw the snowball, grinning when it exploded as it made impact with Thanatos' cheek.

"Right." Was all he said before making a ball himself and ditching it at me.

I darted away, running as fast as I could in the loose snow, quickly dipping to form my own projectile.

It didn't take long before we were in an all out war, building barriers with snow, creating a stock of snowballs, throwing them at each other with complete disregard of whether or not they hit their mark. I ignored my growling stomach and the ache in my shoulder as I continued to lob balls over my barricade at the Prince, enjoying our free moment to have fun. A voice in the back of my mind was begging me to call it quits but the warm feeling of joy in my chest urged me to throw another projectile. I laughed as the Prince made a loud noise of disgust.

"That one went down my shirt!" He called, standing to shake the snow out of his top—a stupid mistake. I pommeled him with snowballs, each one hitting their target and exploding in a fine spray of cold, fluffy snow.

Thanatos was soaked, I was soaked, I couldn't feel the cold of the wetness but my clothing and hair hung heavily off me.

"All right, that's enough," I wheezed between laughing. "We should probably go and eat."

"Good idea. I'm actually getting cold." Thanatos laughed as he wrapped his arm around my shoulders and led me toward the town, the horses following behind us, my love of snow no longer feeling tainted.

The town was quite large considering the environment in which it was situated, the buildings built from stone and wood to withstand the harsh elements. I'd been in such a daze in the last town that I hadn't noticed anything about it, but I assumed it had been similar to this. Despite the buildings having large chimneys, I saw only a few emitting smoke and hoped we were heading to one of those. While I couldn't feel the cold, I still felt the discomfort of wearing wet clothes and longed to change. I was worried, though I couldn't feel the cold, that being in it would still do damage to my body. I'd gotten lucky yesterday, to not get sick after being out in the storm for so long.

As we rounded the back of the village and came to the main thoroughfare, I gazed up at the mountain range setting an almost sinister backdrop for the small settlement. Even from a distance, I could spot the sharp spires of Ravenna palace piercing the sky, the black stone stark against the fluffy white clouds.

I sucked in a breath and slowly released it, calming my pounding heart. It was working until I looked back down at the world directly in front of me and saw the sea of white and varying shades of purple heading toward me.

Dark-Elves.

I froze and Thanatos stopped with me, gazing at me curiously.

So many—there were so many.

For so long, Thanatos was the only one, we hadn't run into any other Dark-Elves on our journey, apart from the one at the inn last night, but I'd barely registered them at all; it was jarring to see so many at once, so many charging toward me.

I wanted to shrink away, to run back to Ajal cave and never come back; my fears of being hated bubbling to the surface of my mind.

A small girl pushed her way to the front of the crowd, her hair was pulled away from her face in various intricate braids, similar to how Thanatos styled his hair. Her clothes were simple; a dress with long sleeves and pants underneath, a vest over the top and flat round hat on her head. The fabric looked too thin, though she didn't seem to be too cold.

"Thanny!" She called over the murmur of the crowd.

"Thanny?" I repeated, dumbfounded as she bolted to Thanatos.

He swooped her up in his arms and lifted her above his head spinning until she squealed with laughter. I couldn't help but smile despite my confusion.

"Amara, this is Evalina," he said, plopping the girl back on her feet. "She's a Princess," he added in a whisper.

Amara's face lit up as the rest of the crowd joined us—it must have been the whole village. "A princess?!" Amara replied, studying me up and down. "No offense, but you don't really look like a princess."

Thanatos burst out laughing at the girl's remark and I joined him.

"And what do princesses look like?" I asked, squatting to be at her level; her eyes were a browner shade of amber than the Prince's.

"Well … I know they're clean," she said matter-of-factly; the crowd laughed and waited for my response. Nerves trickled up my spine.

"That's true but, if I were clean, then it would mean I had never left my castle." A sad truth of my life that she would hopefully not understand.

"Then it is good you are dirty."

The crowd and Prince laughed.

I smiled at the girl, she was not wrong. I guessed the interaction was over because, as the laughing died down, the crowd began to move in closer around us and I suddenly felt like a prize pony on display. The Osirians marveled at my pale skin and dark hair, the opposite of theirs, and fussed over their Prince.

"Have you been eating well?"

"Are you warm?"

"Have you slept well?"

The questions kept coming and the Prince answered willingly, the smile never leaving his face. It was obvious that, even though he was away from home more often than not, he still cared deeply about his people, and them about him. But they didn't treat him like a Prince—he was their friend, their family. It was so foreign to me; to be treated as a regular person and not royalty. I had to admit that I prefered it.

I didn't know when it happened but suddenly there was music, dancing, food, and drink. Someone had pushed an ale into my hand as I sat with a lamb shank in the other, having my hair braided by the village girls. They gushed over the blue and how they wished they could have different colors in their hair.

I gulped down the ale and giggled with the girls as they told me stories of the prince—how he liked to get drunk when he came home from adventures, and tell stories in the tavern, sometimes he'd sing … terribly.

They asked me about Isidia and what it was like to not have snow all year round. I told them what I could, mostly about the palace and how the flowers climbed the walls and bloomed in spring, of the creek that ran through the palace grounds, how the birds sang in the summer. Their amber eyes glazed over as they pictured their own versions of my home, and I got lost in thinking of it too.

It would be snowing there, now, the last of the flowers and trees in the gardens would be dead or dormant, the creek would be frozen over, guards and servants would have changed to their winter uniforms. My mother would be wearing her winter gowns, long-sleeved, thick black and green velvet.

I felt suddenly under dressed, especially for the weather, but I didn't have long to dwell on the thought as I was swept away from the girls by an older Osirian male telling me I had to learn the traditional dance; the girls clapped and followed along behind.

I wasn't a great dancer but it seemed almost impossible to resist dancing along to the Osirian music, the rhythmic drum pounding deeply and keeping a steady beat to contrast with the frantic strumming and plucking of a tear drop shaped instrument with a long neck.

I was instructed to link my pinkies with those on either side of me, joining onto a short line of people gathered in a semicircle. We took two steps left and one step right to the time of the beating of the drum, the person at the end of the line swung a scarf and led us in our dance as we circled around two girls dancing in the center They spun incredibly fast, scarves streaming from either hand, small golden discs dangling from the scarves tinkling as they swirled.

Those around me laughed as I did the wrong steps and tangled my legs with the people next to me, almost causing the whole line to tumble to the muddy ground.

I pulled myself out of the dance, eventually, to get more food and ale, the dancing making me hungrier than I already was.

I downed a bowl of spiced rice and chased it with a whole tankard of ale, the flavors mixing surprisingly well in my stomach.

I watched the dancing and admired the heart of the people, their kindness and welcoming matching Thanatos' exactly. I was again floored by how different they were to what I'd expected, to what I'd been told. How cruel the world was to unfairly judge these people, to be so unwavering in their opinion of them.

The music suddenly sped up and I was glad to have left the dance, I never would have been able to keep up with the new speed. The dancers' feet were a blur, their muddied boots impossible to keep track of. I laughed and joined the few elves scattered around the edge of the party in clapping along to the beat of the drum.

I found all my anxieties and fear disappearing with the sun behind the western mountains, the snow turning red around me as the light shone through bellows of volcanic smoke. I had only been in the village for a few hours but I loved it already; part of me wished I could stay there and never have to return to Isidia.

CHAPTER FORTY ONE
TAKING THE LEAD

My heart soared as she danced the dance of my people, her freshly braided hair bouncing against her back as she stepped in time with the beat. I was sure she thought she'd hid it well, but I knew she was fearful of how she would be received. I wasn't.

I knew the people of this village well enough to know they would welcome all in the same fashion, as would they all. Having an Isidian on our land was an exciting step toward being accepted by the rest of Carynthia; that was really all my people and I longed for.

The village elders had said as much to me when they'd pulled me aside to welcome me back to Osiria and asked how things were fairing in the world beyond the mountains, as they did everytime I returned home. I filled them in with as many details as I felt comfortable providing, warning them of the threat of the Corse but keeping the battle of Kushyam to myself—they didn't need that worry.

"Thank you, Prince Thanatos." Elder Yamajit put a hand on my shoulder. "News travels slowly from Ravenna, it's nice to get it from you." I bowed my head.

Elder Yamajit was one of the oldest living Osirians, so old that no one truly knew how old he really was and, if he knew his own age, he certainly didn't share it with anyone. Elves usually lived to be at least one thousand years old, the healthier ones could live to be fifteen hundred, but Yamajit was past that, or so we assumed.

I laughed as Evalina almost tripped up the whole row of villagers she was dancing with, pink blooming across her cheeks. She righted herself and, after a moment more of dancing, pulled away from the others and headed to the food table. I realized then that she must be starving; I hadn't given us time that morning to eat, my own hunger pushed aside by my excitement and eagerness to finally be home.

I'd been gone for longer periods of time, but never had I been in so much danger. It really made you appreciate home, and friends, and family.

239

I circled the edge of the crowd, keeping my eyes on Evalina but stopping to converse with villagers as I went. I watched the relief come over her as she scoffed a bowl of rice, the delight as the ale trickled down her throat. I paused as she laughed and clapped along to the music, the dancers spinning faster and faster to keep up with the beating of the drum, my heartbeat matching the rhythm as I gazed in awe at Evalina's broad smile, her relaxed posture. My stomach fluttered as her deep, hearty laugh reached my ears over the music; it was a laugh I hadn't yet heard, a laugh of pure joy. It made me forget all the terrible things we'd seen and been through.

I couldn't stand it any longer, it was my fault that she'd felt insecure about what was going on between us. If only she knew how much it made sense.

I had to tell her, but I couldn't work myself up to it. For so long, I had done everything I could to keep my feelings hidden; my anger, my sadness, my helplessness, all for the sake of others. For the sake of appearing strong and reliable, I hid my weakness.

I should have gone to Evalina's room in Kushyam, cried in her arms and told her I felt broken. She should know of my weakness, I knew so many of hers.

I took a deep breath, centering myself and preparing to approach her, it was like this everytime. She didn't notice me as I walked toward her, she was completely absorbed in the music and dancing. The red glow from the smoke-covered sun made her hair look a deep purple, her eyes almost amber, like mine. I held my hands firmly by my sides, hoping she wouldn't notice them shaking.

"Having a good time?" I asked with a false sense of confidence. She jumped slightly but smiled.

"I am," she beamed. Father, she was beautiful. "I can't believe how lively they are, you'd never see a party like this in Lonthia."

I didn't have the heart to correct her. I knew that they did, in fact, have parties like this in the streets of Lonthia—she'd just never had a chance to experience them.

"I'm glad. They're all so excited that you're here."

Her cheeks flushed a deep red, her skin tinted pink from the sun. "I'm surprised they're so hospitable, everything considered."

"I think that's why they are, to prove everyone wrong."

"Taking notes from their Prince?" She nudged me with her shoulder and I could have sworn I felt a spark.

"Maybe, or maybe I learnt it from them." I considered as I watched the dancers pair up and the music slow.

I'd always liked the idea of showing the world they were wrong about us but, no matter how much I'd tried, hatred and fear still followed me So, I'd just learnt to deal with it.

"Dance with me?" Evalina asked.

I stared at her blankly. "Huh?"

"Dance with me!" She insisted, grabbing my arm and leading me into the crowd.

The villagers cheered as Evalina dragged me along before halting in the middle of the group, pairs of dancers spinning around us. "Show me how," she instructed, an excited smile spread across her face.

"Okay, follow my lead." I held my arm out, my elbow bent and fingertips raised toward the sky, my open palm facing her, waiting.

She mimicked and placed her hand against mine. We followed the steps of the dancers around us; two forward, one back, three forward, one back, repeat three times then switch hands and do it all again facing the opposite direction. I could hear Evalina whispering the steps to herself to keep track of them but it didn't help, she still forgot when we had to step forward three times instead of two and switch hands. We ended up a laughing mess in the middle of a circle of twirling dancers struggling not to trip each other over.

"Perhaps this was a bad idea," she called over the music and the laughing crowd.

"I think it was the best idea."

We continued dancing until we were struggling to stay upright.

The village lanterns had been lit and most of the younger villagers had retired to bed, even Amara, though she'd fought valiantly with her mother and father to stay up later.

"We should turn in for the night," I said.

Evalina gazed around the village longingly, but the party was over.

I cupped her face in my hands. "It will still be here in the morning," I said. "The inn is this way." I nudged my head toward the north end of the road.

She wrapped her arm around my waist and followed my lead to the gray, stone inn as I rested my arm across her shoulders. It was a closeness I think we'd both longed for after dancing for hours with only our hands touching. I couldn't help but feel the eyes of the villagers following the Princess and I as we strolled down the road.

I sighed, knowing that the village would be full of rumors by morning.

The inn was warm inside and smelled of snow and sweet spices, the keeper simply nodded at me and I led the Princess up the stairs.

"Don't we need to get a key?"

"I have a key."

"I don't," she challenged.

"Do you need one?" I asked, more genuine than joking.

She shook her head and rested it on my shoulder as we walked down the passage.

The key clicked loudly as I unlocked the door to my room. I'd paid the innkeeper more than he'd wanted to accept for this to be my own private room for when I traveled to and from Osiria. He'd tried to refuse but I'd insisted, it also made it easier for me while traveling. I often came home with no money left.

The room itself was simple; containing a bed, small dining table by the window, and a lounge in front of the small fireplace. Evalina wandered over to the doorway by the bed and gazed apprehensively at the bathtub. I came up beside her, it wasn't a particularly large bath but we could both easily fit.

"We could bathe together?" she suggested sheepishly, reading my mind.

My shoulders stiffened, I tried to keep my face neutral and must have failed.

"I'm sorry, that was very forward of me," she said. "You have already seen me naked—multiple times."

I laughed, maybe a little awkwardly. "That's true. If that's what you want, what you're comfortable with, then we can." I smiled, hopefully hiding the longing that I was feeling.

I wanted her to feel safe, to be safe, but I also wanted to touch her, in all the ways I possibly could.

I filled the bath with hot water as she waited by the doorway, leaning on the frame and watching me a little too intently. I was glad that Glik had let me take one of his enchanted buckets, making the filling of the tub quick work.

"I'll let you get in first." Evalina stepped away from the doorframe. "You're at least still a mystery to me," she said with a smile and closed the bathing room door.

I was frozen for a moment. How had we gotten to this point? Mere weeks ago, she could barely stand to be in the same room as me, now we were bathing together.

I began removing my clothes, taking my time and keeping myself calm, taking deep breaths. I was helping her, that's all this was. I lowered myself into the deep bath, the water rising to the base of my ribs. I called to Evalina and waited.

She slowly opened the door, peeked her head in, and stepped through the door once she saw I was submerged in the warm water.

Her pale skin was beautiful, it seemed to glow in the light of the candles. Her long hair was loose and covered most of her muscular body, but the rest was free for me to admire. My hands itched to touch her, to hold her, run my fingers through her blue-black hair and graze my lips across her cheek.

I was getting too ahead of myself, I took more, subtle deep breaths to calm myself but I wasn't sure it worked.

CHAPTER FORTY TWO
LOST FOR WORDS

I got the shock of a lifetime when I undressed. The second I took the Fire Lily pin off, the air around me had become impossibly cold, my clothes were suddenly icy, almost like they were burning my skin. I'd had to gently peel them off, terrified that they'd stick to me.

My hands shook as I stood in the doorway, because of the bath or Thanatos I did not know. I was thankful that my hair was long enough to cover the majority of my body, though the Prince did not stare as I believed most would have. He looked almost as if he were admiring a piece of art; I blushed at the thought that he may think of my body as art. He turned his head slightly away as I had to awkwardly climb over the edge of the tub to lower myself in—I should have thought of that before I'd planned my grand entrance.

He straightened himself so that he was sitting upright in the tub, touching me as little as possible as I sat across from him, the water just rising to cover my bare breasts.

"Is the water all right?" He asked.

"It's perfect." And it was.

I was once again glad for the length of my hair, it floated through the water like a blanket of tendrils, giving the Prince small peeks of what lay beneath, an unintended tease. We sat awkwardly for a moment, neither of us wanting to make the first move, the Prince most likely out of respect for me and I from the nerves of potential rejection.

I decided to just do it. He never would.

I stretched my arms above my head and my legs out and laid them over his thighs, before relaxing down into the water. I held in my laugh at his surprised expression and he tentatively rested his arms on my shins.

It had been a long time since I'd felt new desire. Lorkin and I had been together for years, and over those years certain levels of excitement were no longer reached. We'd tried many things to keep the passion alive but it only worked for so long.

I was realizing more and more everyday that what I'd had with Lorkin was not love in a romantic way, it was more of a familiarity; he was a constant in my life of constants, something I thought could never change, that would have to stay the same.

Thanatos was different, new, and exciting; and, unlike Lorkin, he didn't want things to stay the same. Thanatos wanted things to be different for me, he wanted me to experience new things and become new myself. What did I want for him? Perhaps he needed a constant, maybe we were opposites in that way; I needed change and he needed stability.

I could be that for him, I'd been a constant for so many already, but this one was different, new and exciting.

I smiled at the Prince as I caught him gazing at me, he snapped back to reality and apologized.

"Don't apologize," I said, hooking my ankles together behind his back and used my legs to pull him to me.

A different look crossed his face, one I matched. His hands traveled up my arms lightly, my hair tangling together in swirls of black and blue in the current the movement had created. I shivered at his touch as his fingers grazed up my torso, my own hands traveling up his arms to link around his neck. It was hard to tell, but I was sure he was blushing. When was the last time he'd been with anyone he really cared about? Was it with Zohar? I forced the thoughts out of my mind; now was not the time to think of ex-lovers, not as Thanatos and I were finally moving forward.

I could feel that he was ready, and knowing that gave me a surge of confidence. I nudged his nose with mine, drawing his attention away from my body and instantly our lips locked. Our touches became less controlled and more desperate. Thanatos pulled me closer to himself, his hands resting on my rear. I ran my fingers through his hair, gripping the roots and deepening our kiss. I hated to admit it to myself but I was desperate. Desperate for touching, for *his* touch, and this was already taking too long, but as I moved to escalate things the Prince pulled back slightly.

"I'm sorry," I said breathlessly, a little embarrassed.

"No, it's fine.," he replied, kissing me quickly. "I just …" he paused, looking for the right words. "Are you sure?" he asked finally, his expression filled with doubt. "With me?"

I was almost shocked. "Of course," I said, brushing stray hairs from his face. "I wouldn't if I didn't want to, believe me." I smiled as his eyes once again filled with desire. "Are you sure?"

"Definitely." He pulled me back against himself and kissed me deeply, his fingers gripping my sides tight enough to almost hurt.

It was as if we couldn't touch enough of the other; our hands moved frantically across each other's bodies, until it was too much. Thanatos slowed and, though I didn't want him to, I was glad for it. We were able to relish in the moment, the moment we finally became more.

The next morning, Thanatos and I woke tangled together beneath a thick blanket. I recalled the events of the night before—starting in the bath. The water eventually going cold around us, Thanatos transitioning us to the bed, carrying me in his strong arms, my wet hair hanging heavily over the crook of his arm.

From the humidity in the air under the covers, I knew that my hair was still damp. I turned to find Thanatos gazing at the roof of the inn, his expression grim.

"Are you all right?" I asked as I moved under the covers and snuggled into his side.

He took a deep breath. "I'm … nervous," he said, glancing sidelong at me. "My mother can be … difficult."

I scoffed. "You think I can't handle a difficult mother?"

The corners of his mouth twitched up in a quick, understanding smile. "My mother is a little different." He paused, considering his next words. "I told you about the Phoenix Priestesses?"

I nodded, not wanting to interrupt his train of thought. Everyone had heard of the Phoenix Priestesses; they were devout followers of the Mother and believed in keeping the elven bloodline pure, particularly the Dark-Elven bloodline, regarding them as the closest race to the Mother and her dark pit.

"Of my mother's … harsh views about humans." I could hear the disdain in his voice, not toward his mother but her beliefs.

"Will she dislike me?" I asked sheepishly.

A strange mix of expressions crossed the Prince's face. "No, but she will try to twist your mind. Just try to be careful around her."

I chewed my bottom lip.

We would be arriving at Ravenna today, it didn't give me a lot of time to prepare. I had almost forgotten where I was, who I was with, and who I would meet today. The King and Queen of Osiria, the avengers of my fathers death … and Thanatos' parents.

I made to get out of bed and sit by the fire to dry my hair, but two violet arms pulled me back down.

"Hey! I need to dry my hair." I laughed, the arms only tightened. "And pee."

"Just go here," he replied, nuzzling his face into my neck.

"In the bed?" I exclaimed.

"Sure, on three we'll both go. One, two, th—"

I pulled myself out of his arms and leapt off the bed. "I don't think so." I laughed.

Thanatos laughed and urged me to hurry up in the bathing room.

The fire was warm on my back as I sat and let my hair dry. Thanatos had offered to rebraid my hair before we left for the palace; the winds would again be strong up the mountain pass and I wanted to look presentable for the King and Queen. Despite my nerves of meeting Thanatos' parents, I could not wipe the smile off my face and it only broadened as the Prince re-entered the room. His hair was freshly brushed and braided, pulled completely away from his face, creating a white halo. I found myself studying him as he moved toward me through the room, his gait a little more confident than it had been in recent days—there was almost a bounce in his step. I smiled as he leant down to plant a kiss on my lips, but I broke it off before it could become more.

"How's your hair feeling?" He asked, moving over to the window and gazing out at the village below.

"It feels almost dry," I said, patting my hair, the ends still damp but the roots dry as a bone. "Excited to be home?"

"I am." From the angle of his head, I knew he was looking up at Ravenna fortress and my mind began to wonder about what was waiting for us there. What was so important? I knew it was more than just collecting weapons, and I wondered if he would tell me now, after last night.

"How long do you think we'll be at Ravenna for?" I asked, hoping he would tell me more than just a number of days.

"I don't know. I know we need to move on quickly, need to get to Minoma, I just … miss my family," he added sheepishly.

I was surprised at first at the sharing, but it made me realize that I had a longing to discuss my own homesickness.

"I understand. I miss my home, too, my family." I took a deep breath, feeling tears pricking at my eyes. "You probably already know, but I haven't seen my Father's family in a long time, and leaving them so suddenly … it was hard." Thanatos moved from the window and squatted down before me. His eyes shone with emotion, the same emotion I felt showing in mine.

"You'll be able to see them soon, I promise." He embraced me and it took all of my self-control to keep my emotions in.

I would not cry, not now.

"We should get ready to leave, so we can see your family." He smiled and pecked my cheek before retrieving a comb.

He braided my hair at a speed I didn't think was possible, given the volume of hair he was dealing with, and though it felt heavy when it was done, it also felt secure and comfortable. He had done a series of small braids starting at my hairline and blended them into one large single braid that ran halfway down my back. Not a single strand was loose.

We left the room not long after, heading down the stairs and into the dining area of the tavern. My stomach was suddenly filled with nervous fluttering. It would be no surprise to the people of the village what had happened between the Prince and I that night; we stood closer together, were more relaxed with each other, the tension between us loosened but not entirely gone. I dreaded the thought of anyone saying something. In Isidia no one dared but here they were so free, there almost seemed to be no sense of hierarchy.

The tavern was empty, save for the barman behind the wooden counter. Light was coming strongly through the windows, the sun reflecting off the snow outside. I was happy that I had the brooch to keep me warm because the small fire definitely wouldn't.

I came to the conclusion that on top of their death gift, the Mother had also blessed the Dark-Elves to feel no temperature—it was the only explanation for how they could live in this land of ice and fire.

I tried to eat breakfast, it was some kind of sweet rice porridge, but I felt nauseous after coming to the realization that I would meet the King and Queen that had previously warred with my family.

This was a momentous occasion in Carynthian history and I was nervous to be part of it, to be partly responsible for it.

I subconsciously placed my hand over the burn on my shoulder; perhaps I would get answers today, for everything. I kicked my pack, making sure I still had the book I'd stolen from Sevah, and sent a prayer to the Father, asking that he could guide me to find the answers I sought and that he could settle my damned stomach.

After poking at our food for half an hour, we decided to leave. It hadn't snowed during the night, the footprints of the dancing still visible in the frozen mud.

I gazed at the tracks and wondered which ones belonged to Thanatos and I, which ones told the story of how we'd ended up the way we had. I found myself wanting to be closer to him, wanting to hold his hand as we walked down the road, my fingers twitching to be linked with his. Did he feel the same way? I thought he did, I had a feeling he'd felt this way for much longer than I had, my feelings for him being clouded by the hatred I had harbored.

I was surprised to have remind myself of that, that I had felt that way, and how quickly my thoughts had changed. But at the end of the day, no one else was responsible for my fathers' death but Orrick and his men, and they were dead. To link the Prince and his people to the acts of few was ignorant, and I saw that now. I smiled as I peeked a small head of white hair poke up from behind a barrel and quickly hide away again.

"I'll meet you at the stable," I said to the Prince.

He glanced at me in confusion but smiled as I nodded my head to the barrel, small lilac hands poking out at the sides. I strolled over to the barrel and sat on a crate next to it. Amara poked her head out to check that Thanatos had left and then joined me on the box.

"My mother says that you're going to help us," her small voice said.

"Help you how?" I asked.

"Help us be able to leave." She glanced toward Ajal cave and my heart sank in my chest.

"The Prince leaves, why wouldn't you be able to?"

"He is a Prince, people respect him. The rest of the world ... Mama says they're scared of us, and fear can be dangerous. So, we're not allowed to leave." She spoke with wisdom beyond her years and from a place that I could understand.

"Mama says you're going to make everything better for us, because you're a Princess and an Isidian."

I gulped at the pressure, how could I tell this girl that I was not her people's savior? The people beyond the cave, even my own people in Isidia, didn't know me, they didn't know if they could trust my judgment.

"Do you love Thanny?"

The question pulled me out of my thoughts and left me speechless.

Amara's large gold eyes gazed up at me expectantly. "Because if you love him, everyone will love him and then everyone will love us." She nodded her head to the road where the village was slowly coming to life.

I was lost for words, my brain in a state of shock.

"You know," I finally began, I wanted to give her hope, but I had to be realistic, "a lot of people don't listen, even if it's a princess or a prince speaking. Sometimes, you have to show them with your actions, and even then it can take a lot for them to see. But, eventually, once enough people see, the ones that don't won't matter anymore. Does that make sense?" I asked, unsure of my words; perhaps they were too harsh for her young ears.

"I think so." She answered, her face smothered in confusion.

I couldn't remember the last time I'd spoken to a child, it could have been when I was one. I had no idea how to dumb things down for them. "But, do you love him?" She asked again, her tone more serious.

I almost wanted to laugh at the absurdity of it all, not the Prince and I but the interrogation the child was putting me through.

"I don't know yet," I said with a weak smile. "It's still new."

She smiled and rose from the box. "I think you do," she said confidently. "You have to." With that, she ran away.

I stared after her, amazed that she could love and care for her Prince so much. I doubted that the children of Isidia would even be able to tell me apart in a crowd.

The stable was made of stone, like every other building in the village, the stalls kept meticulously tidy. Once Faenor was saddled and ready to go, I heaved myself up onto her back; it was a comfortable space now, a safe space. I gave her a pat before gently kicking her sides. She trotted out of the stables and headed north up the center road of the village. Thanatos wasn't far behind but he walked, leading his white mare by her reins. I thought for a second that perhaps I should have done the same and said goodbye to the villagers that had been so kind and accommodating to me but, as we walked, I realized there would have been no point.

His people flocked to him, some begging him to stay longer, others pushing food and gifts at him. A few even slid little trinkets into Faenor's bags as we walked ahead. I called out my thanks and blessings and received warm smiles in return.

We paused at the end of the road; Thanatos gave his thanks to the village and said some quick goodbyes to the Elders and little Amara, whose eyes flicked between me and the Prince the entire time, before swinging onto Serelene's back and coming to join me.

With one last wave from both of us we left the village. I prayed I would one day return.

CHAPTER FORTY THREE
A BREATH OF BRIMSTONE

The air smelled almost poisonous; it took me most of the morning to get used to breathing it. Thanatos said that it was most likely that one of the underground lava lakes had broken to the surface, releasing its toxic gasses into the air. I nodded as if I understood.

The path up the mountains was smooth but dipped awkwardly in some points where it had been overused throughout the millennia. We passed a few travelers on the road and each one was surprised to see me, staring as they shook the Prince's hand.

It was truly amazing to witness the relationship between the Prince and his people. I could only hope that I would someday have that level of familiarity with the people of my kingdom.

Halfway up the mountain, I hopped off Faenor's back and walked up the path on foot. Feeling the solid ground under my boots made me feel slightly better, as if the swaying of being in the saddle had been adding to my nausea. I marveled at the rock formations surrounding me; though they were solid, the shape of them looked fluid. They were formed from cooled lava, the Prince informed me. The higher up we got, the more jaggard the rocks became—some so tall they looked to be piercing the sky.

The air was thick with the smell of smoke and gasses from the volcanoes, making it hard for me to breathe. Thanatos was fine, growing up there he would be used to it, I supposed.

As we got higher up on the mountain, I began to see more of the volcanic side of Osiria. It was a shining, black and red waste but, in its own way, still beautiful. The glow from a lava river flowing through the center seemed to light the expanse, despite being no bigger than a creek. Mt Roark, Osiria's largest and hottest volcano, sat in the center of the land, black smoke billowing out its mouth.

"It won't be long till it erupts again," Thanatos said, tracking my gaze.

"Is it safe to be so close when it erupts?"

"Oh yes, it's fine. The debris barely reaches the palace and, if it does, we have wards." He shrugged.

Of course, he was telling the truth but I was still doubtful—the thought of volcanoes erupting unnerved me.

The closer we got to the top of the mountain, the further apart the Prince and I walked. I wasn't sure if it was done consciously or subconsciously, but I wished it hadn't happened at all by the time we finally reached the top and I spotted what loomed over our heads.

I gaped at what sat before me; it was not at all what I had expected. The sharp spires and general foreboding silhouette of the palace I'd heard of, but the intricate and beautifully detailed stained glass windows and ceilings were a surprise. The whole front of the fortress looked to be made of obsidian which then transitioned into black stone for the remainder of the build.

Past the palace sat the execution square. I walked over to it without even thinking and stood beneath the gallows, staring up at the noose waiting for today's executions to be carried out. My mind was blank as I stared.

Thanatos rested his hand on my shoulder and gave a reassuring squeeze, pulling me out of my daze. Even though it had been over a hundred years since he'd been here and no doubt hundreds of others had died in this same square since then, I spat on the ground. Spat at the memory of him and prayed that Orrick rotted in the Mother's pit.

I let Thanatos lead me gently away from the site of my father's murderer's execution, wiping away tears I hadn't realised had begun to fall down my face.

I paused before the huge doors of the palace to calm myself before we entered.

The entrance to the palace was hauntingly beautiful. The orange glow of the lava on one side and the white light beaming up from the snow on the other made for an interesting lighting situation in the room.

Each stained glass panel on the roof depicted a different scene in Osirian history, some beautiful and some terrifying, but each one cast playful, multicolored shapes onto the ground.

My eyes landed on one of an Isidian King being decapitated on a battlefield; his blood shown with little red triangles of glass, Thanatos flinched as he noticed it too. I moved onto a different panel, my eyes fixed on a young woman in the pane, her long white hair matched by another woman in the same panel, her mother perhaps. The two men flanking her had short hair, common for men during war times. I struggled to pull my eyes from the panel, something drawing me to the young woman.

We continued through the palace. I wanted to take my time to study each panel of stained glass but it would take hours. I could do it after an audience with the King and Queen.

We came to a stop outside two large wooden doors, carved with the same depiction of Osiria as Thanatos' rooms in Sillessia, the fire and ice birds that represented the gods flying above their mountain-divided land. Thanatos took a deep breath and reached over to give my hand a quick squeeze before releasing it and pushing open the doors.

The throne room was much the same as the entry, with stained glass covering the walls and ceiling, but instead of showing histories, it showed the lands conflicting landscapes, casting the room in orange and white light. Tall, wicked-looking columns reached from floor to ceiling and black, stone pews littered the hall, making it resemble more of a temple than a throne room. The thrones themselves resembled the spiked piles of volcanic rock that surrounded the exterior of the fortress; the figures sitting in them fit perfectly with the aesthetic of the room.

King Methuzelah looked identical to his son, the only difference was his thick white beard and stern expression. Queen Omisha was stunning; her features delicate yet striking, she wore her hair loose beneath a red scarf with gold embroidered speckles that resembled falling snow, the same detailing was stitched onto her gown with the addition of the Osirian Sigil on the bodice. Thanatos and I came to a stop before the thrones and bowed, I held my head down until I was addressed.

"Mother, Father, this is Princess Evalina of Isidia, she has accompanied me in returning the treaty papers as a show of goodwill—"

"And she has roped you into a dangerous quest that you did not inform us of." Queen Omisha said bluntly.

I flinched at her words.

"Omisha!" King Methuzelah chastised. "Princess Evalina is our guest and newest ally, the forgetfulness of our son is not her fault."

I suddenly felt very awkward, like a child having to watch their parents argue in public.

"I didn't tell you because I was going to tell you in person and I knew how you would react," Thanatos snapped.

I resisted the urge to sneak out of the room.

"Princess Evalina, we're glad you made it here in one piece." The King said, ignoring his son.

I finally lifted my head. "Thank you, Your Majesty." It was all I could think to say with Thanatos and his mother staring disapprovingly at each other.

"What do you think of Osiria? You must be the first Isidian to walk these lands in quite a few centuries."

"It's beautiful, Your Majesty. Your people have been so welcoming and your land is truly exquisite, King Methuzelah. I would like to thank you for your most kind gift of the brooches, they have been extremely useful on my journey." I bowed.

"Thank Thanatos, he made them and thought it a good gift. I'm glad you have enjoyed your stay so far, I hope you enjoy many more." He smiled warmly, his smile the same as Thanatos'.

I glanced at the Prince beside me, only to catch him mouthing something to his father—he stopped abruptly once he noticed me.

"I'm glad you enjoy the brooches," he said sheepishly.

I nodded. Something seemed wrong about this whole interaction, as if I was missing some important piece of information. It was too casual, despite the formality of our speech. Where were the courtiers and council members?

"We are so glad that your mother agreed to the treaty," Queen Omisha cut in. "It has been long on our minds."

"I am glad, too, from what I have seen of your land and people so far I believe friendship between our kingdoms would be beneficial to both lands."

"Yes, I do agree."

"You two must be exhausted! Go and relax and we'll speak more over dinner." The King boomed, rising from his throne.

Thanatos and I bowed and waited for them to leave the room before the Prince let out a long sigh.

"I'm sorry about my mother." He ran his hand through his hair. "She doesn't like me traveling."

"It's fine, you did warn me." I joked. "Why didn't you tell them?"

"Because I knew how she would react. Father doesn't care but she's ... over protective."

"I understand," I said, gently placing my hand on his shoulder.

"Let me take you to your room." I nodded and followed him through a door and into the corridor of the palace.

The sun must have started to set outside, the light in the corridor now shining more red than orange. I was surprised that it had gotten so late. I'd spent so much of the day worrying that I'd completely lost track of time.

I was glad that the layout of the Osirian palace made more sense than the Sillessian one. I felt that, even though we'd turned many corners, I could still easily find my way out if I needed to.

We climbed two flights of stairs and reached a corridor lined with balconies, the stained glass doors open, letting in a small breeze and the smell of ash and snow. I peeked through one of the open doors and stopped dead in my tracks. I walked onto the balcony and my mouth fell open. At the base of the mountains sat a large expanse of green land. Thanatos came up behind me.

"Disgusting wasteland isn't it?" He joked.

"How is that possible?" I asked.

I'd never heard of there being any plant life in Osiria, we'd always heard that the land was barren and they relied solely on Sillessia for produce; clearly, everyone was wrong.

"The volcanic soil is extremely fertile. People just don't live over there anymore because it's too risky. They used to, thousands of years ago, but too many new volcanoes formed over the years and it became too dangerous. If you look carefully, you may see a few ruined houses."

I tried to spot some but my eyes failed me. The King was right, I was exhausted. I longed to sleep but, if I did, I wouldn't wake for dinner. My shins and calves hurt from the walk up the mountain but I didn't have the energy to heal them.

The Prince eventually pulled me away from the balcony and led me to my room. It was simple but lavish, as you would expect in a palace. I collapsed onto the four-posted bed, the soft mattress and fluffy blankets devouring me. Tonight would be the most comfortable sleep I'd had since we first left isidia.

"I'll leave you to rest." Thanatos laughed, but I called out to him before he could leave the room.

"I need to bathe more than rest." There was no adjoining bathing room to the bedroom that I could see.

"I know the perfect one," Thanatos said with a smile.

The Prince led me back through the palace. Despite the glass ceiling and large windows, the whole place seemed to have a darkness about it; it was almost the complete opposite of Isidia. The structure itself had an overall sinister look to it, nothing was rounded, everything looked as if it would cut you if you got too close. It was a common theme with buildings associated with the Mother. And if anyone was associated with the Mother, it was Dark-Elves.

Part of me liked the dangerous feeling of the palace, the foriegn-ness of it, but being in Thanatos home had made me realize how much I truly missed mine.

We turned a corner and were greeted by two large, black obsidian doors. Thanatos pushed them open and a plume of steam burst through them.

"I hope communal baths are all right," he said. Knowing that questioning was pointless, I walked through the doors and gasped.

The large room was empty, except for the two lake-sized baths carved from the black stone of the mountain.

"Hot springs," Thanatos explained. "They run through the center of the mountain. My ancestors carved these baths. There's a room in the back to change in, you can wear a cover if you're worried but I think we're the only ones in here."

I walked around the baths, staring into the black depths.

I knew they would be shallow, but the black stone made them look bottomless. I went to the back room to change, scoping out the room as I went—it was empty but I needed a private moment to compose myself. I closed the door to the small room and took a few deep breaths, reassuring myself that I was safe. Thanatos was with me, if anything happened he was right there. I undressed and wrapped one of the small coverings around my chest. It barely covered my lower half but kept enough to the imagination that I was comfortable walking into the bathroom.

Thanatos was already lounging in one of the baths when I came out, his clothes discarded against the wall. He smiled reassuringly my way and I slowly stepped down into the water to join him. I took each step slowly, to be sure I was on solid ground, that I was safe.

Once I was fully submerged I rushed through the water to the Prince's side. I could easily reach the floor, but the dark color of it unnerved me. I felt as if it could fall away from beneath me and I would never know.

Thanatos wrapped an arm around my waist and smiled. "It's unsettling isn't it?" He said, giving me a squeeze. "It terrified me as a child, took me years to get used to it."

"I don't think I could ever get used to it." I replied, not taking my eyes off the water and the bottom of the baths. Thanatos gave me another quick squeeze. "The water is lovely though."

It was the perfect temperature, not too hot but not cold in any way. The heat of the water relaxed my muscles; my shins no longer stung, my calves no longer bunched, but I still clung to the Prince. He chuckled when I tightened my grip around his neck as he pushed off the seat of the bath and into the water.

"It's all right, I've got you," he soothed as he slowly pulled me through the water. "I won't let go, I promise."

I tried to relax. I rested my head on his chest, listening to his steady heartbeat and closing my eyes. I tried to focus on the soothing rhythm, on my arms around his neck, his hands on my waist gripping me hard but comfortably. He trod the water as he held me, doing laps of the bath.

With each lap, I felt more and more confident in the water but I still didn't let him go. It felt too right to hold him. Would he stay if I let him go? Or would the monster in the water take him from me?

My mind wandered back to the nightmare that started my fear of water, the eyes that had been stalking me for weeks, haunting my thoughts.

One green and one dead.

They seemed to be stalking the wraith too, whoever owned the eyes. Was it one of the people that had murdered her and her babe? Or was it someone else? Someone hunting me? It frustrated me that I still didn't know where the dreams came from and who was in control of them, but what could I do to find out?

"What are you thinking about?" Thanatos asked.

"The nightmares, I just want to know where they're coming from. The Mother said to listen to the wraith but can we trust her? Can we trust the wraith?"

Thanatos considered this for a moment. "I think if there was anything the Mother said worth listening to it was to trust the wraith, she hasn't led us astray yet."

I almost blushed, remembering that the wraith had pushed me to follow through with my feelings for the Prince. "I just want to know … everything. I'm sick of guessing and never knowing if it was right."

Thanatos ran his hand over the burn on my shoulder, and I resisted the urge to shiver. "I think if we were doing something wrong this would have gotten worse. But, if anything, it's gotten lighter."

I looked down at it. "Really? I haven't noticed that." The handprint burn was still obvious on my pale skin but, as I studied it more closely, I realized that the Prince was right—the color had faded, the skin no longer raised. "What could that mean?"

"I guess that we've done something right, perhaps we've made it to where she wanted us to go."

"Here?" I thought for a moment. The wraith was Osirian, but what could she want me to do here?

"Maybe you're meant to be here with me."

"Yes, I'm sure an ancient Osirian came back from the deadlands just to play matchmaker."

She had indeed played matchmaker but only after a time, there was something else she wanted me to do, some other task that needed to be done.

"So we're a match?" Thanatos poked.

"We were having a serious conversation," I jokingly chided.

He spun us around, sending water spraying. I laughed and clung to the Prince as he spun until we were dizzy and he could barely hold himself upright.

"Serious conversation can wait until dinner with my parents," he said breathlessly. "For now, I want to enjoy your company, I feel like we've been apart all day."

I rested my head on his shoulder. "Are you all right?" I asked, feeling the tension in his shoulders.

He took a deep breath and moved back to the seating at the edge of the bath and plonked down, with me now sitting on his lap. "I'm struggling with something," he said, staring ahead at the wall.

I moved my face in front of his and placed my hands gently on either side of his head. "You can tell me."

He paused, searching my eyes for something I hoped was there. I wanted to know what he was struggling with, what was eating away at him. He let out a long breath. "I should. I need to … I just don't know how."

My chest felt tight, my curiosity clawing to know.

I went against everything my brain was telling me to do. "Tell me in your own time then."

"I'm just worried *my* time is not the right time to go by."

"We'll figure it out when we get there," I said with a smile.

Thanatos smiled weakly but I knew his mind was away from me.

"We should probably get ready for dinner."

The Prince nodded.

Thanatos walked me back to my room and left me to speak with his parents before dinner. I had nothing to wear other than traveling clothes and my Sillessian gown, so I compromised and tucked a clean shirt into the skirt of the Sillessian outfit and left it at that.

I fussed With my hair, staring at my reflection in the mirror on top of a dresser in my room, tucking loose pieces of hair back into the braids Thanatos had done, I tucked and untucked my shirt multiple times and played with adding the sash into my outfit. By the time a servant knocked on my door to take me to dinner, I'd given up on trying to improve on what I was wearing and how I looked. I told myself that they wouldn't be expecting much, they knew we'd been traveling and I assumed that Thanatos had filled them in on everything we'd been through.

The servant was silent as he led me through the palace, glancing my way every now and then. I was once again distracted by the stained glass panels that lined the roof and outer walls of the palace. The colors were vibrant and stark against the malicious looking black of the rest of the architecture, though at times it suited the scene depicted in the panes.

There was so much war in our histories, so much that even I had not been taught about, but it was all here, shown in beautiful works of art meticulously created by glassworkers. Despite the many depictions of Isidians dying gruesome deaths, I didn't at all feel uncomfortable in the palace. Some part of me felt like I was meant to be here. I thought back to the dream I'd had of my father, he'd practically said as much though he'd said nothing. Perhaps that was his way of giving me his blessing, a blessing to move on from the past, to forget and forgive. Or was he pushing me to get the closure that seeing the gallows had given? To see where Orrick had died. Where the tales of my father's last battle ended—with the villain strung up.

I paused at a window, it was the only one that had a single figure. It depicted the same woman from the roof of the entryway, I guessed a princess or queen, Hellebore and Fire Lilies were threaded in her flowing white hair, her hands laid across her middle. She seemed peaceful but, for some reason, the image unsettled me.

"Who is that woman?" I asked the servant as he waited patiently a little ways ahead.

"A princess from a long time ago, I do not know her name."

I stared at the image, something about her jagged face seemed so familiar to me. "Apologies, Your Highness, but dinner will be served soon."

I nodded and followed the servant down the hall to the dining room, the glass woman never leaving my thoughts.

We reached the dining room quicker than I thought we would. I could hear voices through the door, more voices than I thought I would have, and groaned at the thought of this being a formal dinner. I was not prepared for talks of trade and formal discussions of the treaty—and was definitely not dressed for the occasion.

I took a deep breath and tried to ready myself for formal introductions and stuffy council members but, as the door opened, I saw that I couldn't have been more wrong.

CHAPTER FORTY FOUR
BLINDSIDED

The temple's windows had been boarded up with slats of wood, the only light inside the structure coming from candles and braziers. The pews were pushed against the side walls to make room for large tables and beds in the center. The room echoed with the fussing of unsettled children, removed from their daily routines and so desperately trying to make sense of the new thing life had thrown at them. Huddled around the bases of the large pillars were some displaced amputees, already sent back from the frontlines and unable to return to their homes. Priests walked down the aisles of beds and tables, chatting with the people, making it seem like they cared but I knew they felt put out at having to share their temple.

Peverell trailed behind me, taking notes in his journal as we toured the fortified temple, writing down my suggestions as I muttered them, not wanting to say them too loudly in case one of the many children huddled to our sides overheard.

"Those cases there, and the pews there, I want them moved to the doors to be used as barricades if need be. And the door to the catacombs should be left open for ease of escape." I said to Peverell as I was pulled down by a child hanging off my arm. I gripped the child's wrist and swung my arm until they giggled as I swung them into the air before me and placed them back down. More children swarmed toward us, each one wanting to swing on my arms. I obliged a few before we moved into the entrance of the catacombs and the children scurried away back to their guardians.

"I can't believe this has been here all this time and no one knew," Peverell marveled as we reached the doorway to the old goblin tunnels.

"Well, we did. We just didn't share it with anyone. I doubt even the remaining goblins know about these tunnels."

The catacombs beneath the temple were full of past priests and priestesses, their bodies kept in horizontally stacked tombs cut out of the stone. Gold fixings reflected the fire light from braziers that lined the walls and filled the room with an ill-fitting warm glow. The goblin doorway loomed over us, carved from stone and intricately decorated with writings and glittering gems inlaid into the arch. Very few people could read goblin runes but I knew from stories that Eevan used to tell us that Peverell could.

"I wish Eevan had shown me this years ago," Peverell said, crouching beside the stone archway with his quill scratching across his journal.

"I know people have fully ventured through them and survived but I wanted you to make sure they're safe," I said, standing a short distance away, my hands tightly clasped behind my back. The darkness behind the archway unnerved me. It had become a symbol of what would happen if I failed my people.

"It looks to be an entrance to a city and the runes say as much. Is it the only way in or out?"

"I've never heard of it leading to a city, there's a fork in the cave not far from this gate, one side is blocked by a suspected cave in and the other leads under the city and opens along the south-western coast."

Peverell made a sound of realization. "That's why you didn't want us to know about it."

"The *council* didn't," I corrected.

Peverell huffed. "Islina also had sixty years to tell us, then again she wouldn't even speak to us after Eevan died," he added bitterly.

I stared at my feet, caught between agreeing with him and wanting to defend my Queen. I decided to keep quiet and let him vent. As far as I was concerned the Carracallans were an extension of the royal family, though they weren't Isidian, so I would serve them just the same.

"I'm sorry, we must all put you in an awkward position," Peverell said, rising to his feet to join me. "I know you're the Captain, you serve your Queen and people above all else, but to us, well, you're practically our nephew." He placed a hand on my shoulder before walking back through the crypt behind me.

Nephew.

The word sounded strange and the feeling it induced was stranger still. I had considered Islina my mother for many years and always viewed Evalina as the closest thing to family I would ever have again; but, now, I had somehow acquired uncles and an aunty, grandparents even.

"Lorkin, are you coming?" Peverell called.

"Yes!" I answered, pushing the flood of emotions that had crashed over me to the back of my mind.

The sunlight blinded me as Peverell and I stepped through the temple doors and onto the street, greeted by a new wave of displaced elves. The guards stationed in the city were already working to document their arrival and work out where they would be sent until they could return to their homes. I spoke to a guard and learned that they'd come from the outer towns to the east, close to the Shinchaku border. I hoped it wasn't a sign that the Corse were coming from Shinchaku, seemingly the only human place Evalina and Thanatos hadn't visited in their journey. I made a mental note to expand our armies to that area, and hope that we had enough troops to cover it.

The people arriving were dirt-covered and tired. Children either clung to their parents legs or slept on their shoulders. I sympathized with them. After the death of my parents, there'd been a time where I hadn't known where I would end up, who would look after me, where I'd live. But I'd been fortunate enough to have hope that Eevan and Islina would take me in and they had. These people, these children, had nothing. They'd had to flee their homes and the life they knew with little to no hope of returning. It was evident on their faces, the bags deep and purple under their eyes, mouths down turned. I wished there was some kind of solace I could offer but I was sure all they wanted was food and rest.

I wondered how many had seen the horde, and how many had left before they'd arrived. Had they had time to bury loved ones if they'd needed to? Would they be plagued by the same gruesome nightmares as me and the others fighting for their homes?

I tried not to linger on the thoughts, if I let them they would consume me and I had a job to do. I could not allow distractions.

Peverell and I continued through the city, checking in on feed stores and how rationing was going to see if we needed to request more produce from Sillessia. I was surprised at how many of the buildings had been preemptively boarded up, it made it feel as if the city were deserted. I hadn't heard any reports of crime, but most of that news went to Adalric; he'd taken over matters of the city and left the war dealings to me. It was still less than I'd had to deal with previously and I was glad for it.

We were most of the way up the hill that led to the palace when Bellona charged down toward us on horseback.

"Done with your sight seeing?" She said, her blue hair wildly framing her face. "We've gotta go, all of us."

My back straightened. "What's happened?"

"The damn fuckers have gotten through the Aurali boarder, we thought they were just coming through Shinchaku but they threw us off." She paused for a moment, checking that there were no civilians listening in. "They've massacred a whole town. Scouts just got back, absolutely shitting themselves."

"How did we leave a whole border unguarded?" Peverell asked.

"It was guarded," I said hollowly, my mind whirling. How many had we lost?

"They're all dead," Bellona said bluntly. "We need to leave now with a force before this horde can reach the palace."

I nodded in agreement, still partially in a daze from the news. My army was not weak, my soldiers had received nothing but praise from the Carracallans, how had they been defeated? What enemy were we to face on the north-western front?

"What of Islina?" I asked Bellona. "One of us should remain with her."

"My mother is with her. She will keep her calm."

A knowing look passed between the Captain and her brother and I knew not to press. The lineage of the Carracallan Queen, while only rumor, was well known and I would take this as my one and only confirmation of that lineage. I knew Islina would be safe in the care of Zephyrine but it didn't completely subside my worries.

Peverell and I followed Bellona on her horse to the castle as she continued to fill us in on what information she'd been given. And within what felt like moments, we were dressed for battle and once again racing away from the castle.

CHAPTER FORTY FIVE
ROYAL TREATMENT

I didn't know how to react once I saw what was unfolding in the room before me.

The King and Queen were seated on a lounge together, laughing as a Wood-Elf male animatedly retold a story. A young female Dark-Elf nagged at Thanatos as he spun a baby above his head, the infant smiling down at him.

I stood in the doorway, unsure if I should walk in unannounced and feeling as if I were interrupting a private moment.

King Methuzelah noticed me standing awkwardly by the door.

"Evalina! Please, come join us." He waved me over.

I walked around the large marble dining table, feeling even more awkward as the room seemed to hush around me. I was unsure of what to do once I got to the other side of the table, everything was so casual in Osiria, did I still need to curtsey? Before I could ponder on it for too long the King rose from his seat. "This is Daeril, our son in law, married to our daughter, Freyja." He gestured to the woman now snatching the baby from Thanatos.

"I–I didn't know you had other children," I said bewildered.

"Not many people do," The King continued. "She's Thanatos' younger sister, you see, not as important."

"Hey!" Freyja protested, resting the baby on her hip and swaying slightly.

"That is our grandson, Odon."

Odon fought against his mother's arms, trying desperately to get back to his uncle. Freyja couldn't have been much younger than I. I was surprised that she was already married and having children but, I supposed, that's what would have been expected of me had my father still been alive, had my parents produced a male heir.

"He is more important," King Methuzelah added with a wink.

No one protested; they just gazed adoringly at the plump little elf still fighting against his mother. Thanatos came to stand beside me.

"You never told me you had a sister," I whispered.

"You never asked." He shrugged. "Should we sit for dinner? Evalina and I are starved."

I smiled awkwardly, not used to the casualness of the interaction.

Everyone moved to sit around the table, King Methuzelah at the end, his Queen to his left, and Thanatos to his right. Freyja sat to her mother's left, Odon resting on her lap. His brown eyes, the same as his father's, darted between the obstacles on the table and his uncle sitting on the other side, and Dearil took the seat beside his wife and son. I sat next to Thanatos, keenly aware of all their eyes on me, expectant.

I fiddled with my place setting; it matched the rest of the palace in it's dark color scheme. The small side plate looked to be made of thinly carved obsidian, the glasses too. I didn't want to think of how long it would have taken a crafter to make the whole set, or how careful they would have had to be.

A flurry of servants swept through the room, filling cups of water and goblets of wine.

"Th—"

"Ou—" Thanatos and I started and stopped at the same time.

The Prince cleared his throat. "You go first."

"Sorry," I offered, "I was just going to say that the palace is beautiful. I've never seen such intricate glass work."

"We have some of the best glassworkers in Carynthia—it helps that we don't really feel the heat." The King smiled. "How was your journey? Did Thanatos drive you mad?"

I laughed. "Maybe a little bit. We've had quite the journey, but maybe Thanatos would like to tell you himself."

I didn't want to say anything the Prince didn't want his family to know but, as the Prince launched into his story, I realized the only thing off-limits was our relationship and I was glad for it.

Nothing could really happen between us, not when we were both destined to be the rulers of our own lands. King Methuzelah was enthralled with his son's retelling, Queen Omisha wore her usual stern expression, her eyes flicking to me occasionally when I seemed to play a large part. Freyja and Dearil listened as best they could while still struggling with Odon, the infant reaching for anything and everything on the table.

The story caught my attention as he relayed the events of leaving Sevah's house in the woods and the Corse ambush. I'd never heard what had happened after I'd been knocked out, how Thanatos had carried me despite being slowed and injured, the Corse taunting him the entire time, and how he'd healed me before passing out. His mother's eyes again rested on me as Thanatos spoke of me healing him. The moment replayed in my mind. I wanted to reach out and touch Thanatos, to show him I was here with him—reliving the moment as he must be—but I kept my hands to myself.

I was surprised that he skipped over speaking with The Mother but didn't pull him up on it, I was sure he had his reasons.

The table went silent as Thanatos told them of the battle at Kushyam.

"This is the first I'm hearing of this." The King stated, sitting back in his chair.

"I'm sure Keon didn't want to worry you. It was barely a battle," Thanatos justified.

"It's still something we should know, especially when they're so close to our borders," Queen Omisha cut in.

I stared down at my plate.

"I took care of it," Thanatos said simply.

The room again went silent. The King and Queen shared a look, but Freyja spoke first.

"How many, Than?"

I glanced at Thanatos, he'd gone stiff beside me, as if he'd shared too much and knew he was about to get into trouble.

"How many?" His sister asked again, more urgently.

"We'll talk about it later," their father cut in and, by his tone, I could tell it would not be a calm discussion.

"I'm sure the humans could have handled it themselves," the Queen said, taking a sip of her wine.

"I was not going to sit back during an attack, Mother," Thanatos snapped. "We survived and the city and our borders are safe, thanks to us." Thanks to him, not that he would take the credit he deserved. He continued on with his story, though the air in the room felt different, less relaxed.

"It must have been terrifying for you, Evalina, being lost in the blizzard," Freyja said.

"I was a bit worried, yes, but we made it in the end." I bumped my shoulder against Thanatos' and we shared a smile.

I turned back to Freyja, a knowing look plastered across her face. Dinner was brought out and served before I could downplay what had passed between Thanatos and I.

Dinner consisted of roast vegetables and some kind of meat, it didn't taste like any meat I'd had before, but I didn't want to risk asking what it was.

"A toast!" The King proclaimed, raising his goblet into the air. "To Princess Evalina being the first Isidian in Osiria in over a century and to our new friendship."

Everyone at the table raised their drinks into the air and took a sip.

"I look forward to developing the relationship between our peoples further," I replied, bowing my head and taking a sip of my wine.

"Have you heard from Queen Islina while you've been traveling?" The Queen asked, resting her elbows on the table.

"We've had a few correspondences but it's been difficult while traveling. My Carracallan kin are in Isidia, preparing for battle."

"And you are here instead of protecting your home?"

"Mother!" Thanatos warned.

"A simple question," The Queen shrugged.

"I believe I'm doing my part by tracking down the Necromancer," I replied steadily. "We believe slaying the Necromancer will, in turn, dispose of the Corse he has created. And I trust my Grandfather to keep my people and my mother safe in my absence."

"Ah yes, your grandfather, the Great Sea Captain!" King Methuzelah exclaimed excitedly. "I would have loved to meet him at the ball."

"Thanatos told him as much," I said with a smile, glad to be snatched from my conversation with the Queen. "With the peace now between our peoples, you may meet him yourself soon."

"There'll be good reason to, soon, I'm sure. Ouch!" He shot a look at his son. "After the Necromancer is dealt with, I mean."

I glanced at Thanatos but his face was unreadable. I longed to be done with dinner, there was clearly something they all knew that I didn't and it was frustrating to be on the outside.

"How did you and Freyja meet?" I asked Dearil, hoping that speeding up the small talk would in turn speed up the arrival of dessert.

The Wood-Elf smiled at his Dark-Elf wife and their bundle of joy who was gumming a piece of the strange meat from dinner.

"I was part of a convoy for Ambrosia, she was visiting to discuss the use of volcanic soil in Sillessia. I'd never seen snow before and got distracted ... and lost." He chuckled. "A search party was sent out for me and Freyja found me not long after, wandering around the mountain. Boy, did she give me a talking to."

I couldn't hide my smile, the love between the Princess and the Wood Elf was evident.

"After that, I kept writing to her and visiting when I could. I'm sure she was sick of me."

Freyja mock nodded in agreement

"But she was the one that asked me to stay." He grinned at his wife.

She smiled back and handed him the baby.

"He's done a poo," she said with a dazzling smile.

Everyone else around the table broke into a fit of laughter as Dearil took the baby, kissed his wife on the forehead and stalked out of the room holding Odon at arms length.

"I felt bad stealing him from the Sillessians, but he liked it better here anyway," Freyja added after Dearil had left the room, a smile still lingering on her lips.

Her face was beautiful, as beautiful as her mother's, but it held the humor and playfulness of her father's. Both children had their father's long nose and strong jaw.

"Have you had any luck with suitors, Princess?" Freyja asked.

I choked on my wine, badly enough that Thanatos had to give me a good thump on the back. Freyja's easy smile had turned mischievous.

"I haven't really thought about it, to be honest. We had the ball and then we left, and I really only met Soren and then spent the rest of the time with my family." I didn't know why I was sharing so much with them—they felt so comfortable to talk to, like Thanatos.

I took a swig of my wine so I wouldn't say any more.

"I don't think these questions are really any of our business," Thanatos cut in, shooting daggers at his sister.

She relaxed back into her chair resting her goblet of wine against her chest. "I was just curious." She shrugged as she drained her goblet.

Thanatos continued to stare down his sister, their parent's eyes flicking between the two as if they expected one to leap over the table and strangle the other.

"How was the ball?" Queen Omisha asked. "I imagine it was strange to have so many people in your home after so long."

"It was lovely, different but lovely."

"It was a great party, I think everyone had a great time. The Carracallans sure know how to party," Thanatos added, taking over the conversation with his mother.

I'd thought I was well equipped to handle her but, clearly, I was not.

Thanatos launched into telling his family about the ball, describing my home in a way I'd never heard before; even to me it sounded beautiful, more beautiful than the real thing.

I suddenly felt overwhelmingly homesick. I longed to sleep in *my* bed, to wake and have breakfast with my mother, to walk through the woods to the creek. I stared at my pale hands, the only thing in the place that could visually remind me of home.

"Are you all right, Evalina?" The King asked over his son's story.

I shrunk in my chair a little.

"Just tired I guess, it's been a long couple of days." I smiled weakly.

I felt like showing more emotion would lead to an all-out breakdown and I would not do that here.

"Maybe we should call it a night," The King said kindly. He rose and everyone else followed. "Please feel free to explore the palace. If a door is unlocked, you may enter, we have no secrets here. We'll see you in the morning for breakfast," he said with a smile and bowed.

I bowed in return and made to leave, Thanatos trailing behind me.

"Thanatos, you stay."

I looked back at the Prince as he flinched at his father's stern tone. I gave him a sympathetic smile before slipping out of the room and heading back to mine.

CHAPTER FORTY SIX
WINE AND WORRY

I waited until Evalina had left the room and closed the door behind her before turning to face my family. The friendly expressions had faded from their faces and had been replaced with concern and anger. My shoulders slumped as I took my seat at the table again and drained my goblet.

"What in the pit, Thanatos? I thought you were just going there for a damn ball," Freyja exploded. "Now you're almost dying daily?!"

"I'm not almost dying daily." I rolled my eyes and reached for Evalina's unfinished wine.

"Well that's what it sounds like," she snapped.

"She asked for my help, was I just meant to ignore her?"

"Yeah, you don't owe her anything."

My eyes flicked to my parents; my mother wore her usual bored expression and my father looked around the room uncomfortably.

"You haven't told her?" I asked.

"It's your news to tell." My father shrugged, glancing at my mother who only shook her head.

"What? Haven't told me what?" I rested my face in my hands and took a deep breath. Had I ever said it out loud? Had I accepted it yet?

The last few weeks were a blur and I hadn't expected the responsibility to fall to me completely. I hadn't expected things to advance so quickly between Evalina and I, friends maybe, but we were past that—and I was the only one that knew. My mother came to stand behind me and rested her thin hands on my shoulders.

"Thanatos and Evalina are to be married." She gave a supportive squeeze as the last word left her lips.

My sister plonked down into the chair across from me and stared for a moment before pushing her unfinished drink across to me.

"Freyja, don't encourage him," My mother snapped.

My sister ignored her. "I could tell there was something between you two, but marriage? So soon?"

I laughed, a dry, almost sad, laugh. "It was not my choice."

She leaned forward in her seat, her eyes meeting mine. "But you do care for her?" Freyja always had to know everything, always had to have the upper hand.

"Yes." I didn't need to think about it for a second.

I'd known how I felt about the Princess from the moment I pulled her from her first nightmare. She was strong, confident, bold—she knew what she wanted in life and how to get it, she just needed a push.

"What about Thrasos?"

My heart stopped. "What about him?"

"What if …" she couldn't say the words as much as I couldn't hear them.

It had always been a fear of ours, my brother's poor health leading to his early death; it's why I had traveled, why I had made the connections he could not, in preparation for me becoming the Heir in his stead.

"It won't happen," I said sternly, as if I were addressing the very sickness that plagued my twin. "With the new treaty, we have access to the best healers in the world, they will help him."

"Wait. Does she know?"

I looked away from my sister, not ready to face her judgment.

"Thanatos! Really?!"

"I expected her mother to tell her! I thought I was going to be greeted by someone who knew but she had no idea!" I ran my shaky fingers through my hair and my mother once again squeezed my shoulders. "And then, after the ball, Islina still hadn't told her, and then she asked for my help and I thought her mother would tell her before we left, and she didn't." It was getting harder to breathe and my heart was pounding out of my chest. "And then, I thought we could get to know each other on the road and I could break it to her at some point but then we started getting attacked and the blood oath thing started happening more—"

"What blood oath thing?" My father cut in.

I took a few deep breaths to calm myself, my panicking had left me breathless. "She's been having nightmares, we believe they're because of a blood oath but we're not sure, we were going to talk to the mages."

"Nightmares are not usually a sign of a blood oath," my mother said, taking the seat next to me.

"She gets wounded in these dreams. In the first one she got burnt, the second she almost drowned."

My father sucked in a breath. "That sounds more like a curse."

If there was anything Osirians would know about, it was curses. During the wars, my ancestors used to hire witches to curse their opponents, the other races were too scared to deal with the witches but, since most aligned with the Mother, they practically worshiped us.

"I don't think it's a curse but I also don't think it was an oath made by someone living."

Confusion spread across my family's faces.

"She has dreams of an Osirian wraith, in the first one the wraith gave her some riddle to figure out and marked her with a burn."

"Well, that sounds like it would be an oath mark, but it doesn't sound like she entered the oath willingly. There's a higher power involved in this."

I held back the eye roll that my mother's rambling always induced, but perhaps she had a point. I couldn't tell her of the meeting I'd had with the Mother though, it would only result in chaos.

"Can that happen?" My sister asked, the fears of a new mother creeping into her mind.

"Oh, certainly, if one of the gods wills it, it will be done. The Mother may have called on this spirit to make the oath with the Princess and, knowing the Mother, she will likely not give an answer as to why."

Helpful. I finished the wine my sister had given me.

"Have you seen your brother yet?"

I shook my head.

I was always too nervous to see him straight away, every time I came back he seemed to be less than when I left; his color more drained, his eyes duller, bones protruding more, as if the food he ate did nothing to nourish his body. It pained me to see him wither and made me hate leaving, but he got angry with me if I stayed. He loved to hear of my adventures, encouraged me to go on more when I came back, but I always felt guilty.

He was trapped here by his own body and, though he longed to leave, he would never complain, never intentionally make me feel bad.

I was being cautious, if Thrasos knew that Evalina was here he would want to meet her, but then I'd have to tell her. I was not ready and I was a fool for it. Now, when she found out she would hate me and the idea of a loveless marriage was terrifying. Though my parents had different views, they still loved each other; Freyja and Dearil were so in love it almost made me sick to watch them—I longed for that.

"He's doing well, the sickness doesn't seem to have progressed too far this time," my mother said, her voice hopeful.

I smiled, even though it broke my heart to hear her speak of him. Her eldest, her dying son.

"I'll be sure to see him before I leave again. Evalina and I will need to leave for Minoma as soon as possible."

"You believe the Necromancer to be there?" My father asked.

"It's the only lead we have. The first Corse to attack Isidia were Minoman, we'll start there and see if there's any evidence that he's moved, or where he could have moved to."

My father nodded. "It would make sense, that library holds books about everything. Years ago, we petitioned to have some destroyed—they contained knowledge that no one should have, dark magic—but the Minomans refused."

"As you would expect from humans," my mother snapped.

"Omisha, please."

My mother folded her arms and sat back in her seat. The only issue my parents had in their marriage was my mother's hatred of humans. It came from her childhood with the Phoenix Priestesses; they'd warped her young mind and ingrained their beliefs in her so solidly that even my father and her children couldn't change her mind.

"Getting back to the most important task at hand, how are you going to tell Evalina?" My sister asked.

I groaned and my father passed his glass of wine to me.

"Methuzelah!" My mother snapped as I drained it.

"I don't know. Either way, she's going to end up hating me."

"She'll get over it. Do you think I wanted to marry your father at first?" My mother shrugged at his incredulous stare. "Eventually, I got over it, and look at us now! Three happy children, a grandchild and a thriving Kingdom."

I couldn't help but notice she kept the part about the children being healthy out.

"You clearly don't know Evalina very well." Could I even say that I did? Maybe she'd surprise me. My mind was clouding, thanks to the wine. "I'll do it once all this madness is over. Can it wait till then?"

"Of course, darling," my mother said, resting her head on my shoulder and patting my knee. "You do it when the time is right, there's no rush."

I rested my head on my mother's. Though she said there was no rush, I still felt rushed.

Growing up, I knew there was a chance I'd end up betrothed to someone, lady or princess alike, and when it became apparent that Evalina was the only princess this generation, I'd pretty much given up on the idea that it would be a princess. The Isidians had made their hatred of us no secret since the death of King Eevan, so the thought that his daughter would happily marry me had never crossed my mind.

I let out a long breath. I needed to stop thinking about Evalina and the marriage and think about the Necromancer; that was the main goal, that's what we should have been concentrating on, but my mind didn't want to focus anymore. The wine was mixing with my tiredness and bringing my emotions to the surface. I tried to swallow them down. I was with my family and, though it was only for a short time, it was what I'd wanted when we started this quest. To see them, even if it was for the last time.

"I need to go to bed." I slowly rose from my chair, testing my balance.

"See your brother first," my mother instructed. "He's missed you."

I nodded and wished my family a good night before leaving the dining room.

I took my time walking down the halls, the wine affecting me more than it usually would. Thrasos' room was on the opposite side of the palace to Evalina's. Because of his illness we kept him as far away from the volcanoes as possible, hoping the clearer air from the tundra was better for him. We really should have just taken him away from Osiria altogether but to move him was too risky, we weren't sure if he would survive travel.

I ran my hands along the walls and windows as I walked, as I had done when I was a child, feeling the bumps of lead in the stained glass windows and the carved points of the columns that framed them. Part of me hated these windows, their depictions from a time when Dark-Elves reveled in their death powers.

So many showed Kings of the past, my ancestors, using their power on others, their souls leaving the body in a black plume that resembled the smoke of our volcanoes. I loathed them. I wished I could go through the palace and smash every single one that glorified our terrible power.

We were cursed, not blessed.

No one ever spoke of the children that accidentally killed their pets before they even knew they had the power, or the farmers that let emotions take over and accidentally wipe out entire flocks, leaving their families with nothing.

It wasn't easy for some to ignore the stifling feeling of being around people and their souls, it doubled the presences in the room, cornered you until you couldn't take it anymore. Or it piques your interest, draws you in until you draw it out.

Our Neainn were not allowed in Sillessia, even the fairies could not handle the devastation of our gift. Instead, they were kept in the most dangerous part of our land, hidden away so they could do no damage to the outside world.

I knocked gently on my brother's door, entering anyway when I got no answer. The room was filled with everything he could ever need and servants checked on him hourly to make sure his water basin was full and fresh, that he had enough food, books, and paper for drawing and writing.

Both Thrasos and I were quite artistic; I preferred carving and glass work, while he was a talented painter and sketcher. He'd designed most of my tattoos, had even done a few himself—though he didn't like it, complained that skin was too different to paper and canvas.

His walls were covered in his artwork, sketches of our family and the servants, paintings of the landscapes that he was so familiar with he didn't need a reference to paint. He already had a whole corner of sketches and paintings dedicated to our nephew; he'd perfectly captured the exact brown of his eyes and pink-ish hue of his hair, the cheeky grin he'd gotten from his mother.

On the easel near the window, I spied a new family portrait in the early stages of conception. Upon closer inspection, I realized the hold up was caused by Thrasos' own indecisiveness on whether or not he should be painted in his wheeled chair or standing. I ran my fingers down the canvas, feeling the heavy denting where he'd sketched, erased and re-sketched his figure in the two positions. I sighed wishing it wasn't a decision he had to make, I wished he would be content with his chair but also wished he didn't need it. Said chair was sitting empty in the doorway to his bedroom, indicating that he was already in bed.

I walked around his living room, blowing out all the candles before heading into the bedroom. I gazed at my twin and, much to my surprise, he did look relatively the same as when I'd left.

If it weren't for his height and general long-ness, you'd think him a child; he was too skinny, too frail. His breathing was deep and slow as he slept, not ragged and shallow like it was when he was awake and exerting himself. When he painted, he breathed as if he were climbing a mountain but it brought him so much joy, I didn't have the heart to tell him to stop.

I climbed into bed next to him and gently lifted his arm so I could shuffle under it and rest my head on his shoulder.

"Than," he whispered, not even opening his eyes. "Welcome home." His arm tightened around me, as much as he could manage, and I closed my eyes and let sleep take me.

CHAPTER FORTY SEVEN
THE OSIRIAN PRINCESS

I waited for Thanatos for as long as I could be bothered before undressing and curling into bed. Even in the palace, with the fire blazing in my room, I was freezing. I'd asked the maid if they had any warming pans and she'd just stared at me like I was crazy. I shivered under the blankets for a while before I'd fully warmed them up and was able to sleep. I wished that Thanatos had joined me so I could have stolen his warmth but accepted that he was probably not in the mood, given how I thought things were going to go with his family discussion.

He had been quite reckless in Kushyam, though I didn't really know the full extent of Dark-Elven powers. I shivered again, as his face with blacked out eyes slid into my mind. I closed my eyes and thought of other things, trying to push that memory out of my head. I thought of the palace and its beautiful windows, never in my life had I expected something so beautiful would exist in Osiria, despite their gruesome content. I wondered if, now that we had the treaty, Isidia could borrow some of the skilled glassblowers and have them mend the Throneroom roof with stained glass—it would be beautiful with the mages enchantment of falling petals.

I fell asleep with the image of multicolored petals falling from a ceiling made of rainbow glass.

The Palace's vast entry hall was empty, save for the wraith standing in the center, staring at a panel of the stained glass roof. I walked through the hall toward her, gazing at the depictions that littered the walls and roof, the images moving slow and skittish.

Osirian Kings decapitated Isidian in a flash of red triangles, souls sucked from bodies in a plume of gray, glass octagons.

"Who are they?" I asked the wraith once I reached her.

Her face was full, her eyes golden, hair thick but the deep slash across her throat still sat open, exposing the inner workings of her neck.

"My family," she said sadly, her voice echoing through my mind.

I looked at the young elf made from glass and the dead one in front of me. "That's you?!"

She nodded, not taking her eyes off the panel.

"You're—you were a princess."

She nodded again.

"You're related to Thanatos, then," I said, suddenly feeling slightly betrayed. Why didn't she tell me?

"I believe I'm his great, great, great aunt." She chuckled, red blood spurting from the gash in her throat and leaking down her front. "Hard to believe anyone married my brother, he was a brute."

The world around me flashed and I seemed to be speeding through the palace impossibly fast, reminiscent of when I'd been teleported by the fairies.

I stood in front of the other panel of the Princess now, her glass hair blowing in a breeze I couldn't feel, the flowers lifting and drifting through the other windows along the hall.

"They didn't want to show the baby, so they made me pregnant." She ran her fingers down the stomach of her glass-self. "Even in death, they would not accept her."

I remembered cradling the dead infant, her head lolling back as I'd held her, and shivered.

"I'm so sorry this happened to you." It was all I could think to say. "How—"

"What are you doing here?!" The harsh voice came from nowhere.

I spun, looking for the source, and came face to face with a hooded figure, it reached for me with patchwork hands of gray and white. I pulled back with a gasp and looked to where the face was hidden beneath the hood and was met only with two eyes, one green and one white.

I bolted upright in my bed, my breathing heavy. I scanned my room, looking for the eyes, the hand, as if they could have followed me from my dreams. There was nothing, no one.

I pulled off the covers and got out of bed, threw on my clothes and left the room, stalking down the hallway to the panel of the dead Princess. I kept my eyes down as I walked, terrified that I'd see the glass people moving in their stone and lead frames.

I stared at the window, the glow of the volcanoes turning her hair pink like Odon's. I wished for a moment that this one would move, that she could speak to me now and finish her story. I sighed and continued walking down the hallway to the dining room, praying there'd be wine somewhere.

I quietly opened the door and headed straight to the left hand side of the room where the wine jugs sat.

"It seems you and my brother have the same vice."

I jumped and almost dropped my, now full, goblet. I spun to find Freyja on the lounge nursing Odon, the baby suckling desperately on her breast.

"I'm sorry, I thought everyone would be asleep."

She smiled. "I *wish* this one would sleep." She nudged her head toward her son, who grabbed at her mouth with his free hand. "Come, sit with me."

I went to place the jug down but at the last minute decided I'd rather take it with me—perhaps if I was drunk enough I could get some sleep.

"Does that hurt?" I asked, not knowing how else to start small talk.

"A little, at the start, but you get used to it—until they suck too hard."

"Why not get a wet nurse?" I asked, it was what people normally did.

"I prefer to do it myself, I like the time alone with him and it's uncomfortable if you don't." She took a deep breath. "Than told us of your nightmares, did you have one tonight?"

I sighed and nodded. It was nice to have someone else know and I was thankful that I hadn't had to be the one to tell them. I don't think I could have without breaking down.

"The Princess that's shown in the hallway, do you know anything about her?" I asked.

Freyja shook her head. "Not a lot, Mother and Father would know more. I only know that it's believed she was killed during a war with Isidia, but it was so long ago the details are lost."

"What about a man with one green eye and one white?"

She shook her head. "No idea on that one, sorry."

"Thanks anyway, it's just driving me mad not knowing."

"I can imagine."

Odon finished feeding and I looked away for a moment as Freyja adjusted herself, until I heard her patting the baby.

"Do you want children in the future?" She asked.

I smiled. "Maybe, but it'll be in the very far future."

She laughed. "I suppose dealing with your mother is much like dealing with a child."

My face fell and she cursed herself

"I'm sorry, that was rude."

"No, it's true. I'm just still not used to how widely known it is, we thought we'd hid it well."

"I'm sorry, my father always says my mouth moves faster than my mind. I can't imagine what she's been through. Taking the throne at such a young age, then losing your father not long after, I see why she is the way she is." She held Odon a little tighter. "Honestly, if the same thing happened to me I'd probably end up the same."

I smiled weakly. "Hopefully, that will never happen," I said gazing at the little elf, wishing him the best life, a life different to mine.

"Do you want to hold him?"

I started. "Oh no, I've never held a baby before."

She shushed me and thrust Odon into my arms.

I grabbed him around the ribs and held him in front of me for a moment before placing him down on my knee. He stared up at me with his large brown eyes. I was probably the strangest creature he'd ever seen, the exact opposite to the majority of his family.

Freyja took the opportunity to get up from her seat and pour herself a goblet of wine. She took two large mouthfuls before flopping back onto the chaise and smiling at me as I bounced her son on my lap.

"So how long have you and Thanatos been together?"

I froze. "Ah, what?"

"Oh come on, I know when my brother has feelings for someone and you two are terrible at hiding it." She laughed.

"It's only recent," I confessed. "The last two weeks maybe?" I honestly wasn't sure, it was hard to keep track of days and weeks while traveling.

"How exciting," she said gazing at me over her goblet.

"Well, we both know it's only temporary, eventually I'll have to wed."

"Yes." Was all she said, but something about the way she said it sounded like she wasn't convinced.

"I should probably go back to bed, Thanatos will probably want to leave soon. I want to make use of the comfortable bed while I can."

She nodded and sat up to accept her baby back.

I fished my hair out of his mouth and gave him one last squeeze before giving him back to his beaming mother.

"Goodnight, Princess," she called to me as I made to leave the room.

"Same to you," I called back.

I woke to the sun shining brightly through the window. I half expected to roll over and be face to face with Thanatos but there was no one there. I put off getting out of bed for as long as I could, but my bladder betrayed me eventually.

Dressed in travel clothes, not knowing if or when Thanatos wanted to leave, I headed to the dining room. Passing the glass portrait of the Princess wraith as I went, her eyes seemed to follow me as I trudged down the hall.

I slowly opened the door to the dining room and peaked through the gap, scanning the room to see who was already awake and if Thanatos was there.

"Evalina, good morning," the Queen purred, eyeing me over the edge of her tea cup.

"Good morning, Your Majesty," I replied, curtsying as I swung open the door.

The Queen smiled her cruel smile and lowered her cup to its saucer. "Please, call me Omisha. There's no need for formalities here."

I nodded and took a seat by her at the long table.

"Please, have some tea," she offered. "It's a lovely blend from Shinchaku."

"Thank you." I smiled and poured myself a cup, recognising the tea as the same one I'd shared with Queen Anouk.

I wondered if Thanatos had also gifted Omisha the tea and, if so, who had received it first.

"Did you sleep well? Thanatos said you've been having nightmares of late."

"I slept well enough, thank you, but I wonder if you could help me. I asked Freyja last night but she was unsure. The lone Princess, in the window down the hall, who is she?"

If Omisha was surprised by my question, it did not show, she simply poured herself another cup of tea and took a deep breath before speaking in a calm, almost bored sounding tone. Her usual tone, I was coming to learn.

"That is Princess Ossena, she was betrothed to an Isidian Prince, I forget which one, but ran away with a servant, starting a war." Omisha took a sip of tea. "She was assassinated—by your people, it's believed," the Queen explained nonchalantly.

"Oh." I wasn't sure how to react.

"Don't stress yourself, it was millennia ago and her assasination actually sparked the peace we've been enjoying for so long." By 'peace', she meant the lack of all out continent-destroying war.

My mind struggled to make sense of all the information I'd received over the last few days and was starting to ache. I could see no link between Ossena and the Necromancer. Elves lived for a long time, hundreds and thousands of years, but never usually more than two thousand, if they could make it to two thousand. We got sick, just like every other race in this world, and could die from old wounds, but if you were lucky enough to survive all of that you waited until the time was right and then it would just happen. No pain, no fear, it was another blessing from the gods—one more thing for the humans to envy.

"Are you all right, Evalina?" Genuine concern laced the Queen's tone.

"I'm just … feeling lost." I glanced up at her, unsure if I should share my feelings or not.

Despite her cold exterior, the Queen gave off the same openness as her son, the willingness to listen.

"The dreams seemed to be guiding me, I thought they had something to do with the Necromancer but now … I just can't make sense of them."

Omisha sat back in her chair, swirling the tea inside her delicate cup. "It does strike me as odd that the dreams began at the same time as all this. I don't blame you for thinking the two were connected." She leant forward resting her elbows on the table and her chin on her folded hands. "But perhaps they are, just not in the way you're thinking." She studied me for a moment, considering her next words. "I, and the Phoenix Priestesses, believe the Princess was killed by humans, not High-Elves."

I wasn't shocked by the statement, Thanatos had warned me of his mother's hatred for humankind.

"What makes you believe that?" I asked, genuinely; if it could help me, I would listen to any theory—no matter how outrageous.

"The priestesses keep very detailed records of history and, according to accounts from that time, the whole of Osiria had a ward against Idsidians around it. There was no way they could have gotten to her. Humans, on the other hand … ." She frowned. "For millennia, the Osirian royals have consulted with the Kushyami and, while it is profitable, it's risky. They've always been a jealous race, never happy with what they have, always fighting for more. How long before they get sick of paying to use our mines? How long before they get sick of paying for our ice to keep their stores cold? They have magic, but is ours not superior still?"

I wanted to argue, to discount everything she said, but there was truth to it. Humans had been given magic because they revolted once they'd decided we weren't the gods they thought us to be—once they saw that we too could die. Our ancestors could have wiped them out, easily, but they pitied them. So, we taught them how to substitute, how to take a bundle of flowers and tree sap to make paint in an instant—small spells to help them protect themselves and do small things like make their hair grow faster. They'd been happy with that … perhaps, until now.

"What can we do?"

She shrugged and collapsed against the back of her chair. "With people like my husband, Father bless him, siding with them, there's not a lot we can do. Except work to expose them for what they really are, show the others how greedy and irresponsible they are."

It made sense to me; humans were generally fine with High-Elves but was it only because we could be their savior if the situation called? I'd seen the way the humans treated Thanatos, the distance they kept, the hidden glares; how much worse would it be if they didn't have magic? If they really thought they had no defense against him?

I felt anger toward the humans rising within me. After all we had done for them, how could they still not trust us?

I jumped as the door behind me opened.

"Good morning, darling," Omisha said affectionately as Thanatos entered the room.

"Mother, Evalina," he said by way of greeting.

Walking behind his mother, kissing her cheek as he passed her. His usually neatly styled hair was loose around his shoulders, it didn't even look brushed and he was wearing the same clothes as the day before.

"How did you sleep last night?" She asked.

"Well," he stated shortly.

I tracked him with my eyes; he seemed stiffer than usual, each move cautious.

"Evalina was just telling me about her dream last night." Thanatos straightened and spun away from the tea tray to face me.

"Are you all right?" He asked desperately, scanning my face for any evidence of trauma.

"I'm fine, it was just informative this time, but we can talk about it later," I offered, hoping he understood that there was more I needed to tell him—in private.

He barely acknowledged my response, simply going back to make a cup of tea and sit beside his mother. He focused on his tea, occasionally swirling his cup but never drinking as if the act of making it had simply been routine.

Other members of the family slowly made their way in until there were six of us seated around the large table; Omisha, Thanatos, Methuzelah, Daeril, little Odon, and I.

Odon seemed to recognise me from the night before and insisted on sitting beside me, every time his father tried to move away he'd fuss and fuss until Daeril gave up and plonked into the seat beside me, apologizing and warning me that Odon may unexpectedly stick his hands in my food or grab my hair.

"I don't mind," I'd said, poking the baby's nose with the tip of my finger, sending him into a fit of giggles. "Where is Freyja?" I asked the Wood Elf.

"Sleeping in, Odon kept her up very late last night." He bounced the baby on his knee. "Though I'll have to wake her for his next feed soon," he said, more to himself than to me.

Thanatos seemed to be in a daze through breakfast, he spoke to no one, barely ate and didn't touch his tea. I tried to catch his attention multiple times throughout the meal but he almost seemed to be ignoring me. I wondered if it had anything to do with the discussion he'd had with his family after dinner, if he was feeling guilty about being irresponsible with his power or for leaving them for so long, for not informing them of what exactly had been going on on our journey. I was itching to know, to know how I could help him, make him feel better.

The second breakfast was over, I almost shot right out of my seat so I could sequester the Prince and question him; but, before I could, King Methuzelah addressed me.

"Evalina—I hope you don't mind me dropping the 'princess', we're not much for titles here—your mother and I have discussed the treaty at length and agree with everything in it but, as you will soon be Queen, I would like to know your thoughts."

The question stumped me. I hadn't personally read the treaty; I'd not had a chance between the ball and being seated before the Osirian King himself. I thought on it for a moment, whether or not I should be honest, or act as if I had in fact read it.

"I trust that my mother and I hold the same views and, as her successor, I would not want to supersede her rulings—I just want peace. After meeting the people in the villages and speaking with them, I can see that they want it too. I pray that we can have it sooner rather than later."

"I'm glad you feel that way, your mother has said as much. It's time we put our troubled past behind us and moved on, look to the future rather than the past." The King smiled, a smile so similar to his childrens'.

I could see Thanatos's fingers tapping away at the table, and once again tried to subtly get his attention, but his eyes were fixed on the door to the hallway, as if he were terrified of what or who could come through the door next.

"Evalina and I need to speak with the mages," he said abruptly, sitting bolt upright in his chair like a spooked cat. "Are we done here?"

I couldn't hide my surprise at his tone, it was so blunt, so unlike him. The King gave him a disapproving look that Thanatos answered with his own, resulting in a silent conversation between the pair through various subtle facial expressions.

I rose from my seat. "Yes, we do. I hope you don't mind us leaving so abruptly but it is extremely important."

The King pulled his eyes away from his son, his expression returning to one more neutral. "Of course not. Thanatos will know where they are."

I nodded and turned to leave the room and wait for Thanatos in the hallway. Something was wrong—he was hiding something, they all were.

CHAPTER FORTY EIGHT
THE MAGES TOWER

"What is going on?" Evalina demanded as I closed the door to the dining room to join her in the hall.

"What do you mean?" I asked, gently resting my hand on her back and pushing her along the hallway toward the mages' tower.

"Something is up with you. You've been acting strange since we got here."

I ran my hand through my hair. I hadn't braided it, I didn't want to risk being around when Thrasos woke up and having to explain to him why he couldn't come to breakfast. I didn't want to tell him that I was getting married, and my unknowing fiance would be there, and that she thought we couldn't be married because she didn't know he existed … . Just thinking about it all was bringing back the breathless feeling I'd had the night before; I took a few deep breaths and tried to center myself.

"Thanatos? Are you well?" Evalina asked, her hands on my shoulders.

I hadn't even realized we'd stopped walking. We were barely a few steps from the dining room door, how long had we been stopped here?

"Do you need to see a healer?"

I shook my head, closed my eyes and took one more deep breath. "I'm sorry, I'm fine." I hooked my arm with hers and fixed a smile to my face, pushing down my anxieties and savoring our contact.

She wasn't fooled at all by my facade and gave me a stern look. "You can't keep hiding things from me, Thanatos. Eventually, I'm going to get sick of it."

"I'm sorry." My smile faded again. "How about this—I'll tell you everything after Minoma."

She raised a black eyebrow.

"I promise, the second we get back from Minoma, I'll tell you everything."

It was cruel to assume we would be coming back at all, when the possibility of dying was so real. I already had. At least that's what it had felt like. When I'd healed Evalina in Sillessia I could have sworn I'd given her what was left

281

of my life and left nothing for myself. I had felt it pulling out of me and spreading through her and when she'd opened her eyes I could have sworn I'd seen myself looking back at me. Perhaps it was a hallucination and I hadn't seen myself at all, but saw Thrasos watching his only window to the outside die in front of him.

"Then I'll have to make sure we do come back from Minoma," she said defiantly.

And I knew she would.

As I led her through the palace she described her most recent dream to me, giving a shudder as she described the patchwork man.

"I'm sorry I wasn't there," I said helplessly.

"No, it's fine," she said, tightening her grip on my arm. "I was only a little spooked."

"The fact that he knew you were here worries me. Did you tell my mother this?"

"No, I only asked her about Ossena."

I nodded. "We'll have to tell the mages. If he's getting in here somehow, even through magic, they'll know, or at least they'll be able to stop him."

She let go of me and wrapped her arms around herself. "I'm sorry if I've put everyone in danger, now that he knows I'm here he may send Corse after me."

I paused. "This is not your fault. He's the mad one raising the dead and trying to wipe out races. You're the one trying to stop him, trying to save Carynthia." I lifted her face gently by the chin. "If the Corse he sends here are anything like the ones he sent to Kushyam, we'll have them sorted in no time." I couldn't stop the smirk from spreading across my face; as much as I hated using my powers, the idea of foiling the Necromancer was too pleasant of a thought.

"But what if he doesn't? What if he sends ones like the ones in Sillessia, the ones your power didn't work on?" She was fidgeting, pinching at her clothes and shuffling her feet, working herself up into a panic.

I placed a hand on each of her shoulders and stilled her. "There is a reason Ravenna was built in the mountains. Even without the blizzards, the path to the palace is hard to find and if you don't know where the tunnel is, you can't even get through the mountain range, it's too treacherous to try to climb." I pulled her into a tight embrace, needing it just as much as she did. "We're in the safest place in Carynthia right now. No one can get you here." She relaxed into my chest, her breath seeping through my clothes and warming my skin. I wished I could hold her and never let go, but we had to continue on. I wanted, more than anything, for her to be free of the nightmares and if that meant dealing with the Necromancer, then it had to be done as soon as possible. "I'm sorry I wasn't there last night," I said into her hair, giving her a squeeze.

"It's fine, I'm sure you had family matters to discuss."

I know she didn't mean it maliciously but I couldn't help but take it to heart. If only she knew.

After I'd laid down with Thrasos and had a few hours sleep I woke to him throwing up over the side of the bed. I'd pulled his hair back, and held it as he retched, it had grown to be almost as long as Evalinas; it was just one of the many things they had in common.

Had I truly been the Heir and unable to marry her, I would have thought her and Thrasos a smart match. Father knows he could use a healer as a constant companion.

When he'd finished, Thrasos had tried to insist on going straight to the bath but I spent almost an hour talking him out of it. He was too weak to sit in the bath alone and I was too tired to sit with him. He was more worried about my comfort than his own, *again*. I had to tell him stories of taverns covered in vomit, beds that were clean but still reeked before he calmed down and went back to sleep.

"I'll be there tonight, I promise." I said, planting a kiss on the top of her head. She smiled up at me and we continued on our way to the tower.

The tower was nestled into the backside of the castle. The stairs leading up to it were steep and unforgiving but surrounded by beautiful, stained-glass windows depicting various potions and ingredients, as if the crafters had been given a shopping list by the mages and told to put it into the design so that no ingredient was ever forgotten.

I gazed down at the Princess as she followed me up the tower stairs, the stolen book from Sevah in hand, and smiled at her awestruck expression. I was happy to be showing her what life here was truly like and the beauty of my home. I hoped that, on her word, other outsiders would also come to marvel at the beauty of it.

The further up the tower we ascended, the stronger the smell of flowers, herbs, and spices became, until it was a full assault on the senses.

I hoped Evalina wasn't sensitive to smells.

I pushed the heavy door open once we reached the top and stepped into the well organized room. Every herb, flower, and spice had its place and was sorted alphabetically by the ancient Minoman name in open shelves fastened to the walls around the room. The mages were so hard at work crushing, mixing and performing spells, they barely even noticed that Evalina and I had entered. I led Evalina across the room to the Head Mage, Urnaline; her tall, portly figure was bent over an old scroll, scanning it closely.

"Yes, Prince Thanatos?" She said without lifting her head from the scroll.

"Urnaline, Princess Evalina and I have some questions for you, are you free?" She straightened and turned her head to look at Evalina.

"Princess, do you know much about the healing techniques of your people?" She asked Evalina hurriedly. "I wonder, are they much different to ours, or do you just use your gift and barely rely on medicine?"

"Um, we use medicine," Evalina offered. "We tend to only use our magic for the big stuff."

Urnaline wrote the new information down on a scrap of parchment next to her on the desk that was already covered in random, haphazard scribbles. "And what level of pain would you say your people would endure before using their powers?"

"I assume it would depend on the person," Evalina answered, flashing me a questioning look.

"Urnaline, I appreciate your dedication to your craft but it's quite urgent that we speak with you," I interjected.

"It's not everyday I get to question a High-Elf! We know so little of them." I gave her a stern look, to which she sighed. "Oh all right, we'll go to my office."

She quickly jotted something down on the scrap and led us up a rickety flight of stairs to the very top of the tower, the ceiling so low that we had to hunch to stand. It was just as, if not more, organized as the room below, except for the desk, which was littered with pieces of scrap parchment.

"Right, what is it then, Thanatos?" Urnaline said, sounding irritated she'd had to pause her research.

"Necromancy—what do you know?"

She walked around the desk and took a seat, motioning for us to sit in the chairs across from her as she rocked back on hers and thought. "Well, to be brief it's bringing people back from the dead, or if it's a novice it's more returning the soul to the original body. It takes a lot of skill to repair the decay, to fully return someone to the living world."

"So it's not like High-Elf powers?" Evalina asked.

"No. From what I can tell, High-Elven powers don't particularly have a skill level attached, you either bring someone back or you don't, there's no inbetween. And High-Elves have a time limit, you couldn't pull an ancient corpse out of the ground and bring them back, it has to be recent, fresh." She paused, staring at the ceiling. "Necromancers, on the other hand, can bring anyone back, anything back. But they have to be extremely well versed and powerful to be able to resurrect ancient corpses and have them not be skeletons."

"And anyone can do this? Become a Necromancer, I mean," Evalina asked.

Her expression showing clearly how horrified she was that such powers would exist, but Urnaline straightened herself and stared into the Princess' eyes.

"It is black magic, Your Highness," she said sternly, picking up on an emotion in Evalina's eyes that I had missed, "and, besides, no one found your father's body."

"Urnaline!" I chided.

"It's fine, Thanatos, she's right." Evalina's voice was defeated, though I knew that she'd never seriously consider bringing her father back.

"However," Urnaline continued, "I would assume that Necromancy would come quite easily to a High-Elf, given that your powers are practically the same. Dark-Elf however … it would be impossible, completely against nature and the Mother's intentions."

"Dark-Elves can't practice Necromancy?" Evalina asked.

"Of course not, it goes completely against our nature, it'd be like a Wood-Elf trying to use their magic to kill a plant." She snorted.

Evalina's eyes flicked to mine and I knew exactly what had crossed her mind.

"Evalina keeps seeing this man in her dreams, a man with patchwork skin and two different eyes; one green and one white." I paused, considering the words that were about to come out of my mouth and the feeling of downright horror they induced. "Would it be possible to amplify powers by stealing ... parts of another race?"

I saw a shiver go through Evalina and the same horror I'd felt crossed both the women's faces.

Urnaline chewed on her bottom lip and thought for a moment, staring at the roof of the tower. "I–I would assume it could be done, perhaps by using Necromancy to bring each of the pieces back to life before or after attaching them." I felt queasy just thinking about it and was thankful that I had skipped breakfast. "How the magic would transfer is beyond me, there's still so much about how our own bodies work that we don't know." Urnaline said, sounding defeated yet intrigued at the same time.

"Have you heard of the *Nekros Librorum*?" Evalina piped in.

Urnaline gasped. "Do you have a copy?!" She asked desperately. "I've searched for one for years! But the only copy I know of is in Minoma."

"We have a copy," Evalina said, placing the book on the desk. "It's written in old Minoman, we can't read it but, from the illustrations, we believe that if we kill the Necromancer, their creations will die too." Evie flicked to the page with the depiction and pushed it before Urnaline. "Can you confirm that?"

The mage studied it, running her finger over words only she could read, every now and then writing a bit of information down on a piece of scrap. "From this bit of text I can confirm your beliefs. If you are able to kill the Necromancer his Corse will die with him."

Evalina and I let out a collective sigh.

Just knowing that bit of information helped us so much in the long run. It meant that we only needed to focus on one target, not hundreds of thousands.

"In saying that, though"—our faces fell at Urnalines words—"the bodies of those returned will still exist, so someone is going to have to clean that up."

I almost laughed, to worry about something like the clean up seemed petty in comparison to defeating the Necromancer, but I thought to mention it to my father.

"Thank you, Urnaline, this has been a great help," Evalina said, rising from her chair.

"No problem, please feel free to come to me with any question you may have before you leave," Urnaline said, offering Evalina a warm smile. "Now, in regards to that book—"

"You can keep it, for now," I cut in. "Evalina, I'll meet you back at your room. I just have some other matters to discuss with Urnaline."

Evalina glanced between me and Urnaline before nodding and heading down the tower steps.

I waited until I was sure she was out of the tower and strolling down the hallway, probably thinking about how sick she was of my secrets. I collapsed back into my chair and sighed, closing my eyes and pinching the bridge of my nose.

"What is it, Thanatos?" Urnaline asked, sounding only mildly concerned.

"How is Thrasos?"

"Have you not seen him yet?" She asked, relaxing back in her seat, knowing exactly where this conversation was going.

"I have, but I need to hear it from you."

She sighed, it was the same every time I came home—I was surprised she didn't just expect it. "He's doing well. Our latest treatment seems to be working better than the last. He's holding food down more often than not, he's able to stand for longer, and he doesn't tire as quickly." Her eyes shifted.

"But?" I pressed, my heart in my throat.

"But, I don't know how long it will last. He needs constant care from a healer, and a powerful one. Ours are not strong enough."

"Then you'll be glad to hear the news." She raised a single eyebrow in question. "Evalina and I are to be married, so we'll have access to the Isidian healers soon."

Urnaline sat in shocked silence for a moment. "Congratulations?" She offered.

"We'll see. Once Evalina finds out, it may not happen at all."

"She doesn't know?!" Urnaline exclaimed.

"No, and I don't want to talk about it. Just tell me what my brother needs."

She listed off a few ingredients that they were running low on and then filled me in on what they would need healer wise; a trained, non-magic healer as well as a powerful magical healer.

I left the tower full of dread for the future, and it had nothing to do with the Necromancer. I feared for my brother, his condition was still a mystery to us and so we had few answers and even fewer fixes. To have a healer with him all the time would help him immensely—and ease my mind. I had to do all I could to make that happen, even if Evalina hated me afterward.

I just wanted what was best for my brother.

I came to Evalina's door and knocked, it swung open after the first one.

"Is everything all right?" She asked quickly, her green eyes seemed brighter than usual. I nodded and she threw her arms around my neck, hugging me tightly. I fought the urge to break down, I would save that for later, when I was alone.

"I'm so happy we only have to kill him! It makes it all so much easier," she exclaimed.

"We'll still be in for a fight."

"Of course, but it won't be a war, we won't have to fight them all."

I wished I could join her in her excitement, but something felt off. It all seemed too easy, and I'd learnt that, in life, when things seemed too easy they were just about to get hard.

CHAPTER FORTY NINE
PARTING WORDS

Thanatos and I had decided that we should leave for Minoma as soon as possible, given the new information we'd received. We decided it was imperative that we find the Necromancer before he could try a large-scale attack anywhere with Corse like the ones in Sillessia, the ones that had been resistant to Dark-Elven powers. Thanatos left to tell his family the news and I began to pack my things and write a list of any supplies we were lacking.

I felt lighter than I had in weeks, the fear of an unwinnable war dispelled from my mind. Our journey was so clear now, there were no more ifs and buts in our minds, we just had to track down the Necromancer and kill him—simple.

I paused writing my list, thinking of the wraith and once again trying to connect her story to mine. I still couldn't, other than the fact that she was set to marry one of my ancestors. Perhaps it was the father of the child that was the connection, but what connection could I have with an Osirian servant? I shook my head, clearing the thoughts from my mind and continued with my list making.

Once the list was complete I got to work writing an update letter for my family back in Isidia.

Queen Islina,

I am pleased to inform you of my safe arrival in Osiria and the warm reception of the treaty by the King.

We have also confirmed that, in order to destroy the dead army, we must go after the source directly. We leave Osiria now, headed for Minoma where we hope to track down the Necromancer and end this war before it can begin.

I pray to the Father that you are safe and that our land and people are safe, also.

287

I will send another letter once we arrive in Minoma.

It was short and direct but, if I let myself, I would have written pages upon pages, would have told my mother everything—how wonderful the world was, how I hated her for keeping me from it, and how much I wished she could experience it with me.

I took a deep breath, in through my nose and out through my mouth, stopping the tears before they could fall. Being around Thanatos' family had really shown me how broken mine was.

I folded the letter and finished stuffing everything back in my bag. I double checked the room for any fallen belongings and, when I could find none, hauled the pack on to my back and headed to the dining room, where I was sure I would find Thanatos and his family.

I could hear raised voices from outside the door, clearly his family hadn't taken the news very well. I knocked on the door, to at least give them some warning that I was there, and the voices stopped.

"Come in!" Came the King's friendly voice.

I slowly opened the door and edged into the room. Thanatos and his mother were standing at opposite ends, their eyes locked in a fierce silent battle. King Methuzelah and Freyja stood between them while Daeril held Odon toward the back of the room.

"Sorry to interrupt," I said cautiously, "Thanatos said we should meet here." Omisha's eyes narrowed on me and I resisted the urge to flinch.

"Of course, please put your pack down and join us for morning tea."

I nodded to the King and dropped my pack down near the door. The tension in the room made me uncomfortable and I felt very sympathetic to anyone who had ever been around me and my own mother.

Everyone took seats at the table and sat in awkward silence for a moment before Queen Omisha exploded.

"Why won't you take an entourage? Just to be safe? It's so irresponsible to travel with just the two of you."

"We've been fine this whole time, Mother, and an entourage would give us away."

"Because an Osirian and an Isidian traveling together won't." She scoffed. "I don't think you fully understand the severity of the situation, Thanatos."

"Omisha, leave the boy alone," the King cut in. "It's not like he hasn't been in danger before."

Omisha gaped at her husband. "Are you forgetting who is with him?" She flung her hand in my direction. "Evalina is the last Heir to her Queendom, what if something happens to her?"

"With all due respect, Your Ma—Omisha, I was the one who coerced Thanatos into this, it's I who should be worried about what happens to him. It'll be on my head either way." The thought hadn't occurred to me before, but it was true; his life was in my hands.

"I still do not approve," Omisha stated, folding her arms and sitting back in her chair, like a child denied after-dinner sweets.

The room went silent for a few moments, except for the occasional baby babble from Odon.

"Are you excited to visit Minoma, Evalina?" Daeril asked, clearly trying to dissolve the tension.

"I am," I replied with a smile, thinking of all the paintings in my father's study of the great library. "It looks beautiful in paintings."

"The perfect honeymoon destination," Freyja chimed in, shooting Thanatos a look but quickly going back to fussing over Odon, who was grabbing at a knife on the table.

"I've always wanted to see the library," I added.

"It's quite a sight!" The King exclaimed. "Well worth a visit."

"If only it were on better terms," I said, dampening the mood.

"You'll just have to visit again," the King replied with a grin.

I appreciated the optimism of the Osirians, they seemed to always look to the brightest future despite how far away or impossible it may be.

Morning tea continued on quite calmly. Odon kept most of the attention on himself as he tried repeatedly to grab things he shouldn't off the table and throw cake at his grandfather, the King then fawning over the baby's strong arm.

Thanatos and Omisha continued to throw foul looks at each other over the table. I would make him apologize to his mother before we left; I would not allow him to leave here with anger towards her, nor her to him.

As midday approached I could sense the tension once again rising within the room. Methuzelah's eyes flicked between those of his son and his wife, waiting to see which would rise first, who would snap. I took it upon myself and gulped down the last of my tea before rising to my feet.

All eyes fell on me.

"I think it's about time we left, Thanatos." He seemed almost grateful that I had done it, as if he were going to but couldn't quite bring himself to do it. "Thank you all so much for your hospitality. I have enjoyed my short time here greatly and I hope that I will see you all soon."

The King and Queen rose from their chairs and bowed to me.

"Thank you for coming here," King Methuzelah said. "You have no idea what this means to my people. Your very presence in this room signals a shift, a shift that could change a lot of lives."

I smiled at the hopeful King. I shared his hope but part of me felt the weight of his words differently. It felt like too much responsibility.

"I'll leave you to say your goodbyes." I nodded to Thanatos and left the room.

I flinched, as the second the door closed the room behind it erupted once more into a battle of words between mother and son.

I darted down the hallway, my pack bouncing on my back as I made my way back to the window depicting Ossena. I stared at the window; the picture almost seemed to be moving in the midday sun, as it had in my dream. Her hair rippled in an invisible wind, her eyes moving behind closed lids, as if she were sleeping. I thought of how heartbroken her family must have been to dedicate a whole window just to her in a sea of family portraits and battle scenes. It stood out amongst the rest and, even now, gave off a sort of eeriness. I reached out and touched the glass; I expected it to be cool but it was pleasantly warm, as if I were touching her person.

"I will discover what happened to you," I said and could have sworn she'd nodded. I gave the window and hallway one last look, committing it to memory before leaving. I walked back down through the entry hall of the palace, the floor multicolored and shining from the glass ceiling, struck once again by the beauty of the palace and longed to stay. I told myself I would visit again, if time and life permitted.

I was glad to find Faenor and Serelene waiting in the square outside of the palace. I wasn't sure where the stables were, but there they were, saddled up and freshly brushed by the looks of them, their coats shining in the sun. They seemed to be well rested and ready to go. I wasn't entirely sure which route we would take to get to Minoma but I was sure it would lead us through the mountains and I hoped they were ready.

Despite the lateness of the day, the square was relatively quiet. I avoided looking at the execution yard and instead focused on the rest of the square. There were small market stalls sitting empty around the flattened mountain top, and statues of past Osirian heroes and royals, none of which I would know. The doors to the palace swung open and Thanatos came through them, lugging a large travel pack on his shoulder.

"That was a quick goodbye." I said.

"It was long enough, trust me," he said stiffly. "Let's take the long way back from Minoma, give my mother a chance to calm down."

I laughed as we mounted our horses and headed back down the mountain to our next destination.

CHAPTER FIFTY
THE BURDEN OF MERCY

The words of Evalina's last letter rang through my mind like the ringing of blades clashing together. It had been sent well over a week ago, perhaps even two; it told of her arrival in Osiria, her warm welcome, and that she had been leaving for Minoma finally. It had solidified my confidence in the treaty and the Prince, though something about Islina's reaction left me suspicious in a new way. She was too giddy by the news for it to be a simple treaty agreement, but I refused to let my mind wander to what it could really mean.

Since then, we had been battling with Corse daily, barely getting enough time to rest, or even catch a breath at times. The Corse never seemed to tire, but my soldiers did and it had showed.

While the losses hadn't been extreme, they had grown drastically from the previous battles. There was never a time in the camp when soldiers weren't screaming from injury, the healers' tents constantly overflowing. Regular High-Elven soldiers had been ordered to assist the healers to tend to all the injured Sea-Elves, because while they were skilled fighters, they were fearless to the point of fault. Our healers tents were full of the gray-skinned, blue haired warriors but they were looked on as no less.

As well trained as Adalric said my army was, they were nothing compared to his. The Carracallans leapt into the battle with little thought but, when they fought, it was always to win and it was brutal and calculated.

As far as I was concerned, we still had the upper hand—but barely. If we didn't have a big win soon and get some rest, we'd be fucked.

I looked around the battlefield before me, at my feet lay more Isidian corpses than I cared to see. *But many are still fighting,* I thought to myself, because if I didn't I would lose all hope.

It had been two weeks since Evalina had left for Minoma from Osiria, she should have arrived by now and yet we still fought the dead. Hemfain had been able to dig up old records of Necromancers from the palace archives and told

291

us when the Necromancer dies, so, too, will his creations. So, we knew as of that moment that Evalina had not yet succeeded, or that she was dead and we were yet to be informed. I prayed it was the latter, that she was yet to meet him and there was still yet hope.

I brought my sword down through the chest of an Isidian troop. She had arrows sticking out of her head and lower back, her mouth opened and closed like a fish lifted from a creek, her eyes pleading for death. It was the side of war that no one talked about, the side that made me question myself and my morality. Yes, I was doing my duty; but was that enough to justify my actions? And though most of them asked me, no, begged me to do it, did that make it right? What separated me from our enemy?

I pondered the question as I relieved another wounded soldier. Head injuries were difficult to heal and oftentimes things went wrong or simply didn't work. And, on the battlefield, we had no time to try or hope. It was kinder to both the victim and their family to say they'd died valiantly in battle, than to try and fail to heal a head wound and leave the healers to live with the grief. Instead, I would shoulder it. As their Captain, their mentor, their friend.

At this point in the war, I'd lost count of how many of my own I'd killed and it wasn't always for the sake of dignity or mercy, sometimes it was purely accidental. It was sometimes impossible to keep a decent enough distance between yourself and the next fighter and oftentimes, it resulted in my sword nicking one of my own, injuring one of my own and, unfortunately, killing one of my own in some cases. Sometimes I noticed and other times, in the heat of battle, bloodthirst running through my veins, I didn't until it was too late and they were already gone.

I stared down at the she-elf I'd just killed—I remembered her from training. She hadn't been particularly skilled but she had been fast, and, given the direction of her corpse, I'd say she'd tried to rely on that speed to save her from the onslaught of arrows that had taken the lives of almost five hundred soldiers. But it had failed her. If you were quick, you could outrun a sword but very few could outrun an arrow.

Now, her body would join the rest in the mass pire, her family would not get to grieve over her corpse, would not get the closure they would need, because we could not risk the dead returning, would not. And so, her body would join the other reeking corpses waiting to be burned, shit covered and maggot eaten before the flames would even reach her body at the top of the pile.

I wished I could give these warriors the heroes' burials that they deserved but the Necromancer had not allotted us that privilege. I prayed that we could at least do them the honor of remembering. We owed them that much.

The wind shifted through the trees, bringing with it the stench of the undead. I could have cried. I was so tired, so worn down, that I could have broken down in that moment and laid with the dead beneath my feet, accepting whatever fate that would lead me to.

I sucked in a breath and cursed the Necromancer. Nothing could warrant this destruction, whatever his excuse or justifications, it would never be enough. He was lucky it was Evalina going after him, and that she had not seen the things that I had before she left. She would not go easy on him either way, but what I had seen, what I'd had to do … . His death would not be swift at my hand.

I turned to leave the field and race back to the fort before the next onslaught of Corse arrived, ignoring the moans and pleas of the injured and dying around me. They would get their end soon enough, either by the Corse, the stampede of Carracallan and Isidian soldiers, or by my own hand. Unfortunately, for now, they had to wait, as did the rest of us.

CHAPTER FIFTY ONE
GRAVE CONCERN

The journey to Minoma was slow and hard, the descent through the mountains, treacherous. We'd gone straight through the backbone of the mountains and descended to the west, getting closer to the volcanoes than I ever thought I'd be comfortable doing. The heat radiating off the lava lakes was dry and reached us from a considerable distance. I didn't want to know what would happen if we got too close.

Crossing the desert was as uncomfortable as it was the first time. Sand got everywhere, I sweated for a majority of the time and Thanatos was barely affected. I took it as a personal insult and one day, out of pure frustration, threw my soaked sweat rag at the back of his head. He'd laughed and flicked water from his drinking skin at me, which had relieved me for only a moment before the heat once again blistered through my clothes.

I could have sworn the horses had sighed with glee as we finally stepped onto properly solid ground for the first time in weeks. The sand of the desert falling away behind us, making way for the grassy plains of Northern Minoma.

We steered clear of the Orc lands to the east, their crude wooden forts protruding over the hills. I would have loved to see them and experience their ritualistic way of life but we were too close to our target now to stray. I told myself I would visit them another time and make an effort to reach out to the clans that traveled close to Isidia.

We stood on a hill looking over the city, the great Minoman Library towering over us.

I gaped at it.

I had expected it to be tall but it was frighteningly tall. It was hard to grasp that there were enough books in existence to fill the whole tower, and more being written every day. I wished I could find a nice window seat and curl up with a pile of books to be read beside me.

The reality of what we were here to do came crashing down on me and squashed any excitement that I was previously feeling.

We were here to fight the man from my nightmares.

His patchwork skin and mismatched eyes flashed into my mind and made me shudder.

"Are you all right?" Thanatos asked from beside me.

"Yeah. I just want this over with," I said quietly. Despite the fact that we were alone, I felt eyes on me. I had since we'd left the desert but we'd had no run-ins with Corse, or anything else for that matter. It was odd.

We continued on toward the city, picking grapes off the vines that littered the fields and munching them down. It was a real luxury.

Grapes were hard to come by in Isidia, we received too much rain and not enough sun to allow them to grow, but Minoma was perfect, coastal and directly under a desert. I'd never been to wine making areas, but there seemed to be too many grapes on the ground under the vines, as if they hadn't picked the last crop of the season.

I looked around the field, expecting people to be out and enjoying the sun but there was no one. I was about to say something to the Prince when I looked over to see his hand resting on his wicked curved blade. I followed his gaze and saw someone dashing toward us beneath the vines, crouched as if they were hiding from someone.

"Stay where you are." Thanatos told the man as he got close enough to speak to us.

The Minoman raised his hands before him in surrender. "Please," he said desperately, "Your Highness, I had to warn you." Thanatos removed his hand from his weapon and helped the man to his feet. "The dead walk the city." Thanatos and I stiffened. "They've been here for weeks, we don't know what they want. You have to help us!" He begged, his golden hands pressed together, as if he were praying to the gods.

"Where are they?" Thanatos asked.

"Everywhere, they patrol the streets and anyone caught doing something they don't like is taken."

"Taken where?" I asked, stepping forward. The man's eyes widened as he caught sight of my face, and saw the blue running through my braid.

"We don't know, Princess. They just take them." He broke into heavy sobs. "They took my sister—her wife is worried sick."

I took his hands in mine. "We'll get her back." He sobbed harder at my words, at the glimmer of hope they offered. "What are the mages doing?"

"Protecting the tower. They tried to save us but the attack was too much for their magic and they retreated."

I glanced at Thanatos and he nodded, understanding instantly. We needed to get into that tower.

"Is there any indication as to where the creatures came from?" I asked.

The man shook his head. "They just appeared one night. No warning. Some were familiar, people we used to know before they passed but they were not themselves anymore."

"Where are your burial grounds?" Thanatos asked.

I cringed as I pictured dug up graves, corpses lying half in, half out of their final resting places, unable to pull themselves out from the tightly packed dirt.

The man pointed to the other end of the field, away from the city and the tower.

"We will find your sister. Head back to town and act as if you never saw us. Your people will be free soon," Thanatos promised.

He offered us his desperate thanks before slinking back into town under the cover of the vines. I prayed he had the mind to keep his encounter to himself. If word spread that I was here, the Corse would undoubtedly be on the hunt.

"We should check the burial grounds before we go to the library, see if the dead really have risen," Thanatos said after the man had turned a corner and was out of sight.

"And how do you propose we get into the tower?" I asked.

Thanatos ran his hands over his face and tugged his braid. "I don't know. Lets just confirm that people from the town have been raised and then we'll come up with a plan."

I nodded and led us away from the town and the tower.

I'd expected there to be Corse but I hadn't expected to stumble upon a town under their control. It made things a little more difficult. We had to be more careful than we'd thought.

We didn't need to venture far into the graveyard to see proof of the resurrections. Old piles of dirt from the dug up graves could be spotted from half way down the road.

Markers strewn around the yard made it difficult to locate which grave had belonged to who, making it impossible to determine if the Necromancer had brought back people relating to him and his life. Thanatos and I walked through the yard, checking for freshly dug up graves and found none.

The Corse in town had to have been resurrected months ago, meaning the town had been under the Necromancer's control that whole time meaning ... the Minomans knew.

They'd known the Corse were a threat and said nothing, had come to a ball and dined with us, knowing these monsters were attacking. My hands shook at my sides as I stared around the yard. Thanatos met my gaze from across the burial ground, his shoulders falling as he came to the same realization that I had—his mother had been right.

We sat on a mound of dirt, both staring off in different directions trying to make some sense of what we had seen, the pieces that had fallen together. Omisha had been right, the humans had known and hadn't told us.

"Thanatos—"

"We don't know that it's them," he cut in. "They might not have had a choice. You saw how terrified that man was—to ask *me* for help, he must have been."

I turned to face him and rested a hand on his shoulder. "I know you don't want to believe it but this may be a trap." I lifted his face gently. "We have to be careful." His gold eyes were full of sadness, I tried to dull the anger in mine. "We need to get into that tower and speak with the mages."

The Prince took a deep breath and thought for a moment. "I know a back way in. We'll wait for nightfall."

We spent the rest of the day scoping out the city, watching from a distance to see if there were any patrols or guards stationed around.

There seemed to be only one patrol that walked the center road of the city. The people in the city seemed to be living in a kind of forced normalcy, but fled if the guards ever got too close.

The terracotta buildings glowed orange in the light of the setting sun as we finally made our way back up to the mages' tower, sticking close to the outskirts of the city. We tied the horses to a tree close to the back side of the library tower— I prayed they would be kept safe—then Thanatos and I crept around until we came to a large window. All the windows of the library were large, clear arched windows with a center that slid up to open, plain compared to what I had witnessed in Osiria.

"This window is almost always left open," Thanatos whispered to me.

"How do you know?" I asked.

He smirked, "I'll tell you later."

Another thing I had to survive for—my list was piling up. Most things were petty but I added them anyway. Anything that gave me the urge to live and fight was added.

Thanatos stuck the tip of his dagger under the window frame and levered it up before sliding his fingers under and pushing the rest of the way, slowly edging it up as quietly as he could. I held my breath, waiting for it to squeak, or get stuck and come crashing down, but it simply slid up and stayed there. Thanatos and I let go of the collective breaths we'd been holding and quietly climbed in through the window, dropping to the floor as silently as we could.

I looked around the darkened room we'd climbed into and couldn't help but feel underwhelmed. All my life, I'd heard amazing tales of the Minoman library and how beautiful it was, filled to the brim with scrolls and books to study, art from all over Carynthia, and skeletal remains of beasts from all over the world that were said to fill the halls—but this room was empty.

Thanatos crept over to the door, opened it a crack and gazed through, motioning for me to join him. I looked through the small gap and had to stop myself from gasping.

The main hall of the library was everything I'd hoped it could be. Shelves upon shelves of books lined the walls, stone tables sat neatly down the center of the room waiting to have books and scrolls piled on top of them. Candles and vast fireplaces filled the tower with warm orange light, staircases curved down from the balconies above creating a giant spiral leading all the way to the top of the tower. Small rooms protruded from the balconies and I assumed these were small offices or living quarters for the many human mages that studied there.

Down the center of the tower hung a gigantic skeleton of some kind of serpent creature, the skull of the beast above was larger than any living creature I had ever seen.

There was no one in sight, so Thanatos swung open the door and stepped out into the hall.

"What's the plan?" I whispered to him.

"Well, I guess we find someone."

We stepped into the center of the tower and I took the chance to gaze up to the top; it seemed impossibly far away. I pitied the mages that had to trek up and down all those stairs and hoped we wouldn't have to do the same thing to find someone.

We walked up a few floors, I resisted the urge to grab books off the shelves and curl up in one of the rooms to read. It had been so long since I'd read a book, I wondered if I'd even know how.

We found no one and thought no one had found us, until a spell came whizzing past my ear. I dove away as the spell exploded against a pillar behind me and unsheathed my blades.

"How did you get in here?" Echoed a low voice. My eyes darted about the balcony, searching for the owner of the voice, but I saw no one.

"The bottom floor window," Thanatos called back. I heard a murmur of voices echo through the tower, each one equally accusatory of the previous.

"Why are you here?" Asked a different voice.

"We're hunting the Necromancer," I said. "We believe he seeks to destroy my home and my people." I was met with silence.

Then, one by one, hooded figures began popping up in front of me, as if they'd been there all along and we simply couldn't see them. I raised my blades, ready for an attack.

"Princess! We were not expecting you." The hooded figures bowed in unison. "Prince Thanatos, you know you're not to be here unsupervised."

"Yes, yes, but we couldn't really come in the front door now could we?"

I raised my eyebrow at the Prince, what had he done to these people?

"Be that as it may, sneaking in isn't the best impression to be making." A robed figure to my left said.

"We just want answers. What happened here?" I asked.

"The best person to speak to about that would be the Arch-Mage. His office is back down on the ground floor, I shall escort you." A small hooded figure stepped out of the crowd. "Follow me," she said, motioning a small scarred hand toward the staircase Thanatos and I had climbed up mere moments ago.

We began our descent, following the hooded mage. Trailing behind her down the winding stairs. She walked ahead of us for a few floors then slowed her pace to match ours, standing closer than comfortable

"You need to help us," she suddenly whispered, my back straightened at her words. "We're being held here by the Arch-Mage. We believe he's working for the Necromancer."

"And you're taking us straight to him," Thanatos clipped.

"I have no choice, he knows you're here."

"Why can't you all rise against him?" I asked. She almost snorted.

"The Arch-Mage knows all our magic and exactly how to counter it, not to mention he's the strongest one here, probably stronger than the Necromancer."

Thanatos and I shared a look. "Great." Was all I said.

We were prepared to face an onslaught of Corse and possibly two Necromancers but we'd not considered fighting an Arch-Mage as well.

A flurry of nerves filled my stomach. I'd never fought a magic user before, I wasn't even entirely sure I knew the extent of human magic. I shook my head to clear it and ran through my training in my head, trying to prepare myself for battle, but I couldn't shake away the fear or anxiousness. The food I'd eaten that day threatened to rise the second my feet hit the floor of the ground level.

The hooded mage led us across the tower, underneath the behemoth skeleton, and toward a large door. I cast a glance at Thanatos; his face was tight and paler than usual, his hand hovering nervously over his large, curved sword. I tried to calm myself further with deep breaths, breathing deeper and slower the closer we got to the door.

"He's right inside," the mage said. "I don't know if The Necromancer is with him." She paused, her hands on one of the doors, ready to push it open. "If a battle breaks out, we will fight beside you." Thanatos and I nodded. She took a last deep breath in and pushed the door. "Arch-Mage, Prince Thanatos of Osiria and Princess Evalina of Isidia to see you."

There was a brief pause before a low, choked voice replied, "Excellent."

CHAPTER FIFTY TWO
THE PURSUIT OF KNOWLEDGE

The young mage left Evalina and I in the doorway of the Arch-Mage's office, disappearing somewhere deep in the library, hopefully waiting and ready for us to need her assistance.

"Please, sit," said the Arch-Mage. His voice sounded … wrong.

"I think I speak for both of us when I say we'd like to stand," I replied sternly. I wanted this over with.

"Fair enough." He took a seat across from us, his desk dividing the space. "I am Cato, the Arch-Mage of this college," he croaked. "What service may I offer you?"

"What happened here?" Evalina asked, I could hear the nerves in her voice, though she hid it well.

"Many things, but mainly the pursuit of knowledge. Not much is known about Necromical magic and what better way to study it than to experience it first hand."

My eyes widened and Evalina took a step backward.

"You did not notice? Good. We are making improvements!" Cato stopped and jotted a couple of notes onto a scroll before him, then pulled down the front of his robe to reveal a deep bruise across his throat. "I hadn't been open to the idea, at first, but then they made me an offer I couldn't refuse." He laughed an awkward, gurgled laugh, the sound seemingly trapped in his crushed windpipe. "To die and come back is … well, I don't even know how to describe it. At first it felt wrong, an act against the Gods. I swear I could feel the Mother pulling me down, longing for me to join her. But, over time, that feeling dissipated and I felt born anew. I felt stronger, younger! Like I could live forever and learn everything I could ever wish." He stared at his hands, turning them over before himself. "But, we discovered, it does not last forever. I began deteriorating after a few weeks, as if I were a regular corpse."

My mind kept telling me to kill him, to leap over the desk and run him through, throw a knife at the lamp sitting above him and set him alight, but I couldn't move.

I found myself beguiled by his story. The knowledge he was feeding us was almost priceless, it felt a waste to interrupt.

"We tried many different things—spells, potions, enchantments—nothing seemed to work." He glanced at Evalina, it took all of my self control not to kill him; he looked at her as if she were chattel. "Then, we discovered resurrected elves keep their power. All we had to do was look for some High-Elf graves and do some small tests. It took no time really." He lifted the sleeves of his robe.

Evalina gasped at the sight and I almost gagged.

His arm was a patchy monstrosity of High-Elf and human, confirming what we had feared.

The room filled with his choked wet laugh as he stared at Evalina, amused by her utter fear. I unsheathed my sword and pointed it at the abomination before me.

"The reanimated flesh allows me to tap into the elven gifts freely, making my creations stronger than ever, no longer stumbling beasts but fully capable minions, Kushyam was my final test. Of course it's not as strong for me but, for the master, the possibilities are endless! His power is unmatched!"

Evalina shook beside me.

"That's enough!" I called over the Arch-Mage's manic laughter. "This ends now, Cato, can't you see that this is wrong? This goes against everything the Mother and Father intended." I surprised myself at the words but felt them to be true regardless. "Allow me to release you from your madness and blasphemy, before they curse you themselves."

The mage only laughed harder. "Do you really believe that nonsense, Prince? And, here, I thought you were the only sensible one of your kind." He raised his patchwork arms above his head.

I called on my powers, the dark mist gathering at my hands.

"The Gods do not care about us! There is only one who cares, the Master, my Master, only he truly cares for us. He proves it everyday by targeting and destroying elven kind, who have kept us in invisible chains for centuries—left to clean up the mess of your wars, forever caught between the two higher races." He spat at our feet, the saliva black and sticky as his dead blood would be. "No more!" He cried.

I raised my hands, felt my magic latch to his slimy soul and pulled. He paused for a moment and gagged as I strained to rip his soul from his body, then he laughed and, before we could react, Cato shot a streak of lightning at us. Our bodies spasmed, our weapons clattering to the floor. I fell to the ground, my bones vibrating with the current of the lightning, limbs twitching against my commands.

I heard footsteps coming toward me, sandals clacking against the soles of the wearer's feet. Cato's face appeared before mine. I fought against the current rippling through my body so that I could stare directly into his eyes; he smiled, the brown of them turning black.

"Your powers will not work on me, boy, I am no regular Corse." He laughed. "The Master has blessed me beyond what the Gods have ever deemed worthy of a human." He studied me for a moment, his eyes raking my body. "We've never had a Dark-Elf before, it should be interesting. How your two powers will react together in a single human vessel, I wonder." His eyes flicked to Evalina; she, too, had collapsed to the ground and was jerking uncontrollably. My mind showed me an image of her carved up, bleeding on the floor of a grungy healer's room, patches missing from her arms and legs. I tried to kick, lift my arm, anything to gain control of my body again.

Then I was being dragged—I tried to reach out for Evalina but my arms betrayed me and only curled in.

"Thanatos," she croaked. She disappeared as I rounded the desk and saw what had been hidden.

Beneath Cato's desk was a trapdoor. I once again tried to struggle but the spell was still in effect. The Arch-Mage dragged me as close to the hole as he could before resorting to kicking me through it until I was falling.

The air was forced out of my lungs as I hit the grime covered floor, I took a moment to suck more in just to have it knocked out of me again as Evalina's form came crashing down on top of me.

"Sorry," she groaned.

"It's fine." I managed to get out as Evalina rolled off of me. The smell of the room hit us both at the same time "Gods, what is that?"

We were too distracted by the smell to realize that we were able to move freely again. We took in our surroundings and I instantly took Evalina's hand as she gasped.

Surrounding us along the walls were chained mutilated High-Elves and, piled in the corners, were what had to be hundreds of human corpses. The smell was rotting flesh, blood and excrement.

The Isidians I at first thought dead shook in their chains, tears sliding down their faces, but no one spoke or made any noise beyond the odd whimper and sniffle. I pulled Evalina into my chest hiding the view from her eyes. What had these monsters done to keep these poor elves alive? Almost all of them were missing whole limps but some...chunks, as if they'd been picked of their best cut.

I felt Evalina heave a sob against my chest, felt her wet hot tears for her people and let my own leak down my face in solidarity and shared disgust.

One of the chained, a slight female, whimpered toward us, as if trying to get our attention. I tapped Evalina on the shoulder and pointed to the she-elf, who flinched.

"She's alive!" Evalina pulled from my grip and ran to the woman. "It's all right, it's all right," she soothed. "We're going to get you out of here." Her voice was strong but thick with emotion, her hands shaking as she examined the chains and the wounds of the she-elf.

I walked over to them, my movement causing a collective whimper to sound throughout the room. As I got closer to the Princess, the she-elf thrashed against her chains; fear shone in her eyes and she pulled herself as far away from me as the restraints would allow. I paused, my heart falling further than it already had. They were frightened of me, terrified.

The woman began motioning up with her head as Evalina was looking desperately, searching for something to break the chains with, she noticed me looking and opened her mouth.

"Evie, her tongue."

Evalina wasted no time and instantly called on her powers to heal the elfs tongue, her glowing white hands filled the room with bright light revealing the true horror of what lay around us.

Large operating tables lay about the room, all were covered in dirty tools and various dismembered limbs. The walls were coated in layers of blood and grime, caked so thick in areas that it protruded from the surface. Bile rose in my throat but I swallowed it down and tried to focus on the healing, on the new information we were about to receive.

"You must get out of here," croaked a new voice. "It's not safe."

"Not unless I can save you all," Evalina said fiercely ; the woman shook her head.

"No, we are not worth saving. This time is unknown to us, our families are long dead and"—she paused, lifting her head slowly to look at the others chained around her—"I think I speak for all of us when I say I can't live after this. The pain has been ... immeasurable."

"But I can help you," Evalina sobbed. "I can make the pain go away—Thanatos! He can use compulsion to rid you of the terror." She gestured to me and the prisoners whimpered and shied away.

"No. We have been tormented enough by *them*," the chained woman spat.

I shrunk back into the shadows of the room, as I did when I knew my presence would only make others uncomfortable. Given where these people were, I assumed they were warriors of an ancient war—Isidians that had grown up hating my kin, for good reason.

I was not blind to my people's history.

"Thanatos is different, Osirians are different now. We have a peace treaty, there has been no war between us for centuries." Surprise flitted across the she-elf's face but returned to its dull pained expression quickly.

"Be that as it may, it only proves that we are not prepared for this new world where Isidians and Osirians have peace. Please, girl. Let us die again, it's the only peace we've known."

Evalina stepped back from the woman. I could tell by the way she held her shoulders that she'd accepted what the tortured elf had said. "At least tell us what we need to know first." The Isidian gave a weak nod. "Can I heal you more so you're up to it?"

"No. I fear if you heal me more, I may change my mind about returning to death." She gave Evalina a sad smile. It was only natural for her to want to live after experiencing health again, but to live with the trauma of war, torure and mutilation ... I would choose death.

"Where did you come from?" Evalina asked, her voice strong but shaking.

"The battlefields just south of Kushyam—we fought against the Osirian and Kushyami armies"

My mind raced at how many centuries ago that battle must have been, we'd had wars after that but most were at sea or down closer to Isidia, where the land was more suited to it.

"Do you remember who brought you back? Is it the same man that dropped us down here?"

"I don't know, he wore a cloak that covered his face, but he had the patched skin."

"Is there only one Necromancer here?" Evalina asked.

I held my breath, awaiting the answer.

"I believe there are two."

I made to rest my hand on my sword, forgetting that it was not there. Where could the other one be hiding? The trap door was the only way out that I could see clearly. I gazed around the room. There were a few candles scattered throughout but not enough to fully light the space. I walked to the edge of the room, trying my hardest to ignore the whimpers and cries of the High-Elf prisoners. I plucked a candle out of the small sconce on the wall and used it to scan the room for another way out.

"Two, just as we'd thought. Where is the other one now?" Evalina asked.

"I don't know, they both come and go at random and we're always in and out of consciousness."

"I found a door!" I called back to Evalina, my hands resting on the thin wooden door. I reached for the handle and tried to push and pull. I cursed and hit the door with my fist—of course it was locked. I continued to walk about the room, looking for something, anything, that could help us. I came across a table of cruel looking tools, no doubt the ones that had been used to mutilate the Isidians shivering around me. I decided against announcing this particular find, fearing it might distress the prisoners, especially coming from me.

"Do you know what's outside of that door?" Evalina asked the woman.

"No, I'm sorry."

"It's fine, you've helped a lot."

"Can I ask you a question girl?"

"Of course," Evalina answered with a smile, tucking the woman's loose hair back behind her ears.

"Who are you? Both of you, I would like to know the names of my saviors." I paused my searching and looked back at the Princess and the captive. The prisoner gazed at me, she was unsuccessfully trying to hide her hatred and fear.

"I am Prince Thanatos of Osiria."

Her eyes widened.

"And I am Princess Evalina of Isidia."

The she-elf's eyes filled with tears. "Our Princess." Her voice wobbled, "I am glad to have met you, I only hope that this will be the last time … for a long while at least." She gave a shaking laugh and flinched at the jerking movement.

It was then that I found it, our way out.

Lined up against the wall opposite to the prisoners were barrels I pried one open, tearing at my fingertips as I did. The smell hit me like a club to the face and for a moment I'd wished I'd never opened the case.

"Ugh, whale oil." I said more to myself, then my eyes flicked to the candle in my other hand and I quickly stepped away from the barrel. "Evalina! I found some whale oil!"

She rushed over to me, pinching her nose at the fishy scent. "Can we use it?"

"There's a wooden door over there, we can burn it down."

Her eyes lit for a moment then faded. "What about the library?"

"If we're careful it shouldn't spread."

She leaned over the barrel and gazed into its depths. "Can I ask a favor of you?" I gave her a nod, already anticipating what it would be, she lowered her voice to a whisper. "I know you don't like to use it... but"—she paused, her gaze returning to her chained people—"I can't leave them like this and they deserve a painless death."

I rested a hand on her cheek and wiped away a stray tear with my thumb. "Of course," I whispered back.

Her shoulders relaxed. "Thank you. Could we also ... burn the bodies."

I was surprised at first but understood her meaning. If there was no flesh left, there would be no use in bringing them back again, they would finally rest. I took a bleeding bowl from the table of healers equipment and carefully dipped it into the whale oil, cautious not to get it on my skin.

Evalina went back to the captive elves, speaking to each one individually. Their eyes shone as their Princess spoke to them; they'd probably never met a member of the royal family before, even though they'd lost their lives fighting for them. I made my way over to the door and carefully poured the oil over it, holding the candle as far away as I could.

Once the door was doused, I went back to the table and inspected the instruments more closely, sharp fileting knives and bone saws rested on a dirty rag, stained with blood. I shoved a few of the smaller knives into my belt but left the amputation saws on the bench, I would come back for them.

Evalina was now kneeling before the first elf, confirming her wishes once again, trying to convince her to live on one last time.

"This is what we want, Princess, what we need. To be released into the world after experiencing what we have would be more cruel than kind."

Evalina sighed with resignation. "Then please, everyone close your eyes and we'll pray to the Father for the safe passage of your souls." They all closed their eyes, some even began to mouth their own prayers. "Father, I pray to you today to ask that you over-see the deliverance of these souls. Let them pass peacefully into your lands and live there with you among their ancestors." The last of Evalina's words echoed through the small space, she turned and nodded to me, tears falling silently down her cheeks.

I walked to her and embraced her as I called on my powers, shielding her eyes as a black mass surrounded my hand and pulled the souls from her people with a sigh. She shook against me as sobs racked her body. I watched on as the black mist left the bodies; flowing from mouths, noses and eyes, and collected in one large form on the ceiling before dissipating through cracks in the stone, taking a piece of my own soul with it.

The bodies now hung limp in their chains, their eyes forever frozen shut, mouths permanently open. I gave Evalina a moment to grieve, let her sob into my chest leaving my shirt wet and cold with her tears.

"We need to go, we can't hang around any longer," she said, pulling away from me and wiping her face on her sleeve.

I kissed her forehead and asked her to light the oil on the door before I got to work coating the bodies.

CHAPTER FIFTY THREE
DEATH'S DOOR

The door burnt quickly—the wood was old and crumbled almost the second the flames took. I stood and watched it burn, unable to stand the sight of Thanatos dousing the bodies of my kin.

"The smoke will alarm the Arch-Mage," I called back to Thanatos.

"Then we must be ready." I heard him drop the bleeding bowl into the oil barrel and come to stand beside me. He held out a crude looking healer's saw, one so old I'd never seen one like it. It was heavy, the handle made from iron, the blade viciously jaggard. I reluctantly took it; I didn't have much of a choice but it didn't stop me feeling as if I were betraying the memory of my people. Maybe coating it in the blood of our enemies would suffice as my reconciliation.

Thanatos kicked through the charred remains of the door and dashed into the awaiting hallway, checking for guards. He came back moments later shaking his head. "Wait out there while I ... you know."

I nodded and made my way into the hall, breathing deeply to stop the emotion threatening to take over at the whoosh of flames. Light flooded the hall from the small room as did the smell of burning flesh, smoke, and a wave of heat.

"This way," Thanatos said as he passed me in the hall, leading me toward a set of stairs. "This should take us up to the entry level—are you ready?"

"I don't think we have much choice, the smoke will alert them any second now."

"Then let's get moving."

I let him set the pace and followed him quickly up the stairs, our crude weapons in hand ready to start fighting at any second.

We burst through the door at the top of the stairs and halted as we were met with a crowd of decomposing corpses. Their arms hung limply at their sides, their mouths gapped. It must have been every Corse in the city. My stomach turned and my heart raced as I stared out over the crowd.

"I see Cato was incompetent enough to lock you in an easily escapable room." A voice called from the first floor balcony. "Sometimes, scholars are not as smart as we believe them to be." The hooded figure stood surrounded by a guard of five Corse, each one wielding a weapon much larger than what Thanatos and I had available to us.

I gulped at the thought of cutting our way up to them, only to be disposed of in seconds.

"I suppose it would be silly of me to drag this on longer than I need to, no use in prolonging the inevitable." He chuckled like a man who had already won. "Attack them!" He commanded his army of the dead—and they did just that.

Thanatos and I cut and sliced through as many Corse as we could manage, standing back to back and doing our best to protect each other. The first wave were weaponless, they swung and kicked aimlessly.

Our main enemy were our weapons, the jagged edges of the blades catching on bone and tendon. It wasn't long before the floor beneath our feet was covered in black sludge making it near impossible to stand up straight.

Our fighting grew more and more sloppy as time went on, until there was no stance, no structure.

"We need to separate!" I called over the fray.

"I don't think that's a good idea!" Thanatos called back as he ripped through the neck of a Minoman Corse.

"This is never going to end if one of us doesn't kill the Necromancers! If we wait till we've killed all the Corse. we'll be too weak."

"Fine!" He hesitated. "You go. I can handle this."

I didn't hang around, the second the words were out of his mouth I darted for the stairs, cutting down as many Corse as possible as I went. I tried to look around, to see where the mages that had offered help were, but I didn't spot them anywhere, neither did I see Cato.

I was almost to the stairs when a Corse with a large sword attacked, swinging at me blindly, as if she didn't believe she could miss. I caught the blade in one of the notches on my saw and grabbed the tip with my hand, twisting until her wrist was at an awkward angle and snatched the blade from her grip, using it then to cut her head from her neck.

I felt more confident armed with two blades and was filled with new energy.

I reached the stairs and hacked my way through the crowd at the base, none of the dead things particularly skilled with the weapons they wielded.

I began feeling the same way I had at Kushyam, as if this were too easy, more slaughter than battle.

I forced my way up the stairs, not bothering to use flashy fighting maneuvers but resorting to simply pushing my foes over the balustrade, knowing that Thanatos was making quick work of disposing of them at the base.

The library was filled with the smell of burnt bodies and old blood; it was a smell I would no doubt struggle to rid from my memories for years to come. I hoped as I mounted the last few steps that it would be at least tinged with the feeling of victory.

"High-Elf, I had hoped you would be the one to face me." The guards around the Necromancer had a different air about them, more confident and aware, these ones were like the few that had attacked in Sillessia—the ones bound for Isidia. I rolled my shoulders and took my fighting stance, ready and waiting.

While these Corse were stronger than the ones on the lower level, they were still rotting. I still had the advantage of full life, I just had to get past the weapons.

The first guard made her move, striking quickly with her spear-like weapon. I caught her spear between my two blades, the sawteeth snagging in the wood. I used it as an anchor to pull her toward me, using my right arm to guide the butt of the spear to my neck resting on my shoulder for a split second before dropping the handle of the saw and gripping the end of the spear, forcing it through the Corse's neck in a quick slice. She fell, her head rolling to the feet of the Necromancer.

The other guards advanced but kept their distance, now that I had the added reach of the spear. I kept it close, tucked firmly under my arm so I was able to make more controlled movements with it. I lunged into the battle with the four guards left over, careful to keep them in front of me but staying mindful of how close I was to the stairs.

I wanted to peek over the balcony to see how Thanatos was fairing but resisted that urge, I had to believe that he was fine. Had to keep my head in the battle I was already part of.

The guards I was fighting were all wielding heavy, two-handed weapons, deadly if they could land a blow.

It wasn't long before I'd dispatched two more, both had used maces. Their movements had been slow, too slow for my spear and sword work but they'd managed at least to dull my blade and split the staff of the spear, it was now more like a dagger with an extended handle but I still preferred it to single wielding.

The last two guards were trying desperately to seperate, to force me to split my attention between the two of them but I did my best to keep them herded together, backing them up into one of the smaller alcoves along the edge of the balcony. With one swift movement I managed to force one over the edge, knocking him off balance with a blow to the head.

The remaining Corse was not going down so easy.

I was beginning to tire, my hands were slick with sweat and blood, some my own. I hadn't realized I'd been hurt but there was red blood slowly trickling down my arm.

They dodged my lunge and managed to flick the broken spear out of my grasp with the blunt edge of their sword. I regained my footing and we broke into a barrage of attacks, both of us dodging and blocking desperately.

I tried my hardest to force them toward the edge of the alcove but they resisted, viciously forcing me backward with sweeping attacks. I tripped on the body of a Corse I'd killed only moments ago, a cruel grin spread across the face of my pursuer but they made the mistake of making a spectacle, of relishing the kill, it was enough time for me to snatch up a mace and swing at their legs. There was a crunch as the frail bones snapped, their shin collapsed in on itself until their knee hit the ground. They let out a cry of pain and I took that moment to cut off their head.

I gave myself only a second to take a breath before springing to my feet and scanning for the Necromancer—he'd darted away the second I'd killed the first guard.

"Where are you hiding?" I called across the landing. "Too scared to face me yourself?"

I took the quiet moment as a chance to check on the Prince, quickly glancing over the side of the balcony. He was still fighting. Wounded, I could see the blood from my perch. My fingers itched to heal him but the sound of a footfall caught my attention. I spun and ran down an aisle of shelves as a shadow flitted past the end, weapons at the ready, waiting for any sign of where the coward had darted off to.

"I must say, you are far more skilled than I expected, Princess."

I skidded to a halt and listened for where the voice was coming from.

"Those were some of my best warriors."

I slowly followed the echo, peeking around the corners of the shelves before finding nothing and moving onto the next one. My heart was thundering in my chest, the adrenaline of battle slowly seeping out of my system and leaving me fatigued. "This should be an easy war to win then," I called back.

I heard footsteps and darted toward them, dust catching in my nose as I ran. I resisted the urge to sneeze, my vision blurring with tears as my nose begged to be cleared. The torches on the walls flickered erratically as I ran, casting shadows in all different directions, making it impossible to spot any that I should be looking out for. I thought I saw someone move out of the corner of my eye and redirected down another aisle of shelves.

The stone floor was even more worn down this aisle than it had been down the others, it made me curious as to what books were in these shelves, but I would have to find out later.

I reached the end of the row of shelves and stopped abruptly, my ankle shouting out in protest. Before me stood both Cato and the other Necromancer. I took a fighting stance and stepped back, putting as much distance between us as I could without giving them room to escape. The only way to get away would have been through the window behind them.

"Two against one's a bit cheap," I huffed.

"To enact our plan we're willing to take a few cheap shots," the Necromancer stated.

"What have you done with the mages?" I asked, fearing more lost lives.

Cato laughed. "Those cowards! They disappeared, not long after you two arrived. They realized they were too weak to fight us, or to join us." I didn't want to believe it but I could. I just hoped they'd at least saved the citizens of the city. "We don't have to kill you, you know. You could join us."

I recoiled in disgust. "Why the pit would I do that?" I spat.

"We could use someone like you. A skilled fighter, natural healing abilities, high status in the world. You'd be better to us than that Dark-Elf."

"You really think after all this I would join you?" I scoffed.

"Well, if you die here you won't have a choice."

I lept to the side as Cato shot lightning toward me, rolling to safety behind a bookshelf. I wished I had throwing knives, anything to use as a long range weapon.

I rested my head against the books behind me, the tomes solid and heavy. I could've kicked myself for being so stupid. I jumped to my feet and began hurling books at Cato and the Necromancer, using them as a distraction so I could move about without the risk of being hit by magic.

Cato flung magic at the books, bolts of lightning and flames leaving piles of ashes and charred books on the ground. I tried to think of a plan but nothing was coming to mind. Eventually, Cato would stop targeting the books and what would I do then? There were only so many bookshelves to hide behind.

After jumping out of the way of a steam of fire from Cato, I realized that he was the only one using magic, the Necromancer was doing nothing. I decided to test him and threw a heavy book at his face, before it could get close Cato destroyed it. I decided then that I would try to get close to him, I just had to get Cato out of the way.

"I could do this all day, girl," Cato croaked.

I took a moment behind the bookshelf to think through my options, to come up with a back up plan if my first one didn't work. I took a deep breath and sent a quick prayer to the Father before jumping out from behind the bookshelf and flicking two books out in front of me, one aimed for Cato's head, the other for the window behind them. Cato shot the book that was zooming toward his face, completely oblivious of the one about to smash through the window, showering them both with large shards of glass. I ran for the Necromancer, sword out and ready to cut him through.

The window shattered, glass rained down. The Necromancer and Cato let out cries of surprise and pain as the shards sliced on their way down.

I pulled my sword back ready to strike, ready to end this.

He was so close to my blade.

Light flashed in my peripherals and energy coursed through my body. I dropped my sword, as my body spasmed out of my control. I opened my mouth to scream but nothing came out.

All I could hear was the crackle of lightning.

Pain sparked along my spine and my arms as I collapsed to the floor and fell into the shattered glass.

My plan had failed.

I'd thought Cato would be too distracted by the glass but he stood before me, still zapping me with his magic, a shard of glass protruding from his head.

CHAPTER FIFTY FOUR
THE HEAT OF BATTLE

My arm hung limply at my side; the wound on my shoulder was deep.

I swung at the Corse with the blade in my non-dominant hand, struggling with the weight of the weapon I'd commandeered after killing its previous owner.

I couldn't tell how long it had been since Evalina had left me to fight the Necromancer, alone, but the flashing light I was seeing coming from the first level told me that she had also found Cato. I tried to move faster, to fight harder, so that I could join her and keep her safe. We'd already lost to Cato once and I doubted he would be stupid enough to let us live a second time.

I'd made good progress on the Corse on the ground level, more than half were headless beneath my boots, but I was barely holding on. My injury was painful, my eyes threatened to close and possibly never open again. I needed a break, to catch my breath at least. I cursed myself for refusing my Mother's escort, for my naivety of thinking we could do this alone.

I noticed an empty pocket of space, somewhere the Corse were keeping clear of, and realized almost too late that it was Cato's office. Smoke plumed under the door, slowly filling the tower; part of me hoped that someone would put it out soon so that we didn't lose all the books and histories stored on the upper levels.

I cut my way through the crowd before me, slowly edging closer to the door.

My sword was in there, and Evalina's blades. We both had weapons but I couldn't seem to get my mind to focus on the battle before me, knowing that ours were stranded in that room. I'd gone through the pit to get my damned sword from Osiria, I was not going to let it sit unused in a room during a battle I would probably die in.

It was nonsense, my mind was creating nonsense reasons for me to keep fighting, to keep living. I was that close to death.

Again.

Get to the room, I told myself and pushed my tired legs forward. I slashed with my stolen, blunt sword, barely getting it through the Corse's necks, resorting to shattering leg bones with the flat edge so at least they would be slow to pursue me. And pursue me they did, dragging their half mutilated bodies across the ground after me, leaving streaks of black sludge behind them.

The smell of the smoke and burning bodies grew stronger the closer I got to the office until it was almost unbearable. I choked and coughed as I cut my way to the door, finally reaching it and flinging it open, a cloud of black smoke engulfing me instantly. Eyes watering I pushed my way through the smoke until I found our discarded weapons. I threw my stolen blade to the side and seized up my scimitar, relaxing my hand into the familiar grip, worn down to fit the shape of my fingers perfectly. I slid Evalina's blades into my belt and dashed out of the room, the fumes dulling my mind more than the pain from my shoulder.

I felt as if I was filled with a new energy as I rushed back into battle with my own blade, its sharp edge making quick work of the Corse before me. The thrill of having my own blade seemed to distract me from the pain in my shoulder and left me able to move freely and kill swiftly. Heads rolled as I slashed my way to the stairs Evalina had gone up, the flashing light now more solid. I feared that perhaps I was too late.

Ducking beneath a thick arm that swung toward me, I cut through the Corse's back, my blade slicing through her partially decomposed body swiftly. I left her to trail me like the others; I was racking up quite the crowd of legless followers.

I was halfway to the stairs when my shoulder sang with pain.

I cried out, almost dropping my newly retrieved sword and twisted to see what had caused the pain. One of the trailing corpses had thrown a dagger into my already wounded shoulder, the pain spreading quickly through my back.

The moment of pain had cost me, almost instantly I was swarmed, pulled to the ground. Grubby half dead hands ripped at me, leaving scratches over any bare skin. The smell was suffocating, I was suffocating under the weight of the bodies. I could feel the panic rising within me; I tried to bite it down, to use what strength I had left in my good arm to slice through the corpses piling on top of me, but I succumbed to it.

Tears welled in my eyes as I fought desperately to pull myself out from under the stinking pile, my family's faces flashing before my eyes.

Thrasos and Odon stared at me as the air was slowly pushed from my lungs by the weight of twenty or more half corpses. Part of me was glad that their faces were the last I would see but then another joined them.

Her white hair flowed to the ground, her gold eyes, almost identical to mine, shone with tears. She reached for me and tried to speak but all that came out was blood from a wound on her neck, pouring down the beige shift she was wearing.

And then, at once, the three of them disappeared and there was only a group of humans, mages, flinging spells toward me. I gasped as the weight on top of me was slowly relieved, allowing air to return to my burning lungs. A jet of fire shot over me, the heat sweltering. I heard Corse in the distance scream and go silent.

A human mage, the girl that led us to Cato's office, knelt beside me. "Prince Thanatos, are you all right?" She asked desperately, giving my shoulder a shake as if she were trying to wake me from slumber. "Can you go on?"

I tried to respond but all that came out was a rasp.

Black dots began to speckle my vision and suddenly her face changed. Eyes turned the brightest spring green, her skin paled and hair turned to ink.

This was the real face I'd longed to see in death. She smiled at me, her beautiful, insecure smile, as if she wasn't sure she was doing it right. I pictured her in the tavern in Osiria, laying on her stomach on the bed, her hair dripping wet.

Evalina.

I wanted to touch her but my arm couldn't seem to reach.

CHAPTER FIFTY FIVE
EYE OF THE STORM

The lightning coursed through my body. I could feel it reverberating off my bones, shaking my eyeballs in their sockets. I wanted to move, to break out of it, but I couldn't. I was frozen, my back arched and my fingers splayed. It didn't feel enough, a part of my brain was screaming that I needed to do more, bend my back more, spread my fingers until my hand ripped apart and became star-shaped. My breath was caught in my lungs, threatening suffocation, and my mouth opened in a silent scream that I wished more than anything would emit. Everything in my mind told me that if all those things happened I would be free of the pain but, until then, I would suffer.

A flash of movement crossed my blurred vision, a streak of yellow cutting through the blue glare. The blue flashes faded to nothing and my pain lessened, my body relaxed but tensed every few seconds as a residual surge of current ran through it.

My vision returned and, through my sporadic fits, I could see the human mage who had led us to Cato standing before him with a large, yellow crystal hovering in the air between them. Her long, dark hair and robes whipped behind her in the wind as she used magic to redirect the lighting from the crystal into the shard of glass still protruding from the Arch-Mage's head. The glass shattered and a shudder ran through Cato, as it did I felt the mage use her magic on me. It didn't feel the same as elven magic; it was missing something, it felt dull, even duller than Thanatos', but it did the job. She used it to pull the remaining charge coursing through my body out and into the crystal. I stood, shaking my head to clear it further and reached for my weapon.

Cato was trying to speak to the mage but his words weren't forming. He seemed to be fighting with himself for control over his limbs. I felt around in his head with my magic and found the pieces of broken glass scattered throughout; he'd suffered damage to his brain that even Isidia's highest trained healers couldn't help. Though I could have left him to suffer, to feel trapped in his own body

316

as it refused to listen to his broken orders, I stepped forward, blade raised, and raked it across his neck. He gurgled for only a second before he fell silent and slipped down out of my line of vision, leaving only the true Necromancer in my sights.

The Necromancer's previously smug face had fallen into a pained and fearful expression, and I reveled in it. He looked frantically around for an escape but the only ways out were either past me and the mage, or out the tower window where jagged rocks awaited at the bottom. He seemed to submit to me, standing by a wall and not fighting to get past.

"It's over now," I said in a low, frightful voice I barely recognised as my own. "It all ends here."

He looked as if he were about to say something but I didn't give him the chance.

I backed him against the wall, my blade pressed to his chest and, using all my strength, I pushed it through his skin, feeling each pop as it slowly made its way through the layers of flesh, fat, and muscle, never once taking my eyes away from his. I stared into them as they bulged in pain and teared up. Apart from a few whimpers, he was silent.

I wished I could have heard him scream, as I'm sure my people had screamed as he'd carved them up and sewn the pieces of them onto himself—probably right before their eyes—screamed at the fear of coming back and not knowing how long it had been, if their families were still awaiting their return from the war, if their children had survived. I wished he would scream but he did not give me that satisfaction. Instead, I made sure to savor his death, to prolong it as long as I could.

Pausing just before my blade could puncture his lungs, I twisted steadily from the hilt. Tears finally slipped from his eyes as his breath hitched at the new pain, and I drove my blade forward again. My arms were sore, the muscles strained from fighting and the effort of the torturously slow death I was executing. With one last thrust, I let the blade puncture the Necromancer's lungs and watched with delight as he coughed blood.

The light began to leave his eyes as more and more blood flooded from his mouth, his throat began to convulse as he started to choke and drown in it. I removed my sword and let him slump to the floor. I was half tempted to begin carving the parts of my people from his body—while he still had a bit of life left in him—but he was fading too quickly. I had to hope they would be happy enough with his death and the burning of the remains.

As the last flicker of life left the monster's eyes, I found myself overwhelmed with emotion. After hacking off his head, I sank to my knees, tears falling freely as everything came crashing down around me.

The Necromancer was gone.

He was dead.

We were safe.

My home, my people, they were all safe and I had avenged those that had been desecrated and mutilated. I could return home knowing that I had nothing to worry about. I wiped my eyes with my dirty, blood-covered hands that only added to the wetness on my cheeks. I wanted to believe that these were all tears of victory and joy but I knew that they weren't. Part of me had died with the Necromancer, the last hopeful and naive part. It had died and left me and, hopefully, had joined Ossena. I was still unsure as to what part she played but, for her sake, I prayed that it was over. That she could finally be reunited with her child and rest.

"Ichika!" An unfamiliar voice called from behind me. "The Prince needs help!"

Within seconds I was on my feet and dashing down the tower stairs, any joy or sadness I had felt completely cleared from my mind and replaced with terror, terror that, after all this I may lose Thanatos.

He lay on the floor in a pool of his own blood, surrounded by a cluster of mages desperately speaking to one another trying to come up with a way to save him. I pushed my way through them, ignoring the protests. I fell to my knees by his side and instantly began healing him, praying the hardest I had ever prayed to the Father that he would survive, that I could save him, that he wouldn't leave me.

Blood had caked his hair together, his clothes were practically dyed with it, making it impossible to quickly spot the wounds that needed the most attention. So I did what I thought was most suitable and focussed my power into the whole of his body rather than focus on one wound at a time. It was risky, but I would risk it for him, as he had done for me.

"Come on, Thanatos," I murmured to myself as I began to sway, my eyes flitting shut with exhaustion. "Please," I sobbed. "You can't leave me."

I could feel the mages around me shifting awkwardly, believing the Prince to be dead and wondering which of them should be the one to pull me away before I let my magic take hold and do exactly the same thing I had just killed a man for. But, as I was just about to turn and snap at them that he would be fine, his eyes began to move beneath the lids, his heart sped up from its labored beat, and his breathing became more regular.

I let out a strange laugh-cry as Thanatos' eyes fluttered open and pulled him further onto my lap.

"Evie," his voice croaked.

"Shh, just relax," I soothed, patting down his blood soaked hair down with one hand and wiping my eyes with the other.

"Evalina, there's still a dagger sticking out of my back."

"Right." I cleared my throat and unceremoniously yanked the dagger from the Prince's back and slammed my hand down onto the wound and began healing before the blood could start flowing out. Thanatos let out a groan of pain and squeezed my thigh.

"Sorry," I said with a grin, relaxing into the hand on my leg, his tight grip showing me that he was mostly healed, any negative thoughts I'd been having previously had melted away at the sight of his golden eyes opening.

"It's done then?" He asked cautiously.

"Yes," I answered, brushing my thumb down his cheek.

I felt the tension leave his shoulders almost instantly and moved my hand from his back, my magic telling me it's job was done. I sent a prayer to the Father begging for it to be true, all of it. The Necromancer's death, Thanatos and I surviving, my healing magic working.

I suddenly felt exhausted, the world around me seeming to go quiet. I gently removed Thanatos' head from my lap and laid down on the floor next to him.

"Evalina? Are you all right?"

"I'm fine. I'm just tired," I said as my eyes closed.

I felt content for the first time in a long time. I rested a hand behind my head and let sleep take me in a room full of corpses.

Chapter Fifty-Six
UP IN SMOKE

My feet slipped in the mud beneath my feet, the dirt and blood mixture sticking to my boots and pants like tar. I pushed off one of the corpses I'd landed on and blocked the Corse's attack with my blade. At first I had been careful not to stand on the dead but, now, I had little choice and they offered better grip than the sodden ground. I pulled out my dagger as the Corse's sword was hooked between my blade and crossgard and drove it onto the living corpse's head, its fragile, exposed skull shattering at the force. I used the distraction to pull my sword free and remove its head.

"Fire wall!" I screamed over the battle, ordering the archers that lined the fort walls to shoot.

Within seconds, arrows flew over my head and a wall of flame erupted before me in a trench filled with tar coated hay.

We'd slowly managed to get the trench dug between battles, then filled with hay and finally had the first lot of troops from this battle pour tar on it as they'd raced out to fight the enemy. I'd ordered them to be careful not to get it on themselves and, if they did, to be away from the trench when it lit but some hadn't managed. Their screams echoed through the clearing joining those of the enemy that had been climbing through the trenches to get to us.

I couldn't help our troops that had been set alight, there were too many Corse already across and now trapped with us inside the wall of fire. All around me, Carracallans and Isidians were forcing their foes into the fires, setting them alight. In theory, it had been a great idea, one we couldn't wait to put into action. But, now, I saw the flaws. In practice, it wasn't entirely foolproof. Now we were stuck, between a wall of fire and a wall of wood with flaming bodies racing through the space, with little or no regard to our survival.

"Keep them from the fort!" I called over the battle, the order then echoed through the battalion and an informal wall of soldiers formed before the fort, cutting down any flaming bodies that approached, be they friend or foe.

The heat from the fire only added to my overwhelming feeling of fatigue. I tried to fight through it to keep my form but I grew sloppy. Smoke began to blind me and make blocking difficult. Corse were able to get close enough to injure me, slashing quickly at my arms and body, but they were dead moments after. The wounds though only added to my ever growing predicament.

My eyes began to weep, making my vision even worse, and the roar and crackling of the fire was deafening. I was barely aware of what was happening around us; my heart felt as if it would explode, it was beating so fast. I gripped my weapons as tight as I could, my sword in one hand, dagger in the other, and pressed further into the field, attempting to turn my back safely from the wind to clear the smoke from my vision.

A sharp blade came down on my leg. I let out a cry of pain as it sliced a deep chunk of skin from it and knocked the blade back with my own. Wet, warm blood trickled down my calf and into my boot, my steps now becoming squelchy and painful.

The Corse was faster than I expected and more whole than I had seen. Its skin was almost completely solid and flushed, as if it were fully living, but a gaping wound and its trailing intestines gave away its true identity. It swung at my head and I was barely able to block it with my dagger. It then hooked a leg around mine and pulled, sliding its blade until it caught my dagger in the crossguard and pulled it from my grip. I used my now free hand to grip the creature's shoulder and pull it down with me as I fell, rolling quickly to get atop it and wrestling with it to keep its blade away from my person.

I tried as hard as I could, pushed myself with all I had left, but I couldn't overpower the corpse. I was too tired, too drained. The Corse cracked me over the head with the pommel of its sword and rolled us over again so it was now atop me. I struggled, slightly dazed from the hit to my head, and tried to buck it off of me.

The creature raised its arm and angled it down to drive it through my skull, lifting its bent elbow backward. I took the chance and forced my tired leg into the air, hooking it through the Corses arm and yanking it backward. We fought against each other, neither wanting to let go and be at the other's mercy but wanting to gain the upper hand. In our struggles, the Corse managed to flip us over and pin my head into the mud. I choked, breathing in dry dirt and being suffocated by the wet.

In a last-ditch effort to escape, I threw my elbow back, hitting the creature in the head and knocking it off my back. I scrambled to my feet and fumbled for my sword, my heart beating so fast my head was throbbing. My lungs burned as I sucked in as much air as I could to clear the black spots that littered my vision as the Corse, too, rose to their feet. I tried to cough the dirt from my lungs but only choked on it more.

Where had this skilled fighter come from? Why was this Corse so different from the others?

I managed to blocked two, three, four blows from the Corse with my shaking arms. My sword was beginning to feel as if it had tripled in weight.

The bodies that covered the ground were so muddy and trodden on they were as soft as the mud beneath them and no longer offered better grip than the slick ground. I risked a glance at some of the faces around me, white, and gray, and green all stared at me with blank eyes. I was almost certain that I would be joining them soon. A Sea Elf screaming and set ablaze bolted past and, for a sickening moment, my mind placed the face of my King over his. It disturbed me but also comforted me in a way, it made it seem like we were here together, fighting the enemy to save our girls. But it wasn't Eevan. I was here alone; even Bellona was away from this battle. There was no one here with me. I would die alone, with no family.

I raised my blade once more and managed some feeble blocking and striking before the Corse easily knocked it from my hold.

I could barely keep my eyes open.

I tried to focus on the pain in my leg to keep me going but it had turned numb. My boot, now filled with blood, had become heavy.

Black spots spread through my vision and, just as I was about to let myself succumb, pain lanced through my arm.

I cried out, falling to the ground and being met with my hand already there waiting to catch me. I was confused for a moment before I realized that, had my arm been attached, there would be no way it could be at that angle. I felt more warm blood pour down the side of my body from the stump that was left of my right arm. Groaning with pain and effort, I gripped my amputated arm and tried to move toward the fort. All thought of fighting disappeared from my mind, leaving only the desperate urge for survival.

I carried my arm with me, shuffling on my knees across the battlefield, climbing over bodies of the dead, screaming as my raw wound hit the mud over and over. And, just as I thought I was safe, that the Corse had forgotten me and my wounds had numbed, pain shot through my leg.

I tumbled to the side screaming.

My vision blurred.

My lungs froze in a scream of pain that I couldn't seem to get out.

I made to stand but only screamed again when a fresh wave of pain lanced through my body as the wound on my thigh touched the dirt. I rolled onto my back and lifted my left leg, it was lighter, too light.

Looking down at it I saw that it had, too, been cut off and laid off to the side.

The Corse that had maimed me stalked forward. My vision was made up mostly of black specks, my breathing heavy and wet as sobs racked through me. The fresh pain had reawakened me to the others that had dulled and I understood, now, why so many had pleaded, had begged for death rather than healing. Why it was such a good torture technique. I had never experienced pain worse than this. I prayed I never would again. I angled my head back as the creature lifted it's blade, giving it access to my neck, to end it all. I wanted to squeeze my eyes shut and wait for it to happen but, no, I kept my eyes wide open—forced them to focus as best they could, despite their urge to flit shut.

The Corse grinned, the fire light glinting off its blade. I took in a shuddering breath, knowing it would be my last.

And then ... the Corse fell to the side with a great thud, its sword clattering beside it. I stared at its face, so close to mine now on the ground, and it stared back with blank, lifeless eyes.

I heard more thudding, more weapons clattering to the ground, and it was then that a sob of relief escaped me. It dulled the pain for a moment before it flared again and my eyes began to close once more. My mind wanted desperately to block the pain by putting me to sleep, but, if I slept, I knew I would not wake. Cheers began to sound over the field—cheering and a rush of boots as healers burst through the gates of the fort.

A face filled my blurred vision, then white mist. I breathed in the healing magic and, as it faded, I gazed at the face of my savior. Pale, green-eyed, with long, long, black hair. Their magic flowed through me. It filled my veins, stopping my pain. The scratches were the first to heal then the deep cuts pulled themselves together and I felt the tissue knitting itself into one piece again.

A sigh escaped my lips and I reached for Evalina's face but my hand never got there. I remembered that my arm had been cut off and switched to my left, the pain gone thanks to her magic. I tucked the hair back from her face and for a moment could have sworn blue had rubbed off on my fingers. As my vision began to clear I saw that it wasn't blue stains from Evalina's hair but bruises from my fingers being trodden on. And, in fact, it wasn't Evalina at all but the butcher's daughter.

"It's all right, Captain, I'll get you to the healers," she panted, still using her magic to try to stop my wounds from bleeding.

I stared at her face, noting all the differences from Evalina's. Her straight, sloped nose, dull, small eyes, plump lips. How I wished she was Evalina.

"Roana," I rasped.

"Shh," she soothed. "It's over, Captain," she said excitedly. "The Princess has killed the Necromancer."

I tried to reach for my leg but Roana pinned me down and called for a healer. Five were on us in an instant. Roana helped carry me into the fort. She was strong from working in her family's butcher shop, used to carrying animal carcases and lifting them onto hooks. She placed me gently on the healers table and moved out of the way so the healers could get to work reattaching my limbs. As she left the tent I stared after her, imagining that she was Evalina, that we had won this war together.

If I could not die with my King, I would live with my Princess.

CHAPTER FIFTY SEVEN
GRAPES OF WRATH

Evalina began to stir beside me and, before I could reach for her and pull her into my arms, she flicked off the blanket and stood before the window. I groaned. The noise of the rebuilding city had already woken me and I had just been drifting off again.

I wasn't ready to face the world, to accept all that had happened and what was still yet to come. I gazed at Evalina's face from across the room, the excitement that had been there moments ago had faded to a grim, thoughtful expression and I knew exactly where her mind had wandered because mine had gone there too. We'd saved these people, the whole of Carynthia, but who had we killed to do it? Had the Corse been blind to who they used to be or did they remember? Could they have returned to their past lives?

The desecrated Minoman graveyard flashed in my mind; how many had been recently buried and turned? The families were barely given the chance to mourn before their loved ones were hauled back from the Father's lands.

I forced the thoughts from my mind, noticing that Evalina's expression was only growing graver, and decided to pull her from it somehow.

"How do you have so much energy?" I drawled lazily from the bed, baiting her.

A smile slunk across her face. "We did it! Thanatos, we killed the Necromancer!" She exclaimed.

I laughed at her sudden excitement. "You killed the Necromancer, I almost died."

"You played a pivotal role in the killing of the Necromancer," she said, leaping onto the bed and receiving another groan from me. "If you hadn't said yes to being my guide, I would have died before I'd even gotten close." She toyed with one of my braids. "How do you feel?"

"Good, tired but good." I said with a smile. But I could tell by the flicker in her eyes that she knew I was lying. I didn't think I could ever feel *good* again, not after everything we'd been through.

"We should bathe and get ready to leave, though I expect the King will want to see us at some point."

"We don't have to leave so soon, we could take a break for a week … or two," I said quickly, and maybe a little desperately.

"You must want to get back to Osiria … I do," she added sheepishly. "I miss little Odon."

It took a moment for my mind to register what she'd said. She wished to return to Osiria, to see my family. I felt a rush of the same longing. The quick stop hadn't been enough. I missed my nephew, my sister, and brother. For the first time in a long time, I wished to be at home with them. Maybe it was because I knew anytime there, now, could be my last.

I smiled and pulled her into a hug. "I'm glad you feel that way," I said, kissing her hair. "I guess we can head back as soon as you'd like."

She gently pulled from my grasp and kissed my cheek. "What I really want right now …"

I wiggled my eyebrows at her and lowered my hands to rest on her hips.

She grinned. "… is for you to see a healer," she said, slapping her hands on my chest.

I groaned and flopped back onto the bed. I shouldn't have been surprised, but I had hoped she was past her insecurities with her magic.

"What? I just want to know that you're all right!"

"I'm fine! You healed me!" I sat up and sat on the edge of the bed, my back to the Princess. I felt the mattress shift as she crawled across the bed and slid her hands under my shirt feeling her way up my back. "I know you're just checking my wounds." I said in a monotone, wanting nothing more than to lean back into her touch.

"Well can you blame me? The last time I healed large wounds they opened up again and you almost died. I don't have Rangkar here to help carry you to safety."

"That wasn't your fault and you know it," I said as I pulled my boots on and rose from the bed, tucking my shirt into my pants.

"I just want to be sure," she said more quietly.

I turned, giving her an apologetic look.

"You're really heavy," she whispered.

I picked up a pillow and hit her with it. She fell off the end of the bed, control out the window as her body shook with laughter.

I shook my head. "Fine, I'll see a healer," I said, stepping over her giggling form, and made to open the door of our small room at the inn. "I'm getting food, not that I need it, apparently," I threw over my shoulder. "Are you coming?"

I chuckled to myself as the giggling ceased behind me and was followed by the thumping and thudding of Evalina shoving her feet into her boots as she followed me down the hallway.

The inn below was quiet and warm, a change I was sure Evalina would appreciate from the chilly north of Carynthia. All the windows were open, filling the room with salty sea air and the scent of grapes. A barmaid quickly flittered over to us and led us to a table by a window with a view of the ocean.

"What would you like to eat, Your Highnesses?" She asked eagerly. "Anything you ask for we will make—and no charge, not for our saviors."

Evalina smiled at the woman and almost laughed at me as her eyes landed on the shocked expression I was unable to hide. I'd never been treated this way in an inn that wasn't owned by Glik.

"What time is it, madam?" Evalina asked.

"Almost midday, I'm surprised you didn't rest for longer. Your room is free of charge, if that is what you're worried about."

"Of course not, please bring us lunch then, whatever you deem fit, and some wine."

"Of course! You shall have our best wine!" She scuttled excitedly back into the kitchens.

"Are you all right?" Evalina asked, her eyes almost concerned.

I did my best to wipe the surprise off my face. "The last time I was here they wouldn't even let me stay in this inn, I had to stay at the paramour house down the road."

Her smile faltered for a second before broadening. "Well I'm sure you enjoyed that place even more," she joked.

"Ah yes, because I'm licentious and evil right?" I said, rolling my eyes.

"No, because who wouldn't enjoy staying in a paramour house?"

"The more time I spend with you, the more I see how like your aunt you are." I laughed.

"And what do you know of my aunt, Prince?"

"Well, if there's anyone with almost as bad a reputation as me out there, it's her."

"I guess the only difference is that the stories about her are all true. Why let them think the worst of you?"

I took a deep breath. "Sometimes it's easier than trying to argue with everyone." My eyes locked onto the bar maid as she strolled from the kitchen with a large jug. Not at all to my surprise, she hugged Evalina's side of the table as she poured wine for us, and even that was a vast improvement to what I was used to.

When she left Evalina rested a hand on mine. "Give it time," she said gently.

"If I can win you, of all people, over, I can win them all," I said, grinning over the edge of my goblet.

"And so you will," she said, knocking her goblet on mine and drinking deeply.

Our meal was delicious and the perfect thing to eat while staring out at the ocean; cold, roasted vegetables on a bed of soft green leaves, sprinkled with crumbling cheese that paired perfectly with the wine. I wished we could have savored it longer, but Evalina wanted to leave; and what she wanted, I would give her. It was just a coincidence that we wanted the same thing.

The crowd outside the inn practically applauded when Evalina and I walked out the door. We'd both frozen with surprise but Evalina recovered quickly and graciously accepted the praise and outreached hands. It took me a long moment but, eventually, I joined her, making our way down the road to the palace.

It was odd to me, to have people not my own offer me unflinching hands, to thank me. Some still kept their distance, hid their children behind their legs, but the hatred in their eyes was only an ember and, with time, I would snuff that out, too.

I spotted a familiar face in the crowd—the man who'd sought us out. A woman was clinging to his side, her face streaked with tears. I searched his eyes and he shook his head. We hadn't found his sister but he had, in the vast pile of remains in the tower. No doubt it had been the first place people ventured to, after the death of the Necromancer had been confirmed, to search for missing loved ones; and they were gone, all of them—either dead from the demise of their creator or by mine and Evalina's hands. That last thought sat with me as we continued down the road.

With Evalina by my side, I found I was able to enter shops that previously would never have let me in. We were able to restock our supplies with relative ease, the only hassle we kept running into was people insisting on gifting us everything. The people of Minoma seemed to have forgotten that we were royalty and money was of no consequence. I left Evalina to peruse a bookshop that sold books both old and new while I snuck over to a jewelry store, taking advantage of the new found tolerance toward me. I inspected each piece laid out in glass displays as the assistants stared at me with a forced smile. Some pieces were delicate and modest, perfect for my mother, others were more intricately designed but had no gemstones inlaid, the kind of jewelry my sister would like. Nothing in the main counters stood out to me as I made my way around the store and, despite letting me inside, the assistant made no effort to assist me. I was about to give up and leave the store when a pair of earrings caught my eye. They'd been jammed to the side of a display case, as if they weren't meant to be seen.

"Excuse me," I called to the shop assistant, her smile faltering for a second, "can I look at these earrings please?" My over politeness seemed to win her over, either that or the prospect of gossip. "The silver ones, there, with the diamond and—"

"Black sapphire," the assistant finished. "They're not very expensive. Are they for someone special? I can show you some much nicer pieces—"

"No, thank you. They're perfect."

They were silver studs, the black sapphires, cut and smoothed round to reveal a gold star, inlaid in the center were surrounded by sparkling, white diamonds. They couldn't be more fitting. I knew Evalina would pick up on the meaning, I just had to hope that she would appreciate it.

I left the shop, slipping the small parcel into my pocket, and met with Evalina in the book store. She'd found a book of Kushyami history and was already curled up in a corner reading it when I found her. I felt terrible for having to pull her away but we had to speak with the King. I had to know what had happened here, how he had allowed it.

Eventually, the palace came to loom over us, its mammoth form shrinking everything before it.

I'd never gotten so close before, usually I was stopped by guards further up the road and given some lame excuse as to why I couldn't proceed, despite it being protocol that I should announce my presence.

The palace was temple-like in its build, similar to the Kushyami, but more plainly decorated. Where the Kushyami had painted carvings all over the walls and ceilings, the Minomans had large but few paintings, and detailed carvings at the tops of the walls, so high up you could barely make them out. Large, stone columns stretched to the roof structure, some were plain fluted columns and others were ornately carved statues of past rulers, the architrave of the roof resting on their sturdy heads.

We met a guard at the entrance, explained who we were, and were instantly escorted to the King, no questions asked. We walked through a short entrance hall and out into a large courtyard. A shallow pool was situated in the center with two fountains on either end, each one depicting a different god. The statue of the Mother depicted her personality perfectly, though she did not have the false face of the Princess, the statue seemed to hold itself the same way she did. She had her arm raised as if to attack, water spurting out of her palm but her body was seductively posed. The Father, down the other end, was carved muscled, with a long beard and gentle face, holding a vase that water gently trickled out of.

The Father lovingly filled the world with what we needed and the Mother smothered us with it. The mosaic that made up the bottom and edges of the pool showed a picture of everyday Minoman life. Grape harvesting, farming, trade, and, of course, the mages studying in the tower. It was exquisitely detailed, my fingers ached for the artisans that would have worked for months breaking the tile into the perfect shapes and sizes, meticulously placing the tiles until the picture was perfect.

The King sat in a high throne at the back of a large room, decorated with mosaics and tapestries. His two children sat on either side of him, Prince Orazio on the right and Princess Thetissia on the left.

King Arcadio stood as we knelt before him and signaled for us to rise. Facing him as I was, I found myself having to consciously make an effort to keep my mouth shut. I wanted to blast him for not warning anyone about the Corse, for not doing anything about the Necromancer, and leaving him to be dealt with by outside forces. He'd let his people suffer at the hands of the dead and done nothing. I hoped he had a worthy excuse.

"Words cannot express how thankful I am to you, both of you. You have saved me, my family and my people. I do not know what I could offer in return that could even come close to what you two have done for us." His words sounded grateful but his tone was stiff, as if he wished he didn't need to say them.

CHAPTER FIFTY EIGHT
SOMETHING ELSE

The reunion with our horses was more emotional than I had expected it to be. As we'd come over a hill and spotted them, still tied to the tree where we'd left them, I was overcome.

Faenor had nudged me with her nose as I reached her, as if to tell me to stop being silly as tears streamed down my face. I hadn't thought of the horses once during the battle but seeing them afterwards made me realize how much it would have hurt me if they'd died.

Thanatos had chuckled as I'd sobbed into Faenors mane but I could hear the emotion in his voice as he calmed Serelene. They had been on this journey as much as we had and I could have sworn they'd been tense before they spotted us, fearing that their friends had died and left them to die tied to a tree, in the middle of nowhere.

Thanatos and I led the horses to the beach, their hooves sinking into the pale sand. I breathed in the salty air; it always reminded me of my father, he had always smelled of the sea. I kicked my boots off and tucked them away in my pack before running through the sand and down to the water.

I fought down the squeal my body wanted to release as the freezing-cold water brushed over my feet and ankles, the sand beneath my feet pulling away with it. It was too cold to go swimming but I had at least wanted to touch it, the ocean that my father had loved so much—possibly more than he had loved me or my mother.

I couldn't be sure, no one could, but I realized that the part of the ocean I was staring out at could have been the part he'd died in. Burnt alive and dropped into the ocean, lost forever. I was practically at his grave. It gave me an odd feeling of peace, as if he were finally being laid to rest now that I was here to witness it.

I looked back at the Osirian Prince behind me and smiled, one life ends and another begins. I was finally accepting my father's death, finally forgiving those

I once thought to be involved, and preparing to start a new life that involved them heavily.

I didn't want to be a Queen like my mother. I had meant what I'd said in the throne room of the Minoman King; I would take Thanatos' approach, know my people and openly interact with them, travel, meet my allies in person, and form proper relationships with them. I would have none of the stand-offish behavior, staying locked up in the castle like my mother—it had certainly done us no favors. Our allies were barely interested in being involved with us, our only use to them our healing abilities; but there had been no wars, so what use were we, really?

I pushed the thought away; it was something to consider once I returned home. The rest of my travels, I decided, would be time for me to rest, actually enjoy freedom, and enjoy something else, while I still could.

We followed the coast all the way up to the base of the Osirian mountain range, soaking up the fresh, salty air and beautiful sunsets over the water, then followed the mountain range that cut Osiria off from the rest of Carynthia. I was glad to be avoiding the open desert, I didn't think I could have handled the heat again, even with the brooch.

We were only a couple of days away from the mountain pass that would take us north into Osiria when we came up beside the Theisa Jewel mines.

The mouth of the mines was huge; it looked to be a natural cave but I knew that inside, beneath the mountains, there were hundreds of human and elf made tunnels and hollowed out caverns, filled with glittering gemstones and fine metals. The true entrance to the mines, which lay a decent way inside the cave, was protected from outsiders by a large, iron gate.

"Ebele must be running late," Thanatos said, resting his face on the cool bars of the gate. "She'd usually be back by now."

"Perhaps the battle slowed them?" I suggested.

"That was weeks ago, but you could be right," he agreed. "I like to check in on them, both to make sure they're conducting business properly and to make sure they're doing it safely."

"They need that much supervision?"

"We trust them to stick to the mining agreement, it's more of a formality to check that, for the sake of the other lands, really." He sighed. "The safety check is for my own conscience. I had a visit here once and the miners weren't even wearing safety lines while working in the caverns. They were losing hundreds of miners each season. Not to mention the cave-ins that would happen because they didn't support the tunnel roofs while expanding." Thanatos shook his head. "It's improved since I've begun my visits and the head miner, Ebele, sticks to my rules because she can't stand my nagging. Apparently, I can be quite annoying."

"Oh really?" I added sarcastically.

Thanatos ignored me. "We should stay here for the night. The cave will offer extra protection. We're getting closer to troll territory."

I nodded and helped Thanatos set up camp, pulling out my Kushyami book once the tent had been pitched and dinner was stewing over a fire.

It was fascinating to learn the history of our world from another culture's perspective, especially the Kushyami. They'd been so close to the Osirians, unlike the rest of Carynthia, even worshiped them when they first arrived. The stories painted them in a completely different light than how all of my history books had. In Isidia, they were always the villains, always senselessly killing and using their powers; but in these stories they were protectors, only using their magic when truly pushed, as Thanatos had done during our time together. Reading the stories and seeing how the Kushyami saw them, I wondered why the Dark-Elvess hadn't risen up and flattened the world as they easily could; but, perhaps, that was why—it was easy, and predictable, and they were better than that.

The book had opened with a foreword explaining that most of the events had taken place before the Kushyami had a written language and that their histories had relied on the story keepers who would tell the stories of their people; therefore, some details had been twisted or forgotten, as most verbal stories were.

The first story was of how the Kushyami first came to our shores, lured here by spoken stories from other human lands, and guided through the monster filled seas by the Carracallans. It was a time when Sea-Elves having gills was more common. They'd settled in a place similar to the land they'd come from and named it after their King, the King who'd lead them on their voyage, Kushyam. The book did not speak much of their previous home, it only mentioned that the landscape was much like the place they'd chosen here. I would have to ask my aunt if she had been there, my curiosity sparked.

Only Sea-Elves could sail into the open ocean past the horizon, because only they could ask permission from the beasts that ruled the waters.

I read on about old Kushyami Kings and Queens, siblings warring and scheming over the throne, bloodlines being kept pure through incest and intergenerational marriage; it made me almost glad that I had so few living relatives and that, so far, my Carracallan side only had one Heir. There was little to no chance of that happening to me.

Almost halfway through the book, I came across a section that piqued my interest even more than the rest. It spoke of one of the early wars between the Isidans and Osirians, the first one that involved humans directly. According to the story, Isidia and Osiria were preparing for peace, a marriage had been arranged between an Osirian Princess and an Isidian Prince; but the Princess refused the Prince, infuriating the Isidians and leading to them declaring war. Fearful of facing the Osirians alone again, the Isidians convinced the humans to join them by teaching them magic and fooling them into thinking they could win.

It was a devastating war, thousands died and the humans were caught right in the middle, stuck between the two warring nations. Although I had not been involved, or even alive, when it had taken place, I felt the weight of that war, of the lives lost because my kin could not handle rejection. I was glad that the age of political marriages to end wars was over, that Carynthia had been peaceful enough that the most weight a marriage could hold was trade.

In retaliation to the Isidians teaching humans magic, the Osirians created an elite force of warrior priestesses, the Phoenix Priestesses, tasked with hunting down and destroying human magic users. I paused, wondering if Thanatos knew this history of the people who had raised his mother. Did they still hold the same agenda all these years later, or had it dissolved into more of a fanatical group of devoted Mother worshippers? I had seen Omisha's own prejudice toward humans but could it go so far as murderous? I liked to think that people's bark was worse than their bite but was I wrong in this case? I pushed the thought away and continued reading. I didn't want to believe that anyone in Thanatos' family would have these ideals.

The story seemed to jump as if pages of manuscript had been lost before printing; without any reason, the war ended, there was no winner, it was just over and the marriage was forgotten about. It was said that from then on the Dark-Elves stayed in Osiria, few traveled south and the royal family had little to do with anyone outside of Kushyam.

My mouth fell open and I almost hit myself with the book as I realized my utter stupidity.

The story was not lost, I knew the rest.

It was Ossena's story.

It pained me to realize that her parents hadn't recognized her baby enough to even tell the humans of her existence and her demise, that even Ossena's own death was ignored in history—but it made sense why Omisha had known it. The story was the origin of the Priesteshood that had raised her. I had no doubts that she had been told the story since she was a babe. I couldn't say for sure but, from what I had seen of Ossena, I felt she would not be happy to know that her story was tied to such a violent group.

Thinking of the wraith, my hand subconsciously rose to rest on my shoulder, the burned skin smooth against my rough hands. I'd been so certain that her oath had had something to do with the Necromancer, but, clearly, I had been wrong. I still had so many questions, but it had been at least a week since we'd killed him and Cato—Thanatos and I taking our time journeying back—and I was yet to have a dream of her.

What could she want from me? Perhaps it was something to do with the priestesses.

I sat in the tent for a long while, the book placed facedown on the top of my thigh as I stared out of the open flap. The sky had begun growing darker and the desert colder. A shiver ran through me as I tried to piece together what connection the Necromancers had to the wraith, why they had invaded my dreams of her.

"Hey," Thanatos said, poking his head through the tent flap, making me jump. "Sorry"—Thanatos laughed—"dinner's ready."

I nodded, closing the book and tucking it back into my pack.

"Did you enjoy it?" Thanatos added, pointing his chin toward my pack.

"I did." I smiled, I couldn't bring myself to reveal my latest revelations, not while he was finally enjoying himself.

We sat around a fire with our dinner, vegetables and meat skewered on long thin sticks, coated in delicious spices that Thanatos had bought in Minoma. We ate and watched the sun go down outside the cave, the sky going from blue, to the lavender of Thanatos' skin, to pink before orange, and then black. Thanatos and I retired shortly after, the desert wind whistling through the cave entrance and filling our tent with a cool breeze. It was a welcome reprieve from the hot day, though it was cooler at the base of the mountains than it had been traveling through the middle to Nebu.

A single bed roll had been laid out inside the tent, as had been our norm since we'd left Osiria.

"I would have liked to have met Ebele," I commented as Thanatos and I undressed for bed. "I'm fascinated by the mines, seeing them would have been a treat."

"I'd wanted to show them to you but it will have to wait," Thanatos replied.

I watched him undress out of the corner of my eye, I found it hard not to watch him out right, his body still a wonder to me despite the many nights we'd now spent together.

"How long has Ebele been here?" I asked.

"About five years now. She started as a miner and took over operations pretty quickly. I think she prefers to be out here over being in the city." He glanced my way and smiled. "Need some help with that?" He asked as I struggled to find the end of my headscarf to unwrap it. He came over to me and gently pushed the scarf down so that it hung down my back and then lifted the lot over my head, removing it in one big clump of fabric.

"I guess that's one way to do it."

"I can help you with the rest too," he said in a low voice, our faces so close I could feel his breath on my face.

I hooked my thumbs into the top of his pants and pulled his hips into mine. He planted his mouth on mine, his hands reaching for the laces on my shirt. I raked my fingers up and down his back, tracing the dent of his spine between the two sides of dense muscle. Our lips still locked, he deftly pulled my shirt from my pants and ran his hands up my body beneath it, my skin prickling at his touch. I tried not to laugh as he touched a ticklish spot just beneath my ribs.

We pulled apart only for a moment, to pull my shirt over my head, then crushed our torsos together, my bare skin on his. I savored the warmth he provided in the cool night and almost moaned as his large, warm hands ran up my back, encompassing me. He gasped against my lips as I dragged my nails down his back; he retaliated by nipping at my bottom lip.

My blood was speeding through my body, my heart pounding at the thought of what was coming. It was strange, to be so excited for something that had already happened many times before, but each time was like this, like the first. I thought back to our first time as he began to kiss down my cheek, slowly making his way to my neck, how nervous we'd both been—and how desperate.

We were still desperate now, but for another reason; we knew what was coming, what to expect, and it was good. I slid a hand beneath the waistband of his pants, receiving another nip in response. His mouth quickly made its way back to mine, his tongue flicking my lips as I teased him with my hand, touching only gently. In one swift movement Thanatos pulled my hand from his pants and suddenly had me pinned to the bedroll, my hands trapped by his above my head. His eyes searched mine for a moment, seeking consent, I lifted my head and gave the tip of his nose a delicate peck.

Thanatos' lips grazed along my chest as he pulled my hands down to rest behind my head, a silent command to keep them there as his mouth got lower and lower on my torso. He slowly removed my pants, pulling them down my legs and leaving kisses along my thighs as he went. My stomach swirled with excitement and desire—I longed to feel his touch. It took all of my self control not to pull him on top of me and just have it done. I'd learnt over the last few weeks that Thanatos liked to take it slow, sometimes painfully slow, but it was always worth it. The Prince hooked my leg on his shoulder as he rose from removing my pants, his face hovering between my legs.

My breath hitched as I felt his warm tongue begin to flick over my core, my body filling with heat. His hands gripped my thighs as his tongue dove deeper, my body attempting to pull away from him of its own accord. He moved his hands down my thighs, cupping my rear and lifting my hips closer to his face. My head flung back in ecstasy, my heart pounding through my head as my limbs began to quake. My mind went blank as the throes of pleasure took hold. I grabbed a fist full of Thanatos' hair, holding his head in place as I grew closer and closer to release.

Then he stopped.

My body was confused for a moment, I'd been so close to climax and then … it just … stopped. Thanatos' hands moved away from me, a cruel smile spread across his face.

I was on him in an instant, removing his pants and pushing him onto his back on the bedroll. I eyed his body, taking in every single detail, letting my mind wander for a moment on what I wanted to do to him.

Tease or please?

The more I thought on it, the more my body seemed to pulse, to want. My eyes froze on exactly what it was that I wanted. I ran my nails up his chest as I straddled his hips, eliciting a groan. I nudged his nose with mine so that he'd tilt his head so I could kiss his mouth as I lowered myself onto him. He moaned into my mouth, his hands coming to grip my hips, his nails digging into my flesh. I rose and lowered slowly at first, teasing for as long as I could stand it, before I couldn't take it anymore and rode faster, harder.

We freely expressed our pleasure, the tent filling with our deep moans and gasps of gratification. Thanatos' body jerked as he reached completion, his breath shuddering.

I collapsed onto his chest, letting him wrap his arms around me and hold me close. I ignored the slick feeling of sweat beads trickling down my body and onto him. He took hold of my chin and pulled my mouth to his, his tongue snaking into my mouth and tickling the inside of my lips.

After the kiss I rolled off of him, needing to catch my breath, my knees no longer wanting to be bent; they cracked as I straightened them and I sighed with relief. Thanatos rolled onto his side and planted a kiss on my cheek, before his hand made its way down my torso and between my legs.

"Your turn," he whispered into my ear.

Chapter Fifty Nine
THE LONG WAY BACK

We lay facing each other, our hands pressed together and pointing toward the sky.

"When will we arrive in Ravenna?" Evalina asked, her voice thick.

"A week, if not a few days. I just need to inform my family of everything that happened in Minoma and then I can take you home." She sighed, her eyes resting on our touching hands. "You don't want to go home?"

"Not so soon." She paused for a moment, her eyes shifting to meet mine. "Once I go home, this will be over."

My heart raced and my mind flooded with guilt. I should have told her sooner, but now it was too late. I'd have to leave it for when we got back to Ravenna. I knew she would be angry but at least there I had backup and she couldn't get very far if she tried to run—and she would.

"I'd like to live it as long as I can," she added.

"We can figure something out," I offered, wanting to change the subject.

I didn't want to lie to her, not as hope glinted in her eyes. It wasn't unusual for elves to have multiple partners, even when married, but it would have been different for us, being royalty. I was glad that we didn't need to think that way, that we wouldn't be living two lives, but not that I was alone in that feeling.

Evalina had hope but, as we traveled home, she would think on it more, stress, and later decide she was not interested; then, I would inform her of our engagement and she would loathe me.

I wished Rangkar were with me, so that I could vent to him and have him slap wisdom into me. My mind wondered about him as I pushed Evalina's hair over her shoulder, what had he done after he left with the witch? Where was he now? It was odd to be apart from him for so long.

"Are you all right?" Evalina asked, searching my face with her green eyes glinting like the emeralds in the mines.

"I was just thinking about Rangkar." She gave me a look and I pushed her shoulder playfully. "Not like that. I'm just not used to traveling without him, it's odd not knowing where he is."

She ran her fingertips lightly over my arm, tracing the inked lines of my tattoos. "I'm sure he's fine, he's a big orc," she jested.

"I know. It's hard out there for Orcs, though. He plays it off but he takes the attitudes to heart."

"He sounds like someone else I know," she whispered, leaning forward and kissing my shoulder.

"He works as a bounty hunter because he believes that if he does good for people they'll look past his appearance, but they won't. He needs to accept himself and stop worrying about what others think."

"That's great advice! You should take it," she said, giving me a stern look.

I gaped at her, trying to think of a comeback. "Maybe I will." Was all I could say.

She burst out laughing.

I marveled at the sound, at the easy joy on her face. It made me want to scoop her up, hold her close, and never let anything bad happen that might take that laugh from her.

"We can change all that for him," she said suddenly. "When we're ruling. We can make the world safe for orcs, make it illegal to treat them poorly, at least in our Kingdoms. Others will follow suit." She said it with such passion that it almost hurt for me to shatter her hopes.

"Something like that would be very hard to pass and to monitor."

"It will never happen if we don't try." Again, her eyes glinted with hope, hope for peace and love—two things she had never truly experienced.

It made my heart ache for her. I knew my brother would broker for peace, and he would happily follow suit with anything that Evalina pushed, they were very like minded. I just had to hope that he, too, wouldn't resent me once it all came out.

I'd given him almost no time to prepare for my leaving because, despite how much my parents liked to complain that I was never home, I was—a lot—and if anyone were to feel my absence the most, it would be Thrasos. Since we were small, we'd spent almost every waking hour together—as twins seemed to always do—but, unlike other siblings, we'd never fought as children. It wasn't until we were grown that we began to argue, after the sickness had truly taken hold. He grew frustrated with me, that I was well and able bodied but chose to spend my time with him.

He'd never resented me for being healthy, at least not that he'd told me, but he had hated that I was able to leave, to do whatever I'd wanted and never did. The first time I'd left the palace it had been him nudging me out of the door with his wheeled chair, thrusting my sword into my hand and telling me not to come back until I'd had enough fun for the both of us. And I had, and continued to do so by his wishes. When I returned I'd spend the next few days lounging in his rooms, watching him paint and telling him of my adventures. He often expressed that he wished I shared his talent in painting so that I could paint all the places I'd seen, the people I'd met; I simply told him he'd just have to get better so he could join me one day.

It was a dark topic in our household, whether or not Thrasos would ever get better. Healers said he could and I believed he could, but there was always an air of doubt.

I was pulled from my thoughts by Evalina's soft snoring. The uninterrupted sleep she'd had in the last week had greatly improved her mood, despite the fact the burn still lingered on her shoulder.

I hadn't told her yet that I'd seen the wraith during the battle, that I now saw her image in my dreams. She never spoke, just held her hand out to me, tears streaming down her face and blood pouring from her gaping neck.

I looked across at Evalina's peaceful face, how she had managed to keep going after seeing that almost every night I will never know but I would forever admire her strength. I held in a laugh as her incorrectly healed nose began to whistle and closed my eyes to sleep, glad that I even had the chance to still hear her breathing.

"Ugh get off me," Evalina whined, pushing at my chest. "It's too hot."

"Good morning to you too," I said, rolling off her sweat coated body.

It had been so cold in the night she had insisted on me holding her close to me as we slept, but now the air in the tent was hot from the desert sun.

I found it a comfortable heat but others, others who had not grown up near the mouths of volcanoes, did not.

We packed our camp up quickly, both of us eager to continue our journey home. I couldn't help but pause for a moment before leaving the mine entrance. I had hoped to see Ebele one last time, if only to settle business and ease the hand over to my brother, but it seemed it was not meant to be. I wondered if she'd miss my visits or if she truly did find me as annoying as she made out she did.

The wind had shifted overnight, it was now coming over the mountains and sweeping down the face. I took a deep breath and sighed as the air filled with the smell of ash and sulfur, the smell of home.

Journeying home this time felt different.

There was no longer the dread of imminent death lingering over me, I knew I would be leaving again but I would be able to return, if my Queen allowed it. The closer we got to home the more I thought on what married life would be like.

Yes, I would have responsibilities as King but Evalina would be a capable Queen, I would be more of a consort, especially given who I am, what I am. I doubted the Isidian people would take me as their King straight out of the gate. There would be push back, for sure. I wouldn't be surprised if there was rioting and complete pandemonium in the streets the second our engagement was announced. But perhaps I was being too pessimistic, they could react differently, happy even, that our peoples were joined. I suppose it all came down to the reaction of their Princess.

I glanced at Evalina; she seemed lost in thought herself, her brows knitted together, eyes staring off into the distance. I left her to think, whatever it was, and instead used the quiet between us to plan. Plan how to tell her, how to tell Thrasos, and how to deal with the repercussions of both their reactions, be they positive or negative.

We took the long way back to Osiria, cutting over the mountains at the mines and venturing down into the lush valley on the other side. I showed Evalina our farms and introduced her to the fruits that would grow only in Osiria. I also showed her the remnants of a village lost many years ago to the volcanoes, the houses crumbled messes of half-melted stone. Bodies lay about the village frozen in caked layers of ash and solidified lava. She'd been horrified and amazed by their preservation.

We'd then continued our journey up the mountainside, headed straight for Ravenna, only stopping to sleep, eat, relieve ourselves and watch an eruption. It had been a volcano far from where we were on the range, I guessed as a large plume of steam rose from the sea where the lava hit it.

As we rounded the last hill and Ravenna loomed up over us, I found myself growing quite skittish, as if every noise could be Thrasos or my parents ready to break the news to Evalina that she was to be part of the family. Not that Thrasos knew himself, but his very presence would give it away. We were identical, save for his thin frame and longer hair. There was no hiding who he was and what it meant, even if she didn't piece together who was the older one she would realize she was set to marry one of us.

I noticed Evalina avoided the gallows as we passed it, her face passive, as if she felt she couldn't be bothered offering it the time of day. I couldn't blame her, it was not my favorite thing to see when I first came home.

All the faces of the men and women that had been hung there seemed to flash in my mind as I walked past, haunting me. They'd all been criminals, charged with the worst crimes—murder, rape, piracy—but it still seemed almost too cruel to kill them, as if we were stooping to their level.

I stared at my home as we grew closer to it, taking in every tiny detail, in case this was the last time I got to see it. It was afternoon. The skies were clear, for once, so the palace wasn't shrouded in ashen clouds but, rather, it seemed to have a multicolored aura as the sun bounced off the bright windows.

How many times had I come and gone from this place and never truly appreciated its beauty? I could not paint like my brother but perhaps I could sculpt my home. I'd made Evalina's pins for her, I'd carved the doors to my rooms in Sillessia, surely I could make a replica of my home to take with me. If I were to leave.

I tucked my hand into my pockets to hide the fact that they were shaking and strolled through the front doors of the palace, Evalina at my side. I prayed that this was not a day that Thrasos had felt well enough to come out from his room, that he was not sitting somewhere nearby spying on his traitorous brother and his would-be wife.

Tonight. I would tell them both tonight.

"Thanatos!" My mother ran toward me, arms ready to embrace me. "The watchmen told us you were on your way." She pulled me into a tight hug, her head resting on my chest. Despite the fact that we'd left on bad terms, I hugged her back, savoring the familiar feel and scent of her. She pulled away and slapped my chest. "You should have sent a letter," she scolded. "Honestly, I would have thought you'd know better, at least, Evalina."

Evalina bowed. "I am sorry, Your Majesty, the idea slipped my mind." Surprisingly, my mother pulled Evalina into a light hug.

"I'm sure it did. Well done, you two," Mother said into her hair.

My father's broad hand slapped my back and came to settle on the base of my neck. He gave a quick squeeze of affection before insisting that Evalina be taken to a room to write to her family, coming to the conclusion that if we hadn't told them, Isidia also did not know. Evalina had blushed at her thoughtlessness and rushed away as a servant led her to her room so she could write in peace.

I followed my parents to the dining room, staring at my feet as I walked through the halls after them. I knew what was coming, and I was not ready. I'd held it together in front of Evalina but now that I was home, safe and comfortable, emotions that I had swallowed were edging to the surface. I felt nauseous and light headed as my mother closed the door to the dining room, Freyja, Odon and Daeril already waiting inside.

The second I heard the door latch I broke.

Deep heaving sobs escaped me as I fell to my knees, suddenly unable to hold my own weight. Freyja rushed to my side, wrapping her arms around me and smoothing my hair from my tear streaked face. I felt my sister's own tears fall onto my shoulder and heard my mother sniff back her own. I wasn't sure if they were tears of joy at being alive, at home, or grief and horror at everything I had experienced.

Between sobs I managed to explain everything that had happened in Minoma, where the Necromancer was and how he had managed to get away with it for so long. My family's eyes filled with horror as I described, to the best of my abilities, the torture chamber that had sat below the library. Freyja gripped my hand tight as I told them of my mercy killing.

Reliving that moment was now my own torture.

My mother had clicked her tongue and shook her head as I told them of the Minoman King, how he'd known everything and told no one; it was more fuel for her fire.

Everyone in the room around me let out a groan of frustration as I told them that I still had not told Evalina of the engagement.

"Thanatos, darling, I know you've been through a lot but so has she." my mother said, cupping my face gently in her hands. "It may be too much for her to be told now."

"I know, but I can't stretch it out any longer, she'll just be angrier." I pulled the small package out of my pocket. I'd been too nervous to leave such precious cargo in my pack, especially when Evalina liked to dig through it constantly for food. I opened the small pouch and poured the contents into my hand. It was the set of earrings, a symbol of our engagement.

"I got her these in Minoma. They'll not win her over but at least I can propose properly." I gulped as I stared at the earrings in my lavender palm. "I can explain everything then."

"And Thrasos?" Freyja asked.

"I'll tell him after. I'll introduce them. In private, it'll be easier that way."

"That sounds like a good plan, but I think we should still have extra guards posted … just in case," my father added.

I nodded my agreement. No matter how I did it, or when, the reaction was going to be volatile, from both Thrasos and Evalina.

"But you did it, the both of you," my mother said, wrapping her arms around me. "I'm so proud of you," she whispered into my hair.

I was happy to have my mother's approval but I grieved for those that had lost their life for me to gain it, be they Corse or not.

The Corse had not been in control of themselves, they had not chosen to fight us or the Isidians of their own volition, they were commanded. It left a foul feeling in my stomach, as if I had begun to rot from the inside out. Those Corse had been people, had families and friends, and I had slaughtered them. I'd killed before but they were bad people that had made their choices, half the Corse could have been innocent farmers, killed and brought back by the crazed Necromancer out for revenge against a race cursed with powers he wanted. They did not choose to have that power, same as the Dark-Elves did not choose to have ours.

It was forced on us by our very existence.

The conflicting thoughts swirled in my head, making me dizzy and breathless. As if sensing this, my mother helped me to my feet. "Come, you need rest. Tonight, we'll have a banquet to celebrate your return." I nodded, barely taking in her words as she led me through the doors and to my rooms.

CHAPTER SIXTY
RECOVERY

The room was flooded with sunlight, filled with the smell of crisp morning air and pipe smoke. I turned my head to the window to see Bellona sitting in the frame, smoking her pipe and gazing out over the palace gardens, fiddling with her single earring with her free hand. I wasn't in my normal room in the barracks but my old bedroom in the palace. It was exactly as I'd left it, filled with the few things I'd kept from my family home; my mother's jewelry box, one of my father's swords, and some odd bits of decor that I'd liked. I'd never really spent much time in the Norward family home, had never really had a connection to it—or my parents. The palace had always been my true home, the Glenons and Islina my true family.

"Bellona ..." I croaked.

"Lorkin!" She exclaimed with a jump. She snuffed out her pipe and darted to the door, screaming down the hallway before sitting beside me on the bed. "You've been out for a week. Are you feeling well?"

"Water," I gasped. My mouth and throat were dry, my tongue sticking to the roof of my mouth.

Bellona got up again and poured a tankard of water as I sat up. She handed it to me and warned me to drink slowly as she sat back down on the bed, her hand resting on my back as I sipped the water.

"How are you feeling?" She asked.

"Thirsty," I said, sipping more water. "But fine." I realized then that I was holding the tankard with my right hand, the arm that had been removed by the Corse. I studied my bare arm; across the middle of my upper arm was a faint scar from where it had been reattached. I wiggled the toes on my left foot, testing the movement, pushing my magic through my body and examining it from the inside.

346

"The healers did an amazing job," Bellona said, watching my toes moving beneath the blankets. She fell quiet for a moment, her hand pushing into my back. "I'm sorry I wasn't there. I should have been," she said, her voice shaking.

"You were needed here," I rasped and drank more water.

Bellona had escorted me back to the fort and battled with us until she was called back to the palace after Corse had somehow snuck past and gotten into the city. The Glenons had been battling a force within the city walls as I'd led the battle out in the fields; it was exactly what I would have directed had we had time to discuss it.

"I just wish I could have been there for you," she whispered, tucking a hair behind my ear. "You did a good job. We're all very proud."

I fell silent. I didn't know what to say, no one had even been proud of me before. Warmth had spread through my chest as Bellona's words had settled. They were proud of me, I'd done a good job—but I'd almost died. Had the Necromancer been defeated just a few seconds later, I would be dead.

The door to my room burst open and the rest of the Glenons filed in, Islina trailing behind them.

"Good job, my boy!" Adalric cheered, slapping my shoulder as he stood by my bedside.

"Adalric, he's just had his arm reattached, give him a break," Zephyrine chided. "Do you feel all right, Lorkin?" She asked, a glimmer of genuine concern hidden somewhere in the back of her black eyes.

"I'm fine," I repeated.

Islina sat on the opposite side of me to Bellona, one hand coming down to rest on my knee, the other on my cheek. "Are you sure you're fine? I could send for Hemfain."

I smiled into her palm, relishing the clear day she was having. "I'm fine," I insisted. "But thank you."

"Thank you," she tossed back at me. "You kept us all safe, Lorkin. We had no casualties in the city thanks to your sanctuary and from, what I hear the fire wall at the fort was enough to hold back a majority of the Corse horde." She gave my knee a pat. "I knew you'd make a great Captain."

They were all glossing over the fact that I'd nearly died—were it not for Roana I definitely would have—but I didn't want to correct them. I was enjoying the praise and recognition and knew that it would come few and far between in my profession. So I let myself soak it up.

Only one Glenon did not sing my praises, did not rush to congratulate me on a successful battle. Peverell stuck to the edges of the room, eyeing me with concern. It made him look so much like his younger brother. It was the same look Eevan had given me the night my parents had died, like he knew that once everyone was gone, once the mountain of attention stopped, I would cry myself to sleep and have nightmares of being thrown onto a pyre and burnt with the rest of the dead. I offered him a nod, to show that I was all right and he didn't have to worry, but his concerned expression only deepened.

"I'm glad you woke now, I was just about to leave for Osiria," Bellona said.

"Osiria? Why? Is Evalina all right?" I had assumed, with no evidence, that she had been the one to kill the Necromancer but it now occured to me that it could have been someone else. Panic instantly shot through me.

"Evalina is fine," Bellona soothed. "Prince Thanatos has simply requested my presence and asked that I bring her home." Bellona's eyes met with Islina's. I guessed there was more to the journey but didn't want to push my Queen for information, not on a good day.

The city was slowly reopening and going back to normal. The Corpse bodies had been removed, transported north to the battlegrounds and burned with the rest. During the week-long burning of bodies, the sky had been stained red, ash had fallen over the city, and the whole of Isidia had been in mourning for the duration. We'd left the ash to sit for a few days, mourning the lost souls it belonged to, before getting to work cleaning the city for the Princess' arrival home.

I wanted everything to be perfect for her. She'd been gone so long, hadn't seen the town in so long, I wanted it to look it's best.

Word had already spread south of what had happened in the tower in Minoma—of what the Arch-Mage had done to the High-Elves he'd raised and trapped there, of the Minoman King's knowledge of everything. So, too, had the tales of the tears shed by the Isidian Princess for the dying Osirian Prince and the suspected relationship between the two.

I thought I'd be upset, or jealous by the news, but I found myself happy for Evalina. The time apart from her had cleared my mind of any feelings I had thought were romantic and replaced them with a stronger bond. We were family, perhaps not by blood but by what *really* makes a family, being there through everything, witnessing the good and bad and never leaving or judging. I was worried, however, for the outcome. Evalina and Thanatos could never be married, could never be together in a permanent sense, but I was sure they'd discussed that and come to some kind of conclusion already.

Finding out that King Acadio had betrayed us was a blow. I wouldn't say we were particularly friendly with the Minomans, but to hide the existence of the Necromancer and know of High-Elves being mutilated and not telling us … it was grounds for war. And, from whisperings around town, I knew that's where we were headed. At least, in the next war, I could bring the experience gained from this one. I had time to perfect maneuvers and strategies that could help us win. And, though part of me was terrified of another war so soon, another part longed for it and that part scared even myself.

I stopped before Roana's family's shop. I'd begun going there almost daily, seeking updates of her training at first and then just to speak with her father, he was a kind man. Roana was his only daughter and he worried about who would take over the shop when he could no longer run it. He had wanted it to stay in his family but Roana had bigger dreams. I knew where he was coming from, had been on the receiving and giving end of the argument, and was trying to sway him toward taking an apprentice. He had been hesitant at first but, with Roana away at her training, he was growing lonely in the large shop. Today, as I peeked through the store window, I saw him teaching a young girl how to sharpen knives. The blade was almost the length of her whole arm but she held it firmly, studying the old butcher's hands as he ran his own across the grindstone set up in the back corner. I decided not to go in, and instead walked back up toward the palace to stop by the temple.

Much to the priests' displeasure, I'd ordered them to keep it barricaded as a sanctuary and it now housed war orphans, crippled soldiers, and farmers still waiting to be allowed back home.

Much like the priests, I longed for the sanctuary to return to its temple state; not because of the disturbance it caused them but because it would be the last sign of life returning to normal.

But that wouldn't happen for a while yet.

CHAPTER SIXTY ONE
IN GOOD SPIRITS

Queen Islina,

I am overjoyed to inform you of the demise of the Necromancer and his deluded plans. Our people are safe once again. I am also pleased to confirm my health and the health of my ~~companion friend lover guide~~ Whatever he is

I groaned and scrunched up the paper, pulling a new one from the pile and redipping my quill into the ink. I was glad they'd thought to provide more than one piece of paper, though I expect it was because they'd thought I'd write a lengthy letter to my mother, describing in detail the events that had occurred.

I would not.

That would only cause her pain and worry. She would be fine knowing that we were successful. I only had to write a quick note. I am safe. I am coming home soon.

But how do I address Thanatos? I didn't even know. We'd confirmed our feelings to each other, not that it mattered. So what were we? Just temporary lovers? I didn't want to think of it that way. I didn't want it to be temporary.

I didn't want it to be temporary.

Frustration exploded through me at my predicament. We could never end up together, it was impossible. I would have to marry someone else and be done with Prince Thanatos.

But how could I? We'd been through death and discovery together. We were tied together in a way I could never be tied to anyone else.

I threw the top sheet of paper away, as large splotches of ink that had fallen as I'd been lost in thought dried on the corner, and began writing again.

Queen Islina,

I am overjoyed to inform you of the demise of the Necromancer and his deluded plans.

Our people are safe once again.

I am also pleased to confirm my health and the health of Prince Thanatos.

I look forward to reuniting with you in Isidia in peace.

I would like to request, however, that my Grandfather, King Adalric, stay by your side until my return.

Evalina Elsrine Glenon.

It would have to do. I could fill her in when I got home. I folded the letter and passed it to the servant waiting out in the hall. I went back into my room and sat on the bed, unsure of what to do. When I'd first come to Osiria, the King and Queen had told me to freely venture but it felt odd. The palace seemed to be too empty and too quiet, so opposite to the liveliness of the village.

I was sitting on the bed, digging through my pack to see if anything needed to be discarded or replenished before I left for home, when there was a knock on the door.

"Come in!" I called as I pulled a moldy, half-eaten apple from my bag.

"Just me!" Frejya announced as she opened the door. "Just wanted to check on how you were holding up." She came to join me on the bed, picking up my Sillessian skirt and picking at the beading.

"I'm fine. Really," I insisted at her raised eyebrow. "I feel as if a weight has been lifted from me."

She smiled but it faltered quickly, her picking at my skirt grew more aggressive. "Thanatos is not doing well," she said, and it was then that I noticed the blotchiness of her cheeks.

I was surprised but also not. Thanatos had seemed fine since we'd left Minoma but I had noticed he had been quieter than normal, and I'd caught him staring, but not really looking at anything, often. I'd figured he just needed time but, perhaps, I should have checked in.

"He hasn't said anything to me," I said quietly.

"He wouldn't. That's not who he is. He'll suffer in silence and break down in private."

My mind shot back to the inn in Kushyam, after the battle there, when he'd gone with Glik. I'd suspected it was because he was upset and had felt hurt at the time that he hadn't been comfortable to express those feelings to me then. Now, I was almost insulted.

"Don't take it to heart," Freayja added, as if reading my mind. "He doesn't usually talk to me about that stuff either, he usually talks—I mean, he has others with whom he's comfortable." She ran a hand through her hair; I was beginning to believe it was the telltale sign of Helice lies, having seen her brother do it so often. "Anyway, I also meant to inform you of the banquet tonight, a celebration of your success and safe return." She held the green beaded skirt up before her. "You could wear this, or you could find something of mine, though"—she put the skirt down and looked me over—"I don't think your muscles will fit."

"I'll wear this, it's fine." I smiled.

There was no way I was going to fit in her clothes. Though she was in no way skinny, Freyja was only lightly muscled and in different areas to myself. She had the physique of an assassin and I a warrior.

Lorkin had insisted I learn to fight with heavy weapons, so that if I'd lost my small blades in battle I could pick up anything and know how to wield it properly.

"Dinner will be soon, someone will come and find you, but please feel free to roam the palace." She gave my leg a pat and left the room.

I sat and stared at the door for a moment, drinking in everything she'd said to me. I was upset that Thanatos hadn't said anything to me or expressed that he was struggling but I knew approaching it with anger was not the best way to deal with it. I decided to try subtlety, though it was not a strong suit of mine. The idea of him suffering in silence angered me, but not because of him, because of whatever had happened to him in the past that led him to believe it was acceptable.

I sighed and rose from my bed to dress for the banquet. Pulling on my Sillessian garb, I frowned as I got to wrapping the fabric, my fingers dropping the pleats as I tried to make them with my index finger and thumb. I let out a groan of frustration as my door slowly opened.

"You all right in here?" Thanatos asked.

"Have you heard of knocking?" I snapped. He looked me dead in the eyes and knocked, most of his body already through the doorway. "Ha-ha."

"Do you want some help?" He offered, closing the door behind him.

"I just can't get these pleats right," I said, pushing the fabric into his hands.

He laughed and began deftly folding the fabric into sections and tucking them into my petticoat.

With his face so close to mine, I could see the afterglow of flushed cheeks and smell the salt from recent tears.

My heart ached; we had been through so much together, I wished he felt he could talk to me. "You're all right, yeah?" I said as he leaned in close to me to throw the remaining untucked fabric over my shoulder.

"Yeah, I'm fine," he said, offering me a weak smile.

"You're sure?"

There was a flicker of emotion behind his eyes, as if he, too, wished he could talk to me.

"I'll tell you later," he said, kissing my cheek.

"You said you'd tell me everything once we got back. Don't think I forgot."

"I know and I will, but later," he said with a smile, this time, and it seemed genuine.

I hadn't noticed it before but he was already dressed for dinner. He wore all black, a black linen tunic and customary flowing cotton pants tucked into high black boots, all with gold detailing. The colorless outfit made his white hair and gold eyes shine. I stared into those gold eyes for a long moment, pleading for him to actually tell me this time, not palm it off onto another occasion.

"Do you want me to do your hair?" He asked, running a hand through my black mess of hair.

"That would be amazing."

He motioned to a dressing table and I took a seat in front of it. He gently brushed my hair, separated it into sections and braided it into an intricate design that piled it all to the crown of my head. He then left the ends loose to fall down my back, tying it off with the end of a single braid.

"Where did you learn to do hair?" I asked.

He shrugged his shoulders. "I taught myself to do my own after watching my mother do it in the mirror. I used to torture Freyja by doing hers all the time. She hated it, always preferred to wear her hair loose."

I ran my hands over the design in my hair, feeling the tight smooth braids, even the stylists in Isidia couldn't braid like this. "You're very talented at it."

"Too bad I'm a prince, I would have liked to do it for a living. I'll have to save my skills for my future wife and children." He gazed at me through the mirror, nothing but warmth in his bright eyes, but I felt no warmth in my heart. This wife he spoke of could never be me, the children never mine. I felt my eyes begin to prick and rose from my chair.

"Will you go for a walk with me?"

He nodded and followed me from the room.

We walked down the hall toward the dining room, knowing that dinner would be starting any moment now, but took our time.

I wanted to examine the windows more closely and really appreciate the skilled work that went into them. So many had fine details in the backgrounds that I'm sure were barely noticed. They were all gruesome scenes, many featured my own people being executed or tortured, but there was beauty in the way it had been portrayed, the way the glass worker had used two tones of red glass to show the depth of the blood, or the murky green for dead High-Elf eyes instead of the vibrant emerald.

When we came to the window of Ossena, I paused for longer than the rest, the burn on my shoulder seeming to throb at the presence. I wished she'd shown herself to me after it all, so that I'd known we'd done the right thing. Part of me was still sure there was more to the oath than what we had done but her lack of trespassing into my dreams suggested that that was it.

A shiver ran through me as I remembered my last dream and I found myself checking the hallway past Thanatos, just to make sure that we were still alone. I had to tell myself that the patchwork man was dead, we had killed him.

I had killed him.

The doors to the dining room burst open and a stream of servants scattered down the hallway, all of them bowing as they passed us.

"I guess dinner is about to start," I commented. I looked to Thanatos when he didn't reply and found him staring at the depiction of his great, great, great aunt, his face thoughtful. "Thanatos, are you sure you're fine?"

He shook his head, as if clearing it of whatever thoughts he was having. "Sorry, yes, I'm fine. Let's go in, shall we?" He said, guiding me to the dining room with his hand gently resting on my lower back.

The dining room had been transformed. The lounges that usually sat toward the back of the room had been removed and replaced with large tables that matched the preexisting marble one. Each table had been decorated with wreaths of fresh leaves and flowers, ornate, jeweled candelabras were evenly placed down the center, filling the room with orange light. Thanatos and I were the first ones in the room. I followed him over to the wine table, watching as he served us both goblets. I raised my eyebrow as he filled his almost to the top, he winked over the edge as he took his first sip. Perhaps his drinking was an issue, as Freya had said. I didn't dwell on it for long, as more and more people began entering the room. I was surprised that there were this many people in the palace. If they'd been here the whole time, I'd never seen any of them.

Time sped by in a blur. Everytime someone entered the room, they were introduced to me by Thanatos and then we were thanked and congratulated on our success. The more it happened, the more uncomfortable I felt. Yes, we had saved them but who had we killed in the process? Or, rather, rekilled. Judging by the strained expression on the Prince's face, I guessed that he felt the same awkwardness.

Omisha and Methuzelah had been surprised to see us when they'd arrived, expressing that they'd expected us to come later.

"We just thought we'd get a jump on things," Thanatos said, his speech slurring slightly. I'd lost count of how many times he'd refilled his glass but I didn't think it'd be enough to cause him to slur. "And it's easier to meet people as they arrive than when they're already here."

"I apologize, Evalina, for my son. This is not how we'd planned for this night to go," King Methuzelah said, giving his son a disappointed frown.

"It's fine," I said, placing a hand on Thanatos' shoulder. "I preferred it this way. I got to meet everyone one on one." In truth, I would have preferred not to meet anyone new at all.

"Let's not dwell on it," Omisha said, linking arms with her husband. "What's done is done and tonight is for celebrating."

"Then let's celebrate!" Freyja chimed in, holding a silver tray of filled goblets. She handed them to each of us then slammed the tray onto the marble table. The crowd quietened as the sharp ring echoed through the room. "To my brother's safe return!" The crowd cheered. "To peace with the Isidians!" Her voice continued over the ruckus of the guests. "And, finally, to our saviors, Thanatos and Princess Evalina, who so graciously put their lives on the line and saved us all from the threat of the Necromancer!"

The room shook with the loudest cheer yet, goblets raised above heads and clinked with those raised closest, until everyone gulped down their wine to signal the end of the toast.

"Now, before my parents can turn this into some fancy affair, everyone get drunk and have fun!"

Another cheer sounded through the room and Freyja slammed the tray on the table once more to indicate the true end of her speech. My face burned with embarrassment but I was thankful that Freyja had turned the stuffy event into a party.

"Well, I would have put it more eloquently than that," the King huffed. "You kids never let me have a serious moment."

Freyja placed her arm around her father's shoulders. "Serious does not become you, father." She said, sipping her wine and winking at me. "Now, let your children enjoy their night." She called behind her as she pushed Thanatos and I into the crowd.

The air in the room had changed, people were now talking more freely and seemed more comfortable addressing the Prince and I directly. I wished I'd been able to retain their names and converse with them properly but everytime my goblet was half empty either Thanatos or Freyja filled it back up to the top. I had no idea how much I was drinking, or who I was meeting, but I was having a great time.

The room seemed to glow around me and everyone was beautiful; food seemed to appear before me exactly when I needed it too and it all tasted amazing, everything was amazing.

The Osirians broke into circles and began their dancing. Freyja pulled me into the middle and handed me two scarves, I had no idea where she'd gotten them from but smiled as she spun me. I remembered the girls in the village, dancing in the middle of the circles, spinning impossibly fast and never seeming to get dizzy. I mimicked what I could remember of their movements, the way they'd turned their heads quickly before they were forced to face a different direction, tricking their minds into thinking they weren't spinning at all.

I spun and spun as fast as I could manage until my feet tangled together and I fell into a laughing heap on the floor. Laughter erupted around me. Freyja collapsed onto the floor next to me, joining me in my fit of giggles. It felt as if we were there for hours, laughing on the floor, but eventually Thanatos and Daeril came to help us up.

It took all of the little self control I had in that moment not to kiss Thanatos in front of everyone. It was all I wanted to do as he pulled me up and steadied me against his warm body, his mouth so close to mine, his eyes staring at me longingly. I knew he felt the same, could feel it in his tight grip on my arms. He led me to the edge of the room and sat me down on a chair. I tried to protest, telling him all I wanted to do was dance, but he wouldn't listen and just told me to sit there and wait for him to return.

I sat for a moment, with no idea of when he would return, before I decided it was too much. Sitting on the sidelines had made me realize how loud the room was, how cramped. The air was thick and smelled of food, and wine, and bodies. The aftermath of the tower battle flashed before my eyes, corpses littering the ground, blood coating my hands. I rose from the chair, shaking the thoughts from my head as I slipped out of the room.

I took the distraction of the party and the overconfidence that comes with too much wine to explore the fortress, walking down dark hallways and peeking into unlocked rooms, most empty, save the furniture, some very much occupied, the party guests making use of the distractions as I was. I kept venturing through the palace until I came to a room I couldn't help but enter.

The doors were large, carved with depictions of the Father in elf form—which I found odd, as it was not how the Osirians portrayed Him—bent over scrolls and tomes, studying. I guessed that this was the library.

I quietly opened the doors—it was a library after all. The smell of old books and scrolls hit me instantly.

Bookshelves lined the walls floor to ceiling, much like the library in Minoma, the shelves were made of hard blackwood and were filled to overflowing with books. I couldn't see where the stairs were but there was a second storey to the library, visible through an opening in the ceiling of the bottom floor; a roaring fireplace, that stood the whole height of the room, sat at the very end wall, illuminating a majority of the space and filling the room with heat and the sound of crackling wood. Between me and the fire sat tables, and chairs, and lounges—squishy, soft lounges perfect for snuggling into with a good book.

I thought it cruel of Thanatos to have brought me here and never shown me the library.

How could he deprive me of this?

I strolled through some of the aisles and found books from everywhere around Carynthia littering the shelves, even Isidian books. I already had a pile of books in my hands when I found the first staircase; it was hidden in the back of the aisles, as if implying to go to the next level you had to have read everything on the bottom. I lugged myself and my books up the stairs, breathless by the time I'd reached the top, and instantly began perusing the second floor, adding more and more books to my pile until my arms were aching. I moved toward the center of the floor, near the open edge where the tables and lounges had been set up so that you could watch the people on the floor below you, when a sharp smell filled my nose.

Someone else was here.

Surely everyone would be at the banquet—that wasn't so much a banquet as a rowdy party. I followed the scent through the book shelves before I came to a small alcove, rounded with a built-in bench seat, but the person inside wasn't using that seat. I peered in around the edge of a canvas, the smell attributed to the paints being used on it.

The figure inside was slight, so thin I feared they would break if a breeze came through the room, their hair so long it touched the floor in their seated position, the white ends turned slightly gray from dust. Their skin was an ashen purple, as if it were turning white to match their hair. I gazed at their face and dropped my books.

My lungs froze, depriving me of air, and my stomach turned. The face I was looking at was one I was familiar with, one I had seen laugh, and scowl, and cry—one I had kissed.

It was Thanatos' face, only thinner; his cheeks were sunken, his temples protruding through the skin of his forehead, but his eyes were the same, even down the black specks. He turned away from the canvas to find the source of the books that now littered at his feet and, when he saw me, his face fully replicated the same level of shock that I was feeling.

"Who the pit are you?" I demanded.

"I could ask you the same thing," he rasped breathlessly, his voice matching Thanatos' perfectly. He studied me more carefully, his eyes widening as he took in the color of my hair. "Come, sit down." He motioned toward the seat next to him, his voice laced with intrigue. "I have a feeling we have a lot to talk about."

My heart pounded. I stepped around the canvas and took a seat next to him, waiting as he repositioned his wheeled chair to face me.

"You, I'm presuming, are Princess Evalina of Isidia."

I gave a slight nod, words no longer coming freely to me.

"I am Prince Thrasos, Thanatos' twin brother."

"Twin brother?" I repeated, my mind racing.

Thrasos Helice.

The initials on Thanatos's chest were not his own, they were his brother's, his twin's.

I glanced at the canvas to my left, it was a newly started painting, a family portrait. There were no details yet, only blocky colors haphazardly placed, so that Thrasos wouldn't forget who was who. I stared at the two forms at the end, one sitting and one standing, both with longer hair than the rest.

The twins.

I didn't know what to make of this revelation and, by the look of shock and confusion on Thrasos' face, I doubted he did either.

"May I ask why you're here?"

I turned to him wide-eyed. "Surely you know."

He shook his head, his eyes filled with exasperation.

"Thanatos and I have just returned from defeating a Necromancer."

I gave Thrasos a rundown of the events of the last few months, sparing the details of his brother's close calls with death. His face grew darker and darker, his anger rising as quickly as my heart was beating.

"Well, how kind of my brother to tell me," he snapped. I stayed silent, unsure of what to say. "I'm sorry, I don't mean to burden you with my anger."

"It's fine. We've both been wronged. I had no idea you and Freyja existed. I thought Thanatos was an only child and now he has two siblings."

The air between us was full of rage and awkwardness. I wanted to leave, to run from the castle and never return, but something else kept me in my chair.

"Thrasos," I said quietly, "which of you is older?"

His eyes widened and for a moment I thought it was because he'd realized he was one of my suitors but …

"I am."

Everything seemed to crash around me again.

This whole time. Months and months of being together, getting closer and closer until we were as close as two people could be. Had it all been a lie? A trick to woo me, make me love him, so what? He could be King? My eyes flashed to Thrasos' chair and it all made sense.

Healers.

They'd wanted access to High-Elf healers to heal the sick Heir. My lungs burned as I finally forced myself to breathe, angry tears pricked my eyes and I had an urge to hit something, anything.

To lie to me was one thing but to lead me on, to play with my heart. I'd thought this whole time that we could never end up together, that it was impossible, and now it was possible but I didn't want it anymore.

Not now, not after this.

I couldn't stop the tears as they spilled out of my eyes, the sobs raking through my entire body, it was a miracle I could hold myself in a seated position.

"I just don't understand how this could have happe—" Thrasos stopped mid-sentence, his face paled further as he stared at me, as he watched me sob the heavy tears of a broken heart. "They want me to be King," he whispered. "They've arranged your marriage to Thanatos so that he'll leave and I'll *have* to be King …" He took my hand and squeezed it. "I am sorry, I am so sorry you got dragged into this. I can't believe them." A new rage flared in his eyes and the image of Thanatos in Kushyam flashed before me. I wanted to pull away from him but his eyes never turned fully black; instead, just as quick as the anger had come, they changed to sadness.

"It's not your fault. You shouldn't be the one to apologize." I sniffed, wiping at my eyes with the bottom of my skirt.

"But it is, in a roundabout way, If I hadn't gotten sick, none of this would have happened," he replied sadly.

"You can't blame yourself for that."

"If I weren't sick, we would have no need of Isidian healers and you would be free of this arrangement."

"But I wouldn't, he's still a suitor. One way or another we'd have ended up here." It was as if it was fate. To meet him when I had, to go on this journey with him, to fall in love with him.

"He would not have come up with this himself, it had to have been our parents." My head snapped up.

Our parents. Not just theirs but mine, too.

My mother had done this.

I thought back to before the meeting about the Necromancer, the letters she'd hidden from me, the way she'd almost forced Thanatos and I together. She'd anticipated how I'd react, too, that's why she'd decided she'd leave for Sillessia, so she could escape my rage.

"He was just the messenger then," I stated.

Thrasos nodded. "And a bad one, at that." He ran a hand through his hair and, for just a moment, I almost forgot that he was a different person to Thanatos. I averted my eyes, unable to stand looking at his familiar face anymore.

"I can't believe they did this without even talking to us. How dare they choose our lives for us." His hands shook on the arms of his chair. "I suppose now I really have to try to live." He sighed.

"You will live." I reached forward and placed a hand over his as he had done for me only moments ago. "Even after all this, I will still send healers for you, the best we have." He opened his mouth to reject my help but I cut him off. "We have already signed a treaty with your current King, we owe it to our allies to save their future King."

Thrasos was not to blame for any of this and he didn't deserve to suffer because of his brother's incompetence

He offered me a sad smile. "Thank you."

"Little Odon deserves to have at least one uncle around."

"You'll not call off the wedding?" He asked, confusion lacing his voice.

"I cannot. My Queen has arranged it. My mother has sold me." My heart began to ache again. I wished for my father, he would never have allowed this, would be turning in his grave if he had one.

"Then I thank you, sister."

I smiled at the Crown Prince. At least one good thing would come from this situation.

After a few deep breaths, I wiped my eyes and pushed off the bench.

"You're leaving?" Thrasos asked.

"I'm going to find your brother, I haven't decided what I'm going to do after that," I said, stepping around the easel and stalking back through the fortress.

CHAPTER SIXTY TWO
A FEW CHOICE WORDS

I groaned when I returned to the chair and saw that Evalina had wandered off, drunker than I'd ever seen her, and on such an important night.

I wove through the crowd looking for her but not once did I spot the black top of her head in the swarm of white. I made my way into the sparsely crowded hallways and still couldn't find her. I ignored the past panic of losing her in the blizzard that was threatening to rise and continued searching, venturing further and further away from the dining room. Had she gone to bed? Too tired to deal with the crowd and loud music even though she'd seemed to be enjoying it?

I'd rounded a corner that would lead me down a hallway, concerningly close to my brother's room, when I came face to face with her. Before I could even react she'd gripped the front of my shirt and pushed me against the wall by a door. She checked if the door was unlocked, then empty when she could open it, and pushed me through when she realized it was.

I stumbled backward into the room; it was dark and mostly empty, save some old furniture that had been covered with a white sheet. "Well, I wasn't expecting that," I joked as Evalina closed the door behind her and leant against it. "I've been looking for you everywhere," I said stepping toward her, my arms itching to be around her.

"You know what I wasn't expecting?" I paused just before her, her dark tone snapping me from my licentious intentions. "I wasn't expecting to find your *brother*." She stepped forward and pushed me back; it was then that I noticed her tear stained cheeks and bloodshot eyes.

I stumbled again, almost flipping over one of the discarded pieces of furniture. My mouth had fallen open in a wide gape, which Evalina mimicked, her eyes flaring with fury.

"Don't give me that, Thanatos. Don't act surprised. Did you really think you could hide him forever? 'Please feel free to explore the palace, we have no secrets here.' What a load of *bullshit*," she emphasized, quoting my father's words.

I almost felt just as betrayed as she did, why did he have to say that? He knew that she didn't know about Thrasos, that Thrasos liked to paint in various rooms of the palace, I'd just hoped that Evalina's proper Isidian nature would stop her from exploring. I should have known better.

"I'm sorry," I said, stepping toward her with my hands raised in surrender. "I'm sorry I didn't tell you. I meant to, believe me, I did, but I was just as bamboozled as you are now when I arrived in Isidia and, and—" I stopped talking, her face had only grown darker as I'd spoken.

"You had so many opportunities. So many," She raised her hand up before me, counting each time on her fingers. "The first time we met, the dinner, the ball, Oakfell, for Father's sake, even after the tower!" She shouted, tears welling in her eyes.

"I know," I whispered. "I know I was wrong to not tell you, I know it's my fault. But it's not only *my* fault. Had your mother told you, had she told you everything, had you known then," I didn't know what to say, my mind was whirling. Thrasos knew. Evalina knew. But did they *know*? Had they put the pieces together? I wanted to hear it from her first but she would be thinking the exact same thing, it was written across her face.

I took a deep breath and continued, "Had your mother told you of the engagement"— her eyes narrowed at the words—"this whole situation would have played out differently."

"So, it's my mother's fault?" She demanded.

"I—well, kind of—"

"Yes or no, Thanatos?"

"I don't know what you want me to say right now, Evalina." I stressed, "Your mother should have told you before I got there, you should have known. You were meant to know. I was meant to arrive and meet my knowing future wife and have the chance to get to know her before the ball, when it would be announced to everyone in attendance. Not get there, no one having any idea why I'm there, or that I was coming, having to deal with all the bullshit in the town, and from the guards, and Lorkin, have your mother play matchmaker, and then this!" I gestured to the space around us, but she knew I meant the whole journey. True hurt flooded her eyes but I didn't regret my words, not yet. "I've almost died, multiple times, done horrific things that will haunt me for the remainder of my life and—"

"All that but telling your brother and I the truth was harder?"

I sat on the edge of a table behind me and ran my fingers over my braids. Gods, how I wanted to be out of that room. "Yes, it was harder. Telling my dying brother to buck up and be King was harder than facing my own death. And disappointing you was harder than killing innocent people."

"You didn't even know me!" She cried frustratedly.

"I knew you hated me! You didn't even know me and yet you feared me, despised my people, and would have been happier to watch us all burn than to marry me. I was told I had no choice, my brother's life depended on our marriage. I never even wanted to marry!"

Evalina's face pulled back as if I'd slapped her. "I did fear you, and I loathed you," she seethed, "How could I not? You make it so easy with your bullshit act. Swaggering around, picking fights and fucking anyone you want. No wonder an orc and a goblin are your only friends."

It was my turn to look slapped. "Don't you dare disrespect them, they're better people than anyone in your hateful Queendom could ever be." I knew she didn't mean the words against Rangkar and Glik but it was still a step further than I was willing to let this argument go. "And *me* pick fights? When have I ever picked a fight?" I couldn't stop the rage bubbling within me, could feel it burning in my chest. "The only fights I get into are ones started by others, or ones I get *dragged* into," I spat, pushing off the table and rising to my full height. "And if I fucked anything I wanted I would have had you begging for it a lot sooner, *Princess*."

"You're a pig—a lying, self-serving pig!"

"And you're a hot-headed fool who never should have left her castle!" Evalina's face fell, and regret swallowed me. "Evie ..."

She held a hand up and for a moment I thought, even wished, she was going to hit me, but it fell before she could.

"Evalina, wait—" I reached for her but she turned away, stalking toward the door. "Evie ..."

She slammed the door.

"Fuck," I muttered to myself.

CHAPTER SIXTY THREE
THE SIREN'S SHRIEK

I stalked down the hallways till I reached my room, breathing deeply to stay the angry tears that desperately wanted to flow. I swiftly changed into my traveling clothes and pulled on my worn leather boots. I didn't want to rest, didn't want to risk sitting down and changing my mind. The Fire Lily brooch was fastened to the waistband of my pants, I tucked it beneath my belt. I couldn't bear to look at it now, knowing it had been made by his hands, but I also didn't want to freeze. I shoved the remainder of my belongings into my pack, not caring to make it neat or separate clean and dirty items. I just needed everything to be in and ready for me to leave.

I heaved my pack onto my back and left the room, slamming the door behind me. I ignored the windows, whose glass eyes seemed to follow me down the hallway. I retraced my steps to the library, I wanted to speak to Thrasos, wanted someone to know I was leaving, and he was the only one I could bear to see again and still leave. I crept through the library, unsure of whether or not Thanatos would have sought out his brother after our fight, but neither of the brothers was present. I wandered to the area where I'd first found Thrasos and found a door not far from the alcove. My hand halted for only a moment before I opened it. Would I find another secret sibling through this one? Another sister, perhaps?

The faces of the Helice family sprung before me as the door swung open, I froze momentarily but soon realized it wasn't really them, it was life-like renderings. The walls of the chamber were covered in paintings and sketches of the family and other designs, many that I recognised as Thanatos' tattoos. The chambers themselves were larger than most, and, as Thrasos came out from behind a wall, I realized it was so that he had more room to maneuver his chair.

"Princess?"

"You're a very talented artist."

"Thank you. There's not much to do when you're confined to a chair."

"Did you design all of Thanatos' tattoos?"

He smiled. "Yes, but another artist did them. Drawing on skin is not easy."

I nodded, unsure of what else to say as I studied the rest of the art lining every inch of the walls. Turning away only when I reached an especially detailed sketch of Thanatos smiling.

"You're leaving?" Thrasos asked cautiously, as if he were afraid of swaying my decision.

"Yes," I said definitively. "I need time to … think and recover."

He nodded. "I'll make sure the message is passed along."

"Thank you," I said, turning from the wall and walking back to the door I came from, Thrasos following behind in his chair, his arms struggling with his own weight.

I turned to face the Prince as I reached the door; he took my hand in his and smiled up at me. "I know it all seems terrible at the moment, but it will get better. Just give it time."

I squeezed his hand in thanks and, after he'd given me some quick directions to the stables, I left him.

I would send a healer for him as I'd said, it was the least he deserved for being so out of the loop and for being so kind. He would make a great King, just as I'd believed Thanatos would.

I stalked down the halls, ignoring rogue party guests and their invitations of more wine and dancing. I had to get out of there. As impractical as it was, I just needed to leave. I knew the way home but, if I got lost, so be it.

The stables were full, horses, donkeys and mules filled the stalls, the stable hands, having just refilled the hay for the animals, were slumped against a stall sharing a few bottles of amber liquid. I hated to put a damper on their night.

As I cleared my throat, they all jumped, heads snapping my way. "Sorry, I just need someone to help me find my horse." A young boy stood and bowed, his short white hair falling into his eyes.

He led me to the end of the stables, closest to the door. "Prince Thanatos told us to keep your horses here. Said you'd be needing them soon."

I nodded.

Faenor and Serelene were in the stall together, sitting on the floor leaning against each other. It pained me to separate them, but I was sure it would cause too much of a stir if I were to steal Thanatos' horse and I couldn't bear to part with Faenor.

"I'm sorry to take your friend," I whispered to Serelene, holding her face between my hands and resting my head against her nose as I'd seen Thanatos do so many times. "But I need her, especially now."

Serelene huffed and seemed to press her head into mine as if she knew and understood. I wouldn't have been surprised if Thanatos had told the horse before me.

I let the stablehand get Faenor ready to say goodbye to her friend and asked him to bring her to me when he was finished.

I walked up the stoney path along the side of the palace, heading to the square. The stained glass palace beside me glowed like a multi-colored beacon in the night, the many pieces of glass reflecting their various colors on the black stones around me. I truly would miss the beauty of Osiria, even though I'd spent so little time here.

Despite the chaos unfolding inside the palace, the square was quiet. I stepped into it and turned to take one last look at the structure behind me, committing it to memory, in case I never returned.

I remembered the first time I saw the palace. The fear it seemed to instill in me with its pointed spires and sharp pinnacles. But now I saw the beauty in it all. I looked away before my emotions took over again and spotted a lone figure standing by the gallows, staring up at the noose, just as I had done. Something about them rang familiar. I wandered over, averting my eyes from the hanging roping.

"They didn't need to send anyone out, I was just about to come in." The figure mumbled, wiping at their face.

I started.

"Bellona?!"

My aunt spun to face me, her eyes bloodshot and cheeks blotchy. "Flower!" She pulled me into a tight hug, her sea and sweet alcohol scent engulfing me.

"What in the pit are you doing here?" I gasped as she slowly squeezed the life out of me.

"Thanatos invited me. Sent me a message weeks ago saying that you would return with him to Osiria, that he'd like it if I was here when you returned. I guess I got here late." She kissed the top of my head. "Are you all right?" She asked, pulling back as if she could sense my bad mood.

"I could ask you the same thing," I replied, wiping a tear from her cheek.

"It's hard … being here."

"It was my first time too."

She studied me more closely, taking in my pack and traveling clothes. "Are you going somewhere?" She asked, suspicion lacing her tone.

"Home."

"Why?" She asked, her voice hard, eyes flicking between me and the palace, her breath coming fast and short.

"It's just time. I miss Isidia and Mother."

Her eyes focused on me. "Bullshit. What did he do?" Her hand flicked up to rest on the handle of her cutlass.

"Nothing, Bellona, please, I just want to go home." My voice cracked. I took a few deep breaths to calm myself, I would not cry again.

"Did he hurt you?" She demanded, fury flashing across her face.

"No. Please, can we just leave?"

She searched my face, her shoulders tight as if she expected Thanatos to run through the palace doors to attack us.

"I promise I'll tell you everything on the way," I insisted.

"Fine, but if it's anything serious I'm turning around and gutting him." She took one last look at the execution square, toying with her single earring before the stable hand arrived with Faenor.

I didn't look back at the palace until we were miles away, the sun rising over the snow-covered side of Osiria. It was almost a speck in the distance, Bellona and I having walked all night. Thanatos would know I was gone now.

Would he send someone after me? Would he chase me? I doubted it and hoped he wouldn't.

I'd told Bellona everything that had happened between the time I'd had my first nightmare and finding Thrasos in the library. She stayed silent as I recounted what had been my life for the last few months, because it had been months; I hadn't been able to tell while we were on the road, the days seemed to go so fast I'd completely lost track, but her eyes told me exactly how she felt about everything. She was proud, I could see that, but also angry, and worried, and a little happy. It was exactly how I would have expected my father to react.

"Your mother's a bitch for not telling you but, after spending the last couple of months with her, I'm not surprised she didn't. And *fuck* Thanatos, I would have done exactly the same thing you did, pick up and fucking leave." She clinked her flask against my water skin and took a swig of whatever sweet alcohol was inside.

"You didn't know about it?" I asked, skeptical that she truly didn't know.

"I didn't, I swear. I would have never let you leave with him if I'd known."

A tension I hadn't realized I'd been carrying had eased. It was nice to know that I wasn't the only one in the dark.

She filled me in on everything that had happened back home as we continued on a path cut through the mountains to her ship docked north of Ravenna, they had been attacked but it had been small groups, never anything more than a few hundred Corse. There had been casualties, but not many, and Lonthia had remained secure the whole time, the outer walls receiving minimal damage.

My grandfather and uncles had stayed with my Mother and intended to until I returned, though I suspected they would stay long after that as well. Lorkin had also stayed by my mother's side, calming her when she lost control or fell into one of her despairs, but he also had worked diligently to ensure the safety of the kingdom, as I had expected him too. Lorkin would have made a great King, perhaps better than I would make a Queen, but he'd given up any chance of that.

I was glad that I had left my Queendom in such capable hands, that after everything my family had been loyal to me and not held my mother's actions against me. I was itching to get home, to stare out my window at my familiar view, the view so imprinted in my mind I saw it everytime my eyes closed. Traveling had been amazing and I definitely planned to do more in the future but now, after everything, I just needed to be home for a while. I needed to forget the horrors and heartache for a moment.

We rounded the last hill after walking for days and, straight away, I recognized my aunt's ship. I hadn't seen it since I was a girl but it looked exactly as I remembered it.

It was large and extremely well kept. Three tall masts lined the center, rigged with large blue sails. The figurehead was a fierce depiction of the Carracallans' interpretation of the Mother; her face was fashioned into a teeth-baring warcry, her arms pulled back ready to strike, her squidlike lower half fanned out over the bow of the ship. Above water there was not a barnacle in sight and I would bet that there wouldn't be below water, either, my aunt no doubt using her gills to allow her to clean her pride and joy all over.

"There she blows, The Sirens Shriek." She grinned down at her ship as if it were her child, her eyes full of pride and love.

I found myself having to force my feet forward as we walked down to the dock yard, the hill was so steep that stairs had been carved into it in some places to stop people rolling down into the sea, my vision filled with the open expanse of the ocean.

Water, and lots of it.

I had told Bellona of my bath nightmare but left out the details of me developing a crippling fear of water. I'd thought I would be fine given that I was with a well established sea captain, a family member and someone with gills but, as I stared at the vast sea before me, my chest tightened. I tried to fuss over Faenor, who was struggling on the steep stairs, to distract myself but even she could sense my unease. Her large eyes bore into me as if waiting for me to break. I tried to reassure her that I was fine by petting her but she seemed unconvinced.

I had to keep repeating to myself that this was the only way home. I was here now. I just had to get on the ship. I would be fine. Bellona would save me if I went overboard. The Necromancer was dead.

The Necromancer is dead.

CHAPTER SIXTY FOUR
SOLEMN PROMISE

My head pounded as I woke the next morning. I was unsure if it was because of the alcohol consumption or the angry tears that had fallen once I'd returned to my room and replayed my fight with Evalina over and over again in my head.

How could I have been so careless and stupid?

I scrubbed at my face, slapping my cheeks to wake myself further. Water and tea. I needed water and tea and then I needed to work up the courage to speak to Thrasos and Evalina.

I dressed speedily and made my way to the dinning hall, breathing deeply and running through scenarios in my mind, how the conversation with both parties might go. Both were not good, but I was more worried about Evalina than Thrasos, if she was even still in the palace.

I opened the doors to the dining room and sat across from my sister, she laughed at my appearance and poured me a cup of tea.

"You look like shit," she said, handing it to me.

I sipped the warm amber liquid and ignored her. I knew I looked like shit. I hadn't done my hair and, after having it in such tight braids the night before, it was full of kinks and knots. The rest of my family, sans Thrasos, was already seated around the table, most of the way through their breakfast.

"Where did you and Evalina run off to last night? I don't remember seeing much of you," my mother asked.

"We–uh—"

My mother silenced me with a hand. "Perhaps I don't want to know."

"Mother," I chided. "We had a fight. She found Thrasos."

"Well son, you only have yourself to blame for that," my father muttered.

"No, he doesn't." Thrasos' voice cut through the room. He was panting heavily from wheeling his chair, his arms shaking at the effort. "You're all to blame," he continued, positioning himself at the table beside me.

"Thrasos, dear," my mother fussed, "are you all right? You should have asked for your father to get you, do you want breakfast?"

"I've already eaten and thrown it up," Thrasos said with a dismissive wave of his hand, "and I'm capable of getting myself around."

"How am I to blame?" Freyja cut in. "I didn't know about any of this," she whined, crossing her arms and sitting back in her seat.

"Did you know before me and choose not to tell me?" Thrasos paused, waiting for our sister's response but it never came. "Exactly." He reached over a took a sip of my tea, glaring at me over the top of the cup as if he wished I would protest. "Now, I want to be told *everything*, and I mean everything, that has been going on for the last four months." Thrasos said, relaxing back into his chair and glaring at everyone around the table. Even Odon seemed to pick up on the tense energy in the room and remained silently seated on his father's lap.

My mother and father took turns defending themselves to my brother, explaining their reasoning for the treaty and for not telling him, my mother unflinchingly laying the blame on the uncertainty of Islina keeping her word. My father said he'd wanted me to do it, thinking it would be easier to hear coming from me but I cut in and explained that he never expressed that wish to me. Again, my sister proclaimed her innocence and called Thrasos a bastard for thinking that she would have kept it secret had she known. Then it was my turn to fill him in on my journey with Evalina and defend my own hesitancy in revealing the truth to them both; and I was shocked to discover myself that it was the same uncertainty that my mother had felt—a lack of trust that the Isidians would hold true to their end of the treaty. It made me realize just how hypocritical my last few words to Evalina had been.

"You think I can't handle bad news?" Thrasos commented. "My whole life has been nothing but bad news."

"I just wanted to save you from this one," I murmured.

"I'd rather know and be upset than not know at all. Especially when it's in regards to *my* life and *my* future," Thrasos chided. "One day, I'd like to be incharge of my own health and I'll need to know what paths have already been tried or blocked."

"You won't need to do that, Thrasos," my mother cut in. "We're here to do it for you."

"I am a grown man, Mother!" Thrasos exclaimed, slamming his fist down on the table with a light thud. "Despite the chair, you cannot baby me forever. I must be allowed to live my own life, to make my own decisions, as Thanatos has."

"What do you mean as I have?" I asked incredulously "You think I want to be out there? You have no idea what it's like, what I have to put up with, how I have to act to protect myself."

"Well, you always make it sound like you have an amazing time."

"Of course I do! You think I'm going to tell you that I stay in brothels because I have no other choice? Or that children throw shit at me in the streets, if they're not petrified and hiding behind their guardians legs? I'll see a bustling town in

the distance and by the time I get there it looks as if its been deserted for centuries."
My family's expressions had grown dark. Daeril stared down at his son as if this were the first time he'd really thought about how difficult his life would be. "It's not fun out there brother, not for us."

"Then why do you go out there?" Thrasos asked, his voice almost a whisper, exhaustion creeping its way across his face.

"For you. So I can come back and describe what I see for your paintings. So I can tell you what it's like, with some embellishments. And because you've always pushed me out the door! I've got the scars on my ankles to prove it."

Thrasos took a weak, shuddering breath. "I thought you wanted it. You hated being stuck with me as children and you didn't have to be. Once we were grown and I was still sick, it seemed even more cruel. I didn't want you to live the life forced on me when you didn't have to. But I realize now that I simply forced you into another life you didn't want or deserve."

I wasn't sure how to respond. He was right and wrong in that statement. He had forced me in a way but I had been willing, and had I not done that would I have the friends I have now? Would a marriage between Evalina and I even have been possible if I'd stayed home and kept to myself?

Evalina.

"Where is Evalina?" I asked no one in particular, it was practically lunchtime and, even though she was mad at me, she would not skip meals and resist the opportunity to ridicule me in front of my family.

"She's gone." Thrasos said calmly, the complete opposite to how I felt.

My pulse had reached a new speed, my mind almost matching in thinking up ideas of how I could quickly catch up with her.

"She left last night." Thrasos continued.

"She didn't even say goodbye," my father stated, almost sadly.

"I must follow her," I said quickly, rising to my feet.

"No!" My family shouted collectively, causing me to pause with my hand on the back of my chair.

"Than, sweetie, I think it's best to let her cool off," my mother said.

"Yeah," Frejya cut in, "if you guys fought last night, she's probably pissed."

"But running away? She doesn't seem like the type to run from a fight," my father commented, his eyes locking on my uneasy expression, "What did you say to her, Thanatos?"

I collapsed into my chair again and relayed the fight with Evalina, my hands practically pulling through my hair. A collective gasp sounded through the room as I revealed my last words to the Princess.

"You've fucked it," Freyja said unapologetically.

"Gee, thanks," I murmured back.

"Well, she's not wrong, son. You'll be lucky if she ever even wants to talk to you again," my father said bluntly.

"How could you have done this Thanatos?" My mother chastised. "What of the treaty? And your brother? You could have ruined everything!"

"He hasn't," Thrasos said, thankfully coming to my defense. "Princess Evalina was sure to let me know she would still send healers for me."

I stared at him hopefully, praying to the Father that he would continue.

"She also agrees to still go through with the marriage. Though I don't know why," he said, glaring at me, but I was too elated to care. For once, I hadn't ruined everything.

"You lucky bastard," Freyja remarked.

"Will she be safe out there?" My mother asked.

"She'll have taken the brooch, and I wouldn't be surprised if she's been picked up by her aunt," I said, remembering that I had intended to wait for Bellona's arrival the night before to propose before at least one member of her family.

"Bellona? Why would she be here?" My father asked.

"I invited her—weeks ago—she should have arrived last night, and I'm still alive so I assume Evalina left with her." Bellona would have sailed to the docks in the north, it was an easy trek through the mountain pass to get there.

"Well, at least she's safe." My mother paused for a moment, gazing at my brother. "Thrasos, darling, I think you need to go and rest." she said, rising from her chair.

I glanced at my brother, his cheeks were flushed, eyelids heavy.

"Yes," Thrasos said weakly, "but I'm not done. Thanatos will take me to my room and I will finish with you two later." He motioned between our parents.

"So, I'm off the hook?" Freyja asked.

"Barely." Was all Thrasos said as he motioned for me to wheel his chair from the room.

"I didn't mean to hurt you both, you have to believe that," I said as I pushed Thrasos down the hallway.

He sighed, his shoulders still taut with anger. "I know, Thanatos, but sometimes you need to think of yourself, not others, first."

"What do you mean? I was waiting for the right moment."

"Yes, the right moment for *us*, not for *you*. Be selfish, for once," he pleaded.

I didn't know how to respond. I thought I had been selfish, waiting and waiting, leaving them in the dark, but he was right. It would have been easier—for *me*—to have told them from the start. I should have been selfish.

"What can I do to make it up to you?" I asked, desperate for my brother's forgiveness.

He sat silent for a moment. I held my breath, I would do anything, anything to make up for what I had done, for adding yet another stress to his already stressful life.

"*Never* hide anything from us again," he said finally, with an intensity I had never heard from my brother.

"I promise, I'll never do it again," I swore, and I wouldn't. I would be lucky if I could ever win back their trust after this. "I'm sorry. I should have told you. I should have done it the second Mother and Father told me. It was just a lot to take in all at once. I hope you can understand that it was hard for me, too."

I didn't want to shift the blame but I wanted him to understand that being the one with all the information wasn't the easiest either.

It's not like I was just told I had to marry someone I didn't know, I was told I had to marry someone I didn't know, that'd hated my guts, and lived on the other side of the continent to my family. My ill brother, who we had all thought would pass from his sickness, now had to live to be King and, with the way the world was toward our people, there was a chance I would have never see my country or my family again. I was heading into a very lonely existence and, on top of it all, I would miss out on watching my nephew grow up. The thought of missing Odon's life was what made it the hardest for me. As much as I loved my brother and wanted to be there for him, he would remember me; but Odon was young enough that he could forget me after only a few months.

"I understand, but now you've had months to prepare, to think it over, how long do I have? How long does Evalina have? We now have to dive into these new lives without any warning."

"I know," I said, not knowing what else I could say. "I'm sorry."

My mind drifted back to Evalina, her furious face the last time I'd seen her. Gods did I want to go after her.

As if he could read my mind without even seeing my face, Thrasos said gently, "Than, just let her go, for now. She needs time to process."

Thoughts swirled around in my head, my mind coming up with hundreds of scenarios a second, both good and bad.

I stopped pushing Thrasos and moved to stand before him. "I … I can't just let her leave, not like this."

"I know it feels wrong but I think it's for the best. She feels betrayed right now. She believes you've led her on for months, just let her figure out how she feels."

"But I love her," I confessed.

Thrasos's eyes softened, his hand tightening on my arm. "Then you know the best thing to do is give her time." I opened my mouth to argue but he held up a hand to silence me. "A month, give her a month, and if you don't hear anything by then you can go to her."

I thought it over for a moment, pushing the negative thoughts away, the thoughts of her ending up back with Lorkin.

A month.

A month plus my journey time. It was more than enough time. For both of us.

"A month," I agreed.

"Now," Thrasos said, directing me to continue pushing him again, "Tell me what you've *really* been up to these last few months."

I smiled and followed my brother into his room, eager to tell him every detail of my adventure with Evalina, keeping in *all* the details I'd kept from my parents, of how I fell in love with her.

CHAPTER SIXTY FIVE
A SHOULDER TO CRY ON

I'd been back in Isidia for just under a month after leaving Osiria with Bellona. Our journey on the seas had been blissfully calm, though I was careful to stay away from the edges of the deck. I'd spent most of the time in the Captain's cabin, wanting to be alone. I hadn't been for so long.

I studied my aunt's maps and charts, read her few books on navigation, and slept. At night I would emerge and sit with the crew to eat dinner and drink.

The crew on deck were mostly Sea-Elves interspersed with a few Aurali and a Shinchaku man, who spent most of his time up the mast in the crows nest. The cook, however, was a High-Elf.

It had felt odd, at first, to see someone that looked like me, I hadn't seen any of us out in the world, not realizing how much we elves seemed to stick to ourselves. I'd always imagined the world to be so vast and integrated, instead it seemed everyone was comfortable in a sort of self-imposed separation. Perhaps it was easier that way but maybe a marriage between the northern and southern most kingdoms would encourage a change of attitude.

My aunt had questioned me extensively on how I felt about the arranged marriage and everything else that had happened between the Prince and I. I tried to answer her questions as best I could but I didn't really know myself yet. I was still angry at Thanatos, but the longer I was away from him the better I felt about it, or had I simply forgotten how angry I really was?

At the end of the day, I had to go through with it, out of respect for my mother and her treaty arrangements with the Osirians; she was still my Queen, after all. But part of me, separate from all that, wanted to go through with it anyway. I could not deny that I loved him, I did, but it was not for that reason either. It was for an entirely selfish and childish reason, a pettiness I hadn't thought I'd possessed. I would go through with the marriage and I would drive him mad. Any chance I got I would do something to irritate him, a small, cruel pleasure, a revenge without really causing any harm.

Feelings about it though hadn't crossed my mind. I was trying to avoid them altogether, to keep them in check until I was home and could unleash them in private. And I had.

When we'd arrived in Isidia, my grandparents and uncles had met us at the docks. It had been a warm welcome, though, from the way they'd scanned the ship, I knew that they'd been told about the arrangement, that they were searching for my betrothed.

When they didn't spot him they said nothing, as if they, too, knew exactly how I would have reacted. It had almost frustrated me that everyone seemed to be able to predict my emotions and reactions before even I could.

The reception from my people left a lot to be desired after the welcome I'd had from the Osirian village. There was no music or dancing, just a thin crowd of people lining the road to the palace, cheering and praising my accomplishments, but mostly gawking. I'd almost forgotten that they barely knew who I was, had never really seen me. For many of them, this was their first sighting of me and I was riding with my father's family, not their Queen. I tried not to think of how it must have looked to my people and simply waved and thanked them.

My mother was waiting for me in the garden, surrounded by a small council of people and Lorkin, standing tall by her side. Lorkin's face had faltered for a moment as I'd come up the road toward them but had quickly resumed its emotionless facade before anyone else could notice.

My mother stood like a statue, unwavering, a small smile fixed to her face. When she said nothing, the Councilmen greeted me, sucking up as usual. I rolled my eyes and ignored them. Once I was Queen, they would be gone; anyone that had tried to speak for my mother, for me, would be gone. I wouldn't sit back and allow their ridiculous court politics to continue.

I sent the council away and asked for my family and Lorkin to meet in the dining room, where we discussed everything.

Mother said nothing, barely reacted as I unloaded my pent up anger; my Carracallan family's faces were plastered with shocked expressions—except Bellona, who leant against a wall, flask in hand, nodding in agreement with everything I screeched at my family.

By the end of my tirade I was breathless, my face streaked with angry tears and my throat dry from yelling. My hands shook as I pulled out a chair and sat across from my mother, glaring into her blank face.

"Well, if you're quite finished, I would like to explain myself," she said calmly, which only infuriated me more. "I was in talks with King Methuzelah and Queen Omisha for years before this treaty came to be, before you were of age. Once the business side of it was sorted our letters became more personal, we spoke of our children and their grandson. Like you, I'd had no idea they had other children. And when they told me of the twins, of how sick Thrasos is … can you blame me for taking pity? And, all the while this is happening"—she took a deep breath, as if it pained her to speak—"the council were pressuring me to remarry to birth a son, marry you off, or hand over the Queendom. I would *never* betray the memory of your father by remarrying, you know I could never do that, so arranging a marriage for you was my only choice. This Queendom has been ruled by those with Vian blood for millennia and Mother take me if I'm going to be the one to lose it—and you will make a great Queen, better than I could've ever been.

"So, while the Council was pushing for you to marry an Isidian, I was learning what I could of Thanatos. The strength of your marriage to him will throw off the council, many will leave, as they should, and you two can start from scratch. Rebuild this Queendom to what it was before I demolished its spirit. Thanatos is a good match, you know it now, I know you do, but also know that it was not a match I made lightly. I did this for you and for our Queendom."

I hadn't known what to say, the room was silent for three long minutes before I could collect my thoughts. It was another situation of 'if you had just told me, it would have been fine'. But would it have? or would I have flown off the handle?

How could I be so predictable to others but not myself?

I told my mother the same thing I'd told Thrasos—I needed time, to think and to reconcile.

And that's what we had been doing, all of us. I was spending long-missed time with my extended family and slowly working on the relationship with my mother.

Lorkin and I had spoken about our relationship as well and both had, during our time apart, come to the conclusion that what we had was not love in a romantic sense and agreed, especially because I was now betrothed, that there could not be anything romantic between us. He still meant everything to me and always would but now we could focus on just being there for each other.

The garden was long dormant. There were no flowers and the leaves on the floor were long past the crunchiness of autumn. Lorkin and I were walking back to my room after having had dinner with my family; my mother was finally smiling again and I had even hugged her when we'd left. She had seemed like her old self for weeks now, the way I'd remembered her being before my father had died. I put it down to my aunt's presence.

Bellona was so much like my father and her and my mother got on better than I'd seen my mother get on with anyone. It was nice to have my family together; it made the castle seem warmer, even though winter had thoroughly set in.

"I dread the day your grandfather leaves," Lorkin said. "He's helped around the castle so much. I hadn't even realized there was so much wrong and he's taught me so much about commanding the guards."

I smiled, glad that things had gone so well while I'd been away. Slowly during the month, I'd been visiting all the families that had lost loved ones in the battles, all of them had spoken very highly of my grandfather as well. I would have to add him to my list of people whose brains I needed to pick for ruling advice because, even though he'd been a King my whole, life it was easy to forget that he could help with such things.

"I wish they could stay, but they'll have to leave soon. Carracalla must want their rulers back, I'm sure." A breeze cut through the night, lifting my skirt, and I shivered, speeding up my pace to reach my rooms quicker. My fireplace and some books were waiting for me.

We were just about to climb the stairs when a flurry of guards rushed into the hall.

"Captain Lorkin, Your Highness, the wards have been triggered."

I froze for a moment, my hand still outstretched toward the banister.

It was the first time they'd been triggered since I'd returned and it sent a flood of unpleasant memories rushing through my mind.

Lorkin placed a warm hand on the small of my back. "It's all right, go upstairs. I'll come say good night when I get back. I'm sure it's nothing."

I gave him a silent nod and watched him leave the hall and go back into the night with the guards, their weapons drawn.

It's nothing, I told myself over and over again as I walked up the stairs, catching glimpses of the small party as they walked toward the eastern woods.

The Necromancer is dead, I told myself as I sat on the lounge in my room in front of the fire, warming myself from the chill of the gardens. My eyes rested on the black box on my mantle that contained the Lily and Hellebore brooches. I could take out the small black flower and fix it to my dress, the cold would disappear but I would be left with memories of it's creator, memories I'd been ignoring for weeks. What was he doing now? I'd had updates from Thrasos but he conveniently didn't mention his brother, his twin, only spoke of Odon and the rest of the family, his latest painting and how his health was progressing. He'd become a great friend.

I forced thoughts of the Osirians out of my mind, missing them would not help me now, would not alleviate the stress I felt.

It's just a deer, or a rat, I thought as I read my book about how to properly greet foreign dignitaries from each kingdom, the clock on my mantle ticking loudly in the quiet of my room.

The Necromancer is dead.

"Is he?" I spun to face the wraith, her eyes so like Thanatos' it hurt to look into them.

My breathing halted.

She looked exactly as she had the last time I'd seen her, only her neck was healed, her dress no longer tattered.

"How are you here?" I gasped.

"The burn is still on your shoulder is it not?" I nodded, my hand drifting up to my shoulder.

She was the one thing I had forgotten to tell my family about. After everything that had happened, I'd completely forgotten about Ossena, the burn I'd just accepted as part of me.

"I haven't seen you for months. Why are you back now?"

Her expression was uncomfortable, as if she'd walked in on me doing something unmentionable. "I, too, had thought the Necromancer was gone, that you and my descendant had been successful but ..." she trailed off.

In my mind images flashed, dead things stalking toward me, Thanatos bleeding to death, my father's sword hacking through the necks of innocent people, a room full of Isidian corpses.

My breathing became uncontrolled. My head, foggy.

"No, no, no," was all I could get out.

"Evalina, calm down, please."

My head snapped up. *Lorkin.*

"I need to wake up." I began frantically pinching myself, pulling my own hair. "Wake up, damn it!" I resorted to slapping myself.

Ossena grabbed my hand, pulling it away from my face. "Evalina, please!" She yelled. "You must listen to me." Her eyes wobbled with fear and her hand holding mine shook enough to make my own arm shake. "There's another, and I think I'm here because of him—somehow, we're connected. It's why he keeps coming here when I contact you but I don't know how, or why."

Tears were now falling freely from my eyes, my chest so tight I could barely breathe.

"You need to go back to Osiria," she said frantically. "You need to find out the truth."

I wiped my eyes and she was gone.

I stood in the burnt down manor house, two charred corpses on the floor before me, one adult, the other no bigger than Odon. I tried to close my eyes to block the sight but I couldn't, even with my eyes closed they were there, imprinted in my mind, their blackened flesh taught on their bones. I fell to my knees and sobbed, my light pants growing dark with ash. I lifted my lilac hands to my face, but even they couldn't hide the horror of my dead wife and child.

My wife and child.

I bolted up from the couch, almost headbutting my uncle who had been shaking me awake. I felt hot tears streaming down my face. My uncle's eyes were wet, too, though I guessed not for the same reason mine had been.

"It's all right, Evalina."

"Darius? What are you doing here?" I said, wiping my eyes and trying to control my breathing.

He cleared his throat. "Now you're awake, you had better come with me."

My spine straightened at the tone of his voice, deep and serious. I prayed it had nothing to do with Simeon.

We went straight to my mother's chambers, she was sitting on a lounge facing away from me, her shoulders slumped. My grandparents sat across from her, their eyes sad and sympathetic.

I stopped dead.

Looking around the room, Bellona was missing, Peverall was missing, Lorkin was missing. My heart was in my throat.

"What's happened?"

"Evalina, come sit down." My grandmother said, gesturing to sit beside my mother.

I shook my head. "Just tell me what's happened."

My grandparents shared a look and my grandfather rose and approached me slowly. "There was a ward breach, as you know. It ... it was Corse."

In that moment, it felt as if my soul had left my body and that I was watching myself receive the news, like a play that I was the main character of.

"Lorkin was killed, Flower."

The main character fell to her knees, her hands shook.

"But," her grandfather continued, "the remaining Corse took his body."

Every sound was muffled, except a single heartbeat.

A door behind the Princess burst open.

My soul returned to my body as Thanatos' face invaded my vision, his eyes wide. Behind him were Bellona and Peverell; they were all right but Lorkin was dead.

Thanatos was here, but he had lied to me.

I slapped him.

The sound echoed off every wall in my mother's chambers.

I gripped his shirt and brought my cheek to the comforting warmth of his neck, raw grief erupting in a bout of heavy sobs.

His arms wrapped around me tightly. "I'm sorry, Evie, I'm so sorry," he whispered into my hair, rocking me as I wept.

EPILOGUE

I woke to the sound of dripping and a freezing wind whipping through the cave. I tried to sit up but my hands and legs were chained to a bench. I struggled against them but stopped as a laugh echoed through the empty space.

"You're finally awake." I turned my head as the hooded figure stepped into view from the shadows. "Captain Lorkin of Isidia. I'd expected it to be harder to get to you but you practically walked into my arms."

"Where am I?" My throat felt strange, dry but slick.

"I can't tell you that yet," the hooded figure said as he paced around the table.

"Then what can you tell me?" I demanded.

Another laugh echoed through the cavern.

"This one's got balls," a second voice said with a snicker.

"I can tell you that you are very far from home and that you are about to tell me everything I want to know about Princess Evalina."

I spat at the figure as he passed my face, just missing his robes. "I'm not telling you *shit* about the Princess."

"You won't have a choice, pretty boy," said the second voice, the owner now stepping into my limited field of view.

I held in my gasp. I knew his face, I'd seen it many times as a child on posters in Eevan's office, wanted posters.

"I know you," I seethed.

"I'm sure you do, but let me introduce myself nonetheless." He removed his large hat from his head and bowed. "Captain Orrick Ubel." He grinned and something in his neck clicked.

He cleared his throat and stood back.

Orrick Ubel.

The man who killed Eevan.

But he was dead, the Osirians had executed him. And then my mind clicked.

I'd been with Evie when the guards had informed me of the breach. We'd been ambushed. I'd been killed. My head fell back onto the bench and I stared at the ceiling as my realization came crashing down. "He's finally got it." Orrick snickered again.

"Good." The hooded figure said, coming closer to me allowing me to get a good look at him.

I wanted to recoil, his face and hands were a patchwork of grayish-purple and white skins messily sewn together, his hair cut short beneath his hood and, what parts of it were visible, shone white; his eyes, one white and one green, seemed to stare, unblinking.

He was a beast. A monster.

My mind grew foggy as he raised a hand, black mist surrounding it, sucking all light from the already dark space. "Let's begin, then."

ACKNOWLEDGEMENTS

The very first people that deserve acknowledgement are, of course, my partner and my son. Both have been so patient and understanding throughout the five years it took to develop this book. They've had to deal with every single high and every single low, of which there were many at varying degrees.

Dan, my partner, however, deserves extra thanks and acknowledgement. Without him, the world of Carynthia would have been shockingly built, the chapters would not have the amazing titles they do, and the language would be a lot plainer. If it wasn't for his unwavering support I would have given up on this book years ago. So, if you've enjoyed it, you should also thank him, because it would definitely not exist without him.

A giant thanks to my amazing Editor, Danikka Taylor! This chonk was a mess before it met her, and the book needed some work too.

Jokes aside, Danikka did an amazing job on this book and I couldn't have had a better time working and dealing with her. She was a 'Yes Person' when she needed to be but also knew when to tell me no. I could be bias though, because she let me add 20k to an already 150k manuscript, and that is definitely one way to win me over.

I want to thank every single one of my online writing friends, of which, fortunatly, there are many.

I wish I could list you all individually but I'm terrified that I would miss someone, I'm sure you all know who you are though. Without the amazing community of writers, on both Youtube and Instagram, cheering me on from the sidelines I would have lost all motivation to publish this book.

Lastly, thank you to my family and friends, though many of you didn't even know I was writing this. The closest people to me are my biggest inspirations and influences, and each one of you played some part in the creation of this story.

ABOUT THE AUTHOR

E. A. Olivieri never thought she'd be an author, but, after writing out of boredom while on maternity leave, she discovered a passion for it.

She loves all things dark and fantastical, and channels that through her writing.

When E. A. isn't creating new worlds, she's working on an art project or playing video games with her son and partner in their West Australian home.

Coming Soon...

OF
GREED
AND
GLORY
A GARYNTHIA STORY

Ingram Content Group UK Ltd.
Milton Keynes UK
UKHW041202080523
421361UK00001B/4

9 780645 467758